"COLONEL!" A VOICE SNAPPED IN HER HEADSET.

It was Orloffski, in the 80-ton *Victor* holding the gate with her at the moment. "I've got movement! On the left, one hundred meters!"

Lori turned slightly, scanning the smoky ruin there. Yes, she saw them. 'Mechs were moving again beyond the spill of fire-blackened rubble that once had been the far wall of the courtyard. A *Trebuchet* hulked behind the tumbledown wall opposite. As it strode closer, it paused, left and right arms raised to volley-fire their three lasers in rippling spurts of brilliant white light. Other 'Mechs, shadowy figures in the clinging, opaque smoke, moved closer.

Gunfire spat from the shadows as infantry tried to rush the gate under cover of their larger and more deadly comrades. Lori loosed a flight of missiles, the explosions tearing through the tight-knit clots of running men and scattering them like torn, ragged cloth dolls.

Then the 'Mechs closed in. . . .

BATTLETECH®

OPERATION EXCALIBUR

William H. Keith, Jr.

A ROC Book

ROC
Published by the Penguin Group
Penguin Books USA Inc., 375 Hudson Street,
New York, New York 10014, U.S.A.
Penguin Books Ltd, 27 Wrights Lane,
London W8 5TZ, England
Penguin Books Australia Ltd, Ringwood,
Victoria, Australia
Penguin Books Canada Ltd, 10 Alcorn Avenue,
Toronto, Ontario, Canada M4V 3B2
Penguin Books (N.Z.) Ltd, 182–190 Wairau Road,
Auckland 10, New Zealand

Penguin Books Ltd, Registered Offices:
Harmondsworth, Middlesex, England

First published by Roc, an imprint of Dutton Signet,
a division of Penguin Books USA Inc.

First Printing, August, 1996
10 9 8 7 6 5 4 3 2 1

Series Editor: Donna Ippolito
Cover art by Roger Loveless
Mechanical Drawings: Duane Loose and the FASA art department

 REGISTERED TRADEMARK—MARCA REGISTRADA

BATTLETECH, FASA, and the distinctive BATTLETECH and FASA logos are
trademarks of the FASA Corporation, 1100 W. Cermak, Suite B305, Chicago, IL
60608.

Printed in the United States of America

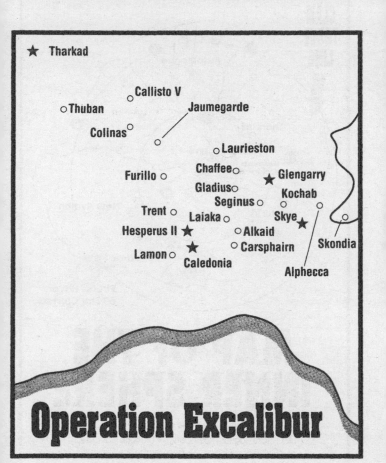

Operation Excalibur

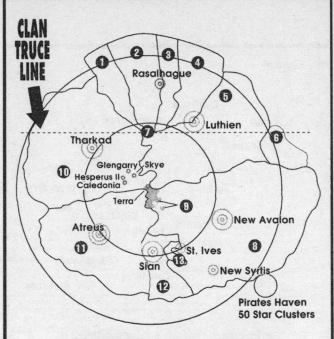

CLAN TRUCE LINE

Rasalhague

Luthien

Tharkad

Glengarry Skye
Hesperus II
Caledonia

Terra

Atreus

New Avalon

St. Ives

Sian

New Syrtis

Pirates Haven
50 Star Clusters

MAP OF THE INNER SPHERE

1 • Jade Falcon/Steel Viper, 2 • Wolf Clan, 3 • Ghost Bear,
4 • Smoke Jaguars/Nova Cats, 5 • Draconis Combine,
6 • Outworlds Alliance, 7 • Free Rasalhague Republic,
8 • Federated Commonwealth, 9 • Chaos March,
10 • Lyran Alliance, 11 • Free Worlds League,
12 • Capellan Confederation, 13 • St. Ives Compact

Map Compiled by COMSTAR.
From information provided by the COMSTAR EXPLORER SERVICE
and the STAR LEAGUE ARCHIVES on Terra.

© 3058 COMSTAR CARTOGRAPHIC CORPS.

Prologue

DropShip* Merlin, *Approaching Glengarry
Glengarry System, Skye March
Federated Commonwealth
1345 hours, 26 April 3057

Field Marshal Brandal Gareth of the Armed Forces of the Federated Commonwealth had reason to be pleased. As the world of Glengarry slowly swelled in the DropShip *Merlin*'s viewscreens, vast and mottled in the greens, blues, and ochers of a living world, reports continued to flow in from the robot probes, the advance DropShip landings, and the aerospace fighter scouts deployed in advance of the main invasion fleet.

He was seated in *Merlin*'s Ops Center, leaning back in an acceleration couch almost completely ringed by screens and readout panels, a high-tech spider at the center of a vast and far-flung web of constantly shifting reports and incoming data. Thus far, all reports from the fleet landing zones on Glengarry remained good. Aerospace fighters were engaged with both air and ground defenses now, but the first DropShips had grounded more than two hours ago, and initial reports from the surface suggested that the defenders had been unable to deploy their 'Mech assets in time to effectively counter any of the landings.

That, of course, was quite according to plan. Contested DropShip landings were relatively rare in modern Battle-

Mech warfare; planets, after all, were *big,* generally offering the invader his choice of landing sites. At last report, Glengarry's defenses boasted only a single BattleMech regiment—the well-known Gray Death Legion—and one of the Legion's three 'Mech battalions had been diverted to the world of Caledonia as the opening move of Operation Excalibur. Gareth's invasion force, a reinforced regiment of three full 'Mech battalions plus a heavy assault 'Mech company, backed up by auxiliary infantry, support units, and an aerospace ground-attack wing, ought to be more than sufficient for a quick, clean, and efficient victory over the rebels.

Rebels. He smiled at the unspoken word. Brandal Gareth was, above all else, a manipulator, a man who always put himself in control of the situation, in control of the people he worked with. For Gareth, people were assets, resources to be quarried, refined, and put to best use, whether they were his allies or his opponents. If the Federated Commonwealth had declared Grayson Carlyle and his Gray Death Legion to be rebels, mercenaries in direct violation of their contract, then it was because Gareth had deliberately maneuvered Carlyle into that position.

Which left Gareth, as usual, in *control.* . . .

A flashing amber light in the corner of one of the smaller viewscreens announced an incoming priority call, flagged for Gareth's attention. He touched a key on the arm of his couch, accepting the communications link.

"This is Gareth," he said. "Go ahead."

A man's face appeared on the screen, peering out through the visor of a heavy neurohelmet. The winged-V emblem of the Fifth Hesperan Aerospace Wing, the Nighthawks, was prominent on the helmet's crest above his eyes.

"This is Captain Umberto," the man said after a brief hesitation; the *Merlin* was still a quarter of a light second out from Glengarry, which meant a half-second pause between each statement and its reply. Umberto's teeth flashed in a tight grin. "Alpha Squadron of the Fifth. Looks like we've got the rebel bastards on the run, Marshal!"

"Give me your tacsit," Gareth demanded.

Umberto's image blurred and jolted. Part of the cockpit of his aerofighter was visible behind his head and the back of his ejection seat. Clouds wheeled through a deep, deep blue sky beyond the bit of the transplas canopy Gareth could see on the screen. "Sorry, sir," Umberto said after a longer space than the speed-of-light time delay required. "Picking up some heavy ground-to-air for a second, there. Okay. We're over the planet's capital. We've got scan traces on what we estimate as one battalion's worth of BattleMechs in this immediate area, mostly at the spaceport, and up the hill at the fortress. Fighting at the three primary DropShip LZs is light to nonexistent. I think we pulled it off, sir."

Gareth nodded. It was supremely difficult to achieve anything like surprise in a planetary invasion like this one. This system's zenith and nadir jump points were positioned some twenty-eight light minutes from Glengarry's orbit, a five-day flight time for Gareth's incoming DropShips that gave the planet's defenders plenty of time to note the approach and prepare their plans. The true tactical surprise in an assault lay in the attacker's choice of DropShip landing zones, a choice that might not be made until literally the last few moments before the deorbit burn and atmosphere entry. Still, Glengarry was a Terra-like world—not as big, but with smaller oceans and larger continents—with over 150 million square kilometers of land surface area.

There was no way a few hundred BattleMechs could cover it *all*.

"How about the locals' aerospace strength?"

"There's not much in the air yet," Umberto replied. "I've lost one in my squadron so far. Glasky got nailed by PPC fire from that damned fortress. If they've got space fighters down there, they're keeping them hidden in shielded bunkers or revetments."

"Any sign of their DropShips?"

"That's negative, sir. There are indications of a pretty extensive underground complex at the spaceport, and there could be some stored up at the fortress." The image jolted and blurred again. *"Whoof!"* Umberto grunted. "Wait one—"

Distantly, Gareth could hear the crackle of radio voices, calls between the members of Umberto's squadron. *"Watch it, Alpha Leader!"* one voice cried. *"Watch it! There's heavy fire coming from that secondary tower!"*

"I'm hit!" another voice called. *"I'm hit and going down!"*

"Punch out, Alpha Five! Punch out!"

The sky visible behind Umberto's head spun crazily for a moment, then steadied. "Make that two downed," the squadron leader said. An aerospace squadron—the equivalent of a 'Mech company—numbered six air/space fighters; Umberto's unit had lost a third of its strength already. "Sir, the ground defenses are wicked, mostly centered in and around the fortress. If they've got mobile assets down there, DropShips or fighters, we haven't seen 'em yet. It's, ah, possible, sir, that the enemy has some of their 'Mech forces and DropShips redeployed elsewhere in-system, and they're laying low."

"Copy that, Squadron Leader," Gareth said, thoughtful. If the advance strike force's scanners had picked up only a battalion or so of Legion 'Mechs in the immediate area around Glengarry, that left another battalion, as many as thirty-six BattleMechs, unaccounted for. "Keep looking. Especially for those missing 'Mechs. We don't want any surprises after we're fully deployed."

"Roger that," Umberto said.

"Report to me directly as soon as you have solid intel. Gareth out."

As Umberto's image flicked off, Gareth thought again about how big a world was . . . and knew that those tens of millions of square kilometers of terrain—of forest and mountain, of ice cap and marsh, of prairie and tundra and city and even ocean—would help the enemy at least as much as it had already helped him. If the sheer size of the planet allowed him to pick and choose undefended landing sites for his DropShips, it also gave the enemy plenty of room to hide. No doubt the defenders of Glengarry were deliberately keeping the major portion of their forces under cover until they knew just how strong the invaders were.

No problem. Gareth's forces would crush those defensive units they could find, then hunt down the rest company by company, even 'Mech by 'Mech if need be. The only real deadline was to complete the work before the rest of the Gray Death Legion returned from Caledonia.

That portion of the plan, Gareth reflected with just a shadow of a frown, hadn't gone nearly as well. The news from Caledonia, relayed to the fleet by HPG a few days before, was not at all good. Not that the outcome posed any real problem to the larger plan; the Caledonian operation had been less certain to begin with, and, given the opposition, more difficult to carry off with complete success. By all accounts, the battle outside the small Caledonian village of Falkirk had been a disaster for Gareth's task force, under the command of the late Marshal Felix Zellner.

But then, Zellner's orders had been to engage the Third Batallion of the Gray Death Legion, to destroy it if possible, yes, but more than that to keep it tied down while Gareth's real blow fell *here,* on Glengarry. Partly, of course, the diversion on Caledonia made Gareth's operation on Glengarry easier, with only two 'Mech battalions to face instead of three. The real significance of the battle between the Legion and Zellner's Third Davion Guards was that it gave Gareth's assault on Glengarry the legitimacy it needed in the name of the Federated Commonwealth.

Of course, the FedCom government had no idea what was *really* at stake here and would not until it was too late. That thought, the certainty of the ultimate success of Operation Excalibur, was part of Gareth's feeling of almost exuberant well-being. So far, each piece of the plan had fallen into place with masterful precision. The situation with the rebel Jacobites on Caledonia had been engineered specifically to force the Gray Death Legion into a violation of its mercenary contract. Marshal Zellner and the Third Davion Guards had been sent in to support Caledonia's legitimate government—and to provoke a fight with the Legion, a fight that would brand Carlyle's mercenaries as contract-breakers.

That provocation, it seemed, had worked only too well. According to the information he'd received so far, Carlyle had pulled off another of his tactical miracles, splitting his battalion in the face of a much stronger force and striking hard and unexpectedly from an unguarded flank. The attack, reportedly, had rolled Zellner's right flank into his center and left, creating a vast, struggling mass of BattleMechs that were easy targets for the attackers while the 'Mechs themselves were unable to maneuver or fire. The Third Guards had been virtually wrecked at Falkirk, and Zellner was dead, his mighty *Atlas* pounded to scrap. If only Zellner could have kept the fight going just a little longer . . .

Gareth sighed. He was a realist and content to deal with situations as they were, not as they should be. It would take time for the Legion's Third Battalion to make the passage from Caledonia to Glengarry, a minimum of three hyperspace jumps. While the jumps themselves were virtually instantaneous, it took anywhere from four to ten days after each jump to recharge a JumpShip's drive coils, depending on the energy flux from the local sun. Add to that the five days it would take the Legion DropShips to travel from Caledonia to the star system's jump point, and five days more for the trip from Glengarry's jump point to Glengarry, and the whole passage would take three weeks or more—plenty of time for Gareth's forces to complete their mission here. The Third Battalion would arrive at Glengarry sometime in mid-May, only to find its landhold firmly in Gareth's grasp. Carlyle and his "rebels" would have no option but to surrender.

It was a pity, really. Carlyle had an exceptional mind, his unit a record unparalleled in the military histories of the Inner Sphere. The man was a tactical genius, with a list of military victories as long as a BattleMech's arm. If there were only some way to get him to join Operation Excalibur. . . .

Gareth swiveled his couch to look at another of the display screens ringing his work station. An unpiloted remote scanner was providing him with a direct visual feed from the planet, an aerial view of the city of Dunkeld. Above the city, on a low and rocky cliff, squatted the object of the invasion, the huge and dull-black sprawl of a Star League–era fortress, the headquarters and operations center for the Gray Death Legion.

Soon that will be my headquarters, Brandal Gareth thought with a heady rush of anticipation. *And then Excalibur can properly begin. . . .*

1

Alexander Carlyle listened to the soft, lonely *peep* of the vital signs recorder, the periodic *hiss-click* of the respirator, the low-voiced hum of the refrigeration units that kept the medical stasis capsule's interior at a chilly eight degrees Celsius, and he wanted to scream. More and more during these past few days, that sleek, oblong capsule with its coils of wires and power feeds had been taking on in Alex's mind the cool, dark proportions of a coffin. *Live,* he commanded, the thought loud in his mind. *You're going to live, damn it! You've got to live. . . .*

Damn . . . damn . . . *damn!* . . . So far, he'd managed to put a careful mask over his feelings, but that mask was at every moment in danger of slipping, and as the days trickled past, it was becoming harder and harder to maintain it.

Grayson Death Carlyle, his father, was encased inside the capsule's gleaming, ceramic and plastic embrace, his features, paste-white and death-still, just visible through the fogged transparency that covered his face. Half of that face, the left side, was further shrouded by the silver-gray metal of a bioplas woundseal; the right side was blotched and puckered by second-degree burns that were still only imperfectly healed. The Legion's medtechs had decided to put Carlyle into cryosuspension in order to stabilize his more serious injuries, even though the reduced heart rate and drastically lowered body temperature slowed the healing of his minor wounds. "Right now," Medtech Ellen Jamison had told him days before, "all we can really do is try to keep him alive. We can't begin to fix everything that's wrong here on the DropShip. We need to get him back to Glengarry."

Initially, Alex had been cushioned by a sense of unreality, a detachment that said this couldn't have happened to his father. Grayson Death Carlyle had always been such a vital, active, keenly intelligent man. To see him reduced to this state, neither wholly dead nor wholly alive, sealed helpless and unmoving inside the coffinlike shell of the stasis capsule . . . it was as though Alex was being forced to witness the drawn-out death and decomposition of someone else, a stranger. *This* couldn't be his father. . . .

As the days passed, though, he'd gradually begun to accept the reality of the situation. With acceptance had come pain.

No one blamed him for his father's condition, no one who'd been willing to confront him face to face, at any rate. Alex had spent much of the past two weeks trying to convince himself that his father's wounds were *not* his fault, and at times, at least, he'd been nearly successful. He knew now, for instance, that it wasn't his being late in hitting the enemy forces at Falkirk that had led to the elder Carlyle's brush with death.

His father had been betrayed on the battlefield in the moment of victory by one of his own men, a mole evidently planted within the Legion by enemies as yet unknown. Grayson had been blasted at near pointblank range from behind, then seriously burned when he tried to climb out of the wreckage of his *Victor*. Most of the wounds he'd suffered had been the result of an unshielded near-miss by the PPC of the traitor's *Zeus*. He'd lost his left arm—removed by the medtechs shortly after the battle. Worse, at least from any MechWarrior's point of view, there was a possibility that he'd never be able to pilot a 'Mech again. No one, least of all Alex, was looking at any of that closely now, though, since there was still no guarantee that the medtechs would even be able to save his life. If they could get him back to the med facilities at the Legion's Glengarry base, then maybe . . .

What gnawed most at Alex was the knowledge that he'd been at least partly responsible for bringing his father to Caledonia in the first place . . . and for the decision that had made the Gray Death Legion change sides, from that of the legitimate government under that bloody-handed Wilmarth, to that of the political and religious rebels who'd been fighting Wilmarth for months. Even now, knowing what he knew, Alex couldn't see how he—or his father—could have made any other choices. Governor Wilmarth had been a vicious and sadistic monster in human guise; to have obeyed his orders would have meant turning the Legion's BattleMechs against all but defenseless civilians in a brutal mass slaughter. To obey that kind of order was unthinkable, no matter what the cost.

At the same time, though, it was impossible not to remember that if the Legion *had* obeyed Wilmarth, the Battle of Falkirk would never have been fought, and his father would not be packed away in a chilled ceramic tube like a bloody slab of Glengarrian aurochs.

What else could I have done? Alex's hands curled into fists, squeezing so hard the nails bit the flesh of his palms. He shook his head slowly, trying to clear it of dark and accusing thoughts. *Damn it! What else could I possibly have done?*

A hand descended, resting itself on his shoulder with a surprisingly light, almost apologetic touch. Alex turned, startled. Major Davis McCall stood at his side. "Aye, it's me, lad," the big man said. "Sorry t' bother you, but there's aye a' bit a' trouble you should know aboot."

Gently, Alex pushed himself back from the med capsule, turning to snag a handhold and brace himself against the possibility of drifting free. The *Endeavor* was in microgravity at the moment, and each movement, each gesture, required care. "Now what?"

Davis nodded his head, indicating the sick bay door. "Let's takit away from here, lad. Up in th' Communications Center."

"I'm coming."

McCall, Alex thought, looked drawn and worn, *haggard* even, if that word could be applied to the big, powerfully muscled man. Though his red hair and beard normally gave him the look of someone much younger, despite the streaks of silver at his temples, at the moment he looked every one of his sixty standard years, and then some. He, too, Alex realized, was shouldering a certain amount of personal responsibility for Falkirk. The arrest by Wilmarth of Angus McCall, Davis's brother, had been the trigger that had set the whole Caledonian campaign in motion in the first place. McCall was a Caledonian whose family's Jacobite sentiments had led the two Legion officers to get involved with the rebellion—and to recommend to Carlyle that the Legion join with the rebels against the tyrant Wilmarth. It had been, without any trace of doubt whatsoever, the *right* thing to do.

But, oh God, the cost!

Alex took a last look around at the sick bay, cluttered with med canisters and electronic monitors. Casualties at Falkirk had been light, considering the odds they'd faced, and only a handful of containers showed the winking constellations of lights and glowing numerals that spoke of injured, cryosuspended, barely living flesh within.

Casualties at Falkirk had been light. . . .

The thought mocked Alex as he pulled his way along, hand over hand through the close confines of the DropShip's partially padded, steel-walled passageways. Even one death or maiming was tragedy to the victim's family. A battle, any battle, multiplied that grief by scores, by hundreds, by thousands or more.

The *Endeavor* was a *Union* Class military DropShip, a 3500-ton sphere measuring less than eighty meters from bridge dome to primary jets. At the moment, she was docked tail-on to the spinal-mount magnetic grapples of an *Invader* Class JumpShip, the free trader *Blue Star*. Balanced atop a tightly focused stream of charged particles, the 505-meter JumpShip was not, properly speaking, in zero-G, but under a constant micro-acceleration of some hundredths of a gravity—the thrust necessary to keep the 152,000-ton starship balanced and more or less motionless against the tug of the local star's gravity, at least for the week it would take to recharge her jump coils. As a result, objects—and people—adrift within *Endeavor*'s close compartments and passageways tended to drift slowly toward the bulkhead opposite the *Blue Star*'s prow. Maneuvering in micro-A could be tricky, but it was something that MechWarriors generally got the hang of by the time they'd made a hyperspace jump or three. Alex barely noticed the low-G tug as he followed McCall out of the sickbay and into one of the *Endeavor*'s passageways.

The DropShip's comm shack was located forward, three decks above the sick bay and just below the bridge, though terms like "above" and "below" carried little practical meaning in zero-G. It was a small compartment, crowded with both flat-screen displays and a large, three-V holoprojection plate. McCall indicated the main flat screen, mounted beside one of the compartment's two acceleration couches. "An HPG message came through from Glengarry a few minutes ago," McCall told him.

His eyebrows arced high on his forehead. "My mother?"

"Aye, lad, it was your maither. She's got the situation in hand right now, but it does nae look good back there. An' . . . well, I should warn you. Her message was cut off, sudden like."

Alex slid into the chair, pulling the harness across his body and snapping it shut. "Let me see it."

"Aye . . ."

McCall touched a control on the arm of Alex's chair. The main comm viewscreen switched on, showing the ComStar logo. At the lower right, alphanumerics appeared.

HPG TRANSMISSION
09 MAY 3057
ONE-WAY, NON-PRIORITY
GLENGARRY TO GLADIUS
RECORDED FOR IN-SYSTEM TRANSMISSION
CODE BLUE SIERRA 2
5

As they watched, the five changed to a four . . . three . . . two . . . one . . .

The image faded out, replaced by the face of Alex's mother.

At fifty-six years standard, Lori Kalmar-Carlyle was still a handsome woman, the hard lines of her face betraying more of her character than they did of age. Her once-blond hair was nearly all prematurely silver now, which made her eyes dark and intense by comparison. She looked tired, and there was a crisp edge of no-nonsense professionalism in her voice that Alex knew covered a well-hidden worry. "Hello, Davis," she said. "And Alex. I presume you're there too. Things are getting worse around here."

The image flickered, then shifted to another view, one obviously taken from an aircraft or drone flier high above the city of Dunkeld. Glengarry's capital was spread out for Alex's inspection like a scale-model miniature, tiny buildings rising among the patchwork swaths of green marking the city's parks. North of the city, a bare-faced and eroded hill rose like the crown of a brown and weathered skull. Sprawled across its crest were the black, slick walls and weapons towers of Castle Hill, the Legion's fortress. Alphanumerics winked at the bottom of the screen, showing date, time, and the legend:

DRONE 7: DOWNLOAD

DIRECT FEED: REALTIME

Transmission of full-color, as-it-happened imagery like this was hideously expensive, and the three-V holocasts favored by the rich and powerful of the Inner Sphere were even more so. Most HPG transmissions were carried out in text only, or with small images, in compressed squirts of data lasting a millisecond or less. Longer messages, three-Vs, or realtime two-V transmissions like this one required much longer transmission times and could be put out over the HPG net only when general traffic was light.

ComStar charged obscene amounts of C-bills for high-data services when they were able to provide them at all, but it was worth it sometimes in the amount of data that could be conveyed. Usually, these techniques were reserved for news transmissions of import to the entire Inner Sphere, but the Great House governments and those independent military units that could afford them sometimes took advantage of the immediacy of the intelligence they offered.

It would be another four standard days, however, before the JumpShip *Blue Star* would have its jump drive charged and able to carry the Gray Death's Third Battalion that final eighteen light years to Glengarry. The laws of physics and of Kearny-Fuchida jump drives being what they were, there was no way they could reach Glengarry's system in less than another hundred hours or so. Why had his mother authorized the considerable expense of a direct-feed, live transmission, knowing that the military intelligence it contained would be four days out of date by the time Third Batt arrived?

Unless she feared that Third Battalion would arrive too late to help . . .

Goaded by a sharp stab of worry, Alex leaned forward, studying the insect-like, metallic shapes that were scrawling white contrails through they sky between the high-flying drone and Dunkeld's tower tops, or stalking along the city's streets. The battle was well under way, and, to judge by the damage already inflicted on the city, it had already been raging for a day or two at least. Missiles slashed through the air like flights of arrows, impacting in silently flaring gouts of light and smoke. A turret, squat and ugly atop one of the fortress towers, pivoted rapidly, and a dazzling sliver of blue light flickered unsteadily from the muzzle of its PPC. Three hundred meters from the fortress, moving along one of the streets of Dunkeld, a ponderous and almost comical caricature of a human lurched unsteadily as flame blossomed close by its left side. Comparison with the buildings on either side showed the machine's height to be something just over ten meters; Alex's experienced eye IDed the thing at a glance: one of the new 30-ton *Battle Hawk*s from Defiance Industries on Hesperus II. That meant the attackers were indeed FedCom, as the first messages from Glengarry had suggested.

"After the initial landings," Lori's voice said as the drone's camera panned across fortress and city, "Gareth's forces moved fast, faster than we really expected. Major Franco's original assessment was that this was some kind of snatch-and-grab raid, but these people obviously had a detailed deployment all worked out in advance. They knew exactly where they wanted to go, and how they were going to get there. We weren't able to assemble a blocking force until they'd already offloaded and started closing on Dunkeld from three directions."

Manuel Franco was the senior intelligence officer remaining back at Legion HQ, a good man with a strong tactical sense, but Alex wondered how good the man's guesswork had been this time. There were a lot more 'Mechs down there than any quick raid would justify.

Alex was counting and cataloguing enemy 'Mechs as the image transmitted from the drone shifted the field of view. Some were older, well-known models—*Marauder*s, a pair of comically stilting *Jenner*s, an ancient-looking but powerful *Thunderbolt*. Most of them, however, were more recent or less common designs. One huge machine, roughly humanoid but stooped, with a dorsal armor plate like a small, disk-shaped aircraft on its back, he recognized as an 80-ton PPR-5S *Salamander*. That was another Defiance Industries design, and a very new one. So far as Alex knew, only a handful had even been built so far, and most of those had been assigned to regions bordering Clan territory.

"They hit us two days ago at Colwyn when we tried to block them," Lori's voice continued, as more 'Mechs, accompanied by a trio of heavily armored hovercraft personnel carriers, moved into view. "At least one full battalion against First Batt's Third Company. They killed three of our 'Mechs at the price of two of their own, and our people were forced to fall back before they were cut off. As you can see, the invaders have a fair number of heavies, along with supporting infantry and armored vehicles. This is definitely *not* just a raiding party."

Everywhere the drone camera panned, more of the invader 'Mechs were visible. Alex had already counted thirty—nearly a full battalion's worth—moving in and about Dunkeld itself.

"We now believe we're facing at least three battalions, plus a battalion of infantry, some long-range artillery, and a wing of aerofighters," Lori continued. "That number is based on the number of DropShips we tracked inbound, as well as the reports brought back by our recon people and relayed by scout drones. With Second Battalion deployed to Kintyre for maneuvers, I ordered the rest of our people to fall back to Castle Hill. I didn't like abandoning Dunkeld to them, but I didn't see that we had much choice."

"Aye, lass," McCall said softly, almost under his breath. "More like no choice a' all."

Two battalions of the Gray Death Legion, the First and the Second, remained on Glengarry while the Third—plus the headquarters lance of the First—had deployed to Caledonia. Houk's Second Battalion had been scheduled to deploy to Kintyre, the smallest of Glengarry's three sprawling, northern hemisphere continents, for training maneuvers, and it sounded as though the invasion had caught them while they were out. That left just First Battalion, minus the headquarters lance, to face three attacking battalions. Lori had done exactly the right thing, pulling her available forces back and hunkering down inside the fortress of Castle Hill. If the attackers tried to dig them out, they'd find it a long, slow, and expensive process.

"That also meant I had to abandon the spaceport," Lori said. Her voice was tight, the words hard-edged and a bit too precise. "I'm sorry about that, but there was simply no other way to save what's left of First Battalion. At the moment, Gareth's people pretty much have the run of both the port and the city. So far, though, the castle's defenses are holding. We have plenty of food, the wells are operating, and if we husband our expendable munitions, we should be able to make them last until you boys get here."

The view shifted to a close-up of the fortress, ebon surfaces gleaming in Glengarry's warm, orange light. Alex was still orienting himself when an attacking aerofighter streaked into view. It was a *Corsair,* a House Davion design, with the bold fist-in-sun emblem of the Federated Commonwealth on its wings. A heartbeat after it entered Alex's field of vision, missiles flashed from beneath the fighter's nose, arrowing into the fortress on tightly drawn threads of white smoke.

"Air attacks have been heavy," Lori was saying. "But so far we're manag—"

Then the volley of missiles struck with a silently pulsing ripple of flashes, and with the third flash the screen suddenly dissolved in a storm of static. Lori's voice, too, was lost in the steady hiss of white noise. Alex waited for his mother's voice to pick up the thread of her monologue again, but the hissing static went on and on until suddenly the screen blanked, replaced a moment later by the ComStar logo and a brief and uninformative message.

TRANSMISSION INTERRUPTED AT SOURCE

Alex wasn't sure what the target had been; he thought, though, that the missiles had been heading for the cluster of communications antennae high atop Castle Hill's vaulted carapace. It had to have been the destruction of an HPG antenna that had cut his mother's transmission off in mid-sentence that way. It *had* to be. . . .

"Davis—"

Alex continued staring at the unhelpful message on the screen, willing the image transmitted from above Dunkeld to return. Gently, McCall reached down and switched off the recording. "Come on, lad," he said. "Let's go doon t' the lounge an' sit a spell."

"Davis, you don't think—"

"*Think,* lad! Those missiles struck fair among the big antennae up on the fortress roof," McCall said with his broadest Scots burr. "Y' must keep in mind tha' it's nae so bad as it seems. Tha' strike we saw a' the end likely put a wee missile or three into th' hyperpulse antennae atop Castle Hill an' damaged it or nudged it oot a' line before th' transmission was complete. It was the antenna tha' went doon, not your maither."

"I know that," Alex replied, taking a breath and trying to steady his reeling senses. "From that bit we saw of her, it looked like she was in Ops when she made that transmission. A hundred meters down and shielded by five meters of ferrocrete and Star League hull metal. But she's cut off. Surrounded by those bastards and outnumbered better than three to one!"

"Aye. But if anyone can hold oot against tha' lot, it's Lieutenant Colonel Kalmar-Carlyle. She's a fighter, tha' one."

"But can she hold out? Against three battalions?"

"In a stand-up fight, probably not. But in a siege? Your mum knows better than t' sally oot against th' likes of Brandal Gareth. She'll sit tight an' make him come t' her. I cannae believe anyone would want tha' wee planet bad enough t' take tha' kind of loss." McCall gestured with a jerk of his bearded head toward the comm shack door. "C'mon, lad. Let's find us a place t' sit an' have a wee talk."

Numb, Alex followed. It was so difficult to banish the

evidence of his senses. And with his father in a medical coma, with enemy forces closing in back home ...

It was beginning to look as though the very life of the Gray Death Legion was at stake.

And Alex could see no way at all to better the odds.

2

DropShip **Endeavor**
Nadir Jump Point
Gladius System, Skye March
Federated Commonwealth
1814 hours, 9 May 3057

The lounge was one of the few places aboard the DropShip where one had an actual, physical view outside the ship, instead of through viewscreen or computer vid display. A long, curved expanse of transplas peered out past armored louvers that were sealed shut during combat. DropShips, especially military DropShips, were designed to be efficient and compact, not comfortable, but ship designers had long ago learned that ship crews and MechWarriors could not spend week after week at one jump point or another, waiting for the batteries to recharge for the next jump, with only cramped cabins or ship working spaces or the 'Mech bays to work in. They also needed a place for downtime.

Only a handful of MechWarriors occupied the lounge at the moment, however. As Alex followed McCall in, pulling himself along the handholds, he noticed Caitlin DeVries and Sharon Kilroy sitting in a far corner, engaged in a flickering, fast volleying game of holographic BattleTech. Sergeant Sergei Golovanov and one of the 'Mech techs were absorbed in an even older game—chess—though the pieces were represented by four-centimeter-tall animated images of black or blood-red BattleMechs.

Otherwise, however, the lounge was deserted. Alex spent a moment floating next to the window, looking out into the star-sprinkled emptiness of space. The *Endeavor*'s orientation was such that he was looking aft along the JumpShip *Blue Star*'s spine. Beyond the sail-rigging spars and yards, the vast, dead-black circle of the starship's energy-collection sail blotted out half the sky's stars. The starship could be pictured as a slender spine of metal and ceraplast balanced on its tail two kilometers above the huge, ebony expanse of its sail. Its stern drives were aimed at the local sun, which was bull's-eyed in the circular opening at the center of the sail, jet black to absorb every photon it intercepted on the solar wind. The hole allowed passage of the thin, invisible stream of high-energy plasma ejected from the JumpShip's station-keeping drive, which kept the entire assembly precariously balanced against the relentless tug of the star's gravity.

Many people, Alex reminded himself as he squinted against the dazzle of orange light peeking past the opening in the sail, perhaps even *most* people nowadays, thought of a star's two jump points as spots defined by the star's north and south poles, places where gravity somehow didn't exist or was canceled out. He'd always found it amusing, while his father insisted it was tragic, an indication of just how far education and the general knowledge of science had fallen during the past few centuries throughout the Inner Sphere.

Gravity, of course, was nothing like magnetism. It had no "poles," and its strength varied inversely with distance from the center of mass alone and was omnidirectional. Direction, whether toward the nadir, the zenith, or simply *out,* had nothing to do with it. The points "above" and "below" a star had come into use as convenient points from which JumpShips could depart a system solely because they offered coordinates as far as possible from the perturbational effects of any planets—especially large, out-system gas giants—that the star might possess, and because they were equidistant from all points of any given planetary orbit. JumpShips required space that was as gravitationally flat as possible, both for the safe operation of their Kearny-Fuchida drives and for the full deployment of their energy-collection sails, which could be collapsed by the tidal effects of nearby worlds. At the same time, the closer they were to the star, the faster they could recharge their drives with solar energy collected by the sail. The compromise between these two opposing requirements—low gravity and high luminosity—determined how far from a given star the jump point could be. The brighter—and therefore more massive—a star was, the farther out a JumpShip had to be for safe operation; at the same time, the brighter the star, the faster the ship could recharge its coils.

Gladius's sun was a K-class star, orange in color and massing a bit more than half of Terra's Sol. It would take eight full days to recharge *Blue Star*'s jumpdrive on that light. The only ways to shorten that waiting period would have been to transfer the Legion's DropShips from the *Blue Star* to another JumpShip conveniently waiting, full-charged, and empty at that point—a hand-off express, as MechWarriors called it—or if a recharge station were positioned there which could transfer a charge already accumulated. There were other JumpShips at the Gladius nadir point, but the chances that one would be available for a hand-off were ridiculously slim, and Gladius was not an important enough world to maintain anything so expensive or high-tech as a recharge station.

As Alex floated in front of the viewport, he found himself beginning to drift slowly toward the transplas, falling, ever so slowly, with the fractional-G thrust of the *Blue Star*'s sunward-aimed drive, and put out one hand to catch himself on a convenient guard rail. Small, scarcely felt impulses, he thought, could nevertheless build relentlessly to an overwhelming force. Each decision made during the past months had seemed insignificant at the time, and yet each had led, step by inexorable step, to this. . . .

"Alex?"

He turned. "I'm here, Davis."

"We should decide wha' we're aboot, lad."

Alex planted one booted foot on the padded bulkhead beneath the transplas and gave a small shove, sailing across the lounge to the curved sofa where McCall had already strapped himself in. "It doesn't sound good, does it?" he said, taking a place next to Davis and buckling his own safety belt.

"Weel, noo," McCall said, rubbing his beard slowly. "I've known less complicated times, aye, an' that's a fact. Still an' all, things could be a damn sight worse. What we do now is figure our next step vurra carefully an' see if we can take back th' initiative from this Gareth person."

"What does Gareth want?" Alex shook his head. "That nonsense about us breaking contract—"

"We *did* break th' contract, lad. At least, by th' strict interpretation of the document's word we did. But tha's for a review board or even a military court t' decide, not Gareth."

The politics of the Inner Sphere, Alex decided, were enough to drive any such body collectively insane. The Gray Death Legion's original contract had been with Archon Katrina Steiner and the old Lyran Commonwealth more than thirty years ago, after the Legion's betrayal by their Marik employers at Sirius V and Helm. That had all been years before Alex was born, of course, but he'd heard and read the story often enough that it was a part of him. The Gray Death Legion took considerable pride in its history as a military unit with a proud past and as a kind of large and extended family for the men and women who served in it. In 3028 the Lyran Commonwealth and the Federated Suns of House Davion had united with the marriage of Hanse Davion to Melissa Steiner. The Gray Death's contract had been picked up by the new government, which was how the Legion had recently found itself putting down the Skye Separatists in the Lyran sector of the Federated Commonwealth.

Alex knew, though, that his father had always believed that the Legion's first loyalty was still to House Steiner— and to the Steiner family rather than to the government that happened to be in power. The elder Carlyle was, by anyone's standards, a rather old-fashioned sort, a man who counted obligations to *people* rather than to any institution. That, in very large part, was why Carlyle had sided with the rebels on Caledonia. In his view, Wilmarth had been acting against the interests of House Steiner with his atrocities and his tyrannical, even genocidal rule; Grayson Carlyle had elected to honor the spirit of his contract to the Steiners by breaking its letter.

And that single act of rebellion, of mutiny, might well have cost him, and the Legion ... *everything*.

"Who is this guy Gareth, anyway?" Alex wanted to know.

"I looked up his bio in the library computer," McCall said. "Th' man has aye an impressive record. Served wi' several mercenary units before going to the Nagelring a' Tharkad. Commissioned First Leutnant in '34. Served with the Second Royal Guards an' saw action against the Clans when they showed up. Credited wi' four Clan kills, an' tha' takes some doing. Order of the Tamar Tigers. Honor of Skye. The McKennsy Hammer."

"The Hammer?" Alex felt an uneasy stirring at that. The award was an actual block hammer of solid silver massing some nine kilos, awarded by House Steiner to officers who'd shown special skill as tacticians or strategists. It was a military award that was not lightly given.

"Aye. Seems he's pulled a wee rabbit oot of a hat a time or two. That's how he got his promotion to field marshal, too. An' of course he's commander of the Planetary Defense Force of two regiments stationed on Hesperus II, including our friends, th' Third Davion Guard."

"That alone says something for his abilities," Alex said. "Or at least for his political skill."

"Aye. Hesperus II is Tharkad's ace in the hole. They only entrust that place to the very best and the most loyal." McCall frowned. "Though there've been a few bootlickers t' win tha' plum as well. Still, Brandal Gareth is, by all accounts, a fine soldier."

"So why does he have it in for the Legion?"

"His record mentions he does nae like mercenaries." McCall grinned. "Tha' seems little enough reason to go to all this trouble, though, eh?"

"Maybe someone else is giving the orders."

"Possibly. Or possibly he heard wha' was happening from Zellner and the Third Guard an' decided to act on his own."

Alex shook his head. "I'm not sure that works logistically, Davis. I mean, we received word that Gareth was entering Glengarry space and demanding the Legion's surrender just after Falkirk. Hesperus II is as far from Glengarry as Caledonia is. Two jumps, two weeks, close enough, plus DropShop shuttle time in-system at either end. He'd have had to leave Hesperus for Glengarry almost three weeks *before* Falkirk to get there when he did!"

"Aye." McCall leaned back in the sofa, looking thoughtful. "Aye, you're right aboot tha'. I suppose he could hae set oot in early April, say, when there was first word aboot our wee risin' on Caledon."

McCall was referring to the brief, savage guerrilla war he and Alex had waged against Wilmarth's ill-disciplined militia with the help of the local Caledonian resistance. It was that fighting that had led to the Gray Death's direct involvement and the elder Carlyle's decision to intervene on the side of the rebels.

"And he obviously set out for Glengarry ready for trouble. Three battalions? Plus auxiliary troops, recon and scouting units, special equipment, supplies for a major campaign. . . ."

"Aye. I'd bet my pension tha' he waited just long enough to know th' colonel had left for Caledonia before lifting th' whole kit an' caboodle for Glengarry. Probably from a spy in th' Legion. Now *that's* an interestin' thought. . . ."

The more Alex looked at the problem, the more obvious it was that Gareth had set out to trap the Legion from the beginning, though he still couldn't begin to guess why. He'd sat back and waited until the Gray Death's commanding officer had left for Caledonia with over a third of the Legion, then made straight for the Legion's baseworld with a demand for its surrender. Alex couldn't help wondering if Brandal Gareth had somehow been behind the trouble on Caledonia in the first place, creating it as a diversion to split the Legion and leave Glengarry weakened. It made sense, in a twisted sort of way. Caledonia was right next door to Hesperus II, less than ten light years distant. It was possible that Wilmarth had been Gareth's pawn, someone who could have been bent into his homicidal ways to force the well-known morality of Grayson Carlyle to rebel against orders.

And then there was the matter of the traitor, Dupré, who'd opened fire on Grayson Carlyle's *Victor* from behind at point-blank range, then tried to fry him with a PPC beam as he climbed out of the 'Mech's shattered cockpit. That man was the best candidate for a spy within the Legion that Alex could think of, ideally placed to report on the Legion's movements. Too bad the bastard had vanished after Falkirk.

"What you're saying, Davis," Alex said carefully, "is that Gareth may well have set up this whole thing . . . and probably tried to have my father killed as well. Why does he want Glengarry, anyway?"

"Weel, it's a nice enough world, but I do see your point. It has no particular industry or other prize worth th' having, save for the Legion itself."

"What it comes down to is he either wants Glengarry for some reason, as a base, or because of some intrinsic value to the place, or his target is the Legion. He wants it dead or disbanded or whatever. I'd give a lot to know why."

"So would I, lad." McCall shook his head. "But for tha' kind of answer, I think we need to investigate th' wee bastard ourselves."

"Which leads us to the next question, which is what are we going to do about it?" Alex drove his right fist into his left palm, a startling slap of sound in the quiet lounge. "About Gareth. It's going to be two weeks before we can ground on Glengarry, and by then—"

"Weel, noo," McCall said, "there's always this." He reached into one of the many pockets in his black combat vest and extracted a palmscreen, an electronic notepad with an eight-centimeter screen, handing it across to Alex. Alex touched the display key, revealing a glowing computer plot of radar targets, each tagged by a cryptic line of alphanumerics.

"A jump-point scan?" Alex asked.

"Aye. This jump point, an' taken this morning." He indicated one of the blips on the screen, representing a kilometer-wide collector sail, glowing squarely at the center of the circular plot. "That one's us."

There were three other targets as well. Jump points were rather vague and ill-defined regions in space, given that their only real identifying characteristic was their distance from the local sun, and the fact that they were more or less in the zenith or nadir direction, as defined by the star's north and south poles. The nearest JumpShip to the *Blue Star,* according to the scale showing in the lower left-hand corner of the display, was about half a million kilometers away.

McCall indicated that nearest blip. "This one's of no use. Steiner military transport wi' a full load, en route from Skye to Tharkad." His blunt finger shifted to another blip, the one farthest out. "An' this one is a civilian JumpShip, but she just arrived aboot twelve hours ago an' won't be goin' anywhere until she's full charged. But this one, noo . . ." McCall's finger slid across the screen to the third blip, a sail tracing perhaps a million kilometers from the *Blue Star*'s position. "This one is the free trader *Caliban*, an' she might just meet our needs. She's ridin' near empty, a fact tha' her skipper made quite clear to me earlier was nae t' their likin'."

"You've talked to them, then?"

"Aye, tha' I did, lad. They'll consider taking on a cargo for Glengarry. Us. For a price, of course."

"What price?"

"Expensive," McCall said, his mouth twisting in a frown behind his red beard. "Expensive enough to curdle a good Scotsman's soul. It may be we'll be able to bargain it doon a wee bit more. But whatever the cost, it'll aye be worth it, considerin' the fact they've been here three days longer than we have—"

Alex's eyes widened. "They're ready to jump tomorrow?"

"In another sixteen hours, more or less. Just time enough for us to effect a transfer, if you follow me."

"A hand-off express!"

"Exactly. An', to put th' gildin' on the BattleMech, as it were, it turns out they've been t' Glengarry before, an' recently. They've a full an' up-to-date ephemeris in their navigation computer."

Alex nodded understanding. "So you're thinking of using a pirate point?"

"Aye. We could do tha' an' save even more time. We hae all the necessary data for it." McCall shrugged. "I may have to convince the *Caliban*'s captain of the, um, urgency of our schedule. . . ."

"If anyone can convince anyone of anything, Davis, you're the one!" Alex felt a savage, exultant stirring within. The hardest part of these past few weeks had been his utter helplessness, his inability to strike *back*. Now, though . . .

"We've got aye a long way to go yet, lad," McCall said quietly, "but we'll see it through. I promise you that." He nodded with his head and eyes, indicating the sick bay and Alex's father. "An' *him*."

"Who is this ship captain?" Alex wanted to know.

"Her name," McCall replied, "is Mindy Cain. An' if half of what I've heard aboot th' lassie is so, we're not going to have any trouble a' all with a pirate point jump."

3

Castle Hill, Dunkeld
Glengarry, Skye March
Federated Commonwealth
0917 hours, 13 May 3057

Deep in the heart of the Gray Death Legion's fortress on Castle Hill, Lieutenant Colonel Lori Kalmar-Carlyle and her commanders were gathered in Ops, a reinforced underground bunker that served as the military nerve center for all of Glengarry.

"Mechdrek!" she said with considerable feeling as she leaned over the shoulder of a tech to study a tactical screen displaying the fortress and the Legion's positions as tiny, three-dimensional images viewed from overhead. Enemy 'Mechs, highlighted in glowing red, were on the move, falling back through the streets of Dunkeld. For days, they'd been tightening the noose on the Legion's stronghold. Now, just when her people were ready to strike back for a change instead of skulking behind ferrocrete and duralloy walls, the enemy was pulling out.

Not *out*, Lori corrected herself as she watched the movements on the screen. But they were shifting their deployment, and it looked to her as though they were moving to block the Legion's incoming reinforcements from the north.

"Do you think they've spotted Houk's people yet?" Captain Vincent Allen asked her. Allen was a prim and fussy sort of man, with a pencil-thin mustache that was probably intended to make him look either dashing or dangerous, and failed both ways. He was commander of the Castle Guard.

"Sure looks that way, Vince," Lori said, voicing at last the worry that had been dogging her for some time now. At first, she'd not been sure the movements she was watching were anything more than the random shuffling of Gareth's BattleMechs as he tightened the noose on the Gray Death's fortress. Now, though, it was clear that more and more of the invader 'Mechs were leaving their positions in and around the city south of Castle Hill and were moving around it toward the east or west, then swinging around into the hills to the north. The land north of the fortress sloped gently down to the wooded banks of the Killross River about eight kilometers away, then began rising again among great, tumble-down blocks of granite and thickly clotted forests, toward the icy, distant peaks of the Scotian Highlands beyond.

The last voice communications Lori had received from Major Houk and Second Battalion had been over two weeks ago, just as Gareth's invaders had been spotted arrowing in from the Glengarry system's zenith jump point. At that time, Second Battalion—currently on the rosters with twenty-eight BattleMechs and two anti-'Mech infantry platoons—had been on training maneuvers in Kintyre. Houk had agreed to keep his unit hidden, to lay low until the invaders' intentions were known. He would have been eavesdropping since, maintaining vid and radio silence while listening in on encrypted tacsit updates broadcast from the fortress.

Four hours ago, just before local dawn, a single, brief burst of radio noise had been picked up by the Legion's comm center, a string of alphanumerics telling Castle Hill's defenders that Houk's forces were close by and preparing to attack.

In two short weeks, Houk's 'Mechs had traversed nearly eight thousand kilometers, slipping unseen through the vast forests of Kintyre, moving along mountain passes south across the twisting Isthmus of Moray, and finally approaching Dunkeld from the north side of the Scotian Mountains. Evidently he'd made it all that way without being spotted by Gareth's patrols.

Now, however, as Second Battalion approached to within a few kilometers of Dunkeld, it was virtually certain that Gareth's patrols had picked up the incoming 'Mechs.

"At any rate, we have to assume that they've seen them," Lori continued. "Second Batt won't be in position for another hour at least, but the bad guys will have both scouts and remote sensors out all across the perimeter, if nothing else."

"If the bad guys did pick up Houk, they'll be moving to hit him when he crosses the river and comes up out of the woods."

"Maybe," Lori said, thoughtful now. "Although if I were Gareth, I'd try to arrange for a surprise in the woods, where Houk's people couldn't give each other support. But, one way or another, Gareth's going to give Houk a bad time, no matter where he lays his ambush. Unless we can give him something else to keep them interested in us."

Vince looked uncertain. "A sortie?"

Lori turned, picking out Christie Calahan, the Ops Officer, sitting at her console nearby. "C. C.!"

The lean, dark-haired woman looked up. "Yeah, Boss!"

"I'm calling a scramble. Every 'Mech the gang downstairs can power up. I also want full alert on all Castle Hill defenses. Stat!"

"You got it!"

Vincent Allen's frown of concern etched itself deeper into his face. "Do you think that's advisable, ma'am? They still outmass us by a substantial margin."

Lori gave him a hard-edged look. "I sure as hell don't see any alternatives, Captain." She nodded toward the display screen. "At the moment, we're in danger of what Colonel Carlyle would call defeat in detail. If we don't poke our noses out from our hidey hole, Second Batt is going to get ground to bits."

Turning her back on Allen, Lori had just crossed the Ops floor and entered one of the elevators plunging down into the bowels of the fortress when the rasping bray of the base alert klaxon began sounding from unseen speakers in the ceiling overhead. As the sound echoed away, she heard Captain Calahan's voice. *"Attention! Attention!*

This is a Class One scramble! All MechWarriors, man your machines!"

The elevator dropped, the sensation raising old memories of free fall aboard JumpShips hanging in space. Castle Hill was some three and a half centuries old, dating well back into the Star League era when settlers from Terra—from the impoverished nation-states of Scotland, Norway, and Canada—had first come to Glengarry. It filled much of the sheer-faced mountain above the city of Dunkeld, with kilometer upon kilometer of underground warrens, assembly and repair facilities, 'Mech bays, and storage chambers.

The sensation of weight surged back as the elevator slowed, and a moment later the door opened onto Castle Hill's Number One 'Mech bay, a vast and cavernous space blasted centuries ago from the solid granite of the mountain. Walkways and gantries covered the cavern walls and stretched from one side to the other across soaring, open spaces beneath a ceiling lost in darkness and the occasional dazzle of a brilliant overhead spotlight. First Battalion's 'Mechs were kept here; a few were in the process of being repaired or re-armed, but most were ready for combat, standing beneath the gleam of multiple worklights, wreathed in the soft haze of steam from coolant feeds and pressure lines. The noise was a brainnumbing cacophony of clanks and shrill metal-on-metal screeches, of hissing, high-pressure gas lines and the heavy thud of multi-ton footsteps on the duralloy-reinforced ferrocrete deck, and, threading through it all, the piercing ululation of alarm sirens.

There was activity everywhere she looked: men and women swarming over the ranks of waiting BattleMechs, completing hasty repairs or loading them with munitions; small tractors trundling about hauling carts piled high with missiles, machine gun ammo, and autocannon magazines; the 'Mechs themselves, one by one edging clear of the gantry towers that enclosed them and marshaling near the towering, heavily armored doors on the north wall of the cavern.

Tech Sergeant Max Dewar was standing on the deck of the bay, waving one of the Legion's *Assassins* forward with swift, precise motions of the yellow chemical light wands he held in his hands. The 40-ton 'Mech pivoted slowly, following Max's signals with careful, almost mincing steps. "Max!" she called, shouting to be heard above the racket.

"Colonel Kalmar!" His eyes widened with surprise. Both the techs and the MechWarriors of the Gray Death called her by her maiden name; lieutenant colonels were addressed as "colonel," and there could be only one "Colonel Carlyle" in the regiment. "What can we do for you down here?"

"Is Boss Lady ready to stride?" She knew it was; she'd checked the ready list up in Ops earlier that morning.

He looked doubtful. "Yes, ma'am. All but for the A/C loads. But, well, are *you* figurin' on taking her out?"

"That I am, Max." Her eyes found Boss Lady, a hulking, 55-ton *Shadow Hawk* standing in a corner of Bay One not far from the tunnel leading to Number Three Magazine. "Surprised?"

"Uh, no, ma'am!" The tech's answer was a bit too quick. "I just didn't have you listed on the deployment sched, is all."

"Well, I'm there now. I'm putting myself on." Fists clenched at her sides, she strode toward the towering 'Mech.

Boss Lady was one of the Legion's handful of supernumerary 'Mechs, a machine that might serve as a walking repository of spare parts, or as a spare machine for a MechWarrior whose regular machine had ended up *hors de combat*. She was also Lori's 'Mech, whenever she cared to take her out.

Lori could understand Max's being nonplused by her demand for a 'Mech. She'd not been in the cockpit of one for more months than she cared to think about right now. There'd been talk in the Legion, she was well aware, to the effect that she'd ceased conning BattleMechs. It had, in fact, been a good many years since she'd piloted a 'Mech in combat. The reasons for that were complex and had more to do with her perception of how she could best serve the Legion—and Grayson—than with any conscious decision to avoid 'Mech firefights.

Her career as a MechWarrior had actually started over thirty years before, on Sigurd, the world of her birth, a frigid planet out beyond the periphery of the Inner Sphere, deep within what was now Clan-controlled space. She'd seen combat on at least a dozen different worlds since then, most of them in the early years of the Legion's history, before Grayson had built the unit up from a single mercenary company to the reinforced regiment that it was today. When she'd become pregnant with Alex, she'd dropped the role of MechWarrior, thinking that it would just be for a time.

Somehow, being a mother had detoured her career as warrior, though she'd continued to serve as the Legion's Executive Officer, handling the unit's internal affairs and bossing the Gray Death from headquarters in Grayson's absence.

The thought of Grayson's absence twisted in her gut, nearly making her miss a step as she reached the 'Mech access gantry. There was no new word from Third Battalion, which by now would be waiting out its recharge in the Gladius system, preparing to make the last hyperspace jump back to Glengarry. There would be no word, not until they could get Grayson back home, decant him from his med capsule, and begin treating him for the injuries he'd suffered at Falkirk. As a military woman, Lori was used to the ideas both of death and of crippling dismemberment, but never before had those realities of war struck so mercilessly close to home.

It was the knowledge that she had to keep the Legion's landhold safe so that Grayson had someplace to come home to, as much as anything else, that had kept her going these past few weeks, had kept her fighting against Gareth's invasion. She'd had to decide early on whether to flee Dunkeld entirely and go to ground in Glengarry's outback wilderness, or to hole up in Castle Hill and hold on until Third Batt returned. She'd decided in favor of the fortress mostly because she knew Grayson would need its medical facilities—by far the most advanced on the planet—when he returned.

She slipped one boot into a footloop and rode the strap elevator up the gantry frame. Boss Lady stood just over ten meters in height, not counting the sleek, black, vertical thrust of the autocannon mounted behind her left shoulder and now pointed straight up at the cavern's dark-shrouded ceiling. The 'Mech was painted in Legion colors, a mottled camouflage of grays and blacks, and with the Legion's grayskull emblem painted on the *Shadow Hawk*'s left breast and both arm pauldrons. She let go of the lift strap and stepped onto the head access gantry; the cockpit was open, the padded seat almost filling the narrow pilot's compartment behind the instrument panel and HUD projector struts.

Max stepped onto the gantry just as she was sliding down into the cockpit. "The Lady's right arm's been stickin' a bit, still," he warned her, squatting on the platform to put his head close to hers. "A bit of a lag when you're acquirin' a target. Watch that, or you'll trigger too soon."

Lori was cinching the straps snug and locking them home. She nodded. "Got it."

"Here comes your A/C."

Autocannon shells were fired in three- to five-round bursts drawn from the *Shadow Hawk*'s wheel-shaped carousel magazines. The 'Mech also sported an Armstrong J11 cannon, a good, reliable weapon with only a slight tendency toward jams if the barrel or receiver group overheated. A crew of armorers bossed by a tech sergeant was slamming a fresh load of 'sels into the autocannon's magazine racks and locking them home.

Lori concentrated on running down her pre-walk checklist, using the printed sheets on a clipboard hanging from the side of her pilot seat, but pleased that, after the first few items, anyway, she was remembering them. The litany was burned into every MechWarrior's mind, as much a part of him or her as flesh, blood, and bone.

Power plant . . . switch on. Temperature optimum. Green light.

Jump jets . . . venturis clear. Plasma jets, green, on safe, overrides set.

Gyros . . . running and at speed.

Engine . . . ready to engage. Green light.

Targeting system. Go.

Comm system. Go.

Tactical. On.

Weapons systems . . .

A/C ammo, check. Weapon on safe, ninety-degree elevation on barrel.

LRM, loaded, missiles on safe, tracking set, green light.

Laser, power connect green. Core temperature green. Safeties set . . .

Reaching up above and behind her seat, she grabbed hold of her neurohelmet in its mount and dragged it forward and down, settling it over her silver hair and bringing its collar pads onto her shoulders.

A long-time dream of BattleMech designers had always been to build a 'Mech that could act in accordance with the pilot's thoughts, that would act, in fact, like the pilot's own body. That goal had eluded even the designers and engineers of the Star League and was certainly well beyond the technological grasp of the Inner Sphere today. While the 'Mech's legs, arms, and weapons systems had to be worked through a variety of control sticks, pedals, and computer feedback connections, one direct link with the pilot's brain was still necessary. The neurohelmet provided that link, feeding a variety of data input from sensors all over the 'Mech's body to the pilot through his audio nerves. Since the inner ear was closely associated with the human sense of balance, it was possible to let the pilot actually feel the attitude and balance of his 'Mech through the helmet's feed. It was impossible, in fact, to pilot a 'Mech without that balance feedback; without it, there was no way the pilot could sense the loss of balance and thus control the motion and attitude of a 'Mech trying to run, to jump, or even simply to walk.

As Lori continued running through the checklist, proving out the helmet's feedback connections and her own sensory input, tears briefly burned at the corners of her eyes. The medical reports she'd seen on Grayson suggested that there was almost certainly serious damage to his left ear, damage that could not be healed and would almost certainly prevent him from ever piloting a 'Mech again.

It was hard for Lori to feel what she knew intellectually that injury must mean for Grayson. After all, she'd made a deliberate choice of family over BattleMechs, but she knew, or thought she did, what piloting a BattleMech meant to him and could imagine what a blow the loss of that would be. Hell, Grayson had been piloting 'Mechs since he was a kid, apprenticed to his father's mercenary unit, Carlyle's Commandos; he was fifty-six standard now, and that was a lot of years spent in 'Mech cockpits.

It would be all right, as soon as she had him back, safe and inside the fortress. . . .

"Boss Lady, this is Ops," a voice said over her radio headset inside the neurohelmet. Part of the gantry structure, the walkways and struts across the front of her *Shadow Hawk,* was swinging back and out of the way. "We've got a green board on your 'Mech. You're clear to march."

"Roger that, Ops," she replied, snapping off the switches that served as movement safeties inside the gantry's embrace. She felt the familiar tingle in the back of her head and recognized the old sensation of balance that felt eerily like the positioning of her own body, but far, far larger. In a way, it was like being the BattleMech, or at least like wearing it, a light suit of armor on a body ten meters tall.

Leaning forward slightly, she took her first step, then the next, and the next. She cleared the gantry, taking short steps until she fully regained the feel of her enormous charge. Shadows cast by the crisscrossing beams of side and overhead work lights slid across ferrocrete walls and the webwork struts of gantries as she moved, vast and weirdly shaped. Below her, reaching up to just below her knees, Max was standing on the deck, tiny and vulnerable as he waved his glowing light wands, directing her to the left.

Pivoting sharply in the indicated direction, she strode with gathering confidence across the 'Mech bay. Ahead, other 'Mechs, the *Assassin* she'd seen earlier, an *Enforcer,* a *Dervish,* a *Valkyrie,* all lined up at the yellow-and-black-striped surface of the bay egress.

"Good luck, Boss Lady" sounded in her helmet phones. She recognized Max's voice. "Good hunting!"

"I'll bring back a trophy, Max," she promised.

"Make it a *Marauder* or an *Atlas,*" he said. "In good condition. I still need a Vlar 300 for that downgrudged *Marauder.*"

She chuckled. "You got it." The Gray Death was pretty well off as mercenary units went—or at least it had been until now. Even so, its techs relied more on parts scavenged from the battlefield—parts up to and including the power plant Max had just mentioned—than they did on shipments from BattleMech factories. That reliance would become even more crucial if it turned out that House Steiner had, in fact, turned against the Legion.

"Boss Lady, this is Ops," a different voice said in her headset. "The approaches to Bay One are clear. We're opening up."

And then with a rumbling whine the massive duralloy doors ground slowly apart, first the inner set, and then the more massive, thicker outer doors, and the blinding glare of morning sunlight spilled through the widening slot. Smoke stained the sky in the distance to the north; it looked as though the battle had already begun.

"This is it, boys and girls," Lori announced over the tactical frequency. "Let's go have a serious discussion with this guy about his penchant for trespassing on other people's planets!"

In close echelon formation, the other 'Mechs followed her into the open. Despite her bantering encouragement to the others, Lori felt a cold, grim deadliness inside.

She was going to close with the enemy that threatened her Grayson. And then she was going to kill him.

=== 4 ===

The four 'Mechs following Lori out the 'Mech Bay One lock were the Fire Lance of First Battalion's Second Company. Lieutenant Dimitri Ivanovich Oretsov, in the ENF-4R *Enforcer,* was lance commander. "Glad to have you with us, Colonel Kalmar," Oretsov said, his accent thick over the taccom frequency. "It makes up for Headquarters Lance's absence, yes?"

"Well, I don't know about that, Dimie," she replied. "I'd love to have McCall's *Highlander* here with us right about now. Or Alex's *Archer.*" First Battalion's Headquarters Lance, of course, had gone to Caledonia with Third Batt. They would miss the firepower of those heavies in the coming fight.

"Hey, no sweat, Colonel," Sergeant Dag Flanders called from his *Dervish.* "What we lack in mass and firepower, we'll make up in sheer charm and good looks!"

At least, Lori thought grimly, their morale was still good, despite two weeks of crouching inside the fortress while Gareth's 'Mechs ran wild through the city. On second thought, maybe that was the reason their morale was good. They were at last going to get their chance to hit back at the invaders. Castle Hill had been under more or less constant, if intermittent, bombardment for most of that time.

The real morale-killer, though, wasn't incoming LRMs so much as it was the steady, wearing knowledge that wives and husbands, lovers, friends, and family were still in the city of Dunkeld and at the invaders' mercy. Glengarry was the Legion's landhold, a world granted to them by the Federated Commonwealth for services rendered over the years. That didn't so much mean that the Legion ruled Glengarry—though Grayson had been awarded the title of Baron of Glengarry the year before—as it meant simply that they lived there, that they'd put down roots on this world and in that city. The Legion, as Grayson never tired of commenting, was people, not machines, and its members had lives outside of the narrow strictures of Gray Death discipline and duty. Normally, the whole Legion and its families lived in the Residence, the largest, grandest building in the warren that comprised Castle Hill. But that had changed with the siege. There hadn't been time to gather all of the Legion families into the old Star League facility when Gareth's forces had closed their net.

The Bay One doors had opened on the north side of the base, on the opposite side of the mountain from the city of Dunkeld. Here, the rugged, barren, cliff-faced hill on which the fortress perched like an old, misshapen beret was less than half the height it was on the south side, overlooking the city. The 'Mech bay, a hundred meters below the topmost towers of the fortress, opened onto level ground at the base of a cliff, a clear fire zone wiped empty of all vegetation—right down to the topsoil itself—by the Star League engineers who'd built the place.

Lori glanced at her main tracking display, a circular screen showing a scattering of blips among the rectilinear smears of building radar traces. Strings of alphanumerics appeared next to each blip; the feed was coming over the tactical channel from Ops, repeating off Display Two but in shrunken, streamlined form; remote sensors, unmanned drone aircraft, and Legion scouts throughout the region were constantly IDing the enemy 'Mechs and vehicles as quickly as possible, but there were far too many targets out there that carried the simple legend UNKNOWN.

A flash through her *Shadow Hawk*'s canopy screen snagged Lori's attention, making her look up. Sunlight was glinting off the angular canopy of the Fire Lance's *Assassin* as it moved past her to the right. Beyond, high in an achingly beautiful blue-green sky, white contrails drew themselves through the air, arcing down toward Castle Hill.

"LRMs incoming, Boss," Sal Donatelli warned, his *Assassin* breaking into a slow, steadily lumbering trot.

Glancing down, Lori noted the long-range missile traces on her display screen, tiny clusters of white dots arrowing toward her position. "Scatter!" she called to the others. No use standing in a clump, making targets of themselves. A moment later, three quick-pulsed geysers of dirt, rock, and smoke fountained into the sky fifty meters to her rear. She turned right, trying to eyeball the incoming LRM smoke trails and backtrack on them to their launchers. More explosions rippled across the plain north of the fortress, and falling gravel rattled across her *Hawk*'s head and shoulders like hail on a tin roof.

Outgoing missiles howled overhead, return fire flashing outbound from the fortress's LRM turrets seeking the enemy launchers. Checking her display again, Lori decided to head for the nearest IDed enemy 'Mechs. In concealment a few hundred meters ahead, they were in a good position to spot for long-ranged artillery, and Lori couldn't think of a better or more immediate target. "Coming to zero-three-five," she told the others. "Looks like we've got some scouts hidden in those boulders up ahead."

"Roger that," Oretsov said. "Stick tight, Colonel. We'll keep your backside clean."

"Don't worry about me, boys," she replied. "Worry about those raider bastards." Conventional BattleMech tactics divided companies of twelve into lances of four, with the four paired two and two so that no MechWarrior was ever alone. By joining Second Company's Fire Lance this way, Lori risked upsetting the carefully practiced and simulation-rehearsed cohesion of the unit, risked having them watch out for her "six," the area at her *Shadow Hawk*'s back, rather than for one another.

Two kilometers from the Bay One exit, the flat plain below the mountain began to fall in ragged, steep-sided steps toward the Killross River. While the fire zone cleared by the fortress's builders remained lifeless this far out, the ground was increasingly littered with boulders ranging from the size of a small vehicle to house-sized blocks and larger, weathered masses of gray and brown granite that sparkled when the sunlight hit tiny flecks of quartz embedded in the rugged surface. The nearest enemy 'Mechs, likely, would be in this area, sheltering behind some of the larger rocks.

There! A burst of dirty-looking coolant steam emerged from behind a tumble of moss-covered boulders, followed a moment later by the head and shoulders of a lone invader 'Mech, visible only for a second as its pilot tried to get a sighting on Lori's *Hawk*. She pivoted left, calling a warning to the other 'Mechs in the lance as she brought her right arm high, sighting with the Martel Mod 5 laser mounted on her forearm. The glimpse she'd had looked like a *Quickdraw*, though she wasn't sure. Her tracking display labeled the blip simply UNKNOWN, at a range of ninety-five meters.

Max was right. Her *Hawk*'s right arm *was* lagging a bit behind her controls, but she got it into position, then edged to her right, trying to spot the enemy. There was a blur of movement, and then the *Quickdraw* was lunging from behind the cover provided by the boulders. Lori triggered her right-arm laser, and an intolerably brilliant dazzle of blue-white radiance seared along the face of the rock. Miss . . . *damn!*

The *Quickdraw* twisted as it moved; four Hovertec short-range missiles streaked across the intervening space, scratching out white contrails as they flashed from the enemy 'Mech's center-torso quad launcher. Lori shifted left, firing again in the same instant. Three missiles shrieked past her right head and shoulder; the fourth slammed into her *Shadow Hawk*'s chest, high up, just beneath the cockpit, with a savage *bang* that jolted her through her padded pilot's seat and rocked her back a step.

No damage, or at least none worth speaking of, though she caught a glimpse of a chunk of armor the size of her head spinning past her transplas-armored windshield. Her laser bolt, she saw, had splashed across the *Quickdraw*'s right hip, peeling open gray armor like a knife slashing through cardboard. She fired again as the enemy 'Mech pivoted to face her square on, at a range now of just under eighty meters. The QKD-4G *Quickdraw* mounted a medium laser in each forearm; two more, Lori knew, were set into its torso facing the rear, a nasty surprise for any opponent who tried to sneak up from behind, but the two she had to deal with now were more than enough. The enemy MechWarrior loosed a quick one-two-one-two, snap-firing his lasers in a manner that was guaranteed to drive his heat gauge to the max but could overwhelm Lori's armor if he connected with accuracy and a bit of luck.

Laser fire blazed, and her cockpit HUD momentarily turned black to prevent the beams, more brilliant than the face of a sun, from blinding her as they flashed through her canopy. Still firing her own laser, targeting on the outlined image gleaming on her HUD, she sidestepped rapidly, ducking her ten-meter mount to take it out of that deadly barrage. A flicker of explosions walked across the *Quickdraw*'s torso and side just as her HUD cleared; Flanders's *Dervish* had moved in close, triggering a double barrage of SRMs that slammed into the bigger *Quickdraw* in a savage fusillade.

Flanders's attack had distracted the *Quickdraw,* possibly crippling him as well. Lori dropped her *Shadow Hawk*'s autocannon into firing position, the servos giving a thin whine as they lowered the long-barreled weapon down across her left shoulder. As she pivoted right, the autocannon's cross hairs glowed green on her cockpit HUD and slid into line with the *Quickdraw*'s comically spherical, armor-belted head, then her thumb came down on the firing button. The Armstrong J11 opened up with its characteristic, deep-throated *thud-thud-thud,* sending a stream of armor-piercing rounds into the enemy 'Mech. Huge chunks of armor spun wildly from an already damaged shoulder pauldron, as deep, punctured craters appeared in a ragged line across its chest. Smoke was spilling from the other machine now, the greasy black kind that told of internal fires and melting wiring and electrical circuits. Once more, the enemy MechWarrior turned, raising both arms and bringing their weapons to bear on Lori's *Shadow Hawk*. She braced herself for the volley to come, ready to jump or dodge. But the shots never came.

Infrared sensors in her *Hawk* were picking up spreading masses of high temperature radiated by the other 'Mech, visible on her left-hand console display as smears of color on a skeleton-frame schematic of a *Quickdraw* that mimicked the real machine's position and angle. Internal fires were raging out of control, and the *Quickdraw*'s heat levels must be approaching critical. Her guess proved right a beat later when the top of the *Quickdraw*'s head popped open, followed by the 'Mech's ejection seat arrowing into the sky atop the stabbing yellow flame of its rocket.

"Good kill!" Oretsov called. He, together with Donatelli's *Assassin* and Bob Wu's *Centurion,* was tangling with an enemy *Apollo* four hundred meters to the east. The enemy 55-tonner was pulling back, flushed by the concentrated fire of its three smaller adversaries. That *Apollo,* Lori decided, with its paired LRM launchers and Artemis IV fire control systems, must have been one of the Gareth BattleMechs that had been bombarding the fortress, probably with the *Quickdraw* serving as spotter.

Suddenly, she *wanted* that 'Mech.

She urged her *Hawk* into a lumbering run, ducking past the *Quickdraw,* which now, standing motionless, was heavily wreathed in smoke and flickering orange flame. The *Apollo* was half a kilometer away, massive, its armor painted in contrasting flavors of dull orange-yellow and olive-drab, moving rapidly at an angle that would bring it across her path in a few moments more, but well out of range.

Crouching her 'Mech slightly, she triggered her jump jets. With a rising whine, her jets powered up, her fusion reactor flash-heating water and air into a violently expanding plasma as hot as the surface of a star. Channeled by powerful magnetic containment fields, the plasma erupted from her jet venturis, kicking her 55-ton BattleMech awkwardly into the sky.

Her flight was brief, a few seconds, no more. Her 'Mech couldn't carry reaction mass enough to keep her aloft longer, but it did carry her across better than 150 meters of open ground. She cranked her jets up to full thrust just as she descended, absorbing the shock of landing with her 'Mech's knees and hip-joint hydraulics, but the landing still jolted her through her seat like a jump off a five-meter cliff.

The *Apollo* had seen her come to earth and slowed its retreat. It pulled up once, turning to duel briefly with its three pursuers, but then its pilot seemed to decide that he would have a better chance taking on the *Shadow Hawk* one-on-one than trying to tangle with an *Enforcer,* a *Centurion,* and an *Assassin* working together—a total combat mass of 140 tons, far more than double his own. Advancing at a ponderous, ground-eating run, the orange and green *Apollo* closed with Lori's machine.

Lori punched up a readout on her primary display, calling up the stats on the APL. The 'Mech was a new one, not often seen on the battlefield, but she took in the data she needed at a glance. Fifty-five tons . . . Dav 220 fusion power plant . . . Maxmilian 44 armor. The *Apollo* had been designed as a long-range bombardment 'Mech, a replacement for the popular *Archer;* its primary weapons were those paired LRM-15 launchers mounted inside the massive, hunched shoulders to either side of its head. For close-in work, the *Apollo* mounted a pair of small Sunglow Prism-Optic pulse lasers in its central torso and had no other weapons at all save its fists.

At a range of three hundred meters, Lori opened fire with her *Shadow Hawk*'s Holly LRMs, sending a five-round volley arrowing toward the target; as the last missile was hissing clear of her right-torso launcher and before the first missile had struck, the *Apollo* returned fire, sending a flight of ten LRMs streaking toward Lori's *Shadow Hawk*. She glanced down at her control panel, checking her 'Mech's heat levels and the pressure in her jump jet mag chambers; both read nominal, so she crouched slightly, flexing her *Hawk*'s knees, then straightened suddenly, kicking in the jump jets as she lifted clear of the ground. The *Apollo*'s missile barrage struck as she jumped; explosions slammed across her *Shadow Hawk*'s legs and feet, jolting her hard and causing her 'Mech to pitch to the right.

The Artemis IV fire-control system vastly improved the *Apollo*'s LRM accuracy, giving it a decided advantage in 'Mech-to-'Mech combat. Had Lori stood still and accepted her opponent's offering, most, if not all, of those

'Mech-killers would have struck home, scouring the armor from the *Shadow Hawk* like paint peeling away in a sandstorm, leaving her nakedly vulnerable to a follow-up attack. As it was, though, her sudden jump had made her a much more difficult target, and only four of the *Apollo*'s LRMs had actually connected, all in her lower assembly.

She battled with the 'Mech's jump controls for a few tense seconds, struggling to keep the big machine from falling over ... and then she felt the balance fall into the proper alignment, and she was sailing across the battlefield once more.

Touching down, she immediately flexed the *Hawk*'s legs, then jumped again; the hit she'd taken had robbed her first jump of some energy, and the distance she was trying to cover was too great for a single jump in any case. She landed, the jolt slamming her through the *Hawk*'s pilot's seat, then jumped yet again. Her heat warning sounded as the jump jets howled for a third time with no respite, but she ignored it, balancing her descending *Hawk* on pillars of superheated steam and plasma, dropping once more to the bare, rocky ground less than sixty meters from the *Apollo*, and well to its right.

Recovering from her landing with a gentle step left, she dropped the autocannon's targeting cross hairs onto the enemy BattleMech and squeezed the firing button. A/C shells slammed into the *Apollo*'s right arm, striking the pauldrons shielding the LRM array above the shoulder, exploding down across the arm's rerebrace and tearing great chunks of ferrofibrous armor from the arm and from the side-torso plate. The *Apollo* staggered with the hit, turning to face her; Lori kept the autocannon in action, slamming round after round into the *Apollo*'s taces and breastplate, the impact knocking the other 'Mech back one step, then another, then still another. She fired her medium laser, again risking a heat overload as she sent three quick-paced bolts of coherent light lancing into the *Apollo*'s right side.

Know your enemy, and know yourself ran the aphorism composed by Sun Tzu, the ancient Chinese strategist whose writings, Lori knew, Grayson had long ago committed to memory. In BattleMech combat especially, knowing the weapons and capabilities of an opponent's 'Mech as well as you knew your own frequently gave you the edge, even in a fight where you were outnumbered and outgunned. How did the rest of that maxim go? *Know your enemy, and know yourself, and in a hundred battles you will never be in peril.* That was it ... a bit over-blown, perhaps, since combat always meant danger, but completely accurate in spirit. The *Apollo*'s key weakness in combat—*especially* in combat at knife-fighting range like this—was the fact that all its weapons were mounted in the torso. The 'Mech could only aim by turning its entire body, a design flaw that perfectly negated one of the few good reasons for building combat machines in human shape in the first place. Lori kept moving, circling around the *Apollo*'s damaged right side, trying to get behind it, and as she moved she could keep her right arm with its Martel Mod 5 laser trained on the target, firing round after searing round into her opponent's machine. Her heat-overload warning shrilled again; alphanumerics scrolled along her console's message board and flashed onto the corner of her HUD, threatening power-plant shutdown.

With one hand, she slapped the override switch, pushing her 'Mech past its set safety limits for the sake of a few more shots, a few more steps. The *Apollo* was trying to turn in place, attempting to pivot faster than Lori could circle him; Lori kept moving, both around the *Apollo* and edging in closer. So long as she could stay ahead of the *Apollo*'s clumsy turn-in-place, the other 'Mech pilot could bring none of his weapons to bear on her.

With a shrill roar of plasma jump jets, Dag Flanders dropped his *Dervish* out of the sky a hundred meters away, and Lori wondered if the new arrival was going to distract her prey. She kept moving and firing, closing the range until she was less than twenty meters away. When Flanders started moving closer, she decided to end that deadly, circling race once and for all. With a jolt that made her gyro shriek, she dug in her 'Mech's feet and came to a dead halt, poised and ready with her autocannon aimed at the still-turning *Apollo*.

Autocannons, especially long-barreled weapons such as the Armstrong J11, were less accurate at short range than at long, primarily because the target's movements across the autocannon's field of fire were exaggerated at ranges much under one hundred meters. Still, at twenty meters and with the *Apollo*'s head and shoulders filling her targeting cross hairs, she could hardly miss. She was already firing even as the *Apollo,* still turning, unaware that she'd stopped short, brought its head around into her field of view. The APL-1M possessed an unusually large windscreen for a 'Mech, a second vulnerability that even thickly layered transplas couldn't make up for. Designed to give the pilot as good a field of view as possible, despite the hunched, heavily armored shoulders to either side, the cockpit was poorly protected; ferrofibrous armor, after all, offered far better protection against exploding autocannon rounds than did transparent plastic laminates.

Cannon rounds hit the *Apollo*'s head and shoulder in a slamming, thundering stream, and to that volleying destruction Lori added repeated bursts from her laser and the loads from both of her *Shadow Hawk*'s short-range missile launchers, mounted to either side of her head. Fist- and head-sized craters pocked the armored gorget, smashed into the right LRM racks. As missiles still in the tubes cooked off under that savage and unrelenting onslaught, the enemy machine's upper works were swiftly wreathed in strobing flashes of light and billowing black smoke. Lori kept firing, even when she saw the *Apollo*'s cockpit visor smashed open and gaping, and then the 'Mech was toppling forward, trailing smoke in a smooth arc behind it as it fell face-down to the ground, as lifeless as a string-cut puppet. She felt the shudder underfoot when the thing struck, and the crash of fifty-five tons of plate armor and heavy machinery was as loud as a high-explosive detonation.

Carefully, she moved closer, watching for the pilot until she saw the wreckage that remained of the cockpit's life support system and seating mount. There'd been no flash of ejection; that stream of autocannon fire must have blown the other 'Mech's pilot into bloody vapor.

"Good God Almighty, Colonel!" Flanders's voice said softly over her headset phones as his *Dervish* edged closer. "I'm sure as hell glad you're on *our* side!"

5

It wasn't until the *Apollo* was dead that a new and disturbing thought occurred to Lori, the sort of jarring afterthought that made her wonder why she hadn't seen the problem, so obvious now, before. Many BattleMech designs—perhaps even most of them—had been around for so long that all the Great Houses of the Inner Sphere had them in their TO&Es. The venerable WSP-1A *Wasp*, for example, had first been mass-produced in 2471, almost six hundred standard years ago, and in that time it had found its way into every military unit on every world in known space, from fifth-rate militias on Periphery jerkwater worlds she'd never heard of—*worlds like the one I came from,* she reminded herself—to the formidable ranks of the Com Guards on Terra. There'd been at least five variants she knew of, and some thousands were still in service.

Other 'Mechs, however, were not nearly so well-traveled. The DRG-1N *Dragon,* for example, was manufactured on Luthien in the Draconis Combine and nowhere else, and in the three centuries since its introduction to the battlefields of the Inner Sphere, Lori had never heard of a *Dragon* in service for any but Combine masters.

She edged her *Shadow Hawk* closer to the smoking junkyard sprawl of the killed 'Mech. The APL-1M *Apollo* was even more limited in its distribution than the *Dragon*. It was a brand new design, no more than a few years old. According to the intelligence briefings she'd seen on the machine, it was being turned out in mass quantities by the Earthwerks facility on Keystone, in Marik space. Large numbers of the 'Mech reportedly had been exported during the past several years to both the Draconis Combine and the Capellan Confederation of House Liao, but word was that Earthwerks had been specifically directed to refuse any orders from the Federated Commonwealth.

So what the hell was an *Apollo* doing with a FedCom unit? She'd not even thought about it before, but now that it occurred to her, Lori couldn't shake the feeling that something here was seriously warped. She wished now the 'Mech's pilot was still alive; as a prisoner, he might be able to tell Legion intelligence a thing or three—like how Field Marshal Brandal Gareth had gotten his hands on an *Apollo*.

Possibly . . . *possibly* the 'Mech had been captured brand new by Gareth's forces during some skirmish between Marik and FedCom troops down on the border, but somehow that just didn't feel right. There were rumors that the Federated Commonwealth was working on their own version of the *Apollo*; if they'd managed to capture one of the originals, it certainly would have been appropriated by the engineers at the 'Mech factories on Hesperus II or elsewhere for research purposes.

The fact remained, and the longer Lori thought about it the more puzzling it seemed. That *Apollo* shouldn't *be* here. . . .

A small convoy of battlefield machines approached from the south, led by a peculiar, low-slung, four-legged walking machine, one of the Gray Death's SC-V *Scavengers*. Other engineering 'Mechs followed, including a pair of troop walkers and a flatbed tractor. Her battle with the *Apollo* had pinned her here not far from Castle Hill, while the main battle lines had swept on toward the woods and river in the north. She was in the rear lines, now, and the Legion's recovery forces were moving into the area to gather what battlefield salvage they could find.

Ramps swung down over the rears of the troop carriers; Legion engineering infantry in black combat vests and helmets spilled out of the vehicles and began breaking out their recovery gear. The *Scavenger* was straddling the fallen *Apollo* now, its flexible drainage tube penetrating a blown-out access panel to reach internal coolant and lubricant storage tanks and drain them dry. In that position, the WorkMech looked like nothing so much as an enormous, four-legged spider feeding on its prey. When all useful or potentially dangerous stores of liquids had been drawn off, the *Scavenger* would use its specialized grippers and arms to hoist the *Apollo* clear of the ground, allowing the engineers to slide the flatbed tractor underneath. By this afternoon, the *Apollo* would be back in one of Castle Hill's 'Mech bays, being rebuilt if the damage wasn't serious, or cannibalized if it was. To Lori's practiced eye, the *Apollo* appeared to have taken most of its damage in the head; it was likely her kill would end up as a Legion replacement, a decidedly valuable combat trophy.

Or would the Legion's FedCom bosses claim it for their own *Apollo* design program? More than ever, Lori wanted to find out that 'Mech's history. She had a feeling it was important—if she could just figure out how to track it down.

Several J27 ammunition carriers were traveling with the engineering convoy. "Hey, *Shadow Hawk!*" the driver of one called over the tacnet. "How you fixed for expendies?"

Lori checked her ammunition counters. Her rapid-paced engagements with two enemy 'Mechs, the *Quickdraw* and the *Apollo,* had burned through her autocannon stores, though she was still well set for missiles. "I'll take some A/C, if you've got it," she replied.

"How 'bout some LRMs?" Flanders asked, his *Dervish* coming up alongside Lori's *Hawk*.

"Stand by, *Dervish.* We'll fix you right up."

It took about ten minutes for the two 'Mechs to have their expendable munitions replenished. Lori used the time to track the course of the battle as it was relayed to her console displays from the fortress. It looked as though the sortie out from the shelter of the castle had indeed caught the Gareth forces by surprise, punching through a relatively thin enemy perimeter about the fortress mountain and striking deep into the rear of the invader forces that were moving to block Houk's Battalion as it came in from the north.

Information. She needed information . . . an overview of how the fight was developing. Lori had worked in combat ops centers long enough to have lost the urgent sense of needing to *be* there, in the midst of the fighting, when a battle was being fought. In any battle, the people out on the firing line generally know less about what is actually going on around them than anyone else. Still, her pulse quickened, and she wondered what was happening down that rocky slope and along the valley treeline, her thoughts chivvying the armorers and assistants who were working on her machine, as though thoughts alone could urge them to move faster.

She spent the time studying the electronic display repeated from Castle Hill's Ops Center. In those patches of colored light scattered with moving blips she could divine at least some of the larger picture. The Legion's sortie from the castle had caused considerable damage to the enemy—at least five BattleMechs killed so far, at a cost of two Legion 'Mechs knocked out of the fight. The Gareth machines moving around the fortress toward the north appeared to have paused, as though startled by this new development and trying to decide what to do.

Houk's 'Mechs weren't on the screen yet—they would be moving with transponders off, which meant they wouldn't show up on the Ops displays and data relays until they were being painted by battlefield radar and other sensors—but Lori hoped they were into the area covered by Legion scans. Crossing the Killross River, say, or moving out of one of the passes in the Highlands and into the woods in the Killross Valley. If they weren't, if they didn't put in an appearance within the next hour or so, the advantage won so far by the Legion would very swiftly be transformed by the enemy's numerical superiority into complete disaster.

Where the hell was Houk's Second Battalion?

* * *

Major Rae Houk paused his *Archer* on the south bank of the Killross River, watching as the last of Second Batt's First Company Command Lance clambered up the bank in great cascades of mud and spray. Gunfire—the thump and hammer of heavy 'Mech weapons and high explosives—rumbled in the distance. Colonel Kalmar, he decided, was doing her best to give his people every chance. They'd discussed the possibility during their last direct-voice exchange, though it had been impossible to coordinate their movements two weeks in advance.

"I'll be there," he told her. *"I'll be there if I have to march my boys and girls over every damned mountain on Glengarry."*

"We'll be watching for you," she'd said. *"We'll move to support you when you enter the DP."*

Evidently, Lieutenant Colonel Kalmar-Carlyle had indeed been watching, and had thrown out an attack with the forces she still held at her command within the fortress when she saw the invader forces reacting to Second Batt's entry into Castle Hill's defensive perimeter, a region roughly defined by the Killross River Valley to the north and the Dunkeld Spaceport in the south.

This sort of coordinated maneuver was always tricky, one demanding sharp timing and perfect cooperation between disparate force elements on an almost instinctual level. Houk had practiced such actions in maneuvers, of course, and worked them out in elaborate training simulations, but he'd never had to do it with real 'Mechs on a real battlefield.

Rae Houk had come by his command of Second Battalion relatively recently, receiving his promotion from captain and stepping in as Battalion CO when his predecessor, Major Hassan Ali Khaled, had been seriously wounded on Glengarry during the Skye Uprising the year before. Houk's record in combat was good, but he knew that both Carlyles were still waiting to see how well he could take a 'Mech battalion in hand and boss it during battle. The training deployment to Kintyre, he knew, had been ordered as much to train him in the fine art of battalion-level command as it was to prepare the troops under his command. Second Battalion had a lot of newbies, new recruits brought in to fill the ranks left vacant by both promotion and combat, and only field exercises like the one they'd been on could get the new hands working smoothly with the old.

And now the efficiency of that training was about to be put to that most brutal of tests of both man and machine—combat.

Quinn Missonak's *Rifleman* emerged from the river, water streaming from its flanks. The entire unit was under strict radio silence, but as the *Rifleman* passed, Houk caught a glimpse of Missonak's neurohelmeted head through the big machine's canopy. Missonak grinned at him and gave a jaunty thumb's up.

Houk jerked his own thumb in toward the south, in the direction of the rolling, far-off thunder. An ancient military dictum held that a unit commander should march to the sound of the guns, and that was exactly what Houk was planning to do. As he turned his *Archer* in place to follow the moving column, he surveyed the terrain surrounding the river crossing—closely sheltered by thick-trunked belum trees, and with granite outcroppings that offered a dozen places of concealment for an anti-'Mech infantry force lying in wait, or even a company or two of 'Mechs.

A perfect spot for an ambush. . . .

At least, this was the place he would have chosen, had he been in Marshal Gareth's place. The invaders knew Second Batt was on the way. The Recon Lance had spotted some enemy infantry scouts earlier that morning and intercepted snatches of coded radio traffic not long after that. Houk had been more than half-expecting a fight for this river crossing. The fact that no ambush had materialized suggested that Colonel Kalmar had managed to upset the enemy's plans.

As for him, Rae Houk intended to repay the favor by placing his entire command precisely where it could do the most good, squarely in the invading force's rear.

He just hoped he'd be in time.

Field Marshal Brandal Gareth studied the colored smear of the terrain stretching from Dunkeld to the base of the Scotian Highlands, and he knew that he'd just committed the worst sin possible for any military commander, that of underestimating an enemy.

He touched a button on his armrest, and with a soft

whine his chair slid down the console, away from the main data display and past rank upon rank of smaller screens, each showing one of dozens of remote-camera views from different parts of the battlefield. Most were being relayed to his mobile command headquarters from BattleMechs—one realtime image from each lance commander in the field. Others were scenes shot by remote drones circling high above the area or from cameras carried by scouts moving on foot or in armored reconnaissance vehicles. In the background was a soft murmur of voices carried from speakers mounted overhead, a babble of orders and counter-orders, of combat chatter and occasional calls for help. Over all was the dull, distant rumble of gunfire, the clash and clank of fast-moving Battle-Mechs, the occasional shriek of someone in pain.

"Phil! Watch your back! You've got two comin' in hard on your six!"

"Hold 'em! I'll circle around!"

"Cover me, boys. I'm running dry."

"Yeah, me too. Where's the ammo wagon?"

"I'm hit! I'm hit! Johnny, watch my back! I'm punching out!"

"One-three, this is One-two. Do you need support?"

"Damn right we need support! Where the hell is One-one?"

"Volansky! Get your lance in there, stat! Plug that hole, damn it!"

"I'm on it, Boss!"

Once, Gareth thought to himself a bit ruefully, it had been possible for the commander of an army—the king, perhaps—to sit on his portable throne resting on a mountain overlooking the battle plain and see his entire army, and that of the enemy, arrayed below him like colorful playing pieces in an elaborate game of move and counter-move. That type of command luxury had probably vanished in the eighteenth and early nineteenth centuries ... about the time of Napoleon. A century later, armies fighting one another on the battlefields of Terra's First World War engaged in actions that covered literally thousands of square kilometers, battles so huge and so complex that individual field commanders could do little but set their forces ponderously in motion and wait to see what re-

sulted from their inevitable collision with the forces of
the enemy.

In the thirty-first century, it was *almost* possible for
field commanders to know what was going on in battles
they'd initiated. Indeed, most of the advances in the past
thousand years of applied military technology had more
to do with C³—Command, Control, and Communications—than with the relatively simple and straightforward
tech required to actually kill the enemy. In some ways, it
was astonishing just how little military tech had advanced
in the past millennium; lasers, for instance, were today
virtually identical to their twenty-first-century counterparts, while most missile technology, thanks to cost and a
lack of necessary electronic components, had actually
taken a big step or two backward from what had been
commonly available even in the late twentieth century.
Even BattleMechs, the kings of the thirty-first-century
battlefield, represented only a relatively modest advance
in maneuverability and firepower over the older tank, and
most modern 'Mech designs were identical to those produced in the twenty-fifth century.

But one advantage resulting from the generally declin-
ing industrial capabilities across the Inner Sphere had
been a completely unexpected one; large-scale military
campaigns were frequently waged with relatively few
BattleMechs. A city might be defended by a twelve-
'Mech company, while a regiment or two, a hundred
'Mechs at most, was usually sufficient for the conquest of
a world. With so few unit elements, it was literally possible to mount a camera on each that would relay to the
commanding officer two- or even three-D images of each
element's situation. Battles on a strategic scale were often
reduced to tactical encounters no more complex than a
meeting engagement between a couple of twentieth-
century tank platoons might have been; the fact that they
were strategic in scope was due to the mobility of
BattleMechs, which could maneuver across vast stretches
of highly varied terrain in a relatively short period of
time.

As was evidenced, he thought wryly, by the sudden appearance of the missing Gray Death battalion. His people
had been searching for that damned unit since they'd arrived two weeks ago, by air, by remote drone, by satellite

surveillance, by careful eavesdropping on all electronic communications frequencies. But a planet was an ungodly big piece of real estate in which a few dozen BattleMechs were all too easily lost. In that regard, at least, modern military units held a significant advantage over their ancient predecessors; a thousand years ago it had been all but impossible to hide anything so large as a brigade or division in a combat Area of Operations, much less an entire army.

Gareth had hoped that his forces could secure the Legion fortress before the "missing" battalion showed up—or that they could find and crush the unit before it had a chance to link up with defenders in the Dunkeld fortress. The first possibility—his preference, since the Legion's HQ would have offered his invading force an excellent and secure base of operations on the planet—had simply not worked out. Military operations by their very nature entailed setbacks, and the partial battalion holed up behind those ferrocrete walls had managed to deal him several. The second possibility had been blocked by the nature of the planet's rough and heavily forested terrain and by the ability of even a battalion of 'Mechs to move undetected through it. Now, it was Gareth's Third Davion Guard that was at risk, vulnerable to being trapped between Castle Hill's defenders and the reinforcements arriving from the north.

One chance remained, and one only. By emerging from the protection of the fortress's sheltering walls, the partial battalion under Lori Kalmar's command had given Gareth the target he'd been trying to find for two long and frustrating weeks. If he could hold the Legion's Second Battalion at bay long enough, he might yet destroy the castle's defenders ... and take their fortress HQ in the bargain.

But as he moved from display to display on his command console, he realized just how slim that remaining chance was becoming. First and Second Companies of the Third Guard's First Battalion had been hit from behind by the Legion's sortie, and if the confusion of blips on his tactical display was any indication, the entire First Batt had been paralyzed by that strike—paralyzed and left vulnerable should the enemy's missing battalion show up any time soon. The screens showing views relayed from his lance commanders were all scenes of combat, some in the general vicinity of the fortress, most further north, in or near the woods masking the river valley. The Third Guard's First was fighting on two fronts now and was in imminent danger of being trapped between two larger enemy forces and utterly destroyed.

The forces he'd detailed to lure part of the Legion to Caledonia had underestimated Carlyle's fighting skills and been smashed at the Battle of Falkirk. Lieutenant Colonel Kalmar-Carlyle, judging from her bio data, didn't possess the tactical brilliance of her husband—that was a very large part of why Gareth had engineered the Caledonian situation, to draw Carlyle away from his HQ on Glengarry—but she'd done very well thus far with the forces she had at hand. With her Second Battalion's sudden arrival, Dunkeld could easily become a second Falkirk for Gareth's 'Mechs.

He thought he saw how he could avoid that, however. Reaching out, he touched a key, opening a communications channel. "Volansky!" he ordered. "Disengage and fall back! You're in danger of being cut off."

"Roger that," Volansky replied. "I'm outta here!"

He shifted to a different combat channel. "Fernandez! Break off! Break off! Fall back to your rally point!"

Light flared on the screen displaying a view from the head-mounted camera on Fernandez's *Thunderbolt*. Gareth could see another 'Mech, one in the gray and black livery of the defending forces, a hundred meters away. Fernandez was evidently chasing his opponent, and at the same time moving deeper and deeper into the woods.

"But, sir! We've got—"

"You've got a full load of trouble if you keep chasing that *JagerMech*! Now break off and get out of there."

"Roger, roger. I'm breaking off. . . ."

One by one, Gareth reined in his lance commanders, pulling them back from the enemy, gathering them at a point halfway between woods and fortress. If he could get them all turned and moving south, they might yet be able to overwhelm the sortie from the fortress, smash through to the open gates, and win. . . .

6

JumpShip **Caliban**
Pirate Jump Point
Glengarry System, Skye March
Federated Commonwealth
1035 hours, 13 May 3057

Captain Mindy Cain opened her eyes, willing the momentary stab of nausea and vertigo to subside. *Did it, by damn....*

"Emergence at ten-thirty-five fifty-one, Captain," her helm officer reported from his couch nearby, checking his console. "Field coordinates match to within accepted limits."

"Good job, Mannie," she told him. "Nice and smooth."

"Thanks, Skipper."

Completing a hyperspace jump always left Mindy feeling a bit giddy, and relieved. Though humanity had in its long and bloody history managed to invent quite a few pastimes more hazardous than leaping across the great, black gulfs of interstellar space, she still felt that small, sharp thrill of danger with each jump. A little thing—a gravitational ripple in space-time from an exploding star far away and long ago, the presence of a clot of matter adrift where no matter should be, a faulty circuit hidden within the kilometers upon kilometers of wiring in drive coils constructed centuries ago—and the JumpShip would emerge, not in the carefully computed volume of space calculated by the ship's computers, but someplace and sometime horribly other—a leap into emptiness completely unknown, since no ship or crew vanished in a misjump had ever returned to report.

But the spectrum of the orange-yellow star shining on one of the navigational displays matched that of the Glengarry sun, and the initial computer star checks indicated that they'd emerged from hyperspace within a few tens of thousands of kilometers of the spot her clients had specified. She double-checked those figures just to make certain; Mindy was no stranger to pirate-point jumps, and she and her bridge crew had the knack of making nonstandard jumps look almost routine. Still, if any of the coordinates had been off by as little as three percent, if the gravitational referents and field strengths provided by her passengers had been in error at all, this voyage might very well have ended quite differently.

Satisfied, she unbuckled her harness and let herself rise above her couch, grabbing hold of a handrail on the bulkhead to keep from drifting free into the center of the bridge compartment.

"Very nicely done, Captain Cain," one of the passengers who'd asked to ride out the jump on the *Caliban*'s bridge said. "Looks like you came out right smack on the call."

He was floating behind the helm officer's position, checking the numbers for himself, then glancing up at the display that showed Glengarry's sun. The screen was stepped way down to filter the blinding light, but the ruddy color of the star shone on his skin and in his yellow hair nonetheless, touching it like the glow of a sunset.

Mindy didn't answer him right away. She still hadn't made up her mind yet about these passengers, and she had reason enough to mistrust their motives. The younger of the two, the one who'd just congratulated her on the accuracy of the jump, was a captain in the mercenary unit she was transporting, a good-looking young man, she thought, though a bit unkempt and obviously worrying over something that was gnawing at him inside. The other, older man was a muscular, heavy-set major with a Scots burr so thick you could slice it with a vibroblade, and a manner so cool Mindy couldn't read any emotion there at all.

They'd both insisted—politely but firmly—on being on *Caliban*'s bridge during the jump, and she had the distinct impression that the request was due less to professional interest than to concern over betrayal. Neither man was armed, but she had the feeling that had *Caliban* emerged into normal space anywhere but at the stated coordinates, she'd have had her hands full with these two. They were professionals, and as cold and as hard as methane ice in a cometary halo. They were also desperate, or, at the very least, very, very determined. She'd not asked what their business on Glengarry was, though she had verified in *Caliban*'s library computer that the Gray Death Legion was a well-known merc unit with a landhold on the one habitable world of this system. The unit's CO, in fact, was Baron Glengarry. She'd heard rumors that the world was currently under attack by some mysterious raiders, but she wanted to keep her nose out of it and hadn't questioned them further. Presumably, they were eager to get their unit back to their home system to meet this threat, whatever it was.

The fact that there might be hostile military forces in the Glengarry system was, in fact, one reason why Mindy hadn't been all that averse to making a pirate-point jump. Out here, away from zenith or nadir jump point and the probable military traffic there, her ship was less likely to be boarded and searched . . . or even impressed.

"Well, *thank* you, Captain," she said after a long moment. She let sarcasm edge her words, immediate and obvious. "I'm sure the crew will be delighted to hear that you approve."

The younger one started to respond to the tone of her voice, but the major silenced him with a slight, almost invisible shake of his head. Mindy turned herself in the air and made a show of studying the navigational readouts, effectively shutting them off from any further conversation.

Normally, she tried to avoid military types entirely, whether they were mercenary units like this one, or the big, well-equipped forces of the Great Houses of the Inner Sphere. Mercenary unit commanders who might approach her all too often couldn't afford her services, while the House Lords frequently resorted to requisitioning independent merchant ships and their crews in times of crisis. JumpShips, after all, were among the most valuable of resources, machines of incredible complexity and technology that were very nearly irreplaceable. And during a major military campaign there were never enough of them available.

The *Caliban* and her crew had been pressed into service for the Federated Commonwealth more than once, and before that, back when Mindy's father had been chief owner and skipper, the ship had been requisitioned three times by the Lyran Commonwealth. Not once had they been offered decent compensation, and since it was military boards and government bureaucrats who put a value on what a requisitioned vessel's services were worth, those figures were rarely within hailing distance of the going rate. The last time she'd had any dealings with the Federated Commonwealth, they'd paid for her services—transporting a trio of DropShips from Hesperus II to Caledonia—in FedCom script instead of C-bills. That meant she had to spend them inside the FedCom or lose even more money to ComStar's usurious exchange rates. And sometimes the requisition was a demand for service, pure and simple. Impressment—involuntary service with the military—had been a tradition in some navies long before man had set sail on the sea of stars. Mindy was only fifteen standard when the military governor of Bolan had requisitioned the *Caliban* from her father in order to escape the rebel mob that was demanding his head. He'd brought along a few incidentals—three DropShips loaded with court sycophants, bureaucrats, military personnel, and part of the planetary treasury—and to accommodate them he'd ordered the civilian DropShips already docked with the JumpShip to cast off. Her father had run afoul of his creditors after that. Years later, she'd looked at the ship's books and learned that he'd nearly had *Caliban* taken from him and sold for transit fees, dock yard costs, and taxes. It was distinctly possible that Bernard Cain's heart attack and death at the age of fifty had been brought on by worry and overwork in the wake of *Caliban*'s impressed service to that military governor.

So Mindy had little love for the military, for *any* military, and she trusted them to honor commitments or debts they might incur just about as far as she trusted that ailing number-four spinneret in the running rigging array, which was to say not at all. It *was* true that this ticket had saved her tail, because *Caliban* had been facing bankruptcy, stark, cold, and simple. She and her entire crew owned shares in the ship and shouldered both its operating costs and its profits—when there were any—together. Which meant, of course, that they also shared the risks and the threat of having their ship impounded by creditors if they fell too far behind. The memory of what had happened after the Bolan incident was never far from Mindy's mind.

So when these two mercs had offered to pay in C-bills, with half the figure she'd demanded up front, and promising the rest upon arrival in the Glengarry system via direct electronic transfer from their headquarters there, she'd had to at least listen to what they had to say.

"But there's aye a catch, lass," the Scotsman had told her before she'd finally agreed to the contract. *"If we don't make it back in time, there may be no headquarters and no funds to transfer. So if you want to hedge your bets a wee bit, you'll help us get there a' the faster wi' a pirate-point jump . . ."*

Maybe it was the man's simple, blunt honestly that had swayed her finally. She'd been tempted to turn him down cold. Pirate points were risky precisely because they pushed the odds beyond what was usual for jumps to or from the traditional jump points of a star system. If the data provided wasn't accurate, the JumpShip could emerge too close to one of the system's outer planets—a gas giant was worst of all—and the gravitational flux could cause a misjump. Too, the zenith and nadir jump points were as far removed as possible from the star's equatorial plane, a region where matter, from planets down to microscopic flecks of dust, was relatively thick. A vessel that emerged from hyperspace with part of its hull simultaneously occupying the space occupied by dust or micrometeorites could be bathed by a burst of intense gamma radiation. And if the intruding body was larger—massing a few tens of grams, say—the ship would simply cease to exist save as an expanding wave front of intense radiation and star-hot plasma.

But the major, Davis McCall, seemed to be laying it all on the line and telling his story the way it was, with no attempt at threats or at deception. While riskier than emerging at traditional jump points, pirate-point jumps had their uses, especially where profits and contraband were concerned. Mindy liked the former and was no stranger to the latter. She had the impression, while talking with McCall and the young captain, that they might be contraband of a sort themselves. She'd heard rumors of some kind of trouble in Caledonia. She rarely paid much attention to such stories, except where they offered her some chance of making some money, and cared nothing at all for politics. But she was pretty sure that the FedCommers she'd ferried to Caledonia a few weeks ago were on the other side from these mercenaries she was taking from Gladius to Glengarry.

It was a strange universe.

Her checks completed, she turned to face her passengers once more. "We have emerged, as you requested, within fifty million kilometers of Glengarry and just a little above the ecliptic. You will be permitted to debark with your DropShips as soon as we have the balance of payment."

"Aye, lass," the major said. He reached into a pocket of his well-worn combat vest and extracted a comcard, which he passed to her with a dexterous flick of his fingers. Reaching out, she snagged the spinning square of plastic. "You'll find th' authorization there," he continued. "An' the communications protocol you'll need t' talk to the' right people on Glengarry."

"I just hope we're in time," the mercenary captain said.

"We'll know in a moment, won't' we?" she said sweetly. "Kathi!" She sent the comcard sailing to her communications officer with the same dexterity the Scotsman had shown. "Run this through. And I want a verification of transfer."

"Aye, Skipper."

"Not that I don't trust you gentlemen. . . ."

"Och, I'm sure we'd do the' same, were we in your position, Captain," McCall replied gently.

"Time lag to Glengarry is five minutes, there and back," she told them. "Ten when we confirm the transfer and wait to get the reply. You gentlemen can just make yourselves comfortable in the meantime."

Privately, she wondered what the hell she was going to do with them if the credit check *didn't* pass. Arrest them for trespass? Claim their three DropShips in lieu of payment? Yeah, right. Her and what mercenary army? A mercenary review board existed to settle disputes of mercenary arrangements, but she had to live to file a complaint first.

Still, they'd given her no reason yet to mistrust their motives, and she decided that she might as well make the best of what must be as uncomfortable a situation for them as it was for her.

"We're positioned for deployment, Skipper," Hans Jorgenson, her Third Officer and Chief Rigger, called from his console.

"Very well," she replied as formally. "You may rig the sail."

Several bridge screens showed views from cameras focused aft along the *Caliban*'s 320-meter length as well as from the rigging arms and yards that branched out from the JumpShip's stern works. As Jorgenson keyed in the computer commands controlling the operation, the starship's solar collection sail began deploying on those screens, appearing first as an immense black doughnut sliding off the ship's stern venturi, rotating slowly, flattening and expanding as it turned. The JumpShip plunged into darkness as the sail expanded wide enough to cast a shadow across the ship's entire length; the central drive stream hole opened wider as it drew clear of the ship, until the sun returned with a burst of orange light.

The sail itself was carried stowed during the jump; the tremendous forces attendant upon the actual hyperspace jump would shred any deployed sail, so those meters of ebon-black, light-thirsty material were kept bundled in the stowage rack array, tightly wrapped and encircling the ship's main drive venturi aft. Set spinning after the ship was safely back in the sane universe of four dimensions, it was gently released from the ship's stern, the deployment collar rotating to impart the centrifugal force that unfolded the billowing mass into a vast, delicate tracery of black webwork and panels against the black backdrop of night.

This was always a delicate part of any jump, riskier even than the transit itself, though with consequences not so grave as those of a misjump into emptiness. Guy wires, power feeds, and running rigging were nearly invisible against the matching blacks of space and the sail itself, though some caught faint, brief, and slender gleams of light as they uncoiled. If any of those cables fouled or jammed in a balky spinneret, it meant hard work in EVA suits to clear the problem before the sail could be fully deployed. Many JumpShips had been helplessly crippled by a sail so badly fouled it could not be cleared.

"How's number four holding?" she asked Jorgenson.

"So far, so good," her rigger replied, his eyes shifting between console readouts and three display screens showing different angles on the deployment. "Running a little hot. As usual."

"Keep watching it."

"Aye, Skipper."

Mindy kept watching it too. The number-four spinneret, one of the rigging yards outstretched from *Caliban*'s stern, caused problems with almost every deployment. They *really* needed to have the thing checked at a shipyard, but there never seemed to be time enough or money enough to take care of it.

"Fouling alert!"

She'd seen it on her monitor just as Jorgenson snapped the warning, the slackness in the unfurling line going suddenly taut. "Maneuvering!" she called. "Roll right, fifteen!"

She felt the answering thump of thrusters firing.

"Rolling to starboard, Skipper. Fifteen degrees per minute."

The deployment collar rotated to unfurl the sail; by rotating the ship against the collar's turning, they canceled both that movement and its attendant centrifugal force without stopping the ring's rotation and risking an even worse fouling. The sail hung frozen in the sky, halfway to full deployment; the stars swung slowly across the heavens, and Mindy felt the gentle tug of simulated gravity pulling her toward the outer bulkhead.

Several attempts to jiggle loose the snagged cable release in number four failed, and ultimately, Mindy had to order the deployment of a pair of work tugs, multi-armed pressure bottles scarcely larger than an EVA suit, which could fly to the rigging array and manually free the snag. It was nearly six minutes before she could give the order: "Helm, cancel spin. Rigger, resume deployment."

"Helm, canceling spin to starboard, Captain."

"Rigging, aye." A pause. "She's deploying okay, Skipper."

Throughout the entire operation, the two visitors to her bridge never said a word, but merely watched with a keen and attentive silence. Had they made so much as a single complaint or cracked a single joke, she would have ordered them off her bridge, but she completely forgot they were there until the great solar sail was almost fully deployed, and the bridge engineering officer had reported a positive current flow to the *Caliban*'s power cells.

"Captain?" her communications officer called. "We've got confirmation on the funds transfer."

"Thank God," she heard the young mercenary mutter, half aloud.

Mindy gave the two passengers a hard look, then pushed herself off from her console to join the comm officer on the other side of the bridge. "Paid in full?"

"Yes, ma'am." Mahmud Li handed her the authorization card. "Authorized by someone named Kalmar-Carlyle, acting military governor. I guess their credit's good."

She returned the card to McCall, pausing for a curious look at the man next to him. He looked ... shaken, she decided. And genuinely relieved, as though some tremendous, pent-up emotion that he'd been fighting to control had just been released.

"Don't mind th' lad," McCall told her as he accepted the proferred card. "His father's been hurt pretty bad, an' we need t' get him back to our base planetside."

"And if the raiders there had captured your facilities on the planet in the meantime ..." Mindy said. "Yes. I understand."

McCall gave her an enigmatic look, his head cocked slightly to the side. "Tell me noo, lass. Hae y' ever considered signin' a long-term contract wi' someone?"

Her eyes widened. "What ... with a House?" Then she thought she saw what he was driving at and her eyes widened further. "No! You mean with mercs? Like you?"

"Aye." He nodded as he replaced the card in a vest pocket. "Not many merc units have steady access to a JumpShip. We've been impressed wi' you an' your crew. I'm sure we could arrive at a fair contract price, if you—"

He broke off as she threw back her head and laughed.

The thought was so comical, so unexpected that she guffawed, causing heads throughout the bridge to turn and stare. "*You've* been impressed!" she cried. She started laughing again.

"I guess that means no," the young captain said.

"I'd heard tha' independents valued their freedom," McCall said with a wry grin.

Mindy wiped her eyes, still shaking as the laughing fit faded. "S-sorry," she said when she could recover breath enough to speak. "But, ah, no. As you say, I value my freedom too much." The mere thought of voluntarily signing up with a merc unit threatened to set her off again, and she bit her lip to keep from losing what little control she retained. She shook her head. "Gentlemen, I'm sure the offer was well meant, but, thank you, no. I must decline." She glanced at Jorgenson, who grinned and rolled his eyes toward the overheard, shaking his head. "I decline both for myself and for my crew. *Caliban* is not for sale. We work for the military when they force us to. Impressment, as they call it. But not by choice."

"Weel, I had t' ask," McCall said. "And I can certainly understand your feelings in the matter. If you ever change your mind, though—"

Not damned likely, she thought, though she managed to swallow the words. There was no reason to deliberately antagonize these two men. "I'll certainly keep that in mind" was all she said.

When she thought about the offer an hour later, as the Gray Death Legion's DropShips were separating from *Caliban*'s spine, she started laughing again. Her? A merc? *Working* for mercs?

Unthinkable.

7

Third Davion Guards Command Section Mobile HQ
Dunkeld Spaceport
Glengarry, Skye March
Federated Commonwealth
1314 hours, 13 May 3057

The interior of the mobile HQ trailer was nearly silent most of the time, though the murmur of voices, radio calls, and relayed orders hung in the close, sweat-tainted air, and the peep and hum of the racks of electronics provided a steady, low background noise that nearly masked the far-off, sound-insulated thump of battle. Brandal Gareth leaned back in his padded seat, staring at the monitors arrayed rank upon rank above his command console, studying them with something approaching a hopeless, almost numbed fascination. The battle had been raging for . . . what? Almost three hours now, and what should have been a fairly straightforward and easily won victory was suspended between a costly win and a far more costly disaster. The question, as in so many other pitched engagements, was how long to keep pushing before giving up the effort and cutting losses.

Though the rumble rarely penetrated the HQ trailer's insulated walls, portions of two 'Mech battalions were locked in savage, clashing combat north of Castle Hill, a running fight where friend was frequently indistinguishable from foe save for the wink of IFF beacons on flowing HUDs, where lasers, PPC fire, and missiles were exchanged volley for volley at near point-blank range. Though he could witness only select portions of the fight, Gareth was able to watch isolated incidents that flickered across the flat, glowing screens of his console displays like dispassionately broadcast documentary movies of some bloody war now lost in time and space.

Here an 80-ton Guard *Victor* collided with a 60-ton Legion *Rifleman,* exchanging burst after destructive burst of autocannon fire and pulses of laser light, until the *Victor* waded in close enough to literally pound on the *Rifleman*'s upper works with a balled, armored fist, smashing away at its smaller foe until armor yielded with a splintering shriek and the Legion 'Mech toppled face-down into swirling dust and ground smoke. There a Davion *JagerMech* leveled both twin-barreled arms at an oncoming Legion *Griffin,* spent shell casings glittering in the sun as they fell away from the breeches of those thundering quad Mydron cannons in golden streams. Snapping and bursting like fireworks across the *Griffin*'s crater-pocked torso, the high-explosive rounds swept away the shoulder-mounted LRM canister, smashing at gorget and pauldron shields and breastplate until the shell-torn Legion 'Mech actually stepped inside the deadly reach of those weapons and fired its PPC directly into its deadly foe, blasting away at point-blank range into an already ragged and battle-damaged patch of torso armor. Gareth watched, fascinated, as the *Griffin* next rammed its massive left fist into the wound in the *JagerMech*'s chest, fingers clamping down on exposed coolant tubes and piping, on wiring and power feeds, clamping and grabbing and yanking hard in a sudden spray of black silicarb lubricant and gushing, steaming green coolant. A moment later, the *JagerMech*'s upper torso split and the pilot boosted clear, his ejection seat trailing yellow-white flame.

Gareth sighed. The *JagerMech*'s savage destruction had been displayed on one of his monitors, the view relayed from a battlefield remote camera, and it was repeated in sundry variations down the console's entire length. He'd not intended for the battle to become this close, but the enemy seemed to be pushing the engagement in a kind of berserk frenzy, fighting to get closer and yet closer to his people.

Pressing the key on his armrest, he slid down the console to another, larger screen, the mobile HQ's main display, where red and green blips seemed to drift about in an uncontrollable swarm throughout the region between the river and the enemy fortress. The picture presented there was an alarming one, with friendly green partly encircled by hostile red drifting in from two directions. Most of his 'Mechs had managed to pull back from the woods to the rally point, but the incoming enemy 'Mechs, the "missing battalion," had followed them up out of the valley, engaging them in a running battle that broke out of the treeline and flowed steadily across the burned-over plain north of the fortress.

Here, the Davion Guard was at a serious disadvantage, pinned between two enemy forces and under a constant, sniping fire from the fortress's turret weapons. Even with half of his force still scattered about the siege perimeter, the Guard companies fighting north of the enemy stronghold outnumbered the defenders by a substantial margin, but they were finding themselves hemmed in, their fields of fire blocked by friendly forces, their numerical advantage nullified by the constricted ground.

And the sheer, vicious *ferocity* of the defenders . . .

"Field Marshal!" One of his staff techs, a young captain named Daley, turned away from his console, one hand pressing the headset of his communications helmet tight against his ear. "Sir!"

"What is it?"

"Emergency call from the *Starfall,* sir. It looks like we've got incoming DropShips."

"From the fleet?"

"Not ours, sir. And not from a standard jump point."

Gareth blinked, unwilling at first to accept those blunt words. It *couldn't* be. "I want that sighting confirmed. With numbers, estimated mass, vectors. . . ."

He thought fast. The *Starfall* was one of his DropShips, an aging *Overlord* assigned to the Third Guard. After she'd disembarked her battalion of 'Mechs, he'd ordered her back into orbit, where her sensors could serve as

longrange warning against the approach of unknown
DropShips or aerospace fighter units.

"Sighting is confirmed. Three DropShips, mass ap-
proximately thirty-five hundred tons under one-point-five
Gs of acceleration. That puts them in the *Union* class.
Vector is non-standard, one-seven-three by one-nine positive."

"A pirate point."

"Yes, sir. Uh, *Starfall* also reports a sail reflection on
radar, right along that same heading. Looks like a *Merchant* Class JumpShip, in stellar orbit nineteen degrees
above the ecliptic."

Three *Union* Class DropShips and a JumpShip in a
non-standard approach. It *could* be Carlyle, returning
with his Third Battalion from Caledonia.

No, scratch that. It *was* Carlyle, could logically be no
one else, and that meant trouble. Brandal Gareth was a realist, one who scorned officers who made assumptions
based on what they wanted rather than on cold, grim fact.
If Carlyle had been lucky enough to pull off a handoff express and to find a civilian JumpShip pilot willing to risk
ship and crew in a pirate-point approach, he could very
well be in-system by now, rather than still to arrive in the
ten to fourteen days that Gareth had estimated.

"What's their ETA?"

Daley consulted a computer read-out. "Assuming they
maintain a steady one-and-a-half Gs, they'll accelerate for
another twenty-eight hours, skew-flip, and decelerate for
thirty-one hours more. Make it just under two and a
half standard days."

Murphy's Law, Gareth reflected, had been written by
and for military commanders, as was the ancient dictum
that no plan of battle ever survives contact with the enemy. Repeated setbacks with Glengarry's defenders had
led to a decidedly disadvantageous situation on the
ground, and now enemy reinforcements were on the way,
big time. Gareth was ambitious . . . but he was also cau-
tious, patient, and completely realistic. If he'd not been
able to break the defenders in the weeks he'd been here
already, two more days would not be enough to do the
trick. As much as he hated admitting it even to himself,
it was time to cut his losses and pull of this rock . . .

Before even that option was snatched away from him.

* * *

Lori Kalmar-Carlyle picked up the pace in her *Shadow Hawk* as soon as she trotted clear of the fortress 'Mech bay and into the sun-drenched open. Pillars of blue-black smoke hung motionless in the green-tinted sky, casting long, slender shadows across the rocky ground where they blocked Glengarry's orange sun.

Sergeant Dag Flanders's *Dervish* paced her. They'd returned to Castle Hill as part of a relay; after reloading several times off J27 ammo supply tractors, they'd pulled back all the way to the 'Mech bay to get a complete "hot" overhaul, to get their coolant systems flushed, and to have some of the worst damage in their 'Mechs' outer hulls covered over by temporary plate tacked on with spot welders. Their 'Mechs not quite good as new but showing less damage than an hour before, they were moving once more into daylight.

And now she had news to share with the rest of the Legion units.

Lori had first learned that Third Battalion had entered the Glengarry system some three hours earlier, when the *Merchant* Class JumpShip *Caliban* had called and asked for a credit transfer for her cargo—three DropShips coming home to Glengarry. After some wrestling with the problem, Lori had decided to keep the news temporarily quiet. Though she herself was wildly elated by the news, it would be, at best, another two and a half days before the inbound Legion DropShips could reach Glengarry or play any part at all in the battle for the planet. The Gray Death Legion had a tradition of always keeping the men and women in the ranks informed and up-to-date, but there were times when information might be edited—or delayed—to avoid adverse psychological effects during the course of a battle and, where possible, to boost any potential increase in morale.

For that reason, she'd not wanted to be premature with an announcement that help was on the way. The knowledge that reinforcements would arrive in two days might make some of the Legion troops slack off, unwilling to risk death or dismemberment when the end of the fight was so precisely in view. In war, no one ever wanted to be that war's last casualty.

In any case, she'd wanted to hold the news as an extra

spur to her people if things started swinging against them, an added reason to hang on at all costs that Lori hadn't wanted to squander. As Grayson had told her often enough in the past, *any* advantage, material or psychological, must be used to best and most efficient effect in combat.

Now, however, she'd just received another piece of news, something more immediate and more strategically valuable even than the word that Third Batt would soon be here. The gang up in Castle Hill communications had just monitored a number of coded enemy transmissions—transmissions that, when put together with the way they were moving right now, seemed to indicate that they were trying to break off the battle.

That changed everything. If Gareth was trying to flee, Lori wanted to be able to take advantage of the sudden shift of balance in this engagement.

"Attention, all Legionnaires," she called over the Legion's general tactical frequency. "Listen up, people! This is Colonel Kalmar. We've just received two interesting bits of news. First. Third Battalion has just been picked up in-system. They dropped in a few hours ago and are heading home at maximum acceleration. Second. It looks like we might not need their help, boys and girls, because the bad guys have seen Third Batt coming and decided to call it a day. According to Legion Combat Ops, Gareth's forces are attempting to disengage and fall back toward the spaceport. Also, the DropShips they've had in orbit appear to have begun deorbit maneuvers. That can only mean they're going to land in order to pick up Gareth and his Davion Guards and get the hell off this planet.

"That means a couple of things, people," she continued. "I don't want any of you to let up for a minute. Keep after the bastards. Make it as hard as possible for them to break free. They may start pulling some fancy stuff soon, trying to get away from you. Don't make it easy for them."

"Don't you worry, Colonel!" an unidentified voice called over the open channel. "We're gonna kick their tails right off our landhold and make 'em all wish they'd never heard of Glengarry!"

There was an answering cheer, echoed several times throughout the unit. Disengaging from an enemy in the middle of a battle was one of the more difficult combat maneuvers. Enemies at close quarters with one another tended to keep at it, and Lori intended to hang on to the enemy as long as she could.

It was an axiom of war old at the time of Nimrod that an army's worst casualties were inflicted during retreat, especially during a retreat that dissolved into a rout. Lori was eager to press the advantage the Legion had won, with reasoning that was both calculating and practical. Most important was the need to hurt Gareth's forces, to hurt them as seriously as possible to make Gareth and his staff think twice about pulling this kind of adventurism again in the future. There was also the matter of battle-field salvage to be considered. The harder the Legion pressed the invaders, the more they would make up for the losses in matériel in smashed and damaged 'Mechs and other gear left by the fleeing raiders, both in the op-portunity to inflict added damage and in the difficulty Gareth's forces would have in mounting salvage and re-trieval operations themselves. The spoils of war ... and the price of failure. Once Gareth's last DropShip lifted off-world, everything they left behind would belong to the Legion.

It was small enough reward for the casualties and dam-age they'd suffered during these past few weeks. *Why?* she wondered, and not for the first time by far. *Why did they do this to us? Why were we ... betrayed?*

A green circle was flashing rapidly on her primary dis-play, pinpointing a particular cluster of blips that ap-peared to be moving southeast, away from the battle zone and in a direction that might be intended to carry it around Castle Hill and south to the Dunkeld Spaceport. The flashing circle was being relayed by Ops, an indica-tion that it might be a target of particular interest. She touched a cursor control, highlighting the blips and press-ing a key to display Ops' assessment.

Alphanumerics scrolled across the top of the primary screen in glowing red: PROB J27 CNVY. The blips moving with them were light and medium BattleMechs.

Excitement stirred at that, a wild pounding in Lori's ears and a thickness in her throat. J27s were used by ev-ery military unit in the Inner Sphere. They were ten-ton tractors hauling twenty-five-ton trailers, low-slung, lightly armored vehicles designed to keep BattleMechs supplied with expendables at the front. Legion J27s had provided Lori with reloads for her missile launchers and autocannon; these machines on the display were probably part of Gareth's logistical train supplying his 'Mechs north of the fortress. If they were pulling out now, chances were they were loaded with goodies that he wanted repositioned closer to the spaceport. Empties would have slipped away earlier singly, rather than moving in a guarded convoy.

"Hey, Dag!" she called. Dag Flanders, in his *Dervish,* had stayed with her since those wild few moments early in the fight, when he'd come to her assistance in the engagement with the *Apollo.* "You see those bracketed bogies?"

"Ammo tractors," he replied. "Easy meat, Boss Lady!"

"Well, it might not be easy. I'm reading a fair-sized escort. But it's meat, and it's fresh."

"Let's go see if we can cut us a piece."

Together, spaced thirty meters apart, the two Legion BattleMechs began vectoring off toward the east, moving quickly to try to cut off the convoy, now about five kilometers ahead, from the spaceport. As they moved, Lori studied the points of light on her primary screen, becoming more and more convinced that the invaders were, indeed, trying to break off the attack.

Her attention focused on the spaceport. Yes, if she were in their boots, she'd have her 'Mechs fall back in mutually supporting lines, until all were inside a tightly defended perimeter within the spaceport. She'd start loading the 'Mechs in sections, shrinking the perimeter as she did so; the last few on the ground would either be sacrificed to get the DropShips away or allowed to escape by a planetary defender who didn't want to unnecessarily risk losing still more 'Mechs in a useless gesture. She already knew she wasn't going to order her people to assault DropShips, not when all they really wanted was to have the invaders off their planet.

A warning sounded in her neurohelmet mike, a rapid buzzing that meant her *Shadow Hawk* was being painted by hostile fire-control radar. Her eyes flicked down to her primary display, picking out a pair of red blips five kilometers to the west and moving straight toward her at twice the speed of sound.

Aerospace fighters. Gareth had several, she knew, though he'd been hoarding them after the first few days of the battle, when Castle Hill's air defenses had bagged four of them in a single day. She slid a targeting cursor over the incoming blips, engaging her *Hawk*'s O/P 2000A targeting and tracking system. The readout appeared an instant later, flowing from her 'Mech's warbook database. CSR-V12 *Corsair*s.

"Fighter alert!" she called over the tac channel. "*Riflemen* and *JagerMech*s, you're up, on point!"

*Corsair*s were among the best aerofighters in service, fifty tons apiece of rugged reliability armed with an array of eight lasers of various sizes and strengths, from small mounts to a pair of big, long-range Exostars in the nose fairing. She knew the design well; there were *Corsair*s in the Gray Death's aerospace wing, though she'd ordered them held back to conserve her assets. Judging by their approach vector, these two were probably on a strafing run. Either they were attempting to lay down a covering fire to let the Gareth BattleMechs on the ground break off from the Legion's 'Mechs and escape, or they were an added escort for those J27s, and they'd seen Lori and Flanders headed for the convoy. Either way, they were trouble.

She considered waiting until the *Corsair*s had committed themselves to their run, then jumping clear. Both her *Shadow Hawk* and Flanders's *Dervish* possessed jump jets. She rejected that idea, though, as probably futile. A *Corsair* was a hell of a lot more maneuverable than a BattleMech and could correct for any evasive maneuvering she did almost up to the last instant.

Streams of tracers crisscrossed overhead, as 'Mechs armed with high-speed autocannon, *Riflemen* and *Jager-Mech*s, mostly, sought to weave a deadly web through the sky ahead of the oncoming *Corsair*s. The fighters didn't swerve or seek to avoid that wall of fire but kept coming; Lori saw them long before she heard them, picking out a pair of dark spots on the western sky above the horizon, now hidden, now revealed by the slow-climbing pillars of oily smoke. One was low and in the lead, the other trailing and high, flying cover for his wingman. She swung her *Hawk*'s autocannon into line, locking on her targeting cross hairs with a radar assist from the O/P 2000A rather than eyeballing it. When the cross hairs flashed gold around the lead blip, she thumbed the trigger.

Her autocannon cut loose with its reassuringly familiar *thud-thud-thud* of high explosive, though the targets were still pretty far off. Raising her balky right arm, she added her Martel Mod 5's snap and flash to the barrage she was throwing into the air at the onrushing craft. An instant later, it seemed, they were growing to fill her HUD, their lasers flickering at nose and wingtips with a pure and deadly, strobing light.

The ground around Lori vanished in steam and hurtling debris; laser bolts struck her *Shadow Hawk*'s torso and upper left arm; warning lights flickered across her console as alphanumerics scrolled across her screens, warning of holed armor, of failing circuits, of damage to heat sinks and power feeds. An explosion, an eruption of armor suddenly turned to white-hot gas, staggered her back a step, and then another, but she held her stance and continued firing as the *Corsair*s death-howled past forty meters above her head, low enough that the concussion of their passage slammed against her 'Mech with the force of a bursting bomb.

Clumsily, she pivoted about to keep them in sight. Dag Flanders's *Dervish* had been knocked down by the strafing run, and smoke was boiling from a ragged tear in his right-shoulder armor. One of the *Corsair*s, the one in the lead, seemed to be trailing a thread of smoke, but Lori couldn't be sure. In any case, they banked toward the south and kept going, showing no sign of swinging about to finish the job.

"Dag!" she called, worried. "Dag, are you all right?"

"I'm still here," Flanders's voice replied in her headset. "I'm not quite sure how...."

Moving across the smoking ground, she extended a hand and helped the *Dervish* to its feet. Flanders's machine had taken a fair amount of damage to its bulky upper torso, and its right arm was hanging limp, the control actuators shot to hell. Overall, however, and despite outward appearances, the *Dervish* was still operational, though at only about seventy percent capacity.

Lori spent several moments more concentrating on

damage control. Her *Shadow Hawk* was overheated after
the brief exchange with the aerospace fighters, and several primary control systems were failing, with circuits
and power connectors melted through. Still, she got the
'Mech moving again, the heat gauge slowly bleeding
down the scale once more, her control and weapons systems functioning on backup or with reserve power feeds
routed around the damaged sections. The *Hawk* was leaking a coolant fluid from its left side, and the hydraulic
pressure in the left leg was falling slowly, a possible indicator of a leak in either the hydraulic shunts or the ac-
tuator assembly.

No problem. Lori would keep going, keep her 'Mech
going. She *had* to, to keep driving the enemy, to keep her
own people moving and sharp.

One way or another, she was going to end this fight
once and for all.

8

The crack and thump and chatter of heavy 'Mech gunfire seemed to be coming from all directions, but it was less concentrated now and less constant, another indicator that the battle was breaking up, the combatants dispersing. Together, Lori and Flanders kept closing on the J27 convoy. As they marched, she coordinated with other Legion 'Mechs scattered across the AO but all closing on the same target.

Tactically, the Legion was in a good position to follow through on its victory and chalk up a good, solid kill ratio. Large-scale 'Mech battles tended to start as tightly concentrated affairs, with large numbers of BattleMechs in close field array advancing in mass formations that allowed tight cooperation and mutual support. In all but the most closely managed battles, however, the initial clash between opposing 'Mech forces tended to scatter the participants, and even the best-planned large-scale battle swiftly degenerated into innumerable smaller firefights.

'Mech battles, Grayson had told her once, started at the level of regiment or battalion but immediately decayed like a radioactive isotope, falling to fights by company, by lance, and ultimately one-on-one contests between individual 'Mechs. There was a Medieval feel to most 'Mech combat, like the confused, chaotic clashes between armored knights and infantry at Crécy or Bannockburn. MechWarriors frequently thought of themselves as modern-day knights and saw single combat between two opposing 'Mechs as both test and rite of passage, a measure of a pilot's stamina, guts, and skill.

That was one reason, probably the single most important one, that 'Mech commanders at anything above the company level found it nearly impossible to keep control of a large and far-flung battle. Master tacticians like Grayson tried holding units in reserve, watching for that critical point of force and timing in a battle when a sudden concentration of fresh and still tightly knit 'Mech companies thrown *here* could tip the balance of the fight to his favor. Lori hadn't had the luxury of that kind of choice, however. To interrupt Gareth's plans against the incoming Second Batt, she'd had to throw all her 'Mech assets, less than a full battalion, into the fight from the start. All she had in reserve were two aerospace fighter squadrons—a total of twelve aircraft—plus elements of the Gray Death's I/A Support Battalion. The infantry/ armor unit might have an application, she reasoned, in the closing moves of the fight, but sending a handful of hovertanks and tracked armor against BattleMechs would be either futile—if the tanks couldn't catch the fast-moving 'Mechs—or expensively stupid—if they could.

I'm sorry, Gray, she thought to herself, and again tears burned in her eyes. She blinked hard, trying to clear them, for the visor of her neurohelmet kept her from reaching them with her hands. *I'm sorry, but I don't know what else I could have done. I don't know what else to do. . . .*

She felt as though she'd let him down, felt as though she were floundering about in this thing like a raw, half-trained newbie. She felt completely inadequate but didn't dare admit that to anyone. After all, the whole of the Legion on Glengarry was looking to *her.*

Judging by the evidence displayed on her primary display, the battle north of the fortress was about over, as enemy BattleMechs, by companies and lances and even singly, streamed to east or west, then swung south, avoiding Castle Hill and the deadly reach of its defensive turrets. She set her display to flash icons at each site where firefights were still under way; there were fewer now north of the castle, more to east and west as pursuing Legion units encountered rearguards and column security elements.

"About a kilometer now," Flanders said. "We might see them when we crest that ridge up ahead."

"Roger that," Lori replied. "Watch it, though. They have a lot of security elements out in a defensive—"

"*Look out!*"

One of those security elements had just put in a decidedly sudden and unexpected appearance, rising above the crest of the ridge just ahead and above the two Legion 'Mechs. It was a Davion Guard *Orion,* a heavy 'Mech massing 75 tons to the 55 apiece of Lori's *Shadow Hawk* and Flanders's *Dervish.*

"Watch it, Boss!" Flanders yelled over the tac channel. "Break left! I'll move right!"

"Keep moving!" Lori called back. "Don't let him pin you!"

"Damn!" Flanders said. "Where the hell did *he* come from?"

The *Orion,* apparently recognizing her *Shadow Hawk* as a greater immediate threat than the *Dervish,* was clumsily pivoting to bring its KaliYama autocannon, the massive, snub barrel protruding from beneath its right arm like an ungainly package, to bear on her.

The monster hadn't been on her primary screen, which meant that so far in this phase of the battle it had eluded Legion surveillance, both electronic and physical. It had already been in a scrape with Legion forces, though; its left hip had been gouged by missile warheads, probably SRMs, and there were grooves and furrows across its side and torso that spoke of hits, probably at close range, by laser fire. Its movements were slower than they should have been, and occasionally jerky; she guessed that its hip actuators had been damaged. There was something hanging as it tried to pivot its torso to track her, too. Her external mikes picked up the grating sound of metal clashing uncomfortably against metal as it rotated, and sparks were striking from the pivot sleeve.

The ON1-K *Orion* was both well-armored and well-armed; besides the autocannon, it packed a medium laser in each arm and both LRM and SRM launchers in its left torso. As in her earlier fight with the *Apollo,* the key to victory here was her maneuverability. If she could circle around on the *Orion*'s rear, she'd be faced by armor only a quarter the thickness of that on the *Orion*'s chest. Pausing only an instant, she triggered a full volley of LRMs at close range, following the rippling, flashing launch with the swift one-two punch of her head-mounted Holly SRM pack. Explosions thundered and cracked across the enemy 'Mech's upper works; most of the surface of its legs was still hidden by the ridge, and several of Lori's LRMs plowed into rock and dirt instead of targeted armor. The *Orion* raised one huge, cylindrical forearm, the right arm with its I.W.W. medium laser, and triggered a megajoule burst of coherent light that tore into Lori's shoulder pauldron, gouging hull metal in a splash of liquid armor and rapidly expanding superheated gas. She kept moving, though, staying ahead of the deadly, slow-swinging muzzle of that autocannon, which seemed to be tracking her with a life of its own.

More explosions crashed across the ridge top or gouged and tore at the *Orion*'s armor as Flanders loosed ten LRMs at the enemy heavy in a long, rippling burst. The *Orion* staggered to its right, and the interruption in its pilot's concentration gave Lori the second or two she needed to scramble to the top of the ridge.

A trap!

The damaged *Orion,* she saw now, had been a lure, something to draw her forces into the open and get them to commit to battle. The reverse slope of the ridge dropped sharply, a twelve-degree grade that leveled off twenty-five meters below her *Shadow Hawk*'s feet. Four of the ammo convoy's screening elements had gathered there, undetected by the scanners that were feeding data to the Legion's 'Mechs. In the second or two before the missiles began striking, she saw and IDed a Third Guard *Trebuchet* and a *Hunchback,* 50 tons apiece, and a pair of ponderously huge, deadly *Stalker*s. Until a moment ago, she and Dag had enjoyed almost a two-to-one mass advantage over the *Orion*; now, suddenly, the mass ratio had flipped to better than two to one against them.

It was definitely, as the ancient combat pilot's saying went, time to get out of Dodge.

The *Stalker*s were the biggest threats. Massing eighty-five tons and packing an impressive array of missile launchers and lasers, even one of those monsters would have been more than Lori's already battered *Shadow Hawk* could handle. The *Stalker*s were having some trouble with the grade on the slope of the ridge; there was a lot of loose gravel, and their digitigrade legs, reversed in cant from the plantigrade stance of a humanoid 'Mech like the *Orion* or Lori's *Hawk,* were having some trouble getting a solid climbing purchase. When her *Shadow Hawk* had appeared above the ridge top, however, both *Stalker*s had shifted their cigar-shaped torsos back in the cradle of their hip assemblies, canting upward to bring both lasers and missiles to bear. LRMs and SRMs crashed together into Lori's left and center torso; warning lights flashed across her console threat and damage displays as some of those blasts were absorbed by her *Hawk*'s internal structure in spots where her armor had already been peeled away.

Lori glanced at her weapons status board just in time to see the legend LRM RELOADING shift to LRM READY. Bending her 'Mech forward, she dropped her targeting cross hairs onto the feet of the nearest *Stalker,* triggering a full volley of five Holly LRMs at a range of less than forty meters. Thunder echoed inside her cockpit; explosions flared; dirt and loose gravel geysered from the *Stalker*'s feet as the ground was literally blasted out from beneath the heavy assault 'Mech. The machine made an almost comical pawing motion in the air with its right leg before it overbalanced to the rear and toppled backward, crashing to the ground in a thunder of clashing parts as loud as Lori's ripple-fire volley.

In the confusion generated by her return fire, Lori triggered her jump jets, intending to translate the forward stoop of her *Shadow Hawk* into a leap above the heads of the *Stalker*s that would bring her down in their rear. A warning sounded almost as soon as she depressed the trigger, however, and several system-failure discretes winked at her. A shrill but dwindling whine told the story better than the array of warning lights. Two of her *Hawk*'s three jump jets were unable to build pressure enough for a jump. Possibly the plenum chambers had failed, possibly she was generating insufficient power; either way, she wasn't going to be jumping clear of this confrontation, and to simply try backing away down the front slope of the hill would expose her to the deadly, thundering fire from that *Orion*.

Thinking fast, Lori let her *Shadow Hawk* absorb some of the impact of the detonations, rocking back on flexed knees, then pivoted ninety degrees right and lunged for the *Orion,* which was just completing its own turn twenty meters off her right side. Its autocannon fired a burst as she closed with it, the shells striking home on her left arm and leg, smashing at her side, threatening to spin her back or knock her off the top of the ridge.

Somehow, she maintained her footing as the impacts slammed into her BattleMech. She kept moving, kept closing in a hard, shambling run, directly toward the *Orion*. The *Orion* appeared ready to greet her, its arms extended wide, but her sudden and unexpected charge seemed to have taken its pilot by surprise. Boldly, Lori slammed into the *Orion*'s armored embrace with the deafening crash of colliding freight monorails, moving inside the reach of the other 'Mech's arm-mounted lasers. In the same movement, she rammed her *Hawk*'s left hand down against the muzzle of the *Orion*'s autocannon, closing her fist around the KaliYama's muzzle just as the enemy pilot triggered a second burst of high-explosive fire.

The blast jolted her, as explosions ripped through her 'Mech's hand, but the explosions that followed as two or three autocannon rounds detonated one on top of the next inside the weapon's barrel were even worse. A hail of shrapnel and fragmenting armor clattered across her *Shadow Hawk*'s torso; something struck her transplas canopy, a ringing, crashing blow that shattered the tough transparency with the violence of an exploding bomb. At almost the same instant, a storm of missiles and laser bolts fired by the *Stalker*s below the ridge tracked across the ridge top and slammed into the *Orion,* which had been spun halfway about by the impact of Lori's *Shadow Hawk,* its back facing the oncoming *Stalker*s. Explosions flared and roared, the noise deafening through the *Hawk*'s smashed canopy. Briefly, flame leapt past her open cockpit and Lori thought one of the heavy lasers had struck her 'Mech full in the head. But then she saw the top of the *Orion*'s head fragmenting in breakaway segments and the neurohelmeted MechWarrior rising on a pillar of ravening fire as he punched out of his back-broken 'Mech.

Lori pushed out hard with both of her 'Mech's arms; the left arm didn't respond at all, and the right was dangerously sluggish, but she managed to break free from the *Orion*'s limp, dead-weight sag and tumble backward down the face of the ridge.

Her BattleMech screamed, a metallic shriek that could almost have been ripped from a human throat. Her left arm stayed entangled in the wreckage of the *Orion*, which remained balanced at the top of the ridge, smoke pouring from savage rents in its torso and from the now vacant cockpit. Her *Hawk*'s body lost all hydraulic support in its legs as it crumpled, massive systems failures flashing across her console like a barrage of missiles peppering a wall ... and then all power failed and her cockpit was plunged into darkness. The impact when the 'Mech slammed full-length and face-down onto the rocky ground nearly finished her; the concussion drove the breath from her body and stars flashed through her eyes. For a long second, she lay there in near-darkness and sudden silence, gasping desperately to draw her next breath.

Then survival instinct kicked in; those *Stalker*s would be over the top of the ridge any second now, and they would be eager to make sure of their kill with a hard-driven kick or stomp to the fallen *Shadow Hawk*'s head. Worse, she smelled a sharpening odor of smoke and melted insulation. It might be nothing, but it was also possible her 'Mech was on fire.

Lori had always had a devastating fear of death by fire. She'd learned to control it many years before, but the mere thought of being trapped inside the cockpit of a burning BattleMech ...

Swiftly, she removed her neurohelmet and slid it into its rack, then unplugged her cooling vest from the life support panel. Next, bracing herself against her dead instrument console, she unsnapped her quick-release harness and hit the emergency hatch handle above and behind her head.

The handle didn't budge; either the mechanism was jammed or the *Hawk* had fallen in such a way that the escape hatch was blocked. She didn't dare hit the explosive bolts, since if the hatch *was* blocked, the explosion might

fry her with the backdraft. Instead, she let herself drop
forward out of her seat and began sliding gingerly headfirst over her instrument console toward the shattered
front canopy. She wasn't well protected for such maneuvers, dressed in garb typical for a 'Mech cockpit, which
tended to become sauna-hot in the course of a long battle:
rubber-soled shoes, red briefs, and a gray cooling vest
with a built-in survival harness. Ignoring the jaggedly
sharp edges of shattered transplas, she wiggled her way
over the instrument panel and through the shattered canopy. There was less than half a meter to spare between
the front of the *Hawk*'s head and the ground, but she
managed to spill through, twist onto her back to slip her
legs clear, and then roll over and crawl on her belly until
she was clear of the wreck.

Then she was up and running, racing across open
ground, desperately trying to put more distance between
her and her fallen 'Mech. Flanders's *Dervish* was ahead,
at the foot of the ridge and fifty meters north. She angled
away from the other 'Mech, knowing just how slim her
odds of survival if she were caught in the open, unprotected, in a firefight between BattleMechs.

A dull, rhythmic thumping and the scrape and clatter of
metal on rock was growing swiftly louder. Once, just
once, she chanced a glance back over her shoulder. One
of the *Stalker*s was standing atop the ridge next to the
burned-out *Orion*; the other was just heaving itself into
view beyond. Clouds of white smoke erupted from the
LRM mounts to the left and right of its blunt fuselage as
it loosed two full volleys of missiles at the *Dervish*.

Flanders's 'Mech rocked back with the impact, then
waded forward, loosing a volley of missiles in reply.
With a stab of horror, Lori realized that Dag was fighting
for *her,* that he was engaging two *Stalker*s in order to give
her time to clear the area. One hand snapped up to the
small emergency radio clipped to her cooling vest's survival harness, then dropped as she remembered that it
would transmit only on emergency channels, not the Legion's tactical frequency. Besides, Flanders appeared to
be totally caught up in the violence of the moment, leaning his chunky *Dervish* forward like a man leaning into a
stiff, sleet-laden wind. The other two enemy 'Mechs were
heaving into view above the ridgeline now, the *Hunch-*

back leading, the *Trebuchet* close behind, all four Gareth BattleMechs keeping up a steady, withering fire. In the next moment, a trio of explosions tore the Legion 'Mech's right arm off, sending it spinning back across the battlefield. Half a ton of armor followed, whirling bits of metal and internal strutwork, plates torn and peeled back like the flaps of a sealed cardboard box, the entire right-side Federated 10-shot launcher system trailing a spaghetti of ripped-out wiring and circuitry . . .

Damn it, Dag! Punch Out!

He couldn't have heard her despairing thought. The torso of the fire-savaged *Dervish* dissolved in white light and hurtling fragments; the thunderclap of noise engulfed her, knocking her to her knees. Somehow, she got up and kept running, her bare knees bloodied by the fall. There was nothing left of Flanders's *Dervish* but the legs and lower torso, still standing on their own and belching smoke. Another volley of missiles shrieked down from the ridge, triggered before the enemy MechWarriors could react to the realization that the *Dervish* was destroyed.

One of the missiles must have gone wild; Lori didn't hear the explosion, didn't even feel it, really. One moment she was running as hard and as fast as she could across open ground; the next she was in the air, arms and legs flailing. She managed to curl up, arms protecting head . . . and then she struck the ground, bouncing hard, pain lancing down her shoulder and arm and side, hammering at her senses.

Her third-to-last thought as consciousness wavered and faded was that now they weren't going to be able to catch that damned ammunition convoy. Her next-to-last thought was a sharp pang of regret at Dag Flanders's death. He'd died trying to save her, a suicidal one-against-four charge, and she still wasn't sure whether it was the bravest thing she'd ever seen, or the stupidest. . . .

Her final thought was one of sour, pain-numbed regret that she hadn't been able to pull this battle together the way Grayson would have. No, she wasn't jealous of his tactical skill, not really.

But she had *so* wanted him to be proud of her. . . .

Brandal Gareth could feel the pace of the battle changing.

To sense it, he'd left the close, warm interior of his mobile HQ, left the arrayed monitors and communications consoles, and stepped out into the open. Dunkeld Spaceport was a clattering, noisy swirl of activity, with BattleMechs moving up to create a defensive perimeter, or standing motionless as techs and armorers completed field repairs or reloaded expendables. Some 'Mechs and armored vehicles were boarding the five DropShips already grounded at Dunkeld. More DropShips were inbound and would be here soon.

To the north, beyond the city, the Legion fortress still stood, defiant and unfallen, a black sprawl of walls and turrets on the crest of the hill. In the distance, to northeast and northwest, there was still the punctuated staccato of heavy 'Mech gunfire, but it was slower now, more isolated, more scattered and random.

Every battle has a tempo, a beat that can be sensed in the flow and interplay of fire and movement, and ever since the unexpected sortie by the Legion BattleMechs from their HQ fortress, the tempo of this fight had been just beyond Gareth's reach ... sometimes almost where he could grab it and wrestle it back under control, but toward the end it was farther and farther from his grasp until it was all he could do to maintain even a semblance of control over his own farflung and scattered forces.

The 'Mechs of the Guard's First and Second Battalions, most of them, at any rate, had finally managed to disengage and were falling back toward the spaceport. The Legion forces had been pursuing them, sticking close, never letting up in the insane savagery of their attacks.

Then, as though a switch had been thrown, the enemy's pursuit had faltered. Individual firefights continued, pursuit continued, and yet the planet's defenders seemed to have lost that all-important tempo of mass, maneuver, and fire. More and more of Gareth's 'Mechs were breaking free and gathering in the perimeter he was forming about the spaceport. More and more of the Legion 'Mechs had broken off, and many appeared to be milling about almost aimlessly.

He thought none the less of his opponent for that; such things happened in combat, and victory or defeat could turn on some tiny and unforeseen twist of coincidence or human failure.

He looked up at the mighty fortress. Who had been his opponent, the mind on the other side of the game board, he wondered? Lieutenant Colonel Kalmar-Carlyle? His intelligence sources had confirmed that she was in charge of the Glengarry garrison in the absence of her husband, but he'd not expected such tactical skill from her. Those same reports indicated that she'd not participated in active ops very much over the past few years, and people who were good at something rarely just gave it up. The reports said that she tended to lead from her Ops Center, but the best 'Mech commanders knew you had to lead from the front, not the rear.

No matter. If Kalmar-Carlyle had been his opponent these past weeks, he saluted her. She had done well. If it was someone else, then perhaps that unreported change in the enemy's organization charts had just been responsible for his defeat.

As for Gareth, his attempt to grab Glengarry to further Operation Excalibur had failed, but that failure was no more than a minor setback. With the return of the rest of the Gray Death Legion—and of Colonel Carlyle—it was time to leave.

Other plans were already in motion, plans that would bring Glengarry into his net . . . along with a dozen other worlds throughout this region of space.

Even the Gray Death Legion might soon be his. If he couldn't beat them, perhaps he would have it given to him as a prize. With a wry grin, Gareth tossed an ironic salute toward the brooding fortress of Castle Hill. Then he turned and climbed back up the ramp into his headquarters.

There was a lot remaining to be done.

9

Lori had not expected to live.

Even now, almost three full days after the battle, she found herself genuinely surprised from time to time that she'd somehow managed to survive. Well, she reasoned, she'd fought her hardest to make certain that Grayson had a place to come back to, and it would have been tragedy bordering on the pathos of comic opera had she succeeded, only to be killed herself in the last moments of the battle. Maybe there was justice in the universe after all.

Lori had regained consciousness a few hours after the destruction of her *Shadow Hawk,* strapped into a cot in one of the Legion's field mobile aid stations, a combination ambulance and emergency room on tracks that had been dispatched to the scene by several Legion 'Mech pilots who'd seen the last part of her fight. All things considered, she'd been remarkably lucky. She'd suffered a mild concussion, she was told, and there was the chance that the broken ribs she'd suffered in an assassination attempt the month before had been broken again. The medtechs who'd picked her up had air-injected her with a painkiller, wrapped her chest in meters of white gauze, and immobilized her in the cot with assurances that she would be just fine.

She'd not wanted assurances about her health at the time. Eager for tactical information, she'd plied the techs with groggy questions until they'd consented to establish a data download link with Ops. The *Stalkers*, *Trebuchet,* and *Hunchback* had all moved on, she'd learned, following the ammo convoy they'd guarded so effectively. The *Orion,* one of the medtechs told her, remained where it had fallen, sprawled across the top of the ridge. That made Lori smile. Max had told her he needed a Vlar 300 power plant before she'd left the base that morning, suggesting that she take down a *Marauder* or an *Atlas*. Well, *Orion*s were powered by Vlar 300s too, and Gareth had been in too much of a hurry to take his dead 'Mechs with them.

Max Dewar would have that power plant for the downgrudged *Marauder* after all. The cost had been high, though. Dag Flanders had been a tough, sharp, and experienced NCO. He would be missed.

All of that had been two and a half days ago, and though Ben Watson, the senior medtech at Castle Hill, had ordered Lori to remain in the dispensary for observation, as base commander she'd countermanded those orders and was back in the Ops Center, watching the incoming DropShips on the main viewer. All three had arrived on schedule, completed their deorbit burns, and were inbound now through Glengarry's ionosphere. An aide had woken her forty minutes ago with the news that they were on their way in.

"Colonel Kalmar?"

She turned sharply at the voice and winced, her hand going to her side. Fortunately, it turned out that her recently electro-knitted ribs were only badly bruised, and not broken a second time, but the sharp pain when she inhaled still brought a catch to her breath, especially if she moved too quickly.

Major Rae Houk's lean and mobile face showed his concern. "Colonel? Are you all right?"

She managed a smile, straightening slowly. "Still a bit tender there," she told him.

"Damn it, Colonel. You should be down in the dispensary."

"I belong *here*, Major. What'cha got for me?"

He didn't look convinced. "I just wanted to hand in my final report." He handed her an electronic pad. "I guess Second Batt got a stiffer training session the other day than we expected, huh?"

Lori chuckled. "You certainly did. And passed the test with flying pennants, I should add. That was a remarkable feat of arms, Major, marching your battalion all that way. And through such terrain. It should stand right up there with the Long March. Or Xenophon's *Anabasis*."

He seemed embarrassed, an almost boyish "aw, shucks" look on his face. "It wasn't as though we had an alternative, Colonel. We did what we had to do. Nothing more than that."

"Hmm." Now Lori didn't sound convinced. She'd known plenty of mercenary officers in her forty-plus years of service, and damned few of them held anything like the devotion to duty or to comrades that had been revealed in Houk's march. "Well, you pulled our skittles out of the fire, that's for damned sure, and I'm grateful." She touched the pad's presentation key and scanned the figures that came up on the screen. "So . . . seven 'Mechs fell out of the march on the way here. Mechanical failures. And eight 'Mechs destroyed in the fight, or so badly damaged they'll be out for major repairs. Seven more downgrudged with combat damage. That's steep."

He nodded. "I heard you lost five here, Colonel, counting your own."

"That was just on the last day. We lost four before that, in the opening rounds. Right now, my friend, the Gray Death is down by almost a full battalion, and that's not counting the losses Third Batt took on Caledonia. I'd say we're going to be hanging out the recruiting posters pretty soon."

He made a face. "And more training."

"*Always* more training." Lori set the report board aside. "Expendables?"

"We're restocking okay. Ammo and missiles are in short supply, of course, like they always are right after a big fight. I wouldn't want to take the battalion into a major battle, just yet. But we'll manage."

"I know you will." She winced, touching her side. "Colonel?"

She waved off the question. "I'm fine."

Grimacing, she considered the reserves of expendable munitions, missiles and autocannon rounds, in particular, a number she'd been mulling about with concern ever since she left the base dispensary. Any battle larger than a skirmish—and the fight around Castle Hill two days before had been far more than that—used up the munitions stored in base or DropShip at an appalling rate. One reason mercenary units valued landholds was the simple fact that such worlds or large tracts of land provided a powerful industrial capacity for the unit, factories to turn out A/C shells and missiles and belt-fed machine-gun rounds literally by the million, not to mention plate armor, electronic components, circulating machinery, myomer bundles, and all the rest of the industrial output necessary for a modern war.

The Gray Death was lucky in that regard, Glengarry having been presented to the Legion as landhold, the fief of Grayson Carlyle when he'd been named Baron Glengarry. Most mercs relied on purchases made on thread-slender budgets, or on supplies provided by contract with wealthy employers. The Great Houses of the Inner Sphere, of course, each had numerous worlds to draw on for their military-industrial requirements, some almost entirely dependent on the government's military purchase orders and contracts. Hesperus II, just two jumps from Glengarry, had been one of the most important sources of BattleMechs and military expendables for the old Lyran Commonwealth for as long as it had been in existence and was nearly as important now for the entire Federated Commonwealth. Glengarry had no facilities for manufacturing whole BattleMechs, but the factories at Dunkeld and Ross and Inverurie could produce key components, and a brisk trade with other, similar worlds purchased more.

"Looks to me like a good six months to get our expendie reserves back to full stock," Lori said after thinking through the problem for a moment. She shook her head. "Damn. Two weeks of skirmishes capped by one four-hour battle, and it's going to be November before we're ready to campaign again."

"Maybe Third Batt—"

She stopped him with one arched eyebrow. "From the

reports I've seen, they're coming home damned near empty. They fought a battle of their own, remember, on Caledonia, and it was a negotiated truce."

Meaning that the other side had agreed to a cessation of hostilities—meaning further that they'd have recovered their salvageable 'Mechs, gathered up any stockpiles of expendables left behind their lines, and generally cleaned up after themselves—a no-good state of affairs for the munitions-hungry victors.

"All things considered," she went on, "Gareth might have been better off staying put. I'm not sure how much firepower Third Batt and the HQ Lance could have brought to bear on him."

"He probably had some ammo limitations of his own, Colonel."

"Could be." *Or he just lost confidence in himself,* she added to herself, a little fiercely. The psychology of command could be a fearsome thing, with decisions made on perceptions of the course of a battle, perceptions so easily misled.

"Colonel Kalmar?" Lieutenant Whitney Ronga, the duty comm tech, called from her console. "First Drop-Ship's out of LOS."

"Excuse me, Major," she said, nodding to Houk.

"Of course, Colonel."

LOS—Loss of Signal—was that window when ionization caused by the high temperature of atmospheric entry blocked radio communications with incoming spacecraft. If the DropShips were back in contact with Castle Hill, they must be nearly overhead by now.

She walked over to the comm desk. A radio voice, a bit scratchy and faint, sounded from a console speaker. *"Homeport,* Endeavor. *We have your beacon and are on approach vector delta three. Speed eight thousand kph, altitude two-five-eight-nine-five meters. Please advise with a met update. Over."*

Lori recognized the voice. It was Captain Ilse Martinez, captain of the *Endeavor,* one of the Legion DropShips that had carried Third Battalion to Caledonia.

"Endeavor, Homeport," Ronga replied, her voice brisk and professional, though Lori could still hear the excitement there. "Sky mostly clear, with scattered cirrus at

one-eight-thousand meters. Ceiling unlimited. Wind at the port is northwest at five and steady."

Lori leaned over and held her lip mike, turning it slightly so she could speak into it. "And welcome home, *Endeavor*," she added.

"Colonel Kalmar!" Martinez said. "Is that you?"

"None other. We're planning a bit of a party in your honor, *Endeavor*. If we can just catch that damned fatted calf."

"Ah, roger that. Say, Colonel. We have a passenger aboard here you'll be interested in. The doc says to tell you his readouts still look good."

Lori sagged inwardly with relief, though she knew Grayson had a long fight ahead of him.

"Thanks, *Endeavor*. So tell me, where did you come from? And how? We weren't expecting you for days yet!"

"It's a long story," Martinez said. "Basically, we found a JumpShip going our way and hitched a ride. Then we made a pirate-point jump. Gareth's people never even saw us coming."

"Actually, I think they did. And then they broke all kinds of records getting loaded up and boosting out. They must be halfway to their JumpShips by now."

"That's affirmative. We have them on radar . . . just keeping an electronic eye on them to make sure they don't try anything funny. They're running for it, it looks like."

"Safe landing, *Endeavor*. We'll be waiting for you when you ground." She glanced at Houk, still waiting nearby. "Major? Care to accompany me?"

"Of course, Colonel. It'll be damned good to see them again."

He's still alive. . . .

The thought remained with her as she left Ops with Houk and a two-man security detachment, catching an elevator for Castle Hill's entrance level. For weeks, ever since word had arrived after Falkirk, she'd been trying hard not to think about it, trying not to dwell on the fact that Grayson might not even survive the voyage back from Caledonia. But he had survived. *He's still alive. . . .*

Ten minutes later, Lori stepped out of the monorail pod that had whisked her and the others from Castle Hill across the city to Dunkeld Spaceport. The sun was just peeking above the Scotian Highlands to the east, huge and deep orange in hue. The crowd already gathered in the public areas was enormous; most of the city's population had fled when the invaders had descended on flaming jets from the sky, but they were coming home now, returning to a city badly damaged by battle. The air was brisk and still carried the stink of burning rubber and oil.

It was obvious that the fighting in and around the spaceport field had been especially savage. A couple of BattleMechs, their structures reduced to carbonized wreckage and the stark, bare skeletons of internal frameworks, lay in sprawled heaps, still smoking. Armored vehicles had circled here and died; the burned-out hulk of a Pegasus lay with its nose buried in the ground, its ducted fans shredded in a litter of gleaming silver metal. The spaceport had been a prime target for Gareth's 'Mechs and troops, who'd enjoyed a brief orgy of destruction on the way out, smashing windows, burning what couldn't be smashed, and littering the field with wreckage. Work crews laboring through the night, assisted by volunteers from the city, had begun restoring some order to the place, but there was still so very much to do.

All work had ceased, however, when word had begun spreading that the Legion DropShips were inbound. The crowds waited silently behind the safety barriers and fences, faces turned to the early morning sky.

Waiting.

They're waiting to hear about Grayson too, she thought. Lori sighed. If Grayson didn't recover . . .

She shook her head. She'd given a lot of thought to what would happen if Grayson couldn't resume command, and she didn't like any of the answers she'd come up with.

As executive officer Lori was next in line for command of the Legion, but she knew her own limits, or she thought she did. She was a good administrator, a good organizer, even a fair MechWarrior when it came to that, but she didn't have what it took to command a regiment, to inspire the sort of wide-eyed awe that Grayson could raise in new kids and jaded veterans alike. Certainly she couldn't follow in his steps; the inevitable comparisons, the litany of "Grayson Carlyle wouldn't have done it that way" would follow her, would plague her until the day she died.

The logical choice was Davis McCall, despite the grizzled Scot's insistence that he was a command company exec, *not* regimental leader material. Of the others in line command . . . Rae Houk, she thought, was still inexperienced, though he was coming along fast. Major Jonathan Frye, CO of Third Battalion, was an exceptional commander, experienced, battle-hardened, and loved by his men, but an injury a few years back had left him deaf in one ear and unable to wear a neurohelmet. Grayson had always been adamant that a good CO led his men from the 'Mech cockpit. Frye agreed, and more than once had tendered his resignation because of it. Grayson had rejected those resignations because he valued Frye so highly, but Gray and Jonathan would both probably reject him for regimental command.

So who was left? Some merc units followed a hereditary line, with eldest sons or daughters following in the lineage of command. Lori gave a small, ironic smile at that. Alex was certainly being groomed for command, and he did well as a company commander, but he wasn't ready for battalion-level work yet, much less a regiment.

Which brought things full circle back . . . to her.

God help us if I have to be the one to boss this unit, she thought.

The truth was that the Gray Death Legion was in a terrible position right now, squarely between the proverbial rock and the hard place. Quite apart from her own personal feelings in the matter, if Grayson died, even if he simply didn't recover from his wounds sufficiently to resume regimental command, the Legion might well be finished. There were going to be legal problems in the wake of the unit's changing sides on Caledonia; that much was clear from Davis McCall's HPG transmission right after the Battle of Falkirk. Mercenary units simply did *not* attack the forces of the people who'd contracted with them, no matter what the rights or wrongs of the situation might be.

And morale had been low throughout the Glengarry contingent of the Legion when it became known that Grayson had been seriously wounded. She knew that if it were possible to chart morale levels on a graph, the chart would have shown a sharp, upward spike marking the battle just fought here on Glengarry as the Legion's members rallied to ensure that Grayson and the other wounded from Caledonia would have a place to return to. But she knew, too, that within a few days, once Grayson was back and under medical treatment, morale would fall off again. If he didn't recover, or if the prognosis turned out to be poor over the long term, a great deal of the Gray Death Legion's fighting edge could be lost, perhaps for months. The men and women of the Legion loved Grayson with a passionate enthusiasm that was a little bewildering sometimes to the people, like Lori, who knew him best. She loved him deeply, but she also knew his flaws; most newcomers to the Legion had joined because of Grayson's reputation more than anything else. Hell, even the civilians here in Dunkeld worshipped the man. The Legion, after all, provided employment for well over three quarters of the population, one way or another, with jobs at the factories, at the spaceport, and the civilian positions up at Castle Hill.

What, she wondered, would happen if the Legion were forced to disband, or move elsewhere? The people here would suffer if that happened. No wonder they were waiting in such great, anxious, and silent mobs. She knew exactly how they felt. Sometimes, the waiting was worse than the bad news in the end.

Thunder pealed, high overhead in a bright, green-tinged early morning sky. The first DropShip thundered across the zenith, tiny with altitude and drawing a white contrail behind it. Pivoting in the sky as the last of its forward velocity bled away, it brought its four massive stern jets to bear on the ground and, from an altitude of less than a kilometer, began backing down on a shrieking pillar of white fire toward Dunkeld Spaceport's landing field.

It was a *Union* Class, a squat, dull-silver sphere bristling with turrets, antennas, and assorted bulges that gave the vessel a battered, almost organic feel, as though it were something alive rather than another machine. Soon it was low enough for Lori to read the name picked out in script on the stained and age-mottled hull: *Endeavor*.

The flame and thunder intensified as the ship lowered itself to within a few tens of meters above the shallow depression of a blast pit. Landing legs unfolded from cowled fairings, reaching out to touch the ground, then yielding beneath the DropShip's tremendous weight. The flame died away; coolant steam vented from external ports; the sharp, metallic ping of cooling metal could be heard even across the kilometer of open field between the ship and the spaceport terminal.

Lori turned to Houk, who'd been standing silently at her side throughout the landing. "Let's get out there" was all she said.

A ground tractor transported them to the waiting *Endeavor*. As she stepped out of the vehicle in the long shadow of the ship, other DropShips filled the vaulted Glengarry sky with echoing thunder as each, in turn, shifted venturis toward the ground, then drifted toward the landing field on ravening plasma jets. One by one they touched down on the spaceport so recently controlled by Gareth's forces. Ramps lowered, 'Mech bay doorways slid open, and the Legion's gray and black BattleMechs began striding out into the sunlight, weapons at the ready.

A ramp was already down from the grounded *Endeavor*. A familiar 'Mech, a 90-ton *Highlander*, stood at the top of the ramp, as though surveying the lay of the land. And beside the 'Mech . . .

"Alex!" she yelled.

The young man's face lit up, the expression visible even from here. "Mom!" He trotted toward her.

"Where's tha' wee bastard Gareth?" McCall wanted to know, his voice booming from his 'Mech's external speaker. The *Highlander*'s armor-shrouded head swung back and forth, as though he were looking for the leader of the invasion forces.

"Gareth pulled out when he heard you were coming," she shouted up at him. "All of their forces pulled out while you were still inbound."

The top of the *Highlander*'s head split open, and Davis McCall appeared, rising from his cockpit. "Tha's nae fair!" he bellowed down at them. "We bring th' cavalry all th' way here from Caledon . . ."

McCall scrambled out of his *Highlander*'s cockpit and began clambering down the outside of his 'Mech, using the footholds down the side torso and leg. He let go and dropped the last couple of meters to the ground, then walked toward Lori and Alex, his cooling vest flapping over a black T-shirt and khaki shorts.

"It *was* a bit of the old cavalry to the rescue," Lori told them. "When he realized you were only a couple of days out, I think he broke the all-time air-space speed record getting his gear together and moving out."

"We were tracking DropShips lifting off planet as we entered orbit," Alex said. "Figured that was what had happened."

"So Captain Martinez told me." Lori's eyes strayed to the DropShip towering above them, its dull gray and silver hull casting a long shadow in the afternoon sun. "How . . . how is he?" she asked.

Alex's jaw tightened at the question, and for a moment she imagined the worst. Then Davis touched her arm, nodding. "Still hangin' in there. You've got y'sel' a fighter there, lass. A *real* fighter."

"The ship's doc said he'd be all right if we could get him back here," Alex added. "He . . . he doesn't look real good, Mom. But there's been no change since we lifted from Caledonia." He obviously meant no change for the worse.

Lori nodded. Her last update on Grayson's condition had been from Caledonia, when she'd learned the extent of his injuries. If he was no better now, weeks later, then at least he could be no worse. That was the wonder of medical stasis . . . and the curse. All it did was keep the patient alive, or perhaps a better description was that it kept him not dead. Not quite. As if on cue, a hover transport whined up to the DropShip, its ducted fans howling as they sent a storm of dust and flecks of gravel across the field. A team of medtechs, identified by the caducei on their jackets, vaulted from the vehicle as soon as it grounded, sprinting up the DropShip's main boarding ramp and into the cavernous bay beyond.

Lori wanted to go to him, to see him, to be with him, even if he was totally unresponsive in the icy embrace of the med capsule. But the team would be moving him now, and she'd only be in the way. She consoled herself with the thought that if anyone could bring him back, the Gray Death's med team could.

She grinned at McCall, then nodded toward his empty

Highlander. "You didn't really expect to find Gareth here waiting for you, did you?"

"Weel, noo, Colonel, y' ken how I feel aboot security. . . ."

"We discussed it coming in," Alex added. He nodded toward the fence keeping the crowd of civilians at bay, a good two kilometers off. "The major thought it would be best if we had a perimeter display, at least."

Lori nodded, understanding. The possibility that Gareth had left commandos, saboteurs, or snipers behind when he'd boosted for space was very real, as was the possibility that some few, at least, of the locals had supported Gareth's brief military rule of the area and might seek to take out their frustration at being on the losing side through paramilitary action. Having some of Third Batt's 'Mechs deploy in a defensive perimeter about the DropShips as they touched down was a simple precaution, and a means of overawing any possible non-'Mech resistance.

"Besides," McCall added, an impish grin tugging at the corner of his mouth behind the bushy red beard. "It was just possible tha' Gareth had won an' was holdin' you hostage. I was nae in th' mood for takin' damn-fool chances."

Lori smiled. "You always were a bit paranoid, Davis."

"Th' Colonel taught me tha', lass," McCall replied. "Besides, just because you're paranoid—"

"Doesn't mean the bastards aren't out to get you," Lori and Alex said, completing the old joke in chanted unison.

A team of medtechs was bringing a medical stasis capsule down the DropShip's number one ramp now, wheeling it ahead of them on a powered cart. "Excuse me," Lori said. Swiftly, she hurried to the side of the cart, leaning over to peer inside the transparency over his face.

"Uh, sorry, Colonel," one of the techs said, recognizing her. "He's in the *next* one."

"Of course . . ." It was a little disconcerting. She'd been focused so tightly on Grayson's injuries, she'd momentarily forgotten that all three Legion DropShips were crammed with wounded. The face of this one, partly visible behind a thin rime of ice on the transparency, was that of a young woman, looking as cold and as pale as a likeness sculpted from white marble.

The second stasis capsule down the ramp was Grayson's. She walked swiftly along beside the cart as the techs steered it toward the hovercraft, unwilling to delay its progress, yet wishing she could just reach inside and *touch* him. . . .

Frost rimed the inside of the transparency. From what little she could make out, he did look bad. His eye—the right one, the one eye she could see—was closed. The other was covered by a wound seal, and she remembered the report on the extent of his injuries. He'd lost his left eye, possibly the hearing in his left ear as well. The skin on the left side of his face was charred in places, blistered in others, and coated with thick gobs of yellowish burn ointment.

McCall was there, one hand on her shoulder as the techs trundled the cart up the rear ramp of the medevac craft. "He'll be all right, lass. If there's aught I can do. . . ."

"Davis," she said, so softly that no one else could hear. "Davis, what are we going to do?"

"Keep going" was his reply, curt and grim. "It's called survival. . . ."

10

Castle Hill, Dunkeld
Glengarry, Skye March
Federated Commonwealth
1017 hours, 18 May 3057

McCall looked up as the door to his office chimed. "Come."

The door slid open, and a man walked in, one Davis had never before seen. He was Oriental—Japanese, McCall thought—with a dark and wary look about him. "Isamu Yoshitomi," the man said with a crisp, precise bow. "You wished to see me, sir."

McCall grunted, gesturing toward an empty chair opposite him at the desk. "Good morning, Mr. Yoshitomi. Thank you for coming."

Yoshitomi nodded once before taking the seat but said nothing, patiently waiting. McCall had the impression that the man was studying him with a nearly microscopic scrutiny, yet without revealing anything in the way of interest or, indeed, of any emotion at all.

"I appreciate you coming at such short notice," McCall prompted. "I'm told you're vurra good a' this sort of thin'."

"I am . . . a specialist," Yoshitomi replied. "If you are looking for someone with my particular background and training, it is perhaps fortunate that your man found me. I know of no other freelancers with my level of skill on Glengarry at the moment."

"Hmm. Indeed." McCall's impression was that Yoshi-tomi was not given to boasting or displays of ego. If any-thing, his manner was low key and self-deprecating. The man's blunt self-appraisal spoke of a complete and abso-lute confidence, one born of an exact knowledge of himself and of his own abilities.

McCall couldn't help wondering how accurate that as-sessment was, though. *No other agents?* Despite his flip reply to Lori the other day about paranoia, it was all too possible that Gareth had left someone behind on Glen-garry. At the very least, there would be infantry scouts now masquerading as Glengarry citizens, positioned to report on the Legion's strength should Gareth be inter-ested in it in the future.

And McCall had no reason to assume that Gareth had lost his interest in the Legion's landhold. He just couldn't figure out what was the reason for that interest in the first place. That was why he'd told Henderson to put out a dis-creet word in certain quarters, looking for a man like Yoshitomi.

It then occurred to him that Yoshitomi had specified "no other freelancers with my level of skill." Perhaps he was speaking what he perceived to be the exact truth.

Though McCall functioned as head of Legion Security, that was not—thank God—his primary responsibility. Lieutenant Henry "Hank" Henderson held that thankless title and the responsibility for dealing with such head-aches as personal security details for Grayson, Lori, and other top Legion personnel, and watching for would-be assassins, saboteurs, or enemy intelligence operatives within the Gray Death's ranks.

It was a job made damned near impossible by its very nature, and by the fact that Grayson Carlyle and most of the other high-ranking Legion brass, Davis McCall in-cluded, refused to isolate themselves from the men and women they commanded. Recently, McCall had stepped in as a kind of unofficial security consultant, working on the theory that old MechWarriors like himself tended to acquire a fairly good arsenal of survival traits, techniques, and tips along the way—which was how they got to be old in the first place. To his credit, Hank hadn't felt threatened by McCall's trespassing in his bailiwick. To the contrary, he'd requested help in the first place, and

Davis had begun spending some time each week reviewing the Legion's security measures and regulations, as well as making spot checks in all departments from time to time and passing on his recommendations as needed. Overall, the system had worked well enough—at least until the assassination attempt two months ago.

Hank had tried to resign after that one. McCall had been off-world at the time, on his way to Caledonia, in fact, but Lori had convinced Henderson to stay. That had been a particularly nasty incident, though, when assassins had tried to take out Grayson here on Glengarry in the middle of a holovised BattleTech exhibition match staged between Grayson and another famous mercenary commander, Jaime Wolf. The match had been prematurely ended by the attack, during which both Grayson and Lori had been slightly wounded and the assassin killed.

What was intriguing about that case, however, was the fact that the Third Batt officer who'd killed the assassin had been Walter Dupré, a newbie lieutenant in the Legion—and the man who'd opened fire on Grayson's *Victor* with his *Zeus,* striking from behind, at the height of the Battle of Falkirk. Dupré was the bastard who'd nearly killed Grayson, and McCall took it as a personal affront that the would-be assassin had masqueraded in Third Batt for months before making his move, and then had the effrontery to make a clean getaway afterward. McCall, personally, had taken down Dupré's *Zeus* in a fiery exchange with his *Highlander,* but the son of a bitch had ejected. Though Legion troops had scoured the battlefield, they'd found nothing but his ejection seat and parachute long hours later, which meant he'd probably managed to slip across the lines to the enemy camp.

Gareth had been taking one hell of a keen interest in Legion activities lately, had involved them in a lose-lose confrontation on Caledonia guaranteed to make them come out looking either like traitors or like monsters, and had used that diversion to create a pretext to invade Glengarry. Assuming that he had indeed been the paymaster behind Dupré, he'd set up one assassination attempt against Carlyle, and then, when that attempt was clearly unsuccessful, Dupré had engineered the situation to make himself look like a hero, putting him in the ideal position for a *second* assassination attempt at Falkirk.

McCall was growing heartily sick of Gareth's plots and machinations. To the best of his knowledge, neither Grayson Carlyle nor anyone else in the Legion had ever crossed swords with the field marshal in the past, so the reasons for his interest and for his animosity both remained mysteries. It was time, he'd decided seconds after hearing that Glengarry was under assault by Gareth's forces, to take the offensive.

But the Legion couldn't strike back until they knew just what it was they were striking back against.

Yoshitomi might be the means for providing some of that necessary intelligence. McCall didn't like using spies, though he readily conceded that every army since Joshua's had needed them. This one was a freelancer, a man who, according to the reports Legion Intelligence had given him, had served for several of the Great Houses, including both the Federated Commonwealth and the Draconis Combine.

"So," he said after a long and increasingly uncomfortable silence. "Tell me some wee bit about y'sel', Mr. Yoshitomi. Who was your last employer?"

The spy bared his teeth in what might have been an approximation of a smile. "You don't really expect me to answer that, do you, Major?"

"Um. Maybe not. But I'd like some idea of your background, where you come from, what y' do. Both military and otherwise."

Yoshitomi appeared to consider this, then gave a small shrug. "My military record is undistinguished, as you have no doubt learned from the file information you have already collected on me. I graduated from the Wisdom of the Dragon, then served for a time with the Draconis Combine Mustered Soldiery, where I had the honor of attaining the rank of *tai-i*."

McCall nodded. *Tai-i* was the equivalent of captain in the Legion, or a *hauptmann* in the old Lyran Commonwealth. A company commander, in other words.

"I was born and raised on Shimosuwa, in the Buckminster Prefecture. As a child, I was apprenticed to the Tatikaze."

"What is that?"

"The name means . . ." Yoshitomi hesitated. "It is a poetical concept and difficult to translate, but the reference

is to the wind caused by the stroke of a sword. It is . . .
you might call it a religious sect, though my understanding of that term suggests it to be a pale and somewhat
empty translation. In any case, it is an order that vener-
ates purpose, discipline, and skill at arms as means both
to self-knowledge and to enlightenment. Bushido . . . you
know the concept?" When McCall nodded, he continued.
"Bushido, the way of the samurai, was my path to enlightenment.

"At twenty-five, I was assigned to the staff of Lord
Tai-sa Shotugama, of the Draconis Combine High Command, himself a member of the Tatikaze. Several years
ago, well, let us say simply that the Luthien government
did not agree with us, precisely, on some interpretations
of the proper and honorable practice of bushido. Tatikaze
was disbanded, its members scattered, its leaders disgraced.

"When the Lord Shotugama committed seppuku, at the
direction of the Coordinator's Office, I suppose I too
should have followed him into an honorable death. It
would have been customary, rather than accepting the status of ronin, a samurai without a master. That, however,
was my choice to make, and I made it, as you can see."
He gave another small shrug. "In truth, there is little
more to tell."

McCall studied Yoshitomi for a long moment. He
would've been willing to bet that there was a great deal
more to tell. He had the feeling that the man was a master
at this sort of verbal warfare. While appearing to be quite
free with his information, Yoshitomi was not telling everything by any means. Not that his prevarication was at
all obvious. McCall only knew that there must be more to
the story because he'd had some dealings in the past with
various bushido-aligned cults.

There were a number of those—no one knew how
many. Large numbers of Japanese had emigrated to space
in the early days of the Great Exodus from Terra, and
many, though by no means all, had brought with them
various conservative traditions, teachings, and ways of
thinking old long before humanity first traveled to the
stars. Bushido—the way of the warrior—tapped traditions
now well over two thousand years old. The planet
Yoshitomi had mentioned, Shimosuwa, was the name of a

world and of a system deep within the Draconis Combine, itself a star empire well known for its revival of ancient Japanese philosophy, culture, and martial arts.

This . . . what was it called? Tatikaze. McCall had never heard of the sect before, but that was scarcely surprising. Both within the Combine and without there were innumerable cults, sects, and organizations revolving around tradition, conservatism, and reverence for the ancient Japanese ways. Most were tolerated or even absorbed into the mainstream of Draconis thought and culture. Some, inevitably, opposed aspects of House Kurita's rule over the Combine or its tolerance of other races, other cultures, other beliefs. The Combine, as McCall understood the situation over there, could ill afford open criticism of its methods, so opposing voices were generally dealt with in a direct and uncompromising fashion.

McCall pursed his lips, absently stroking his beard as he thought about that. Did the fact that Yoshitomi had indirectly claimed to be a refugee from Drac justice make him more trustworthy, or less? He honestly wasn't sure, especially when it was obvious that there was a hell of a lot more to Yoshitomi's story than he was willing to admit.

The Gray Death Legion had never served under merc contract to the Dracs. In fact, they'd squared off against the Draconis Combine military more than once in the past thirty years, but there'd been incidents of cooperation, too. Several times, in fact, Grayson had actually shared lostech finds with the Dracs, a bit of philanthropy McCall had privately thought stupid—or at best outrageously naive—but which, in all honesty, he had to admit had always worked out in the best interests of the Legion.

In fact, McCall had been pretty sure from Henderson's initial contact report that Yoshitomi was recently arrived from the Combine . . . possibly an expatriate Drac, but a Drac nonetheless. The question now was not so much whether the man could be trusted as whether the Legion could make effective use of his services.

If he was as good as Henderson had stated in his report, there was no doubt of that fact at all.

"You would be willing to take on a long-term assignment for me?" McCall asked. "One answering to me, personally, rather than to a House or other government body?"

Yoshitomi gave a curt nod in the affirmative. Curious. He'd not even asked how long "long-term" might be. Nor did he question the unspoken possibility that service in opposition to an established government would be, by its very nature, illegal.

"One that might involve some personal danger if you happen to be found out?"

Again that same, sharp nod.

"Do you have relatives? Family?"

There was the barest hesitation, as though Yoshitomi were considering several different ways of interpreting that question. Then he shook his head "no."

"Do you have any questions about the assignment?"

"I assume that I will be given what information I need to carry out my mission."

"Of course." McCall considered Yoshitomi for a moment, wondering if it was *he* who was drawing *McCall* out in this interview, rather than the other way around. "Do you know the name Brandal Gareth?"

"It would be difficult to have been on Glengarry these past few weeks and not heard that name."

Was Yoshitomi actually cracking a joke? McCall couldn't tell. His facade of imperturbable calm seemed unbreakable.

"I suppose so. Tha' wee bastard hae been screwin' wi' th' Legion, an' we dinnae ken why."

As McCall spoke, his Scot's burr, held somewhat at bay during the earlier portion of the interview, began reasserting itself. Yoshitomi's eyes narrowed slightly, and he leaned forward a bit as though trying to catch and decipher each word, but he revealed no other outward sign of his thoughts.

"He's aye anglin' for somethin'," McCall continued, "but I cannae make out wha' it might be. But I have this feelin' that I'd damned well better find out before the man tries to take us down again.

"Accordingly, I intend t' send you to Hesperus II wi' credentials that should suffice to get you a place in his organization. Ideally in Communications, Ops, or even on Gareth's staff, though tha' might be a wee bit hard t' swing from here. I'll want you to stay there then, possibly for six months, possibly for a year. We'll arrange codes and communications protocols tha' will allow you to report back to me by HPG, probably through innocuous-looking messages to relatives tha' will hae a secret code to them."

"I know a number of routines that might be appropriate for that."

"Aye. Aye, I imagine you do," McCall said dryly. "Weel, lad, I expect tha' you'll do for our purposes just fine. There is, of course, the matter a' money...."

Without preamble, Yoshitomi named a figure, and for the first time, McCall was nonplused, not because the figure was high, but because it was low. Five thousand C-bills per month was less than the operating cost of a single BattleMech lance, figuring in maintenance, repair, and ammo.

"That is more than reasonable," McCall said slowly after a moment. "We'll leave a bit a' leeway in th' expenses. I would nae want you feelin' y' shortchanged y'sel', lad."

"I assume I will have a salary while on Field Marshal Gareth's staff," Yoshitomi said reasonably enough. "Besides, I have no wish to drink this particular well dry."

It was a long time before McCall stopped wondering exactly what Isamu Yoshitomi had meant with that cryptic reply.

The Highland Lassie was a typical spaceport bar, dimly lit, the air thick with smoke from the burning and inhaling of various recreational plants. Isamu Yoshitomi made his way toward the back of the main room, where a rough-looking man with blond hair and a wary expression sat in one of the booths. A bargirl, also blond and vacantly pretty, perched in his lap with one arm around his neck and the other moving seductively inside his open shirt.

"Lose your friend," Yoshitomi said, walking up to the table. "We have business to discuss."

The blond man looked at him a moment, his jaw working silently. Then he nodded, pushing the woman off his lap and giving her rump a swat. "Later, sweetheart. I got business to attend to."

The woman shrugged, turned, and walked away, giving

Yoshitomi an appraising glance as she passed him. No matter. Yoshitomi was well aware that Occidentals could rarely identify individual members of his race. There were thousands of Japanese living in and around Dunkeld, and by this evening he would be on a DropShip, bound for the nadir point and jump passage to Hesperus II.

"Well, Mr. Nakamura?" the man said, using the name Yoshitomi had given him. "What's on your mind?"

Yoshitomi slid into the booth, deliberately taking the seat next to the man in a move calculated both to threaten his personal space and to block his escape.

"I have decided that I am interested in your offer, Mr. Lang," he said quietly. "I should be able to carry out your, ah, reconnaissance, with little chance of detection."

"Good, good. I thought you'd see things my way." Lang flashed a glance past Yoshitomi, checking to see if anyone else were near.

Yoshitomi had spotted Lang yesterday and, from various clues the man had dropped, had decided he was almost certainly either a deserter or a drop-off, a member of Gareth's invading forces left behind for some reason. After initiating a casual conversation with the man last night, he'd gradually worked the talk from women and sex—which seemed to be Lang's favorite topic of discussion—to other, more serious matters.

Lang was, indeed, a drop-off, though he'd never admitted the fact, not in words, anyway. Yoshitomi suspected he was a member of Gareth's military intelligence unit. He still wasn't sure whether he was here to infiltrate the Legion strictly to gather intelligence or to set up another assassination attempt, but the man had been extremely interested in the layout of the Castle Hill dispensary. Yoshitomi had mentioned that he worked in the fortress and should be able to obtain entrance to the dispensary section. And that had led almost at once to an offer of a job, one that would pay fifty thousand C-bills. Lang wanted a detailed map of the dispensary patient area, together with names of patients and their locations, staff schedules, and a timetable of hospital routine.

It sounded like an assassination, though it was possible that Lang's masters simply wanted to confirm some information they had about the presence of some particular

Legion officer under medical care. It didn't really matter one way or the other to Yoshitomi. He already had his orders.

Isamu Yoshitomi had told the precise truth in his interview with the Gray Death officer, and he was well aware that McCall knew he'd not told him everything. The news that he was ronin, a masterless samurai, would go far in explaining his rather strange and impressive list of skills without raising McCall's well-honed suspicions to the point where they would become dangerous to Yoshitomi's mission.

Yoshitomi belonged to another organization besides the Tatikaze, an organization far more secret, far more secretive, and infinitely more focused in its agenda than that philosophy-oriented group. Yoshitomi was Nekekami, a Spirit-Cat.

"How do you intend to get in there, anyway?"

"As I told you, I have a pass. I do work at the facility, you know."

"Yeah. Yeah, so you said." Briefly, Lang began running through the list of specific things he needed.

"Very well," Yoshitomi said, when Lang completed his list. Turning, he extended his right hand in the fashion employed by Occidentals. "I will have what you need by this time tomorrow night. Here?"

Lang accepted the hand and shook it. His grip was limp, his palm cool. "Better not. You know the Ryman Hotel? Up on Edinburgh Street?"

Yoshitomi nodded once.

"Room two-eighty. Come on up the back way so no one sees you. Give a knock like this." Lang rapped the table in a simple code, two quick, two slow, two quick. Yoshitomi maintained his expressionless mask, keeping to himself his thoughts about the man's almost boorishly amateur performance. Gareth's intelligence forces must be hard pressed just now to use idiots such as this one. "I'll give you the money then," he continued. Something about the way Lang held himself as he said that confirmed what Yoshitomi had already guessed, that the man had no intention of honoring the agreement. He imagined that Yoshitomi would be a convenient and useful . . . what was the Anglic word? Patsy, yes. "And maybe I'll have another job for you, if you do good with this one."

"I would like that."

Yoshitomi slid from his seat, then turned to bow to Lang. The man was looking strangely at his right palm, rubbing thumb to fingertips and making a faintly sour expression with nose and mouth. "Have a good evening," Yoshitomi said.

Lang looked up, unthinkingly wiped his palm on his shirt, then his eyes twinkled. "Oh, I plan to, little buddy. I definitely plan to. You see that honey who was with me?" He winked, then made a quick, double clucking sound with his tongue against the inside of his teeth, as though he were riding a horse.

"Then I will say, Mr. Lang, have an *enjoyable* evening."

Yoshitomi proceeded immediately to the bar's bathroom, where he leaned over a sink and proceeded to wash his right hand with very great care, paying particular attention to the spaces between his fingers and beneath his nails. The layer of oil with which he'd coated his hand before coming here tonight both resisted water and imparted a greasy feel to his skin. That was probably what Lang had been reacting to, without knowing what it was.

What Lang could not have reacted to, not yet, was the light dusting powder Yoshitomi had sprinkled over his oiled palm. The powder was so fine it was nearly invisible and certainly impalpable in such small amounts. It was also deadly . . . eventually. Absorbed directly through the skin, it would begin breaking down into long-chain proteins as it circulated through the unfortunate Mr. Lang's bloodstream. It was actually harmless in that state—harmless, at least until those circulating proteins began bonding with large amounts of adrenaline. Any strong emotion, any excitement, any arousal, and the protein would bond with it, transforming itself into one of the most powerful vasoconstrictors known. Lang's arteries would literally pucker up, and in the space of seconds the flow of blood to lungs and brain and heart muscle would be sharply reduced. Blood pressure would soar . . .

Yoshitomi thought of the blond woman in Lang's lap and gave a faint smile. She was in for a surprise. Sometime tonight, Lang would be dead of a heart attack—or possibly a major stroke. It was impossible to tell in advance exactly what the drug's end effects would be. But one way or the other he would be dead, and Yoshitomi's first Nekekami assignment on Glengarry would be complete.

And by accepting McCall's offer, he'd already begun his second.

=== 11 ===

Sometimes, Grayson Carlyle wished he'd died on Caledonia.

It wasn't that life wasn't worth living any more, but life, his life, anyway, certainly seemed to have lost both direction and purpose. Sometimes, lately, he felt like a rudderless, engineless boat adrift in one of the big coriolis storms that sometimes swept up suddenly out of the Scotian Sea, completely at the mercy of currents and winds that he was powerless to deflect or control.

Colonel Grayson Carlyle, commander and founder of the Gray Death Legion. *Mechdrek!* What good was a regimental CO who couldn't pilot a BattleMech?

They'd brought him out of the medical coma nearly two months after Falkirk, and months more had followed as he'd learned to use the new plastic and alloy hardware that had replaced his left arm.

Grayson looked down at the new arm, the one hand a perfect match for his other. He could even feel with it, thanks to neural feedback and receptor site boosting, and the micromyomer bundles gave it the feel and strength of a flesh-and-blood arm. What he would never, *never* get used to was the loss of his ability to pilot 'Mechs.

And now, with his professional life already looking about as bleak as it could, he'd been summoned to Tharkad, together with his executive officer, to face charges.

Charges including treason. . . .

He floated in microgravity in the spacious and tastefully decorated lounge of the civilian passenger DropShip *Orion*. There were others in the lounge, most of them civilians who, after as much as five weeks out from Glengarry, were familiar faces. He still knew very few of them by name, however. He'd not exactly felt . . . *sociable.*

Others, though, numbered among those closest to him. Lori. Alex, their son. Davis. Jonathan Frye, of the Third Battalion. Caitlin DeVries, who'd come along to be with Alex. As the Gray Death Legion's executive officer, Lori had been directed to accompany him to Tharkad—not that anything could have made her stay away—but the others had come voluntarily. To testify on Grayson's behalf, if necessary.

Or to share his punishment.

He doubted that it would come to that. As regimental CO, he was responsible for the abrupt change of sides on Caledonia, and for the Battle of Falkirk that followed. His actions had prompted Gareth's subsequent attack on the Legion's landhold, and Lori's defense of Glengarry had been justifiable self-defense no matter how you looked at it. If the government needed a proper sacrifice in the name of justice, discipline, and propriety, they would find it in him, and in him alone.

The shutters of the *Monarch* Class DropShip's lounge viewport were closed, blocking out the intense radiation of this system's primary. Instead, a flat-screen display occupying the entire forward bulkhead had been set to show the view aft, toward the JumpShip's solar collection sail and the twin suns beyond, with filters to step down that brilliant light to an intensity merely dazzling rather than literally and permanently blinding.

Thuban—Alpha Draconis, a name drawn from a constellation visible in the northern hemisphere skies of Terra and therefore having absolutely nothing to do with the far-flung Draconis Combine—was a type A0 double star, both components blue-white in color and demonic in their radiation output, circling one another at a distance of thirty-two million kilometers with a period of fifty-one days. Even at the distance of the system's nadir jump point, the radiation levels were uncomfortably high; they would be higher still on the surface of the system's inhabited planet.

Not that that was a problem for the inhabitants. The world called Thuban, Carlyle had read, was a manmade world, one of a number of engineered planets scattered across the Inner Sphere. Originally it had been an airless, radiation-blasted rock the size of Terra's moon, but its core had been hollowed into a vast, rock-enclosed cavern, its spin hastened until the centrifugal force of its rotation provided an artificial, out-is-down gravity, its interior filled with a breathable atmosphere distilled from native ice and rock. Like numerous other planets throughout the Inner Sphere, it was an inside-out world, an enclosed environment you entered through an airlock, a place where you could stand on the ground and look *up* at farmlands and forests and small, landlocked seas spread across a floor that steadily rose ahead and behind into walls that, in turn, merged with the distant, cloud-hazed ceiling; where the "sun" was a thin, intensely radiant thread across the land-encircled sky that literally piped light in from outside, as needed. A world created by the hand of Man . . .

The engineers of the old Star League had practiced numerous varieties of large-scale terraforming, from the crude dropping of moonlets of solid water ice onto barren, frozen desert worlds to warm and wet them into bloom, to hollowing out moons or asteroids like Thuban and shaping them to their will. Many, perhaps most, of the inhabited worlds of the Inner Sphere had been engineered to one degree or another to make human life possible on them. Nowadays, though, humankind was hard-pressed even to *survive* on worlds as perfectly suited to it as Terra herself; war, it seemed, had a way of undoing everything humanity had won, as it ground on and on for year after year after destructive year.

Such technology as that required by terraforming, Carlyle thought glumly, was now far, far out of man's reach. How much more would be lost to the idiocy of continuing war?

The subject had always been guaranteed to raise Grayson Carlyle's passions. *Lostech,* the technology and the science and the learning vanished in the centuries since the fall of the old Star League, had occupied his full attention more than once in his career. But somehow, even that just didn't seem important any longer.

He stared at the display screen, watching the dance of shifting shadow and blue-white radiance as the sail's thrust aperture rotated slowly beneath the JumpShip's fractional-G boost.

It had been a long voyage. Glengarry to Laurieston. Laurieston to Jaumegarde. Jaumegarde to Callisto V. Callisto V to Thuban, and with a four-to-eight day wait at each system, as the JumpShip recharged its drive coils. Grayson and his companions had been aboard ship for over a month now; with one more jump scheduled in another four days, from Thuban to Tharkad, plus an eight-day DropShip transit time from jump point to Tharkad, they should make planetfall on the capital of the old Lyran Commonwealth by the end of the month. They'd left Glengarry aboard the *Orion* on August 10, and Grayson Carlyle was becoming sincerely sick of the *Monarch* Class DropShip.

The ship was certainly comfortable enough. To a man who'd spent a hefty percentage of his whole life aboard one DropShip or another in passage between the stars, it seemed downright luxurious, a slender leaf-shape aerodyne with a smoothly sculpted central fuselage, massing five thousand tons total and with space aboard for 266 passengers. Her mass was better than eighty percent that of a *Fortress* military DropShip, but she mounted little armor, no facilities for transporting BattleMechs, in fact, no weapons at all.

That had been one of the provisions in the orders. Grayson and Lori Carlyle had been directed to take *civilian* passage to Tharkad, there to stand trial for the events on Caledonia and Glengarry the previous April and May. FedCom Military Command seemed to fear what might happen should one or more of the Gray Death's military DropShips be allowed to ground at Steiner Spaceport.

At the thought, Grayson gave a thin smile empty of humor. Some of the men and women in the Legion were about ready to march on Tharkad and take the place apart with their bare hands, so strongly did they take exception to the orders requiring Grayson and Lori to stand trial. It had taken an explicit directive from him personally to ensure that they didn't try it, or something equally harebrained.

Some sort of court of inquiry or court-martial had been inevitable, of course. The entire system of using mercenaries throughout the Inner Sphere demanded some guarantee against mercs accepting one government's money, then immediately switching sides, whether out of conviction or simply for profit. From the moment he'd made his choice on Caledonia, Grayson had known he'd one day have to face retribution, either from the Mercenary Review and Bonding Commission on Outreach or, possibly, from the Federated Commonwealth itself. Being called to Outreach could have resulted in fines and hardship for the Legion, but being called before a military tribunal on Tharkad promised more serious punishment.

Grayson might have protested that this was a matter for the Mercenary Review Commission, but in point of cold, steel-edged fact, he didn't really care what happened to him, not any more. He would fight with all of his strength to save Lori and Alex and Davis and the rest from the consequences of his actions, but if the FedCom military tribunal decided to shoot him, it just wouldn't matter much to him one way or the other. He cared about nothing anymore, nothing beyond the security of those he loved, and the good name of the Legion.

Grayson turned, positioning himself so he could watch Lori for a long moment. She was several meters away, floating at one of the rec lounge tables, talking with Alex, Caitlin, Jon Frye, and McCall. Once, she shot him a quick, almost furtive glance; when her eyes met his, though, she replied with a warm, if somewhat worried smile.

It had been damned rough for her, he knew, having him come back from Caledonia ... *crippled*. Half-crippled, anyway. He knew well how worried she'd been before he'd woken up from his medical coma back at the Castle Hill dispensary, yet somehow in the past couple of months they'd drifted apart, become more distant. It was harder to talk, harder to share things with her.

Hell, a lot of it, he knew, was his own inability to accept what had happened to him, which tended to make him moody and distant to begin with, but there didn't seem to be much he could do about it. It would require more *caring* than he was really capable of just now.

He turned his gaze back to the display, where Thuban glared balefully beyond the drive aperture of the sail. Grayson knew the numbers by heart. At an A0-class star's jump point, the *Stardancer*'s solar sail would require 161 hours to recharge the Kearny-Fuchida coils, just under one full week. They'd arrived insystem three days ago; they would be able to make the final leap to Tharkad in another four days.

Then an eight-day passage from jump point to world, and after that it would all be settled, one damned way or the other.

"I'm not going to offer you a C-bill for your thoughts," a voice said at his side. "Judging by the expression on your face, I have the feeling you'd be shamelessly overcharging me."

Grayson turned, looking the other up and down. "Hey, Jon," he said, voice dull.

Major Jonathan Frye was a tall, lean, leathery-skinned officer in his mid-fifties, a bit on the balding side, gray-mustached, and possessing the twinkling, catch-all eyes of some improbable bird of prey. Commander of the Third Battalion, he'd been with Grayson at Falkirk, commanding his unit from the cabin of a Pegasus hovertank.

He'd insisted on being with him now.

"So, what do you think?" Frye asked, gesturing to a newscast showing on one of the smaller displays. He paused to take a sip from the drinking bulb he held in his right hand, then eyed Grayson speculatively.

Grayson shrugged for answer and turned his attention 7toward the screen. He'd been following the political news lately with less than intense interest, with an apathy, in fact, that was completely atypical of him. Normally, he studied political developments quite closely indeed, if for no other reason than that wars and rumors of wars were the mercenary's literal bread and butter. The Legion was always employed when the various Great Houses were busy rattling sabers at one another.

And the current situation was a beaut, a guaranteed widowmaker. The Federated Commonwealth had been under joint Steiner-Davion rule for thirty years now, in a political union that had never been entirely embraced by the people of either of the former states. Marriage between Melissa Steiner and Hanse Davion had sealed the alliance, and now it was two of their children who were threatening to tear it apart.

Last year when the worlds of the Skye March had risen up against FedCom rule, the rebel leaders had accused Prince Victor Davion, among other things, of assassinating his mother. In the midst of all this, his younger sister Katrina had suddenly emerged as a potent force, offering to serve as peacemaker. This only served to heighten her enormous popularity among the Lyrans, while Victor's continued to plummet. The Skye Rebellion had been put down, of course, but Victor still lived in the shadow of suspicion and the Lyrans continued to chafe under his rule.

And now his most recent political machinations had led to outright war with two other Great Houses, the Free Worlds League of Thomas Marik and the Capellan Federation of Sun-Tzu Liao. Just two days ago, Thomas Marik had stunned the Inner Sphere with the announcement that he would invade the Federated Commonwealth to take back the worlds his realm had lost to Hanse Davion thirty years before. Joining him was Sun-Tzu, who intended to recapture planets the Capellans had lost in the same war. Even as Marik was making the announcement, Marik and Liao DropShips were already on their way to hit a number of those FedCom worlds.

"That's no answer," Frye said, persisting. "Come on. What does the great Grayson Carlyle say is going to happen to the Federated Commonwealth?"

"Victor's got his hands full—as usual," Grayson said with another shrug. "And it's his own damn fault for trying that wild scheme to hoodwink Tom Marik. Who can blame Marik for turning on him?"

"No argument there. What about Katrina, though?"

He sighed. "God knows what the Steiners are going to do with this. If they could disown Victor, I think they would."

"Yeah, that's what we were talking about over there." Frye gestured toward the table where Lori, Alex, Caitlin, and Davis were continuing an animated conversation. "Care to come over and join us?"

"I don't think so. Katrina's going to make up her own mind, whatever we might think."

"We were considering the possibility of a civil war. Lyrans against Victor."

"It'll never come to that."

"No?"

"No offense, Jon, but I really don't have much to say about all this. I couldn't care less what Katrina or Victor do, say, or think."

Frye's mouth tightened. "You'd damn well better start caring about *something,* man. Or are you feeling so sorry for yourself that you've decided to abrogate all responsibility?"

The words stung. "I'm not feeling sorry—"

"The *hell* you're not! Look at yourself, Colonel. You've been in a clinical depression since they woke you up. What is it? The arm?"

Grayson glanced down at the arm, flexing his hand, *feeling* it. "It's not the arm and you know it," he said quietly, daring at last to admit to himself what the real trouble was.

"It's your ear, isn't it? And not piloting 'Mechs again."

"Damn it, Jon," Grayson said softly. "I'm feeling so damned *useless.*"

"I know." Frye nodded slowly. "I've been there too, remember?"

Grayson scowled and looked away, his fists, both of them, clenched hard. Frye, too, had been badly wounded a few years back, losing his left audio nerve in a firefight. There were MechWarriors, Grayson knew, who'd lost legs and arms in battle, had them replaced with bionic substitutes, and kept on piloting 'Mechs as though nothing had happened. He continued to look at the arm, turning the hand over, studying the fine crafting of the hand and fingers, the skin, even the fine hairs on the back of his hand and between the second and third joints of his fingers as natural-looking as the real thing. A perfect replacement, as perfect as modern medical technology allowed.

But with all that medical science knew, it still couldn't stimulate dead or severed nerves and make them grow, and a MechWarrior needed both left and right audio nerves to translate the signals from his neurohelmet into something his body could sense as balance, enabling him to pilot a 'Mech from a tiny cockpit ten meters off the ground and not fall flat on his BattleMech's face.

"I'm sorry, Colonel," Medtech Ellen Jamison had told him in the recovery room back at Castle Hill. *"There's just nothing we can do. The nerve damage in your left ear can't be repaired. Without it, I don't think you're ever going to be able to pilot a BattleMech again."*

Grayson shook his head, the thought painful. Never pilot a BattleMech again? Hell, he'd learned to pilot 'Mechs as a young apprentice to his father's old mercenary 'Mech company, Carlyle's Commandos, out on the Periphery more years ago now than he really cared to think about. It was what he did, a hell of a lot of what he lived for. He wasn't ready to be retired to some staff position, pushing holographic images around the tactics table back in Ops.

"I know it seems like damn near the end of everything," Frye said. "Take my word for it, Colonel. You'll live. And you'll get over it. *If* you don't let it drive you out of your head *now*."

"You're the expert, I guess."

"Yes, Colonel. I *am*."

"Hey, Colonel?" McCall said, pulling himself hand-over-hand along the back of a sofa so that he was within conversational range. "There's aye somethin' you'll be wantin' to see here."

Grayson looked up, one eyebrow askance. "What?"

Holding on with one hand, McCall jerked a thumb over his shoulder. "Word just came through tha' Katrina Steiner hersel' is aboot to make an announcement. Apparently she broadcast it by HPG to every world in the Lyran Alliance—maybe quite a few outside, too—an' it's makin' its way oot to the outlyin' regions noo."

Thuban's jump point was over forty-eight billion kilometers from the system's inhabited world, a bit over seventy-two light minutes; Katrina's transmission would take that long to crawl out to the *Stardancer* at the snail's-pace crawl of light.

Grayson was about to tell McCall just what he could do with Katrina's announcement until he caught a hard look from Frye. "Sure," he said. "I'll come."

Out the corner of his eye, he caught Frye giving

McCall a jaunty thumb's up; he ignored the gesture. *Let them play their games,* he thought. *They can't engage my enthusiasm because I haven't got any.* He'd read that old joke somewhere, but he couldn't remember where.

The transmission was just arriving, received by the *Stardancer*'s main communications antennas and fed through to the DropShips that rode her spine like improbably huge, metallic leeches. It led off with the Federated Commonwealth emblem; the words LIVE FROM THE ROYAL COURT were prominent at the bottom of the screen though, of course, the events now being viewed had transpired at least seventy-some minutes earlier, longer if there'd been a delay in the HPG transmission schedule.

Emblem and caption faded to a new view, and Grayson, despite himself, leaned in a little closer, his heart beating a bit faster. Katrina Steiner stood behind a podium, a look of both weariness and sorrow on her lovely face. Her fair hair was brushed back and fell loosely against the Steiner blue of her simple dress. Slowly, the camera zoomed in, and only Katrina's head and shoulders filled the screen, her icy blue eyes looking out at an unseen audience that must have numbered in the hundreds of billions.

"My fellow citizens . . ." she began.

Watching her, Grayson had to admire her manner, strong, confident, and commanding. As she continued speaking, he had the impression she wasn't reading her speech from a prompter or having it micro-fed to her retina by laser. The words themselves were a product, no doubt, of her speechwriting staff, but she had apparently taken the time to memorize them. Briefly, she recapped some of the recent events that had dragged the Federated Commonwealth into war—including the rumors that her brother had concealed the death of Thomas Marik's young and hostage-held son and replaced him with a double as part of some dubious plot or other. Grayson had heard those rumors but dismissed them as too wild and paranoid for belief. Katrina, however, seemed concerned that her brother had yet to answer the charges.

"For the good of you, my people, however," she continued, "I cannot afford to wait passively for Victor to account for his actions. He has broken faith with you, and

I will not have you suffer while I cling to the faint hope that my brother can justify himself."

"Th' lass should get hersel' a new speechwriter," McCall said softly, staring at the screen with his arms folded.

"Shush, Davis," Lori said. "I want to hear."

"What's she going to do?" Caitlin asked. "Declare war against her brother?"

Katrina was still talking, her voice steady. "To guarantee that the Lyran people do not suffer, I have given the following orders.

"First, I have decided to declare our Lyran districts to be in a state of crisis. This gives me greater powers under the regency, which include the right to sever the connection between Lyran agencies and their Federated Commonwealth counterparts. We will function in the interim as an independent political unit, which I have designated the Lyran Alliance."

"Great God in heaven," Frye said softly. Lori gave a hiss, a small, sharp intake of breath. Katrina Steiner-Davion had just declared independence for the old Lyran Commonwealth. "Prince Victor is *not* going to be amused."

"I want all my people—from Northwind to Poulsbo, Loris to Barcelona—united and allied together, for we must work hard to safeguard ourselves in these dangerous times," Katrina was saying, her hands grasping the sides of the podium. "Second, any Lyran military unit serving in the Sarna March or elsewhere in the Federated Commonwealth is invited and urged to return here, to the Alliance. As long as Lyran forces offer no resistance to Free Worlds League troops, they will be considered noncombatants and allowed to withdraw."

"There it is," Frye said. "She's breaking with Victor and signing a separate peace with Marik."

"Sounds like th' lass has already talked things over wi' Tommy Marik," McCall commented. "She said tha' piece about th' Lyran troops bein' allowed t' withdraw like it was already an established fact. Like she knows they'll be able t' leave unhindered."

Slowly, dramatically, the camera zoomed even closer on Katrina; she faced it, clear-eyed, proud, and perhaps a little defiant. "My brother, the warrior, has taken *his* half

of the Federated Commonwealth into war. I will not bleed
my people to defend his actions. It is my sacred duty to
ward your welfare—the same duty my mother honored
before she was so cruelly cut down. . . ."

McCall groaned, but before he could make further
comment, Carlyle silenced him with the nudge of an elbow. On the screen, Katrina Steiner-Davion continued to
face the camera squarely, her blue eyes unflinching.

"I hereby lay claim to her mantle, though aware of the
dangers inherent in doing so. Anything less," she con-
cluded with solemn grace and dignity, "would be to deny
my heritage as a Steiner and my responsibility as your
Archon."

There was a long silence in the DropShip's rec area.
On the screen, the announcement clearly at an end, the
camera zoomed out, then cut to the talking heads of several news commentators babbling about the significance
of Katrina's statement, mindless noise snapped off in
mid-sound byte when someone finally muted the sound.

"My God," Frye said, shaking his head. "She did it.
She actually did it!"

"Will it mean a war?" Alex asked. "Alliance against
FedCom?"

"Weel, young Victor's nae goin' t' be keen aboot losin'
half his realm to his little sister," McCall said, rubbing
his beard thoughtfully. "I'd say civil war is a possibility,
at least."

"More than a possibility," Lori put in. "Katrina just cut
the ground right out from under him."

"How's that?" Caitlin wanted to know. She'd moved
closer to Alex, Grayson saw, and he'd slipped his arm
around her shoulders.

"She's ordered Lyran troops in the Sarna March
home," Frye said, "and by removing herself as a threat to
the Free Worlds League, she's freed up one hell of a lot
of Marik's troops. You can bet they'll be on their way to
join the invasion, at double time."

"Maybe not," Lori said. "Marik's no fool. Chances are
he'll play a waiting game, see which way things settle
out."

"The real question," Alex said, "is what happens here.
To this new Lyran Alliance. And to us."

Carlyle was just beginning to digest some of the ramifications of Katrina's speech. "Technically," he said slowly, "those new powers she talked about give her the right to declare martial law. She could even dissolve the E. G." The Estates General was the parliamentary body of the old Lyran Commonwealth that both advised the Archon and served as the government's legislative branch.

"I doubt she'd go that far," Frye said, his arms crossed in front of him. "Hell, they may have put her up to it. I don't think the E.G. has ever been solidly behind the Davion-Steiner alliance."

"Alex has a point," Caitlin said. "What does this mean for us? For the Legion?"

Carlyle blinked. He'd been so caught up with Katrina's announcement that he'd momentarily forgotten about his own problems. "I guess it still depends on what Gareth's game is," he told her.

"That's right," Lori said. "Is Gareth working against Katrina? Is he working for Victor? Or for Katrina? Or is he in it for himself?"

"Here's another conundrum," Frye said. "Who are *we* working for now? Katrina? Or Victor? The Legion's contract was with the Federated Commonwealth."

"That was updated when the Lyrans and the Federated Suns decided to form one big state," Lori said. "Originally we worked for the Steiners."

"We *still* work for the Steiners," Grayson said, his tone gruff.

Grayson had never cared much for Victor, despite the fact that he'd received a barony the year before at the Archon Prince's hand. The young Prince seemed too inclined to make reckless decisions without considering the consequences, too prone to military adventurism, and too egotistical to admit he'd made a mistake. And dragging the Federated Commonwealth into an essentially useless war with Marik and Liao wasn't going to do much for his dismal standing among his own people. They were sick of war, what with the Clans and then the Skye Rebellion. Victor was *not* an especially popular fellow at the moment, and the hell of it was, he didn't seem to care.

Grayson had long ago decided that his first obligation was to the Steiners, since it was Katrina Steiner—*the* Katrina Steiner back in the late 3020s—who'd given the Gray Death Legion both shelter and a long-term contract after the unit had been betrayed by an ambitious officers' cabal in the Free Worlds League.

The memory stirred a vague uneasiness in Grayson. That betrayal thirty years ago had involved an earlier landhold world of the Legion's, a planet in Marik space called Helm. That time, the Legion had been set up, with the unit blamed for an attack on civilian facilities in order to have them declared outlaw so that others could seize Helm. The pattern here was eerily similar; the Legion had been directed to put down a revolt on Caledonia, deliberately placed in a damned-if-you-do, damned-if-you-don't situation that had ended with Carlyle choosing to disobey orders and support the popular rebellion. That decision had put him into direct conflict with the forces of the Federated Commonwealth and resulted both in the Battle of Falkirk and in Gareth's abortive invasion of Glengarry.

And now, Carlyle was on his way to Tharkad to face charges of treason and breaking contract.

Where did Gareth stand in this sudden break between Katrina and Victor?

Grayson had the uneasy feeling that his personal survival, not to mention the survival of the entire Gray Death Legion, might very well rest upon the answer to that question.

He thought again of that rudderless, engineless boat, and frowned. . . .

Tharkad City
Tharkad, District of Donegal, Lyran Alliance
22 September to 30 September 3057

Four days after Katrina's announcement, the *Stardancer* vanished from normal space in the Thuban system, rematerializing instantaneously—if that word had any real meaning within the context of Einsteinian space-time— thirty light years away, at the zenith point of the Tharkad system. Shortly after that, the *Monarch* Class DropShip *Orion* broke free from the *Stardancer*'s spinal mount, the shock silent in the vacuum of space but ringing like a deep-throated gong through the interiors of both vessels.

Tharkad was one of those fortunate systems with massive deep-space facilities and sail-rigged recharging stations positioned at both the nadir and zenith jump points; the *Orion* was directed to pause long enough to exchange electronic greetings with security and naval forces at Tharkad Alpha-Three, the nearest jump point base. The locals, it seemed, were a bit touchy about any traffic in- or out-bound in this rather sensitive star system, and the *Orion* was given a thorough outward inspection by a quartet of SYD Z2 *Seydlitz* fighters, backed by the heavy firepower of a silently watching, blunt-prowed *Overlord* Class DropShip.

Grayson was interested in the markings on the *Overlord*. It looked as though the fist-on-sun insignia of the

Federated Commonwealth had been crudely and recently painted out. In its place was a new emblem—the symbol, he presumed, of the Lyran Alliance.

Outward inspection complete, the *Orion* had next been approached by an NL-42 transport, one of the tiny, 200-ton smallcraft sometimes referred to as "battle taxis." Technically a troop transport designed for planting landing parties on enemy vessels, it mounted six lasers of various sizes and could carry up to three platoons of marines. Two platoons at least boarded the *Orion* and carried out a careful search, looking, presumably, for hidden BattleMechs or other serious weaponry. When done, they reboarded their taxi, which cast off from the *Orion*'s dorsal lock. A blunt "*Orion,* you are clear to proceed" was transmitted moments later.

Everybody was nervous—the port authorities at the jump point, the marines searching the *Orion,* the passengers. The entire political structure of the Federated Commonwealth had just been turned completely over, and no one knew exactly what the end result would be.

Perhaps even more stunning than Katrina's secession from the Federated Commonwealth had been Victor Davion's follow-up announcement, broadcast via HPG throughout the realm the day after Katrina's speech. In his address, the Prince had admitted that the rumors about a double of Marik's son were true, that Joshua had died of natural causes but the death had been covered up in order to buy time—time to cool the still-simmering passions of the Skye Rebellion, time to pacify the seething Sarna March, inflamed by Liao agents.

He'd also announced that he would not oppose Katrina's withdrawal from the Commonwealth, nor would he block the return of Lyran troops to Alliance territory. Victor had said simply that he accepted his sister's decision to protect her people from war.

The uncertainty, though, was still unnerving. Most people were willing to accept Victor's assurances that there would not be war between the FedCom and the new Lyran Alliance, but there still seemed to be a lot of hard feeling between pro-Davion and pro-Steiner factions. News reports for the first few days after Victor's speech told of riots on various worlds with divided loyalties, and on several worlds in the Skye March, Davion officials had been harassed and threatened and, in one notable instance, brutally murdered. Then, miraculously, on the day the *Stardancer* was scheduled to make the jump to Tharkad, the news stories had vanished as though they'd never been. The censorship, so far as Grayson could tell, did nothing to alleviate either concern or speculation aboard the DropShip *Orion*. If anything, the tension, the not knowing, became worse, charging the atmosphere with a dark foreboding.

After an eight-day flight at a comfortable one-G, with the usual midpoint flip to kill the DropShip's velocity, the *Orion* slipped stern-first into low orbit around the world of Tharkad.

From two hundred kilometers up, Tharkad was a magnificent sight, a dazzling glory of clouds and ice sheets glittering in the cool, yellow sunlight. The oceans had a gold-to-green cast about them, partly from the light, partly from the planktonic organisms adrift on the surface.

It was a cold world, not an ice planet by any means, but cooler than the norm for most of the worlds populated by humanity. Fifth out from a G6 dwarf sun, Tharkad was perched precariously at the edge of a planet-wide glacial age, the eternal ice just barely held at bay by the greenhouse effect of an atmosphere both somewhat thicker than Terra's and more richly tainted with methane, water vapor, and carbon dioxide. Ice caps extended from both poles to within thirty degrees of the equator; the equatorial region, according to the computer ephemeris aboard the *Orion*, ranged from twenty degrees Celsius in summer down to over one hundred below in the depths of the long, long winter.

Possessing a much stronger magnetic field than Terra's, Tharkad generated brilliant auroral displays, even though its sun was somewhat cooler and less active than was Sol, and the world was considerably more distant from its primary than Terra was from its sun. As the *Orion* drifted across the planet's night side, a shimmering, shifting circlet of greens, yellows, and reds glowed in an arc encircling the pole, the light strong enough to weakly illuminate the masses of clouds gliding silently beneath the DropShip's keel.

With an axial tilt of thirty-one degrees and a period of

revolution of very nearly two standard years, the planet tended to have long, long seasons. In the hemisphere experiencing summer the days were long but cool under the wan and shrunken sun, and the nights never got wholly dark beneath the silent, flaming dance of the auroras. In the winter hemisphere the nights must seem to go on forever beneath the cold, celestial fires of the auroras, while days were short and bitterly cold. At the latitude of Tharkad's capital, twenty-four hours out of each of the planet's thirty-hour days were in darkness during midwinter, with snow remaining on the ground for fourteen of the year's twenty-two months.

Naturally, Tharkad's calendar, involving thirty-hour days and twenty-two-month years, was not in sync with the standard calendar used throughout the Inner Sphere; few, if any, worlds could be, save for Terra herself where the system had originated millennia before. According to the ephemeris, it was currently the thirty-third day of the month of Spätkalt, and early spring in Tharkad's northern hemisphere. That meant it would still be cold there, with plenty of snow on the ground. Much of Tharkad's intercity transport, Grayson understood, was by subsurface highway or maglev trains, or above ground by VTOL.

After one orbit, the *Orion* fired her stern drives briefly, flipped around so as to approach the world nose-first and chin-high, and started her long descent, skipping three times off Tharkad's atmosphere like a stone popping across the surface of a pond. With some of its velocity dissipated, it settled lower, riding the denser air like a hydroplane skimming the waves as it slowly descended. Eventually, flying now like an aircraft rather than a spaceship, the *Orion* dropped to an altitude of five thousand meters, racing east across the gold-green waters of the great Marsden Sea, going feet-dry as it passed over Breman's west coast, and still descending, arrowed toward Steiner Spaceport, a sprawling, modern complex erected on the outskirts of Tharkad City.

From the air, the capital city was spectacular, despite a driving snow that occasionally masked the view. Grayson had the vidscreen in his and Lori's cabin dialed to the *Orion*'s nose-camera view, which showed the huge urban complex laid out in glittering steel and ferrocrete and transplas triangles hewn from what once had been a continent-spanning forest. The complex was dominated by the Triad, an immense civil and government facility composed of over three hundred buildings, anchored at the three corners by the Royal Palace, the Royal Court, and the Government House. Ten kilometers to the south lay the older planetary capital center at Olympia; eight kilometers to the north was Tharkad City and Steiner Spaceport. West, positioned to keep a close watch on spacecraft approaching the capital complex and rising above the city from the crest of ice-clad Mount Wotan, was Asgard, House Steiner's military headquarters, its main central tower eighty meters tall, flanked by four lesser towers, all thickly armored and bristling with heavy weapons. Grayson studied the fortress with a keen, professional interest as the *Orion* passed overhead to the north. The architecture, though considerably larger and more grandiloquent, was outwardly similar to that of Castle Hill; the two might have been the product of the same military engineer's mind.

Moments later, the *Orion*'s landing gear dropped with a whine and a thump; the dark gray surface of the circular spaceport field, nearly five kilometers across, was revealed ahead, as immense, wedge-shaped slices of the weather dome sheltering the entire field slid back. With a shrill hiss of belly jets and a final swerve that brought the ship's nose up, the last of the *Orion*'s velocity was killed and the craft settled to a gentle VTOL touch-down at the center of a white cross-in-circle on the pavement.

The entire passenger complement disembarked into a large, tracked crawler that trundled out onto the field to meet them with a telescoping passageway that docked to the DropShip's portside-forward lock. The segments of the spaceport's sky shield had closed again overhead to keep out the snow, but the temperature outside was still ten below and not all of the passengers were prepared for such brisk weather. Grayson easily spotted the native Tharkans, though; the men wore fur coats crisscrossed with chains and metal plates, giving them a fierce and barbaric look, while the women favored long gowns trimmed with fur and coats or stoles made entirely from the pelts of some fur-bearing animal. Even within the close confines of the transport vehicle, he noted, the temperature was kept fairly low. Possibly, the powers that be had decided that it was too expensive to warm vehicles or building interiors that were repeatedly exposed to the cold. Certainly, the natives seemed used to lower temperatures, even inside, and had set things to suit themselves. Whatever the reason, the newly arrived offworlders, Grayson, Lori, and the other Legionnaires included, were shivering by the time they reached the Steiner Spaceport terminal.

The crawler deposited the *Orion*'s passengers in a broad, high-ceilinged lobby with ramps leading down to an even larger mall area. As they exited the transport, however, they were immediately approached by two armed men in the green and blue uniform of Tharkad's Royal Palace Guard. The leader wore the blue and black spearpoint rank insignia of *leutnant,* which, in the old Lyran system, made him not quite an officer, but more than an enlisted man. His companion wore the blue hunter's point of a corporal.

"Colonel Carlyle?" the leutnant asked. He was holding an electronic pad and glanced several times from Grayson's face to the pad's display screen, as though double-checking a photographic image.

"I'm Carlyle."

"Will you come with us, please." The leutnant cast a quick glance at the others, who'd closed in on Grayson protectively. "You and your party, of course."

"Am I under arrest?"

"No, sir. But I am directed to escort you to the place where you will be staying."

"We thought we'd stay at the Reichhaus," Grayson said, naming one of the finer hotels in Tharkad City.

"Sir, I am directed to escort you to the place where you—"

Grayson waved the man silent, grimacing. "Yes, yes. Of course." He considered testing the soldier's canned statement a bit further but decided against it. There was no advantage in having himself branded as a trouble-maker, not this early in the game.

Their escort led them from the lobby down the ramp and through the mall area. A public forum center or plaza appeared to be the site of some sort of political rally. Grayson noted a banner screen, easily four stories tall, displaying a full-color, full motion video loop of Katrina

Steiner, resplendent in her persona as warrior Archon, clad in black and gray battle armor, field officer's cloak, and holstered sidearm.

In fact, he saw, there was quite a bit of martial fervor evident throughout the spaceport's public area. Signs in both Anglic and Deutsch—some on immense cloth banners hung from walls or ceilings, others projected in glowing, holographic characters each meters tall—proclaimed a variety of patriotic or inspirational thoughts. LYRAN ALLIANCE: PEACE, PROSPERITY, SOVEREIGNTY, read one. Another showed a head-and-shoulders shot of Katrina Steiner, chin high, expression solemn, and the words, A STEINER AT THE HELM ONCE MORE.

That last was an amusing distortion, since Victor was as much a Steiner as his sister was. It appeared that the considerable Steiner public relations apparatus was in full swing; in the nearly two weeks since Katrina's announcement, her transition from Katherine Steiner-Davion, sister of the Prince of the Federated Commonwealth to Katrina Steiner, Archon of the Lyran Alliance, appeared complete. The breakup of the Federated Commonwealth might eventually turn out to be a peaceful one, if Victor's speech had told the truth, but it was clear that on a personal level there was a great deal of animosity between the factions, at least here on Tharkad.

Grayson could understand that. In the thirty years since the alliance of the old Lyran Commonwealth with the Federated Suns, many in the Lyran half had continued to bitterly oppose what they saw as their second-class status. The seat of government had followed Prince Hanse Davion to New Avalon while paying only lip service to Tharkad, the Davion military never entirely overcame their contempt for their Lyran counterparts, and it was the Lyran worlds that took the brunt of the brutal Clan invasion while not a single Davion planet was touched. And the Lyrans remained vulnerable even after the signing of the truce, since it was their border that fronted on the Clan-occupied zone.

The people in many districts—such as the Skye March—simmered angrily at what they saw as Davion callousness and neglect, while the Steiner military resented their relegation to second-class status and the loss of over six centuries of Lyran martial tradition and history.

At an underground garage reached by a deep-diving elevator, Grayson and the others boarded an armored land cruiser with Lyran Alliance markings, the corporal getting in the back with the five of them, the leutnant joining the driver up front; in another few moments, they were speeding along a subsurface highway.

"Weel noo, lad," McCall said to the corporal as they picked up speed, throwing him a friendly grin. Tunnel lights flashed overhead, gleaming along the cruiser's transparent canopy. "What's the low-down here, eh? How are things going since th' Archon's announcement?"

The corporal ignored them.

"If we're not under arrest," Lori said, folding her arms in front of her and leaning back in her seat, "you can at least tell us where you're taking us."

"Someplace where you'll be safe," the corporal said after a long hesitation. His lip curled a bit as he added a final word, heavy with scorn. *"Merc."*

Grayson caught Lori's eye and shook his head, ever so slightly. These people would know nothing about the case, nothing useful, anyway, and obviously cared little for mercenaries to begin with. Arguing with them would accomplish nothing.

Inwardly, he shook himself, battling the depression that had closed ever more tightly around his heart and mind and soul during these past few months. Again, he held up his left arm, examining the careful mimicry of skin and hair, and nails and wrinkles and palm lines. Gently, he stroked the back of his left hand with his right. The sensation wasn't quite right in a vague and indefinable way, but it was damned close. He was no less of a man for what had happened. He knew that. And Frye had been right a few weeks ago, talking about how he was feeling sorry for himself.

So why couldn't he accept what had happened?

Glancing up, he met Caitlin's eyes. The young Mech-Warrior was sitting next to his son, but she was watching him closely. "It's going to be all right, sir," she said, apparently taking his distraction for worry.

He smiled reassuringly. He had found himself fretful

lately. He wanted to do ... *something*, something to take his own fate and the fate of the Legion firmly in hand.

But he didn't know what. Worse, he still couldn't muster the interest or the passion to force the issue. It was easier to sit back in the cruiser's rear seat and watch the lights of the subsurface highway flash past with the rhythmic regularity of a monotonous pulse.

Their destination, it turned out, was Asgard itself, the enormous Star League–era fortress perched atop the icy rock crags of Mount Wotan. The cruiser deposited them in a cold, underground garage area, where an elevator whisked them up level after level after level, and still they were on sublevel five when the elevator doors slid open and let them out, with four sublevels and twenty regular floors more above that. Asgard was a literal self-contained and completely enclosed city, a military city with a population numbering in the tens of thousands.

Grayson had expected that they would be assigned quarters in the military barracks section, but Asgard boasted a considerable number of both civilian inhabitants and visitors, military and otherwise. Their lodgings on Tharkad were a VIP suite in the Bifrost, one of Asgard's larger internal hotels. The suite arrangement allowed all six visitors to share a single large, common room, with three adjoining bedrooms and space for more to sleep on the sitting room's sofas. McCall laid claim to a sofa immediately; he wanted to provide a first line of defense should uninvited visitors try to force their way in.

Obviously, though, he would not be the *first* line of defense; Grayson noted that two armed guards stationed themselves outside the suite's sole exit. If they weren't prisoners, they were certainly well-protected.

From what, Grayson wondered?

Archon Katrina Steiner was seated at the desk console of her private quarters in the Royal Palace, writing a letter—*hand*writing it with a stylus on the display screen of an electronic notepad rather than using the desk's terminal. A Chopin nocturne lilted in the air, achingly sweet, but she scarcely heard it. Her stylus made tiny clicking sounds as it skipped across the notepad's screen.

The room was tastefully decorated in subdued colors, grays, greens, and Steiner blue for the most part. One wall, opposite the door, was dominated by two enormous full-length holoportraits, each three meters tall. On the left was Katrina's mother, the Archon Melissa Steiner-Davion. On the right was her grandmother, Archon Katrina Steiner. Two very different women, but both strong and smart in their own ways. And Katrina took from each one what suited her best. Between the portraits was the symbol of the Lyran Commonwealth, the clenched, mailed fist descended from the emblem of Polish freedom fighters a millennium ago.

Once she stopped, shivering a bit. She was wearing a long, silver dressing gown trimmed top and bottom in white althis fur, but the thin material was scarcely proof against the chill that always seemed to permeate the Palace. She adjusted a control on her desk, raising the room's temperature. It was all nonsense, really; it wasn't as though the immense fusion reactor beneath Tharkad City couldn't provide power enough to heat the population centers above. Sometimes, she thought the Palace Chamberlain and the environmental engineering staff were engaged in some kind of conspiracy aimed at bringing back the glory days of old Tharkad, when one Archon had actually boasted about ice forming on the walls and on the two guardian *Griffin*s in the Throne Room, deposited there from the smoky breaths of a thousand Lyran citizens attending a public grievance gathering. Katrina had always imagined that the Archon had deliberately kept the heat dialed way down just to keep the proceedings short and to the point.

Letter complete, she read it through, checking both spelling and content before signing it with a flourish of the stylus. Satisfied, she entered a code group in the notebook's alphanumeric pad. The screen blanked and then displayed the flashing word ENCODING. Seconds later, a five-centimeter memcore rose from the top of the notepad. She took it, hefted it a time or two, a smile playing across her features as she thought about how the message would be received. Then she set it on her desk and touched the call button.

A servant woman answered the silent page, stepping through the door as it slid open and giving a small curtsy at Katrina's back. "Yes, Miss?"

Katrina turned, smiling. "Hello, Anna. I have an errand for you."

"Yes, Miss."

She picked up the memcore and passed it to the woman. "I want you to take this to Asgard. Give it to Leutnant-Colonel Willy Schubert. You know him?"

"Yes, Miss. I've delivered messages to him before. He works in Asgard's Security Unit."

"Good. Give him this. And give it *only* to him, right into his hand. Understand?"

"I'm to give it only to him. Yes, Miss."

"Quickly, then. I want it there before twenty-five hours tonight. Report back to me when you return. No matter how late it is, come get me. I'll be here."

"Very good, Miss." Anna showed no hesitation. She'd performed similar tasks for her mistress before, and she was clever and competent, precisely the reasons Katrina had hired her in the first place. "Is this . . ." she started to say.

Katrina cocked her head to the side. "Yes? Go ahead, Anna."

"I was wondering, Miss, if this had something to do with that trial coming up in a few days. Of that mercenary."

"What do you know about that, Anna?"

"Perhaps I shouldn't have asked."

"No, Anna, that's all right." Katrina valued Anna Logan's intelligence. "I just wanted to know what you'd heard, and where."

"Well, I only know what's been on the holovid lately, Miss. They say that mercenary was working for *you* and he changed sides."

"Not quite, Anna. But . . . yes, the message you're carrying does have a bearing on the trial. An important one."

Anna frowned. "I hope they find that mercenary colonel guilty, take him out, and shoot him."

"I doubt that it will be anything so drastic, Anna. However . . ." Katrina paused, grinning mischievously. ". . . the verdict on the trial has already been decided, and I think I can promise you that Colonel Carlyle is going to get exactly what he deserves."

Smiling, Anna nodded, placed the memcore in her belt pouch, curtseyed again, and quickly left.

===== 13 =====

Lori was growing more and more scared, not of the legal nonsense surrounding this board of inquiry, but for Grayson personally. Something was *wrong,* something in his mind, something in his heart and soul. You couldn't be married to a man for over thirty-five years and not be able to read him pretty damned well.

To begin with, he'd been depressed throughout the seven-week voyage out from Glengarry. Lori had tried everything she knew to get him to snap out of it, but it only seemed to make things worse. Grayson had been so damned withdrawn lately that he scarcely even spoke to her, and that—next to knowing how much he must be hurting inside—had been rougher on her than anything else.

And since two nights ago his depression appeared to have given way to something else, some emotion less readily identifiable, less easily catalogued, and far less easily dealt with. Was this just another phase in his recovery?

Or had something happened to him that night, when the Steiner officer had come to their room and asked Grayson to go for a walk with him? And then the man had come again last night, this time asking for Grayson and McCall, claiming loudly that he needed to go over their recollections of events on Caledonia before the actual hearing.

Ever since his return from that first stroll, Grayson had been . . . changed. More intense. More watchful. And after the second stroll, it had seemed as though he'd recovered something of his old bearing and humor.

Even so, she couldn't tell if the depression had lifted once and for all or not.

One of the sillier myths of the modern age, a statement Lori had heard more times than she cared to remember, was that MechWarriors who'd had various parts of their anatomy replaced by mechanical parts tended to become machinelike themselves, emotionless and ruthlessly precise. While there might have been a few people like that, they were, in Lori's opinion, almost certainly the exception rather than the rule, people who'd been a bit stiff and passionless to begin with.

Grayson, if anything, had become *more* emotional since being wounded, not less. Unfortunately, it was not a good emotion; depression tended to be destructive, gnawing at its victim from inside, like cancer. Ever since she'd known him, Gray had always tended to be somewhat introspective, even moody at times, but overall he had a fairly outgoing and basically positive disposition. The change in him since Falkirk had been starkly evident from the beginning, though, simply because his manner had changed so, becoming a kind of bleak withdrawal punctuated by flashes of anger, tears, or even mild hysteria. Once, aboard the *Orion* on the passage out, he'd started laughing at something—she no longer remembered what, but it had been something insignificant and not really calling for that reaction—and he'd not been able to stop laughing for fifteen minutes afterward.

And once he'd become angry—again, she didn't know the cause—and slammed his clenched fist into their cabin bulkhead so hard that she'd taken him down to sickbay afterward, fearful that he'd broken his hand.

The past couple of months had been hard on Lori as she'd tried to find some way of restoring Grayson's old outlook on life, all the while watching him sink deeper and deeper into a self-made morass of despair.

His depression seemed to be following its own evolutionary path. Initially, just after he'd been revived in the Castle Hill dispensary, he'd seemed worried about whether or not he was still a whole man. Ellen Jamison had warned Lori about that after Grayson's surgery, trying to prepare her for what it would be like when he woke up to find one of his arms missing, replaced by a look-alike of plastic and electronic circuitry.

Lori had thought she'd taken care of that particular bit of bleak self-deception. Their lovemaking after his return to their quarters had been both passionate and sweet and fully energetic enough to put to rest any fears that he was somehow no longer *qualified* as a man.

But then, afterward, he'd become more distant. . . .

Ellen had warned her about that, too. 'Mech Power Transference Syndrome, or MPTS, was a fairly common psychological condition—more of an attitude, really, than a neurosis—especially among male MechWarriors. Men tended to identify on some level with their BattleMechs, as though the 'Mechs were extensions of both their bodies and their personalities; in their dreams, they often stood ten meters tall, possessing strength and size enough to tear down walls or crush opponents underfoot. Outside of a BattleMech cockpit, however, they felt . . . vulnerable. Exposed. Weak.

Lori had trouble identifying with that set of perceptions. After all, she'd been able to simply walk away from piloting 'Mechs, once she'd decided that family was more important. Though there were plenty of exceptions, Ellen believed that women were far more likely to think of a BattleMech as a very large and useful tool, a vehicle tailored to a specific and deadly purpose. As a result, they were often colder and more calculating at their 'Mechs' controls, moving and fighting by the book, with precision, and with unemotional deadliness. Men, on the other hand, tended to *become* their 'Mechs during combat; that sometimes made them better *instinctive* fighters, achieving much higher levels of coordination between their brains and the machines they controlled.

Learning that he could never again strap on a Battle-Mech, learning, in effect, that he'd been forever cut off from that *other* Carlyle, the powerful and commanding Grayson Carlyle who could kick over buildings and cross the landscape in ground-eating, five-meter strides, must have generated the same psychological shock as had losing his arm—worse, really, since the arm could be replaced. *Nothing,* from the perspective of a MechWarrior like Grayson, could replace the ego-coddling testosterone-charged glory of piloting a BattleMech.

The psychologists called the effect 'Mech withdrawal, as though the 'Mech itself were some kind of addictive drug.

Was Grayson suffering from withdrawal symptoms? Ellen couldn't know for sure, since diagnosis was not so simple a thing as running a blood test or probing a physical wound for shrapnel, but she'd thought it a definite possibility. There wasn't much that could be done for it, either, except to give moral support and to try to control the symptoms, the worst of which was chronic depression.

"Grayson," Lori had said suddenly that morning, as they got ready to appear before the court. "*Please* tell me what's wrong."

He was across the bedroom from her, standing in front of the full-length mirror as he adjusted his ribbons. At her plea, which she realized must have seemed to come out of nowhere since she'd not said anything for the past ten minutes or so, he glanced at her, his eyes meeting hers in the mirror.

She thought again how handsome he looked. He was wearing the Legion's full dress uniform, two-toned grays with black trim and half cloak. By contrast, the ribbons, most specific to the Legion, but others awards from the governments of several different worlds and states, flashed and glittered, a large rectangle of brilliant, sectioned color splashed on his left breast.

When he didn't answer immediately, she spread her hands. "Damn it, Gray, I can't *stand* it when you shut me out!"

"Lori . . ." he began. Then he snapped his mouth shut and shook his head. She saw the pain in his eyes.

"Sometimes, love," he said softly after a moment, "it's best not to say *anything.*"

What had he meant by that? That he didn't want to talk about it? Or . . .

Another possibility occurred to her, one that made her shiver with something more than the wintry chill of their quarters. Could he know that they were being watched? The possibility that their Asgard quarters were bugged had, of course, occurred to her. In fact, she'd taken that for granted as soon as she realized that the leutnant at the spaceport intended to take them to rooms specifically prepared for them.

"We really shouldn't talk about this right now," he told her. He spoke softly, scarcely above a whisper, though she could tell he was still choosing his words with care. Listening devices the size of a fingernail could detect heartbeats at forty meters, she knew, and a spy camera that could read lips and estimate fluctuations in skin temperature—a fair first step in determining whether or not a subject was telling the truth—could be built into a cylinder no wider or longer than the first joint of her thumb. "All I can say right now is that it's going to be all right."

She looked around the room, an initial flash of vulnerability and embarrassment giving way to anger. There could be cameras everywhere here, watching everything they did, the watchers analyzing each expression, each exchange, even zooming in over shoulders to read notes written to one another in silence.

There could be no privacy here and no chance of sharing secrets. Possibly, Grayson didn't want to say anything because he couldn't, because any signal he made to her would be picked up and deciphered by the unseen watchers.

Grayson glanced at the chronometer on his left wrist. "We'd better go," he said heavily, "unless we want them to send some goons in to drag us there." As Lori crossed over to his side of the room, he reached out and patted her shoulder. "Don't worry, love. *Trust* me. . . ."

And now, two hours later, Grayson and Lori sat side by side in a wood-paneled box to the left of the long and imposing desk behind which the adjudication board sat. In front of the desk was a low table where evidence could be displayed, though this hearing would be judged only on the testimony of the various witnesses, not on any physical evidence. Above the board of inquiry, on a wall that might once have been white but that showed its age now in its layer of pale gray grime and dust, a sword crossed with its own scabbard hung in display, a reminder of the martial intent of these proceedings. Military justice, Lori reminded herself, was rarely concerned with the niceties attendant upon civilian trials. Decisions would be made here not on questions of right or wrong, but on principles of duty, of discipline, and of military expediency. What was best for the service frequently took precedence over what might be best, or even just, for the individual.

The inquiry board consisted of a panel of five, two Lyran military officers, two Davion officers, and one lean and elderly man in the formal long robes and pointed hood of a ComStar precentor. The officers, of course, were present both because they knew the demands of military life and because Grayson had attacked Davion troops in the service of the Federated Commonwealth; both Davion and Steiner officers were present so that both factions in the FedCom split could be represented. The two groups, two men in Davion gray and a man and a woman in Steiner blue, didn't seem to like one another very much. Lori wondered what effect the politics of the recent breakup of the Federated Commonwealth would have on the outcome of these hearings.

The precentor seated between the two factions was probably intended as a more or less neutral party. Ileus Horne was the local precentor in charge of ComStar affairs on Tharkad, a rather high-ranking and important official to be bothered with a relatively minor breach-of-contract hearing, Lori thought. Horne, clearly and from the beginning, was in charge of the hearing. He opened the proceedings by reminding those present that this was *not* a formal trial and that any findings made by the board were not binding. The board would submit its findings, and the prisoner, to the state—meaning the Lyran Alliance, within whose jurisdiction the presumed crime fell.

"If punishment of any kind is warranted," Precentor Horne said in solemn tones, "then it will fall to the state, specifically, in this instance, to the Judge Advocate General's Office of the Lyran Alliance, to review the evidence and to render a final verdict and sentence."

"My Lord Precentor," one of the Davion officers, a colonel, said. "Surely the Federated Commonwealth, which is, after all, the party that was wronged in this incident, should have some say in any future dispositions of—"

"This board will *not* be used as a political forum," Horne said sharply. "Your objection, Colonel Dillon, is noted. And overruled."

When the male Steiner officer turned his head to stare at Dillon, Lori recognized him: Leutnant-Colonel Willy Schubert. He was the man who'd come for Grayson the previous two evenings, taking him out somewhere for a long discussion, one extending into the wee hours of two long, cold nights. She thought some flicker of recognition—a glance, the slightest of nods—passed between Grayson and Schubert, but she couldn't be sure.

The rest of the large room, despite the seemingly endless rows of seats arrayed in ranks like the pews of a large cathedral, was empty, save for two Steiner guards flanking the tall double doors at the back of the room, and a proceedings recorder seated at the electronic booth to the right of Grayson's and Lori's box. There were no advocates as there would have been in a real trial; Grayson and Lori would speak for themselves, while the adjudicator board served as prosecution, judge, and jury. "A great way to save money on an expensive trial," Lori noted wryly, after wondering aloud to Grayson whether or not they would be allowed to have legal counsel.

"I have a feeling," Grayson told her, "that they're not so much interested in justice as they are in nice, tidy packages, with no loose ends."

"Colonel Grayson Death Carlyle," Horne intoned from the bench. "Lieutenant Colonel Lori Kalmar-Carlyle. Please stand."

When they had done so, Horne continued the recitation. Lori reached over and took Grayson's hand as they listened. "Colonel Grayson Death Carlyle, you are charged with one count of violating the terms of a legal and binding mercenary contract between the Gray Death Legion and House Steiner, with five counts of illegal military assault upon forces then in the service of the Federated Commonwealth, and with one count of treason against the state of the Federated Commonwealth, to which you were bound at the time under the terms of your mercenary contract."

Treason. Lori's heart beat a little faster at that word, and her knees and stomach felt weak. That was a capital offense. If Grayson was found guilty, he would be taken out and shot, a summary execution with no chance of appeal. She'd tried desperately to persuade him to argue that this was a matter for the Mercenary Review and Bonding Commission on Outreach, but he'd just shrugged. Was it possible that some part of him wanted to be punished?

"Lieutenant Colonel Lori Kalmar-Carlyle, you likewise are charged with one count of violating the terms of a legal and binding mercenary contract between the Gray Death Legion and House Steiner, with three counts of illegal military assault upon forces then in the service of the Federated Commonwealth, and with one count of treason against the state of the Federated Commonwealth, to which you were bound at that time under the terms of your unit's contract."

Schubert, at this point, reached over and lightly touched the precentor's shoulder. A low-voiced consultation followed, the two men whispering back and forth. Twice, Schubert gestured at the accused, and once Lori was certain he was looking straight at her, that *she* was the subject of the debate. After a moment, Dillon, the Davion colonel, got into the discussion as well, turning it into an urgent and harshly whispered three-way debate. "I object, sir!" Dillon said once, loudly enough to be heard across the room. "I strenuously object!"

"Overruled." The debate continued. Lori looked at Grayson, but he appeared to be somewhere else entirely. His eyes were closed, and his head was lowered.

Finally, the precentor said something unintelligible but sharp, and both of the military officers sat back in their chairs. Dillon looked disgruntled; Schubert appeared smug.

"Lieutenant Colonel Kalmar-Carlyle," the precentor said, folding his hands before him on the bench. "In the interests of expediency *and* of justice, I am dismissing all charges against you. From the evidence I've reviewed so far, it seems obvious to me that you were acting only in the best of military traditions. Your orders were to protect and administer the Gray Death Legion landhold on Glengarry. You were in no way responsible for your husband's change in loyalties at Caledonia. Indeed, I am surprised, in fact, that these charges were filed against you in the first place." He paused to give Dillon a hard look, which the Davion colonel did not meet.

"Normally," he continued, "I would ask you to leave at this time, since these proceedings are officially closed. However, in view of your relationship with the accused, if you wish to remain, you may."

"Why don't you step outside?" Grayson whispered to her. "This won't take very long—"

"I want to stay, Precentor," Lori said, ignoring him. Her mind was racing now. What had been the point of that hurried consultation? She suspected that the Lyran officer, Schubert, had been urging that the charges be dropped against her. Had that been the subject of Schubert's discussion with Grayson the other night? She shot him a quick glance from the corner of her eye. Had he agreed to something on the condition that she be left out of it?

"Very well. You may be seated. I will take this opportunity to remind you both once again that this is not a formal trial. If there are no further objections from the bench, we will proceed with the inquiry."

He was right, Lori thought. This was nothing like a trial, and she had the impression that he was supposed to remind them all of that fact from time to time. There was no chance for Grayson to plead guilty or not guilty, no formal prosecution, no defense. Still, the process carried all of the weight and ponderous legal terminology of any regular military court. If Grayson was found guilty here, there would be no reason for any Steiner military court to reject that decision. Quite the contrary, in fact. It would be politically expedient for JAG, the office of the Judge Advocate General, to accept the board's ruling point by point to the final detail. This would be just one more nail in the coffin of the Steiner-Davion alliance.

One by one, witnesses summoned from Caledonia and Glengarry were called into the room, each taking his place before the bench where he was questioned by the panel members. Everything was very formal and correct; the adjudicators interrogated each witness thoroughly, sometimes reading from electronic pads on the bench before them, sometimes apparently addressing them with new questions suggested by the testimony.

Lori had wondered whether Brandal Gareth would be

here. He wasn't, but a colonel named George Irwin from Gareth's staff was present to give the field marshal's side of the story, as was Marshal Seymour, the commander of the Third Davion Guard at Falkirk. Both men testified that Grayson's attack against the militia and palace guard units belonging to Caledonia's Governor Wilmarth had taken them completely by surprise, that their orders stated that the Gray Death's Third Battalion was supposed to assist them in putting down the popular revolt against Wilmarth, and that the Gray Death's operations had caused heavy damage and loss of life to elements of the Third Davion Guard.

After that, it was Major Frye's turn. He was questioned closely about his part in the Battle of Falkirk and about what he'd known of Grayson's decision to turn against Governor Wilmarth's forces. McCall was next, and his testimony turned out to be the lengthiest of all, for he and Alex had gone to Caledonia weeks in advance of Third Batt to scout out the political situation and find out just what the Legion was getting itself into.

"It was my decision," McCall said with a quick, almost furtive glance at the box where Grayson and Lori were sitting. Grayson frowned and shook his head quickly. Lori knew that Grayson had already told him to keep quiet about that aspect of things, but McCall pushed ahead anyway. "Caledonia is my home world, y' ken, an' tha' wee bluidy bastard Wilmarth had arrested my brother an' was holdin' him for no good reason."

"Please refrain from prejudicial comments or descriptions, Major," Horne said mildly. "Continue."

"I was th' one who suggested tha' Governor Wilmarth was the problem, y' see. He was the man causing the rebellion among the people wi' his beastly bad manners. Kidnapping, torture, murder. I saw it wi' my own two eyes."

"And so you took it upon yourself to right this wrong? Rather than reporting the situation to a higher authority?"

"Sir, the situation had been reported time an' time again. To the Skye March Command. To an official of the Federated Commonwealth serving as Wilmarth's attaché. And people were dying. The Gray Death had been ordered to attack civilians. It was nae *right*!"

When Alex took the stand, the questions directed at

him tended to be phrased so as to confirm the replies the board had already gotten from McCall. Alex had been with McCall throughout the scouting assignment on Caledonia, and he, too, tried to take some part of the blame for bringing the Legion in on the side of the rebels.

Finally, it was Grayson's turn to speak on his own behalf. He approached the bench and stood at attention before it.

"Colonel Carlyle," Schubert said. "Do you deny the charges made against you here this morning?"

"No, sir."

"Would you care to explain your actions to this board? Why did you choose to violate the terms of your mercenary contract?"

"Sir, I have no excuse."

Lori's blood ran cold at those words. She'd thought that he would at least explain the position he'd found himself in, with direct orders from Wilmarth to fire on an unarmed civilian crowd. . . .

Damn it, Grayson! Defend yourself!

"I would like to make one statement, however."

"Proceed, Colonel."

"I reject the statements made on my behalf by both Major Davis McCall and Captain Alex Carlyle. The latter is my son and spoke out of filial devotion. The major is a very old friend of mine and no doubt hopes to deflect some of the blame from me." He shook his head slowly. "I was to blame for everything that happened on Caledonia . . . and on Glengarry. I accept full responsibility for my actions."

"Very well, Colonel," Horne said. "It is so noted." He turned to the recorder. "The board recorder will delete the entries made on the accused's behalf . . . those statements where they tried to take responsibility for Colonel Carlyle's decisions."

"Yes, sir."

"Colonel Carlyle? Do you have anything to add?"

"No, sir."

"Wait a minute!" Lori shouted, leaping to her feet. "You haven't heard what *I* have to say!"

"The questioning sequence of this board of inquiry is closed. Colonel Carlyle, you and your wife will wait outside while the panel completes its deliberations."

"Yes, sir."

"Precentor!" Lori called "Wait!"

But one of the Lyran guards had already come up behind her. "This way, Colonel," he said softly. He sounded gentle, even sympathetic. "There's nothing you can do now."

And with a cold, sick certainty, Lori knew he was right.

14

Adjudication Chambers
Royal Palace, Tharkad City
Tharkad, District of Donegal
Lyran Alliance
1165 hours (local), 3 October 3057

They were led into an anteroom, one with Spartan furniture and a temperature kept so cool that Lori could see
their breaths puffing from their mouths in the cold air.
The room had a window—one of real glass or transplas—
that looked out through frost etchings over the mountains
and snow-clad forests of the countryside to the east.

"Grayson?" Lori said, studying him carefully. "What
do you think?"

For just a moment, she caught a flash of . . . something.
Of excitement, of *eagerness,* perhaps. Something she'd
not seen there in a long time.

But then it was gone, fading behind the dull and expressionless lack of feeling she'd come to hate so much
of late. "Everything will be all right," he said. "Believe
that."

"Damn it, why didn't you defend yourself?"

"Because it wouldn't have done any good."

"You don't know that! You could have tried for a
higher board review! An appeal! You could have requested a formal court-martial! Or a special trial by your
peers as nobility, as Baron Glengarry!"

"Believe me, love. None of that would have changed anything. I *know* what I'm doing."

"I'm not so sure you do!"

Ten minutes passed. Then fifteen. The tension was unbearable, but Lori dreaded hearing the decision almost as much as she wanted an end to the waiting. All too soon, then, the door opened and an aide in Steiner full dress walked in.

"Colonel Carlyle?" the aide said, speaking to Grayson. Then he nodded to Lori. "And Colonel Kalmar-Carlyle. Will you both follow me, please? They're ready."

"Time to face the music," Grayson said.

"If they find us guilty," Lori said, "they're going to have a damned hard time with—"

"If they find *me* guilty. You're not a part of this."

"The hell I'm not. I'll *make* myself a part—"

"Hush," Grayson said.

Side by side, they walked back to the council chamber. The aide palmed a door open, then stepped aside as they walked through.

Lori's eyes went at once to the desk in front of the seated panel of five. Resting directly in front of the cowled ComStar precentor was a sleek, keen-bladed sword, its furniture of gold and its hilt tightly wrapped with black sharkskin, a relic, no doubt, of some military collection or other. The sight struck her an almost physical, palpable blow, and she hissed with the sharp intake of a breath. *No! . . .*

Once, well over a thousand years ago, officers had been identified by such swords and, on some rare occasions, had even used them in battle. There'd been a tradition, she'd read once, in the ocean-going navy of some one or another of Terra's countless warring nation-states. If an officer of that navy was accused of some wrongdoing—of running his ship aground, say, or of cowardice in the face of the enemy, he would face a court-martial with brother officers as his judges. As a prisoner, he was required to surrender his sword, which was his badge of authority and of command, for the trial's duration.

The tradition held that after the tribunal had completed its deliberations and the accused was called back in to hear the verdict, his sword was placed on the table before the court. If the verdict was an acquittal, the sword was placed with the hilt turned toward the officer, so that after the decision was announced he could reach out, pick it up, and return it to his scabbard. If the verdict was guilty, however, the sword was left with the blade pointed at the officer as he walked in the door.

It was a tradition that some militaries had picked up and made their own a millennium later. Looking up at the dingy wall behind the board, Lori saw that the sword had come from there—she could see the dust-outlined shape where it once had hung—and had been placed on the table, as dictated by tradition.

The blade was aimed directly at Grayson.

He said nothing, though he plainly had seen the symbol and knew precisely what it meant.

"Colonel Grayson Death Carlyle of the mercenary regiment known as the Gray Death Legion," Horne said when they stopped in front of the bench, with the table and that accusatory sword before them. "On the charge of treason, this board of adjudication finds you innocent. There is insufficient evidence to suggest that you acted willfully against the Federated Commonwealth.

"On the charge that you violated the terms of a legal and binding mercenary contract between the Gray Death Legion and House Steiner, the board of adjudication finds you guilty as charged.

"On five counts of illegal military assault upon forces then in the service of the Federated Commonwealth, the board of adjudication finds you guilty as charged on all counts."

The precentor looked up from his electronic slate, fixing Grayson with wintry eyes. "It has been suggested that since you were technically working for the Federated Commonwealth at the time of your offense, you are not guilty of violating your principal agreement with House Steiner. This board has decided, however, that you be found guilty on all applicable counts nonetheless. We are interested here not in the letter of the law so much as in the spirit, and it is clear that you, Grayson Carlyle, violated the spirit of contractual law when you willfully changed sides on Caledonia, entering combat against the military forces you had been directed to support. It is for this reason that we have no alternative but to find you guilty.

"This adjudication board is neither a civil nor a military court of law and, as such, has no power to pass final judgment or to mete out legal sentencing. Our recommendation, however, will be that the office of the Judge Advocate General find you guilty on all counts save that of treason, that the mercenary contract between the Gray Death Legion and House Steiner be officially declared null and void due to noncompliance, and that your personal properties, Colonel Carlyle, be handed over to the Barony estate.

"I have before me a message from the Archon Katrina Steiner, further stating that should this board find you, Colonel Carlyle, guilty on even one count, she intends to declare an official disinvestiture, which will strip you of all rank, titles, and privilege associated with your former position as Baron Glengarry, including the Landhold of Glengarry itself. A new baron will be named within twenty-four hours.

"Further, it is our strong recommendation that the Gray Death Legion be disbanded, by force, if necessary. This order would not need to be carried out if Colonel Carlyle agrees to voluntarily give up his command of the unit." Horne's cold eyes fell on Lori. "It was my thought that command could fall upon Lieutenant Colonel Kalmar-Carlyle."

Lori opened her mouth to speak, to refuse point-blank, to tell Horne exactly what she thought about his offer when Grayson, at her side, closed his hand upon hers and squeezed, hard. When she looked sideways at him, he shook his head, warning her to be silent.

"In any case, the Gray Death Legion will have ninety standard days to leave its former landhold and find work and basing elsewhere. Any resistance to this command by any member of the Gray Death Legion will result in the forceful disbanding of the Legion. Do you have anything to say for the record at this time, Colonel Carlyle?"

"Yes, Lord Precentor," Grayson replied. "I accept the judgment of this board, and I would like it noted that I do hereby resign as commander of the Gray Death Legion, in favor of my executive officer, Lieutenant Colonel Lori Kalmar-Carlyle."

"I refuse," she said. Turning, she favored Grayson with a dark scowl. "Grayson! What the hell are you do—"

"The decision is mine to make," Grayson said, still addressing the board, "and I wish it recorded as such."

"It is so ordered. Colonel Kalmar-Carlyle, I remind you that you are present at these proceedings as a courtesy of this board. Any further outburst on your part, and I will order you ejected from these chambers. Am I clear?"

"Yes, damn you," Lori said, breathing hard. If she could have reached the precentor's throat in that moment . . .

Horne ignored what he might have called the "prejudicial comment" on her part. "Colonel Carlyle? Have you more to say on your behalf?"

"No, Lord Precentor."

"Then I declare these proceedings are closed," he said.

"I'd like this message sent," the man said, passing a small electronic pad across to the clerk at the message desk of the Asgard HPG station. "Priority-commercial."

"Just this?" the clerk asked, looking up.

The client was a military officer in the uniform of the Davion Guards. His epaulets bore the rank insignia of a colonel. "That's it. Here's my account card."

The clerk nodded, accepted card and pad, and began keying in a code sequence at his terminal. He wore the white uniform of ComStar, with that organization's device worked into a patch on his left breast and on his shoulder. "I can fit you into a routing slot going out at 2330 hours standard, tomorrow. That's just about thirty-four hours local from now. Unless you want to pay extra for—"

"Tomorrow's fine." The cost of full-motion HPG transmissions might routinely be borne by the likes of Katrina Steiner and interstellar governments, but he was on a limited budget. He was willing to accept the costs of commercial-priority transmissions, which meant he wouldn't have to wait until the next routine package transfer, probably in a week or so. He would have to see about getting a raise. He was worth it by now, surely. But he would keep his messages to text only and as abbreviated as he could manage.

"Need your signature," the clerk said, pushing a screen

tablet and stylus across the counter at him. "And confirm your destination address."

Swiftly, the officer scrawled out his signature: Charles Dillon, Col., AFFC. The destination of the message was correct.

Brandal Gareth, Defiance Industries, Hesperus II.

The collective mood of the Legion officers was subdued as they entered their visitors' quarters once more, escorted by Lyran Alliance troops who took up their accustomed positions outside the door. "Weel, we gave it th' good fight," McCall said heavily.

"Good fight nothing," Lori snapped. She whirled to face Grayson as soon as the door was shut behind them, eyes sparking. "What the hell is going on, Gray?" she demanded, her voice low and fast. "It's not like you to just—"

She broke off, practically in mid-word, as Grayson held up one warning finger. He glanced back and forth, then looked at her and winked. Casually, he tugged at one ear with his hand—his artificial hand—and she realized that he was concerned about spy devices and unseen watchers. "I don't really want to discuss it," he said.

She hesitated, then nodded, a bit sharply. In her anger she'd forgotten the danger. Still, how much more damage could they do now? The worst had already happened. Grayson had been found guilty, ordered to renounce command of his precious Legion, and the Legion itself was in danger with its landhold, with its *world*, forfeit.

No large military force could survive for long as a unit without some planetary base to call its own. It was more than a matter of having someplace to call headquarters, and BattleMechs needed more than pilots and techs to remain operational. They needed vast amounts of ammunition, silicarb lubricants, replacement parts, circuitry and electronics, fusor packs and power couplings. They needed a vast support infrastructure, people to produce the spare parts and manufacture the ammunition. Farms to grow the food needed to feed all of those people. More people to run the farms . . . truck the produce . . . handle transport logistics and communications for the unit.

And most of those people had families. . . .

The Gray Death Legion, with orders to depart from

Glengarry within ninety days, had just lost *all* of that. They would have to disband, unless they could find another employer, one well-to-do enough to feed and equip a regiment numbering hundreds of BattleMechs and thousands of people for as long as it might take to get established once more.

"Listen to me, Lori," Grayson said softly. Reaching out, he took her by both shoulders, looking into her eyes with an intensity and a depth that she'd not seen in the man since, well, since before he'd left for Caledonia. Something had changed in him, but what?

"Listen," he said again, for emphasis. "I can't tell you everything, not now. But it's going to be all right."

"But Gray—"

"And the reason I know that is because you're going to be in command of the Legion now."

Her eyes widened and she fumbled for the right words. "Gray, I don't want . . . I mean, that's crazy!"

"*You* may be the best for th' job, lass," McCall said. "The lads, they'll aye listen t' you."

"*You* would be the better choice, Davis," Lori said. "But it's not going to come to that. Grayson has been moping around for months, and now he ups and decides to quit on us. Well, I'm not going to let that happen!"

"Lori, you may not have the choice," Jon Frye said gently. "If he won't do it, no one can make him."

"Grayson!" Lori said. "Don't you *care* what's going to happen to the Legion?"

"Yes, I care," he said, slumping into a sofa. "I care very much. God, it's cold in here. Alex, dial us up some heat, will you?"

"Dad," Alex said. "What are we going to do? The Legion, I mean. We can't get along without you."

Grayson gave a wry smile. "At this point, you can't get along *with* me. That's one of the conditions of the judgment. I'm out."

Caitlin DeVries looked from Grayson to Lori. "But we can't just give up. We've got to *fight* this somehow!"

"Was that what you discussed with that Lyran colonel during those late-night strolls . . . what was his name? Schubert. You talked about your stepping aside in my favor?"

"Among other things," Grayson admitted. "Lori, I really want you to do this."

She glanced from one side of the room to the other, wondering who might be listening in, wondering where the unseen cameras might be. Had she already said too much in her anger and frustration? She decided she didn't care. "You mean I'll pretend to run the regiment, while you—"

"No!" He pointed a finger squarely at her face. "You. I'll run off the papers tonight, promoting you to full colonel. And you'll be in charge as of immediately, because I won't be going back with you."

He's slipped a primary cam, Lori thought, suddenly even more worried than before. This wasn't *like* him. *The stress had pushed him too far. . . .*

"Grayson, I know this has been hard on you—"

"Don't patronize me, Lori. I know what I'm doing."

"Damn it, let's at least talk about this!"

"Mom's right," Alex began.

"No!" Grayson brought his fist, his left fist, down hard on the low table in front of the sofa. There was a sharp crack of splintering wood, and the tabletop shattered. "Damn."

"You dinnae ken y' ain strength, lad," McCall said.

"Still getting the hang of the damned thing," Grayson said, rubbing his left hand ruefully. He shook his head. "Lori, listen to me now. You're just going to have to trust me on this one, love. I want you to take the promotion. And the Legion."

Her jaw clenched. Defiance flamed, hot and sour. "I will *not*—"

"Damn it, Lori!" he flared. "I'm giving you an order! Take command of the Legion and see to my people! And don't give me an argument, hear?"

She stared at him for a long moment, tears stinging her eyes. "Yes, *sir,*" she snapped, and without another word she turned on her heel and strode off to their bedroom.

Alex Carlyle no longer knew his father.

The change that had come over him recently was inexplicable. For as long as Alex had been able to remember, the Gray Death Legion had been Grayson Carlyle's passion, his whole reason for life, a love surpassed only by what he felt for his own family—and even there, in terms of demonstrativeness, the Legion had often taken precedence. Alex had grown up in the Legion, playing in the shadow of ten-meter-tall war machines locked in their access gantries. When kids his age outside the Legion compound were playing sag or touchball, he'd been running miniatures simulations on a discarded BattleTech holotac board McCall had scrounged up for him. He'd piloted a 'Mech for the first time at age twelve, sitting in his father's lap inside the close, oil-and-hot-metal-smelling complexity of a *Marauder*'s cockpit.

From the beginning, Alex, along with everyone else he knew, had assumed that he would continue with the Legion, that he would even go on to command it someday. After all, where else would he go? Oh, there'd been some doubt in his own mind a year or two ago; he'd been worried for a time by the natural question of whether or not he owed his promotion to captain and his assignment as company commander to his father instead of to his own abilities.

Well, that was all changed now, that was for damned sure.

The toughest part, though, would be breaking this to Caitlin. He'd been trying to think of a good way to go about it, until finally he'd just plain run out of time. There'd been no place at Asgard where they could talk, and no time, either. The Legion officers—all save Grayson—had been rounded up early that morning by their Lyran hosts and hustled off to the spaceport with an almost indecent haste. They'd spent the time since in the spaceport terminal, waiting as the *Orion* was readied for boost.

They'd been kept together by a half dozen armed guards, escorted to meals and washrooms as though they were dangerous prisoners. Perhaps their hosts were afraid they would try to strike back somehow. To Alex, it felt as though the fight had drained out of all of them, even McCall, even his mother.

And what he had to do now would just make it harder. On *all* of them.

Leaning back in one of the seats in the spaceport terminal lounge, he eyed the trooper in charge of the guard detail. He was an older man, forty, Alex guessed, maybe forty-five, and he wore the rank of leutnant.

Many leutnants, Alex knew, never advanced beyond that twilight rank between commissioned and non-commissioned officers within the Lyran military structure. Those who had no ambition to reach a higher rank, or those who for one reason or another were simply passed over for promotion or a chance at command, could remain leutnants for their entire careers.

This one wasn't young, which meant he wouldn't be as stiff or as scared of the system as a newbie might be. His cheeks showed a shadow of stubble and his uniform was rumpled and stained here and there, a clear indication that he wasn't out to impress anyone. If he was still a leutnant after—what, twenty or twenty-five years in the military?—it might be because he was a troublemaker already, or simply because he had no ambition. Either way, he would be more amenable to a bribe than some kid fearful of his CO looking over his shoulder. Alex glanced down at himself. He was wearing civilian clothing, a white jumper, trousers, and leather boots, with a shoulder cloak as proof against the cold. He'd thought it best, that morning, not to emphasize his connections with the Legion. With Alex in civilian garb, the leutnant shouldn't be put off by his captain's rank tabs, even though the man surely knew the ranks of everyone in the Legion party.

Hell, it was worth a try.

The leutnant watched him suspiciously as he approached. "What d'you want, merc?"

"Some time alone with my girl friend," Alex replied, turning to stand next to him. He indicated Caitlin with a sly nod, then nudged the man in the ribs with his elbow. "Just a few minutes . . . know what I mean?" He opened his hand just enough to reveal the fifty C-bill note hidden there. "We haven't had any privacy since we got here."

The leutnant hesitated, but Alex caught the avaricious glint of interest in his eye, and the way his tongue flicked once swiftly across his lips. "Hey, kid. What kind of scam you tryin' t' pull?"

Alex sighed and produced a second fifty. The leutnant pursed his lips, then turned his back on the lounge, covertly taking the money from Alex's hand as he pivoted. "Ten minutes, kid." The man jerked his head, indicating a direction. "There's a room over there, through that door. A *private* room. Make it a quick one. Haw!" He laughed, a salacious guffaw, as he thumbed the two bills, then made them vanish into a belt pouch.

Alex nodded, then hurried over to where Caitlin was sitting before the officer could change his mind or think of an excuse to up the price. He reached out and caught her hand. "Caitlin? We need to talk."

"What? What is it, Alex?"

"Over here. I fixed it with the guards."

The door had a small keypad lock; the leutnant tapped out a code and the door slid open. "In there," he told them, leering. He winked at Alex. "I guess I could let you have twenty minutes, kid. Have fun!"

The door opened into a small storeroom of some sort. It was dimly lit by a single glowstrip up high on one wall and was cluttered with empty boxes, some cleaning equipment, and a stained and dirty mattress lying in one corner on the floor. The air stank faintly of detergent and urine.

When the door slid shut behind them, Caitlin turned to face Alex. "What's this all about?"

The only way to do this, he'd already decided, was to blurt it right out. "Caitlin, I have to say good-bye. I'm staying here."

She blinked. "What . . . staying with your father?"

"No, actually. He's going . . . somewhere else. He won't tell me where. He won't tell me anything. But last night, he gave me this."

Reaching into his belt pouch, he extracted the printout his father had given him last night and handed it to her. She read it silently, holding it up slightly to make out the words in the faint, dirty light. "This is a commission," she said, "in the Lyran armed forces. . . ."

"That's right. They're offering me the rank of hauptmann, based on my experience with the Legion. At least it's not a demotion, huh? I'll be serving with a Guards receiving unit here on Tharkad, at least until I get my new 'Mech broken in and my gear squared away. But after that, I've got a straight shot at the First Royal Guard!"

Caitlin shook her head but didn't seem to pull her eyes away from the printout. "I . . . I don't understand. You're just . . . leaving? Leaving the Legion?"

"I talked it over a bit with my father last night," Alex said with more confidence than he really felt. "Like I said, he's the one who gave me that. Seems this Colonel Schubert, the guy on the adjudication board? He's the one made the offer to my father. Said it was mine if I wanted it."

She looked at him then, over the top of the printout. He couldn't read the expression on her face. When she said nothing, he pushed ahead. "Look, it's clear enough I'm not going to get anywhere if I stay in the Legion, right?"

"Are you asking me or telling me?"

"Telling, I guess. I mean, even before all this happened, there was a big question about whether I was getting promotions and stuff on my own merit, or because of who my father was. He agrees, by the way. He told me I should take the chance and get while the getting is good."

"Damn it, Alex!" Her voice was intense, scarcely above a whisper but as hard and as cold as ice. "How *could* you?"

His jaw tightened. "How can I do anything else? It's not like I'd be doing anybody any great favors by staying. And it's clear enough that staying here is a dead end."

"And just what do you expect me to say about all of this?"

"Well, I was hoping you'd come along. You're a great 'Mech pilot. I've been checking around, and the word is that the Royal Guard is actively looking for experienced personnel, MechWarriors and aeropilots with good kill records. I'll bet we could find you a billet, maybe even in my new company. I thought—"

"You . . . malfing . . . *bastard*," Caitlin said, the words so low Alex almost couldn't hear. "You're actually going to walk out on your family now, when they need you most?"

"It's not like that," he said.

Inside, though, he wasn't so sure. He'd been up most of the night wrestling with this one. Go? Or stay? If his father hadn't been so dead certain that taking the commission with the Guard was a good idea, Alex doubted he'd have been able to make himself leave. This *was* a tremendous opportunity for him, for any career soldier. Had he been offered this chance under any other circumstances, he certainly would have accepted it, with the idea that after serving a tour or two with the Royals, he'd be able to return to the Legion. Lots of mercenary officers rotated back and forth between their units and regular line regiments that had room for them. The regulars valued the added combat experience most mercs possessed, even when they professed to look down on mercenary warriors as somehow lacking in devotion to any cause but money; the merc units benefited by having men return to the unit with new skills and experience, and possibly new insights into how the line units—and potential adversaries—operated.

Invitations to join the First Royal Guards were not generally extended to mercenaries, however. Damn it, he'd *had* to say yes.

"Take it, Alex," his father had told him at last during their discussion late the previous night. "You'll never have an opportunity like this again, and you know it. *Especially* if you stay hitched up to the Legion."

"I don't want to leave the Gray Death," Alex had replied. "Not like this."

"Look, I'm going to do everything I can to make sure that the Legion manages to hold together. If it doesn't, though, it could drag down everyone with it when it goes. If that happens, I'll be counting on you to take care of your mother, at least until she can get on her feet again. Somebody's going to have to pay the bills, and if nobody hires her because she's linked to a blackballed unit, that somebody's going to have to be you."

A blackballed unit. A mercenary unit so disgraced that its members could not find work anywhere, even as freelancers. Surely, it wouldn't come to *that*.

"Damn it, Dad, you make it sound like you're never coming back!"

"I may not, son. War's like that. You've been there. You know the odds." Then Grayson Carlyle seemed to read his son's expression and chuckled. "Don't worry, Alex. I'll be fine. So will the Legion. We'll survive. And you'll be the best help to yourself and to me and to the Legion if you take this billet with the First Royals."

That had settled it, and Alex had agreed. Simply saying yes, however, had not ended the debate in his own mind.

Nor did it help explain things to Caitlin.

"Caitlin, I don't—"

She slapped him, hard, the blow rocking his head to the right.

"Ow! What was *that* for?"

"Maybe I'm just old-fashioned," she told him. "But I always figured I owed something to the Colonel. Like *loyalty*."

"But he *told* me to go!"

"He gave you an order?"

"Well, no. But—"

"And obviously he's going through a really bad time right now. Maybe he thinks he's doing you a favor. But damn it, he needs you. He needs all of us. And you're just—"

"I told you, Caitlin. It's not like that. I think—"

Suddenly, the door to the storeroom slid open, spilling light across the floor. The leutnant stood in the opening with three of his troopers crowding in behind, craning their necks to see past him. "Hey, you two!" the leutnant boomed. Then, seeing Alex and Caitlin standing next to one another, fully dressed and talking rather than engaged in any other, more interesting activity, his face fell. "Time's up, kid. Get the hell out of here."

"Good-bye, Alex," Caitlin said in a voice that might have had liquid nitrogen behind it. "I'm sure you'll do very well in your new posting." Turning, she marched past the soldiers, brushing by them with a no-nonsense manner that pushed them aside like an invisible hand.

Alex had the distinct impression that she'd just told him good-bye for good.

Great, he told himself. Taking a deep breath, he walked out of the storeroom. He still had to find time to talk to his mother, and he was wondering if that would be any easier. His dad would have already broken it to her, but still. . . .

Just malfing great!

15

Planetary Defense Command
Hesperus II, Rahneshire
Lyran Alliance
1975 hours (local), 4 October 3057

Field Marshal Brandal Gareth stood in his office, looking down on the Defiance Industries factory complex and on the city of Maria's Elegy. The sky was as clear as it ever got on Hesperus II, which was to say patches of violet sky showing here and there through the roil of blue, purple, white, and yellow clouds. The factory—one of the largest, busiest, and most important of such facilities in the entire Inner Sphere, was almost, *almost* his entirely. . . .

The view was spectacular.

In fact, his office was heavily armored and buried nearly a kilometer beneath the hostile and mountainous surface terrain of Hesperus II, but the wall screen gave the illusion that he was standing high up on the western flank of Mount Defiance, looking down on one of humanity's greatest engineering achievements from something like eighty stories above the world's capital city. Though the greater part by far of the Defiance Industries complex was underground, enough had emerged from its subsurface caverns and tunnels to create a titanic sprawl, a literal metallic forest of cooling, stripping, scrubbing, or fractionating towers, of circulating pumps and storage tanks, of cracking stations and smelters, of warehouses aligned in rows measured by the tens of kilometers, of gantry frameworks and blast furnaces and exhaust stacks and cranes and compressors and dozens of squat, black defensive works. From up here, it all looked a little like some colossal jumble of jackstraws, blocks, and toys dropped in heaps by some wayward giant's child, though with greater order than might have been expected of a completely random scattering of parts.

Maria's Elegy, the planetary capital, appeared tiny, even primitive by comparison, a small tangle of buildings, towers, quonset huts, domes, and other structures tacked onto the edge of the larger industrial complex, a ragtag huddle of disparate parts that looked more like a frontier outpost than a city.

Measured by standard time it was late evening, but the world of Hesperus II, like both Tharkad and Glengarry, had a rotation considerably longer than the ancient rhythm of twenty-four hours to the day inherited from Terra, and the standard calendar had nothing whatsoever to do with the local one. By local time it was 1975 hours—with each of twenty-five hours divided into eighty minutes. On the South Whitman continent, at this longitude, it was late afternoon, and the Hesperan sun was a dazzling pinpoint of diamond blue-white light hanging in the sky just above the Myoo Highlands to the west, setting the tormented clouds aflame.

Hesperus II was a world of mountains, vast mountains, immense, towering mountains, a planet with continental plates in constant, slow-motion driftings, grinding up against one another to raise a labyrinth of crisscrossing mountain peaks and ranges that from space gave the world the look of an apple dried in the sun. There were four major continents and innumerable smaller island chains and archipelagos, and all were heavily crinkled by young, upthrusting mountains, some volcanic, most the product of active plate tectonics. The Hesperan sun was an F2 subgiant, and though the planet was second out from the primary in this system, it was also remote from its star—it *had* to be, or its surface would have been seared lifeless by the torrent of radiation washing across it. The Hesperan sun scarcely showed a visible disk, so distant was it from its world, yet it was still impossible to look at that intense, laser-brilliant light without special filters or vision-protectors; where it touched the glaciers high up among the tallest mountain peaks, it struck shimmering white fire.

Temperatures were intolerable for unprotected humans near the Hesperan equator, where swamps steamed and native life adapted to eighty-degree-Celsius-plus temperatures and atmospheric pressures of three bars plus thrived in its hot-blooded, sulfur-metabolizing way. Centuries before, human xenobiologists had classified the highest forms of native Hesperan life as reptilian, but that was only because their most recognizable features—scales and claws, flat heads and toothy jaws and questing, air-tasting tongues—seemed more reptilian than any other variety of safe, homey, familiar, *known* life.

Humans rarely ventured into the Hesperan Equatorials, and then only in specially designed exploration 'Mechs, heavily armed, armored, and refrigerated, equipped with ranked batteries of heat sinks to deal with the oppressive temperatures. Of those exploration 'Mechs that had ventured into the Hesperan swamps, fewer than thirty percent had ever returned. The last expedition had gone north from Point Vallejo nearly two centuries ago, which made it considerably overdue. Since Hesperus was primarily a commercial venture, a partnership between government and industry, there seemed little point in wasting precious resources on scientific research.

North and south of the Equatorials the climate was milder, especially at altitudes above three thousand meters where the air pressure was close to one standard bar and the temperature hovered around thirty Celsius. There were even glaciers at the highest altitudes, say, at six thousand meters, though the air up there was too thin for breathing. Back in the twenty-sixth century, human terraformers had attempted to remake the world into something more pleasantly livable by importing various native Terran and gene-engineered varieties of microbes, plants, and animals. The project had been, at best, only partially successful and only at those higher elevations where humans could live without special protection. The deep valleys, the oceans, and the Equatorials remained unexplored, for the most part, the domain of the great Hesperan "reptiles." In the uplands, weaker, native

Hesperan forms had given way before the alien invasion of hardier, more adaptive gene-tailored life forms; even so, there were still precious few places anywhere on the world suitable for human habitation. The only regions available for cultivation—requiring as it did fertile soil rich with nitrogen-fixing bacteria—were the breathtaking Melrose Valley complex stretching across nearly a thousand kilometers of the Sulden Uplands and the heavily terraced mountain slopes around Maria's Elegy, here in South Whitman.

There was really no need for more arable land, however. The Melrose Valley and the region near Maria's Elegy provided food enough to feed the planet's population, which had never numbered much above fifty million, if that. Hesperus II was a world with only one industry and one export, and that was military hardware—BattleMechs, especially.

BattleMechs, or, more specifically, the factories and casting plants and smelters and assembly lines needed to fabricate them, were the only reason people stayed on this hellhole. Defiance Industries had been founded in December of 2577, its ownership passing to House Steiner with the fall of the Star League. Over the years, no fewer than fourteen full-scale attacks—and numerous raids—had been mounted to capture or destroy the industrial facilities on Hesperus. The primary factory, occupying as it did level upon level upon labyrinthine level of a vast cavern complex hollowed out beneath the Myoo Mountains, was a warren of hardpoints and sophisticated defenses, laser cannon and PPCs, missile launchers and radar networks, so tightly interlocked that the proverbial gnat would be hard pressed to make an unauthorized landing at Morningstar Spaceport.

Gareth stroked his chin as his eyes traced a line of ferrocrete abutments and walls up the flank of a mountain to a battery of laser turrets a kilometer from his position. Defending a world against an invasion or a raid from space was never easy. As had been the case at Glengarry, there were always plenty of landing sites to choose from, whether they were empty forest clearings, a wide stretch of beach, a wind-polished stretch of glacier, or a smooth patch cleared by chance in a boulder field. Even a world as rugged as Hesperus II had an abundance of such spots.

But the Hesperan environment posed a special consideration for any would-be raiders. Men serving with the 'Mech units stationed there—traditionally the Fifteenth Lyran Guards and, a more recent addition, the Third Davion Guard—joked that the terrain and the environment were at least as much a threat to invaders as were any defending 'Mechs. Any attempt to land in the immediate area of Maria's Elegy or the main Defiance plant would bring the descending DropShips into the defense batteries' crisscrossing fields of fire; any attempt to land farther off, making an approach out of range, exposed the invaders to the hellish Hesperan terrain. The Russians of Terra had long ago hailed General Winter as their most valuable and implacable defender; on Hesperus II, it was General Heat and General Terrain, the dread twin nemeses of any who dared attack that world.

And it was a world that Brandal Gareth now virtually controlled. That, and that alone, made him without question the most important man, the most powerful man, in the entire Lyran Alliance, the one man who, at a word, could destroy the Alliance before it was even properly begun.

Turning from the wall screen, he walked back to his desk and read once again the message glowing on the terminal display.

CMSTR HPG TRANS. PRIORITY-COMMERCIAL
CIVIL PRIORITY, CLASS 2
RELAY VIA: THUBAN, TURINGE, CIOTAT, HESPERUS II
DATE: 4 OCT 3057
TO: BRANDAL GARETH, FLDMRSL,
COHESPERAN DEFENSE FORCE,
DEFIANCE INDUSTRIES, HESPERUS II
FROM: CHARLES DILLON, COL, AFFC
ASGARD, THARKAD
MESSAGE:
    VERMILLION
SIGNED: DILLON

Regrettably, the message had not read ALIZARIN, which would have indicated that the Kalmar-Carlyle bitch had also been charged and convicted in the hearing on Tharkad. Gareth wondered what had gone wrong there. Dillon was supposed to have had that fixed.

No matter. The woman was definitely of secondary importance to the plan, and, even now, Gareth could recognize that his desire to drag her down with her husband had been motivated by the petty dictates of revenge; he was still smarting from the mauling she'd given him some four months ago on Glengarry. Besides, with her husband stripped of his title, she wouldn't be in a position to cause trouble any more.

Clearing the computer screen, he began typing rapidly on the work station's keyboard, setting up a list of new orders for electronic routing to Culligan, Samules, and Blaine. With Carlyle and the Gray Death neutralized, it was time to get on with the next phase of Operation Excalibur.

It was, he thought, about scagging time. The Caledonian operation—and the follow-up invasion of Glengarry—*should* have taken care of that particular problem in short order. That it had not was due mostly, Gareth decided, to plain bad luck, the one thing that had plagued every military leader who'd ever formulated a plan of battle since the time of the ancient Sumerians. He'd considered launching a second assault against Glengarry in order to take advantage of the likely confusion and drop in morale brought on by Carlyle's wounding, but decided against it. The Gray Death Legion could still fight; the last invasion attempt had demonstrated that. If he could have confirmed that the Legion's stores of expendables was as low as it should have been after that campaign, he might have attacked anyway. But through mischance or enemy action—he couldn't tell which—the agents he'd left behind on Glengarry had all stopped reporting within a very few days of the battle. Without reliable intelligence, Gareth wasn't going to take his forces into that hellhole again, especially since he no longer needed to. Within three months, the Legion would be gone from Glengarry; if they refused to leave, they'd have the entire Lyran Alliance to answer to and not just the two regiments now controlled by Brandal Gareth.

A tone sounded from his computer, accompanied by a light winking on the console. Gareth sighed, tapped in a security command to keep the orders locked from anyone save himself, then got up from the desk. The secret suite of rooms adjoining his office was reached through a hidden panel, one keyed to accept only his handprint on the access screen, or the palm print of a handful of others.

The suite was luxuriously furnished, fifteen large rooms trimmed in various hardwoods, as tastefully decorated as the best, most expensive hotel on Tharkad. Brewer was waiting for him in the first room as he came through the door.

"Hey, Brandal!" the young man said, excited. He was holding his violin tucked under his arm, the bow in his right hand. "I was wondering when we could go down to the floor on Bay Seventy."

"Your grace," Gareth said, bowing slightly. "I know I promised, but it's not convenient just now."

The duke's face clouded. "Damn it, Brandal, if I stay cooped up in here much longer, I'm going to *rot*!"

"I know how you feel, your grace." Gareth gestured at the door behind him, and the office beyond. "Right now, I have work piled up so deep I don't think I'm ever going to see the end of it." He brightened. "You know, your grace, you could help. Maybe with a vidtalk to the workers in Bay Seventy. The new prototype is behind sched and I haven't been able to get things moving. But they'll listen to *you*."

Daniel Brewer, Duke of Hesperus II, drew himself up a little straighter. "You think so, Brandal?"

"I *know* so, your grace. They love you, almost as much as they hate your family!"

Daniel smiled. He was a tall, slender, delicate-looking man with ebony-black skin, black hair fashioned into twin braids in the now out-of-date fashion of Lyran MechWarriors, and the long-fingered hands of a musician. He was also young—just twenty-two standard years old—and he still possessed a young man's impatience.

Not that Gareth could blame him. Daniel didn't get out much and had no companions save the servants and bodyguards assigned to his suite. He could see any part of his domain at any time, of course, at the touch of a key; the wall screens in the suite could show both entertainment and real-time displays from cameras, drones, and remotes throughout the vast complex that was Defiance Industries. But Gareth didn't dare let him venture out. Not yet. Daniel Brewer was the key to *everything*.

"We will go down to Seventy," Gareth promised him.

"But I'm going to have to arrange special protection for you when we're there. We don't want another attempt like the one four months ago, do we?"

"No, Brandal. And I . . . I'm sorry about that."

"It wasn't your fault, your grace."

"Well, it *was* my *family*." The young man spoke the final word as though it were a curse. "It cost you some good people."

"But we stopped them. It's just, well, we don't want to invite another . . . incident, do we?"

"No, Brandal."

"So. If you help me by delivering that speech—I'll have my staff write it up—we can get Bay Seventy moving again. And then maybe I can arrange for you to make a personal visit down there, let you thank the workers in person for getting back on track."

"I suppose if I went down there now, it would just slow things down more, huh?"

Gareth chuckled. "Well, now that you mention it . . ."

The young man looked crushed. "Well, I'm sorry I interrupted you. I know you have better things to do than babysit for *me*."

"It's always a pleasure talking with you, your grace. But I'd better get back to the old desk before it misses me."

"See you later?"

"Count on it."

Gareth sealed the door behind him, then walked back to his desk. He touched an intercom key.

"Sir?" a woman's voice replied at once.

"Yes, Marta. Have the public relations staff put together a speech. Nothing fancy. Just the usual work-hard-and-prosper drek. Have Jensen approve it, then forward it to the duke."

"Yes, sir."

"And hold further calls."

"Yes, sir."

Keying off the intercom, Gareth walked back to the wall screen, thoughtful. He was going to have to find some way to get the boy out more, or risk losing his affection. The question was . . . how, without letting his family get its claws into him again . . . or managing to kill him outright?

Daniel Brewer was the seven-times-great grandson of Gerald Brewer, an ex-MechWarrior and the CEO of a BattleMech production plant on Coventry who, shortly after the fall of the Star League, had been named baron and granted the fiefdom of Hesperus II by no less a personage than Archon Jennifer Steiner. The Brewer family had managed Defiance Industries ever since, running everything like a tight little feudal empire, from the main factories here at Maria's Elegy to the fusion plant works out on the Tatyana Archipelago.

The tightness of the Brewer operation, in fact, had given Gareth the wedge he needed to gain de facto control of the world himself. In fact, he never would have been able to carry it off if Defiance Industries had been run with anything like a sensible business hierarchy, with its leadership slots filled by executives chosen for their competence instead of passed on generation to generation as inherited titles.

But then, after three centuries it was unthinkable that anyone but a Brewer could be the company's CEO. When the boy's father, Duke Randolph Brewer, and his mother, the Lady Clarissa, had both died in an unfortunate VTOL accident in the Tatyana Islands, Daniel had been named both CEO and Duke of Hesperus II—even though he'd been only sixteen standard years old at the time.

No one save a few trusted confederates knew that Gareth had been behind the accident, or behind the string of deaths that had led eventually and inevitably to the election of Veronica Kelly to the head of the Hesperan Council, and the appointment of Randolph Chang as Operational Head of the Defiance Board of Directors.

Gareth had been working toward this moment for a long time, for ten years, in fact, since his original assignment to Hesperus II as a military liaison officer from Tharkad. He'd first made Daniel's acquaintance when the boy was just twelve. With Duke Randolph's permission, he'd taken the boy for a ride in his *Warhammer,* and he'd used that and numerous subsequent opportunities to fill young Daniel's head with glory-stories of 'Mech combat, especially those of his illustrious g'g'g'g'g'g'g'great-grandfather.

Today, Daniel all but worshipped Field Marshal Brandal Gareth, the man who'd been more than a father to him for the past six years, and who'd promised to make him a MechWarrior one day soon. The truth was that Daniel hadn't had much of a childhood—no friends his own age, no trips outside the various family compounds without bodyguards in close attendance, no real life at all save school and the unbearable monotony of knowing that things wouldn't be getting any better. As heir to the Brewer holdings, the future Duke of Hesperus II had had to be sheltered from kidnapping or terrorist assault; as heir, he'd been meticulously groomed for the position he must one day hold, no matter what his personal feelings in the matter might be.

Brandal Gareth had seen the opportunity here ten years ago and taken it, even though it had meant investing the rest of his life in the project. The rewards of that investment were astonishing in scope. Once successful, he would be among the most powerful men of the Inner Sphere and able to write his own ticket to whatever he desired.

All that had really been required was patience and a near-infinite tact.

Getting the young duke's signature and thumbprint on several key sets of legal papers had actually been easy, once Gareth had won his complete trust. The hard part had been dealing with the rest of the Brewer family, which, naturally enough, had seen Gareth as an interloper, a greedy and ambitious outsider trying to split Daniel— and his inheritance—away from the small army of relatives who made up the upper ranks of the Defiance Industries administrative complex.

Old Greydon had been the worst threat of the lot. Daniel's grandfather had tried to come out of retirement after Randolph's tragic accident; it had taken *another* death in the immediate Brewer family, this one an apparent heart attack, plus several more key deaths among the Defiance Industries Board of Directors, before Daniel could be confirmed as both duke and CEO. After that, well, Gareth had only been forced to play his trump card a single time—in the form of a direct order issued in person by a carefully rehearsed Daniel—to confirm Gareth's position as the real power behind the Brewer throne.

The situation now was somewhat precariously balanced. Some elements within the Brewer family empire still hadn't accepted Gareth's position, operating under the assumption—a correct one, as it happened—that he would eventually find a way to dispense with the entire Brewer management apparatus and install a directorial system of his own. They'd made a number of appeals to the Federated Commonwealth government, and then to the Lyran Alliance, he knew, but he'd expected nothing serious to come from *that* direction. So long as Hesperus II was turning out BattleMechs, the powers-that-be were happy. Four months ago the Brewer family had actually tried mounting a commando raid aimed at capturing or killing the duke. That had been right after Gareth's return from Glengarry, and he'd been in no mood to put up with what amounted to a minor civil war on his home ground.

The commandos had been freelancers—mercenaries hired by Thadeus Brewer, a cousin who stood to be named CEO if anything happened to Daniel. Gareth had rounded up a handful of Companions, his personal elite guard, and held out for two hours against the commandos as they stormed the command complex in heavy battle armor. The last of the attackers had been gunned down just outside this office; by that time, Gareth's 'Mechs were in the streets of Maria's Elegy, hunting down the mercenary BattleMechs operating in support of the raiders.

Thadeus had been captured at the spaceport trying to escape; Gareth himself had shot the would-be duke after his interrogation was complete. The body had been destroyed, partly to hide the evidence of torture, partly to scare the rest of the family, who would never know for sure what had happened to him. After that, the opposition had gone underground, and Gareth had thought that perhaps he was finally getting the upper hand.

But things were changing now with lightning speed, and maintaining his current advantage had taken formidable powers of manipulation and persuasion. Katrina Steiner's declaration of independence from the Federated Commonwealth raised the possibility that the long list of Brewer family grievances would be addressed. The Brewers had always been among the Steiner family's most ardent supporters. Too, Defiance Industries had offshoots on other worlds than Hesperus II, including Defiance Motors on Tharkad itself. There were plenty of people in the Tharkad Royal Court who had Katrina's ear, who would profit from continued Brewer control of the Defiance empire, and who either owed Gareth nothing, putting them beyond his control, or else hated or feared him for one reason or another, making them enemies.

That was the reason for Gareth's current haste. Naturally, he'd sworn fealty to Katrina in September when she'd made her announcement, and again, a few weeks later when she had named him Baron of Glengarry, but his very next act had been to set Excalibur rolling again at full speed. He had to work fast, and not just because there was a greater danger now of the Steiners intervening in the affairs on Hesperus II. Gareth saw opportunity here, as well as danger. Katrina's succession and the creation of the Lyran Alliance was simply a continuation of the Skye Rebellion on a larger scale—and evidence of a drastic acceleration in the breakup and collapse of the entire Inner Sphere.

A touch of a desk control wiped away the view of the Defiance Industry complex outside. In its place, a star map showed in three dimensions the sweep of space extending for fifty parsecs out from Hesperus II, a scattering of colored points of light, each tagged by glowing alphanumerics identifying that system and its attendant worlds and deep space facilities.

Chaos and anarchy. Those would be the dominant political forces of the future, of that Gareth was convinced. Operation Excalibur was aimed at nothing less than the creation of a new interstellar state, one carved from the dying carcass of the Federated Commonwealth and stretching—initially, at least—from Hesperus and Caledonia all the way to Skye. Another opportunity like this one might never come again, as the old holdings of the Great Houses crumbled. Reportedly, that was happening already in the old Sarna March, where worlds once belonging to the Free Worlds League and the Capellans were being reclaimed or splintering into tiny, war-torn and scattered shards. *That* was the future of the Inner Sphere.

Except in places where a strong man could seize and hold power now, before the breakup had gone too far.

Lovingly, he studied each point of light, each representing its own set of problems, its own challenges. He'd color-coded them according to their place in Excalibur. Hesperus, for all intents and purposes, was already his and would be his base for further conquests. He'd wanted Glengarry next, some sixteen parsecs distant, partly because it held a strategic location in this stretch of space, partly because it was home base and headquarters for the Gray Death Legion, a mercenary unit with an atypical—and therefore worrisome—loyalty to House Steiner. Laiaka and Alkaid, Gladius and Seginus were the next four systems on the list, lying between the first two and creating a solid base for further operations in several directions.

And beyond—Kochab, Carsphairn, and Chaffee, certainly. Caledonia, lying as close as it did to Hesperus. Lamon and Trent. Possibly several worlds closer to the border with the Draconis Combine, like Alphecca and Skondia. By then, he would be in an excellent position to move against Skye itself, and then the capital of the entire Skye region would be his.

As the Great Houses crumbled, new ones would arise, supplanting them, feeding on their bodies. He clapped his hands together, rubbing them briskly. House Steiner, House Davion, House Marik. They were all old, old and doddering and growing more feeble by the year.

His house, House Gareth, was destined . . . yes, *destined* to be first and greatest of the new, a beacon that would light civilization's way for the next thousand years.

And it was just possible that by eliminating the Gray Death Legion, he'd removed the final barrier to that glorious future.

16

Approaching Morningstar Spaceport
Maria's Elegy
Hesperus II, Rahneshire
Lyran Alliance
0912 hours (local), 15 November 3057

The *Seeker* Class DropShip punched down through high-piled clouds that dazzled the eye with their reflection of the actinic light of the Hesperan sun. The main drive lit with a thunderous, bucking roar. Grayson Carlyle lay in his cabin, strapped down against the accelerations and thumps of the DropShip's atmosphere entry maneuvers, watching the cloudscape unfold below on the viewscreen mounted above his couch. From here, the face of Hesperus II presented a dazzling white surface, a vast expanse of sun-gleaming clouds interrupted only occasionally by patches of emptiness through which the surface beneath could be briefly glimpsed.

With gunshot suddenness, the spherical DropShip punched into the cloud deck, flooding the cabin with misty white light.

And then an instant later, the clouds parted beneath the falling DropShip, and Grayson saw for the first time the mighty mountains of Hesperus.

It took a moment—and a fast keyboard query of the computer displaying the image on-screen—to orient himself. Assuming that this was South Whitman, those would be the Myoo Mountains down there . . . and so *that* peak should be Mount Defiance. The landscape had a seared, tortured look to it, all rugged mountains, deep and sinuous valleys with floors of thick, purplish vegetation, ice-glint from the tallest mountains, some of which must be well over ten thousand meters tall. Mount Defiance had an artificial appearance from the air, its sides shaped by other than natural forces, with the patchwork of factories, storehouses, and defense nets laid out in chessboard patterns covering hundreds of hectares around the mountain. He could see the spaceport and the gray knotting of buildings and streets that must be Maria's Elegy fanning out from the western face of a cliff in the early morning shadow of Mount Defiance.

Defiance Industries. *Every* MechWarrior knew about Defiance Industries. It was one of the largest, perhaps *the* largest, of all 'Mech manufactory complexes. Ever since the fall of the Star League, House Steiner had depended on this complex, one of the precious few remaining factories where fusion plants, high-tech weapons, and BattleMechs were still manufactured.

And the 'Mechs they made there . . . The newer designs, the *Battle Hawk, Gunslinger, Salamander,* and *Nightsky* (which Grayson always wanted to pronounce night-ski, as though it were a Slavic design). Among the older, time-tested and battle-proven designs, there was the redoubtable *Zeus* and the incomparable, the unforgettable hundred-ton *Atlas*.

And who could forget the *Hatchetman*? Grayson grinned to himself. Well, six out of seven wasn't so bad, though he had to admit the *Hatchetman* was a decent enough 'Mech, if a bit under-gunned. It was the right-hand hatchet gimmick that had always bothered him. In his book, club weapons were the absolute last recourse in 'Mech-to-'Mech combat; he'd always insisted that any Hatchetman serving in the Legion dispense with the thing in favor of some extra torso armor in the rear, where the 'Mech was pitifully weak, or an upgraded right-arm laser.

It was still an impressive list of BattleMechs. And to that list several varieties of armored vehicle and transport, a number of BattleMech weapons, communications, power, and targeting/tracking systems, and the fusion packs produced by Defiance Motors, and it was immediately clear just how important Defiance Industries was to House Steiner.

Grayson turned his head in his acceleration couch, taking a sidelong glance at his traveling companion in the rather close confines of the DropShip cabin. Colonel Charles Dillon had accompanied him out on the passage all the way from Tharkad, along with an escort of twelve troopers. Dillon had been one of the members of the board of inquiry.

And, according to Schubert, he was Brandal Gareth's man.

Grayson turned his head back and watched the wall screen. The vibration and the thunder increased as the DropShip's pilot throttled up to 110 percent, riding the *Seeker* down on its ground-pointed pillar of star-hot plasma.

The *Seeker* DropShip—Grayson never had learned the vessel's name and thought it was probably a number rather than something more picturesque—was supposedly registered in Gareth's name. That in itself was impressive; DropShips were fairly precious technological resources, and owners, whether governments, mercenary unit commanders, or private operators, did not lightly refit them from their original specs. Though the *Seeker* was normally a military fast transport designed to carry scout battalions in and out of hostile zones, this one had been converted to courier service by pulling out troop and equipment bay fittings and replacing them with passenger modules. Massing 3,700 tons and measuring about 90 meters across, it was only a bit larger than the ubiquitous *Union* Class DropShip, but its powerful Quad RanTech fusion drive accounted for a good third of that mass. The *Seeker* had a steady-boost acceleration nearly twice that of a *Union,* which had cut the passage time from Tharkad to Tharkad's nadir point, then from the Hesperan zenith point to Hesperus II by considerable margins, shaving several days off the entire trip.

The journey, Grayson reflected, had been a tedious one nonetheless. The long, empty recharge times had been the worst. The JumpShip *Enif* had made the passage in four jumps: Tharkad to Thuban, Thuban to Colinas, Colinas to Furillo, and Furillo to Hesperus, but that was still nearly three weeks of hanging useless in micro-A, waiting . . .

and fretting. He thought again of Lori and McCall and the others. They ought to be back in the Glengarry system by now, though the DropShips would just be beginning the journey from jump point to world. He called to mind again the various ship schedules he'd studied with Lori back on Tharkad. Yes, the timing was just about right.

And Alex. How was he getting along? There was no way to maintain communication with him. Not that Alex wanted any, just now. Grayson wondered if his own behavior seemed as bizarre to Lori and Alex and Davis and the rest as it felt to him.

God, he *hated* the waiting.

Well, the waiting was almost over, though Grayson still wished to hell he didn't have to go through with this. If there had been any other way under heaven . . .

The DropShip was descending faster now, still balanced on its pillar of fire. The camera transmitting the image to Grayson's screen was mounted somewhere amidships and aimed aft past the torch. He couldn't see the flame, but the picture was wavering now as the *Seeker* descended through roiling currents of superheated air created by its ravening jets. The Morningstar Spaceport appeared centered in the screen, a roughly circular gray patch occupying the lopped-off top of a mountain just outside the cramped, uneven urban sprawl of Maria's Elegy.

"It can get really hot down there, y'know," Dillon said from his couch. Grayson glanced at him and the FedCom colonel gave a wide, oily grin. "Especially in the deeper valleys. Sometimes I think that's why Gareth was so eager to grab Glengarry for himself, y'know? I hear it's a lot cooler there."

Grayson didn't rise to the bait. Throughout the passage, it had seemed to him that Dillon was testing him, pushing him, seeing how far he must go to provoke some sort of response to his jibes.

"The temperature's largely pressure-dependent, y'know," Dillon continued. "Because the gravity's a bit higher than standard, the pressure gradient is steeper with altitude. The air gets thinner, faster, as you go up, know what I mean?"

Grayson remained silent, merely continuing to stare at

the screen, hoping that Dillon would take the hint and shut up. It didn't work.

"So in the day, it gets beastly hot, thirty, maybe forty degrees. At night, though, the temperature drops a bit and that makes the atmosphere thicken up in the lowlands, where it's always hot. But it gets colder up on the heights where the cities and factories are. And then there's winter. Hesperus doesn't have much of an axial tilt, but its orbit's a bit eccentric. In wintertime, that sun can be so tiny and far off, and the temperature up at Maria's Elegy can drop to twenty below or worse. Doesn't snow much, 'cause the air gets thin and dry in winter, but that wind comes whipping down off the glacier and, I'll tell you, it'll freeze a 'Mech's silicarb solid in twenty minutes flat. . . ."

Grayson let the man prattle on, making uncommunicative grunts from time to time. Dillon had been garrulous and overfriendly throughout the voyage from Tharkad. At first, Grayson had wondered if he was trying to make amends for having been on the tribunal that had judged him. It was hard to tell for certain, but as time went on, Grayson suspected that Dillon was trying a bit of applied psychology; the authority figure who'd passed judgment on him was now extending the hand of friendship and equality. Such a shift in attitude could knock its victim off balance, setting him up for something else.

And, just possibly, it was the prelude to a real scam.

Grayson had used similar tactics to good effect himself more times than he could recall.

" 'Mech operations are always a bit hairy on Hesperus II," Dillon continued. "It's either too hot or too cold, and it's always too rugged. Still, I think you'll be impressed by what you see when we land."

"I'm sure I will be."

Grayson had been as noncommittal as possible throughout the past month of traveling. It was Gareth he wanted to talk to, not this garrulous, sycophantic underling. Grayson despised the man, not so much for his part in the tribunal on Tharkad as for his evident duplicity, working both for the Federated Commonwealth and for his real master, Brandal Gareth.

The DropShip's roar increased, assaulting Grayson's ears and body and mind. He closed his eyes, trying to lose unpleasant thoughts in that shuddering, bouncing thunder.

Moments later, when he opened his eyes once more, there was nothing on the viewscreen save jet-scorched ferrocrete seen intermittently through billowing clouds of smoke. The *Seeker*'s landing legs were out; when the pads touched down, there was the slightest of jolts and the yielding sensation of hydraulic jacks taking up the Dropship's weight.

"Well," Dillon said, unbuckling his harness. "We're home."

Grayson kept his thoughts carefully to himself as he gathered his gear—a single carry case with a couple of changes of clothing and his toiletries. The case felt heavier—*he* felt heavier—than what he tended to think of as normal. The surface gravity on Hesperus II, he recalled, was a nagging, unpleasantly wearying 1.34 Gs, a third again greater than Tharkad's. It wasn't bothersome at the moment; he'd had several days aboard the DropShip under a higher acceleration than this to get his G-legs back. Still, months or years of this could wear at a man. He much preferred Tharkad's surface gravity, or Glengarry's, where he didn't feel as though he were carrying a large child on his back.

The DropShip's other passengers were debarking from the vessel's lower bay. A crewman stood inside the inner airlock door leading out, passing out electronic goggles. "Better take these, sir," the rating said, handing a pair first to Dillon, then another set to Grayson. "You glance at that sun up there by mistake and you're not wearing these babies—"

He left the sentence incomplete. Grayson accepted the goggles and slid them into place over his head. The lenses gave him a clear and undistorted view of his surroundings, even in the low light of the debarkation area. Their electronics, however, would filter out any harmful radiation before it could damage his vision.

As he stepped off the boarding ramp and onto the ferrocrete, Grayson immediately noticed two things. First, and most demanding, was the heat, a sweltering, humid, steaming heat that struck him like a physical blow as he left the air-conditioning of the DropShip. The sun was an intense, blue-white spark glaring down through a rift in the clouds, uncomfortable to look at even with the goggles' self-adjusting filters. Strangely, the sun looked *cold,* so shrunken did it appear, like an intensely brilliant, ice-blue star that could not possibly give off any heat. The heat felt more like a product of this thick, clinging, steamy atmosphere than something given off by that chill-looking sun.

The second thing he noticed, once he'd gotten clear of the DropShip's overhang and had a chance to look around, was a long, long line of other DropShips grounded at the spaceport. The nearest was perhaps half a kilometer away, and it towered above its landing pit like a mammoth, inverted top, squat and rounded at the base, longer and more elongated toward the blunt prow. He knew that design.

The *Excalibur* Class was one of the largest DropShips in general service, a titanic vessel measuring 124.9 meters from stern jets to bow, with a diameter of 113 meters across the fattest part of the waist. The monster massed 16,000 tons; a single *Excalibur* normally carried one complete combined-arms regiment, composed of an infantry battalion, two tank battalions, and a BattleMech company. A relatively simple conversion could extend that to a 'Mech battalion—thirty-six BattleMechs—plus technical crews, spares, and an infantry company in support.

Grayson could see nine *Excalibur*s lined up in a row, sitting along the port's ferrocrete horizon like immense, squat eggs. Depending on how they were configured, that represented transport for either three or nine 'Mech battalions.

Was that array planned for another try against Glengarry, he wondered? Or did Brandal Gareth have some other target, some other prey in mind?

"Gareth has big plans, Colonel," Dillon told him, following his long gaze at the *Excalibur*s. "Big plans. Play your cards right, and you can be a part of 'em!"

"That," Grayson said carefully, "is exactly why I'm here."

Reluctantly, he followed Dillon across the spaceport field toward a waiting transport vehicle.

Brandal Gareth studied the two men on the monitor screen on his desk. They were on their way to his office,

traversing the passageway on Level Eighteen, followed
every step of the way by a security-monitor drone. He
watched as they stopped at a checkpoint, then touched a
key so he could see the security scan as they walked
through. Seen from the side now, instead of from overhead, the men's figures were shadowy, their skeletons visible as shifting black bones embedded in the lighter grays
of clothing, muscles, and internal organs. A pistol, all
black in hard-edged angles, the internal mechanism and
bullets seen as even blacker shapes inside, was clearly
visible riding under Dillon's left arm; the security monitor zeroed in on the weapon with red brackets—then immediately overrode itself with a winking green light and
the weapon's authorization code.

Grayson Carlyle was carrying no weapons, though his
left arm showed as a complex and tightly organized mass
of metal parts, circuitry, and wiring. The security system
gave the artificial arm an extra careful going-over, but
turned up no obvious weapon parts. It was certainly possible that a small gun of some sort, or the disassembled
pieces of a weapon, could be hidden in there, but Gareth
was pretty sure that this was no assassination attempt.
From what Dillon had told him in his last HPG transmission, the former commander of the Gray Death was indeed desperate, but not so desperate as to be looking for
a spectacular means of committing suicide.

Stroking his chin, Gareth thought about Felix Zellner,
the Lyran marshal who had been a part of his cabal,
working to turn the Skye Separatist Movement into a
power base for Gareth's revolution. A year ago, Gareth
and Zellner together had discussed what to do about the
founder and commander of the merc unit known as the
Gray Death Legion.

Something had to be done. The Gray Death enjoyed a
formidable reputation. In existence for over thirty years,
the unit had racked up an impressive list of campaigns,
victories, most of them, and even the defeats had been
masterpieces of tactics that had extracted advantage—or
survival—out of seemingly hopeless situations facing impossible odds. Seven years ago, they'd fought the Clans,
and the fact that they still existed as a combat unit itself
said something about their abilities. They'd fought on the
side of the Federated Commonwealth in the Skye Rebel-

lion, holding onto Glengarry when the Separatists had seized that world, waging a savage guerilla war in the planet's hill country until reinforcements could break the Separatist blockade and lift the siege.

So they were good. *Very* good. And they were loyal to House Steiner, loyal to a degree that transcended anything Gareth had ever heard of in a mercenary unit. So loyal that Gareth had from the start ruled out trying to hire the Gray Death himself.

Of the various other military units in the Excalibur Area of Operations, or EAO, most were either strictly local defenses, planetary militias and such, or regular Lyran troops and 'Mech forces. There were a few other mercenary units in the area, but none of the same caliber as the Gray Death.

The local militias were scarcely worth Gareth's notice. Small, poorly equipped, with only handfuls of outdated and much-patched 'Mechs, they would offer no resistance at all when the time came and Excalibur's final phase began to roll.

And Gareth expected that he would be able to handle the regular Lyran units without much more trouble than the militias would cause. Once the commit order was delivered, his military forces would be moving swiftly to secure key points in several key systems, including the zenith and nadir jump points to prevent any large-scale movement of troops in or out of a given system. Tharkad would be paralyzed for a time and would hesitate to move any of its garrison forces off-world, wanting to wait until they knew exactly what was happening, what was diversionary and what was real. By the time they began to move in anything like an organized fashion, Gareth's people would be in position on and around a dozen worlds, ready for anything Katrina Steiner could throw at him.

The only unknowns—as was very often the case in long-term strategic planning—were the mercenaries.

Zellner, Gareth thought with a half smile, had hated mercs. He'd been fond of quoting a passage from Machiavelli's *The Prince* that described what scagbags mercenary soldiers really were. "If any one supports his state by the arms of mercenaries," that passage went, "he will never stand firm or sure. . . ."

Despite that, Zellner had suggested an alternative to

simply assassinating Carlyle and his senior officers. None of the other merc units in the EAO posed much of a threat. They could be bought . . . or they could be crushed with little trouble. The Gray Death Legion, however, was something else, a full regiment strong and enough to cause Excalibur some serious trouble, loyal to the opposition, apparently unbuyable. Simply getting into a standup fight with the Legion at this point, no matter what the final outcome, could well weaken Gareth's forces to the point where they'd not be able to hold against the Lyran Alliance troops when they inevitably arrived on the scene.

Gareth had tried assassination, hoping to cripple the Legion by eliminating its commander, but without success. He'd been planning on trying again, but Zellner had proposed something else, a way of getting the Gray Death out of the way without further assassination attempts. Gareth had agreed to it only reluctantly.

His alternative had been brilliant. If the Gray Death could be crippled by forcing it into a situation where it would disgrace itself no matter what happened, or what it did . . .

That had been the idea, and it had worked. Gareth had gotten Carlyle assigned to Caledonia, but Zellner had not lived to see his plan come to fruition. He'd been at Falkirk when Carlyle split his forces, sending most of his troops on a flank march through thick woods to hit Zellner's force in the flank and rear. Zellner's *Atlas* had been blown apart after a hard fight, and he hadn't been able to eject in time.

Briefly, Gareth had considered going back to assassination. The people he'd tried to plant on Glengarry after the recent fight there were intended as assassins, if the opportunity presented itself, as well as intelligence agents. Unfortunately, none had reported in after being left behind, and Gareth was forced to assume that the Legion's intelligence corps had spotted and picked them up. The Legion still remained a potentially deadly obstacle to Operation Excalibur.

And then, almost as if through a miracle, Zellner's plan had borne its fruit. Carlyle, critically wounded at Falkirk by another assassination attempt made during the battle, had been a long time recovering. And then he'd had to present himself to the tribunal on Tharkad, to answer for that damned-if-you-do, damned-if-you-don't situation he'd found himself in on Caledonia. Working through his influence on Tharkad, Gareth had been able to plant Colonel Dillon on the tribunal, simply as an extra precautionary measure. In fact, the precaution hadn't been necessary. The case, from what Dillon had been able to report, had been pretty much open and shut; Katrina Steiner herself had contributed to Carlyle's collapse by stripping him of both his title and his landhold.

Which had effectively removed the Gray Death Legion from the equation, exactly as Zellner had predicted.

And now, if Dillon's supposition were true, it was just possible that Gareth would have the Legion working for him instead of Steiner after all.

The two visitors were now through the security scan area and on an elevator, descending through the mountain's core toward Gareth's office.

Smiling, he prepared to receive them.

17

Planetary Defense Command, Maria's Elegy
Hesperus II, Rahneshire
Lyran Alliance
1165 hours (local), 15 November 3057

The door to Gareth's inner sanctum slid aside, and Grayson followed Colonel Dillon through. The office was expensively decorated, he saw, its sleek and modern furnishings contrasting sharply with the view of Maria's Elegy showing on the wall screen.

Though he'd heard a lot about Brandal Gareth, Grayson had never met the man, and the information in his public biography was somewhat lacking in anything beyond the rather dry facts of military academy and campaign service. He was a large man, somewhat overweight, but brawnier than he was fat, with meaty hands and a muscular build. He wore the closely tailored, green and blue uniform of a Lyran Alliance Armed Forces officer, with the four-pointed device of a hauptmann-general on collar and epaulets. Medals gleamed at his left breast. A large, heavy, silver hammer hung on the wall at his back, and the matching decoration rode on his uniform jacket just above the rack of medals. The McKennsy Hammer.

"Field Marshal Gareth," Dillon said, saluting, addressing him by his old FedCom title. "Good morning, sir."

"Colonel Dillon," Gareth acknowledged, looking up

and returning the salute with a casual toss of his hand. "Did you have a good trip in?"

"Excellent, sir, if tedious, as usual. Field Marshal, may I present Colonel Grayson Death Carlyle, of the Gray Death Legion. Colonel Carlyle? Field Marshal Brandal Gareth, Commander of the Hesperus Defense Force."

"A pleasure, Field Marshal," Grayson said, snapping off a Lyran military salute.

"Colonel Carlyle," Gareth replied, nodding, but not bothering to return the salute. "I've heard a great deal about you."

"And I feel as though I already know you, sir. Colonel Dillon here has told me a lot about you on our flight out."

Gareth glanced at Dillon, then gave a frosty smile. "Nothing too unflattering, I trust."

"Not at all, sir."

"Colonel Dillon tells me you wanted to meet with me," Gareth continued, "and that you had an interesting proposition you wished to discuss."

Grayson smiled. "I hope something of mutual benefit, sir. And mutual profit."

Gareth sighed, shifting back in his seat. "Perhaps Colonel Dillon did not explain to you, Colonel, that I *don't* care much for mercenaries. I have no use for them, in fact. I can't imagine what you have to offer that I might be the least interested in."

Grayson hesitated before pushing ahead. Dillon had been a bit more encouraging when he'd talked with him back on Tharkad, shortly after Lori and the rest had departed for home.

"I'm sure you know by now what has happened to me," he said, "and why. I don't know why you were interested in Glengarry, but it's obvious you are. Sir, I'm here to offer you Glengarry on a platter."

Gareth smiled, an unsettling showing of teeth in his fleshy face. "You've been in transit for some time, Colonel. Perhaps you are not aware that I have already been named Baron Glengarry."

"I heard." Grayson paused a moment for effect before adding, "Your grace."

"So I don't really need your help, do I?"

"Possibly not. But I do hear you're looking for 'Mechs.

And good men and women." He hesitated again, before deliberately adding a single word. *"Excalibur."*

Gareth's bushy dark eyebrows came together, and his bland expression molded itself into the darkest of scowls. He looked at Dillon, who raised his hands and shook his head, as though saying, *"I* didn't tell him."

In fact, that word had been dropped in Grayson's ear by Davis McCall, scant hours before he'd boarded the DropShip for Glengarry. Grayson jerked his thumb back over his shoulder. "I saw that line of *Excalibur*s out at the spaceport. I'm assuming you need some 'Mechs to go in 'em, right?"

Gareth regarded Grayson in silence for a long moment, as though wondering exactly what to do with him. "I think, Colonel Carlyle, that you had better explain yourself."

"I don't know that much, your grace," Grayson told him. "But I know that you're, well . . . *ambitious* isn't too strong a word, is it?"

"One doesn't rise to the rank of field marshal without being ambitious, Colonel," Gareth said quietly. "But there *are* limits to ambition."

Grayson shrugged. "Maybe I've made a mistake, then. I thought you were trying to put together a sizable 'Mech force. A bigger force than you would need just to make up your losses at Glengarry."

Gareth's face clouded darker at that gentle dig. "Yes, well, we did suffer substantial losses at the hand of the Legion," he said. "This is supposed to incline me to look favorably on your people?"

"Which would you rather have, Field Marshal? The Gray Death Legion as enemies? Or as part of what you're trying to do out here?"

"I thought you only worked for House Steiner?"

Grayson shrugged and folded his arms over his chest. "Thirty years, almost. And what thanks do I get?" He nodded at Dillon. "He can tell you. They wouldn't even let the Legion remain intact unless I promised to resign. They *did* let me turn operations over to my exec, who also happens to be my wife, so they had to know they weren't cutting me out of it entirely, but the Legion is in serious trouble now."

"Can't your wife handle it?" Gareth said, partly masking his smile with one hand.

"Oh, she can handle it fine, thank you. She handled *you* well enough, while I was in a medical coma. Right?"

"That's hardly germane to the issue." Gareth started to rise from behind his desk. "Colonel, I regret you made such a long journey here to see me with nothing to show for it at the end, but—"

"Sir, please. Hear me out. I've got—*Lori's* got, I should say—three BattleMech battalions, a combined arms infantry battalion, an armor battalion, scout and intelligence units, nine DropShips, and two wings of aerospace fighters. Damn near two thousand people, the very best. They're based right this moment on Glengarry, on *your* world, sir.

"Now think about all those people. Two thirds, maybe three quarters have roots on Glengarry. A lot of them were from Glengarry in the first place. Others have married local gals or guys or at least set up housekeeping with them. Given the choice, they'd rather stay on Glengarry, no matter who they're working for."

"Colonel Carlyle does have the reputation, sir," Dillon said, "of always looking out for the best interests of the people in his command."

"I am well aware of Colonel Carlyle's reputation," Gareth said. He continued to study Grayson, as though measuring him with his eyes. "I repeat, Colonel. Why should any of this be of interest of me? I have everything I need without your, ah, *help*."

Grayson clenched his jaws so tightly that his teeth ached. He'd thought he was above such testosterone-laced idiocy as proving himself worthy, beyond hindrances like ego and pride. He was realizing now that he couldn't simply dismiss such emotions. He was doing this, had come here to meet this man for this purpose, because he was convinced that it was right, not to mention that it was likely the only way he could save the Legion. Love of the Legion was what was driving him now. He'd thought that in the name of the Legion, he could easily do whatever was required.

But to *grovel* before this man, to beg for the lives of his people . . .

"I . . . I'm begging, Field Marshal," Grayson said. He

stopped, swallowed, then tried to put more strength, more firmness into his words. "I'm begging you, sir, for the lives of my people."

Gareth favored him with an oily smile. "I . . . see. And what could your people do for me, once I'm officially invested as Baron of Glengarry?"

Grayson shrugged, spreading his hands. "Our combat record is unsurpassed, Field Marshal. As I'm sure you're well aware."

"You are mercenaries."

"Technically, yes, sir. We started out as a merc unit, a long time ago. But if you'll look at our record, you'll see that the vast majority of our service was to the same employer. House Steiner."

"Which is why I fear I will not be able to use your people, Colonel. My interests and House Steiner's . . . may well diverge at some future date."

Hit! Grayson thought to himself, fiercely. It was the first admission he'd heard that might point to Gareth's true plans.

"Of course. Permit me, sir, to put it this way," Grayson said, presenting the words with the care of an unarmored man stepping through a minefield. "If we . . . if the Legion, I mean, is forced to leave Glengarry, it means the destruction of the unit. Most people will have to leave, because there won't be that much left for them on Glengarry. The area around Dunkeld, well, the Legion is pretty much what keeps that whole district alive.

"Now some of those folks are liable to stay, and I won't be able to vouch for their behavior once the Legion's gone. And they're liable to resent the change in the guard."

"Are you actually threatening me, Colonel?"

"Not at all, sir. I'm merely pointing out some possible consequences of your decision that you may not, in fact, have anticipated. Maybe you'll end up needing a larger garrison on Glengarry than you're allowing for in your plans right now. Or take damage that you weren't anticipating. All I'm suggesting is that you have an opportunity here to *add* a sizable and experienced force to your inventory, rather than tie one down."

Grayson was watching Gareth closely. He saw the man's nostrils flare slightly, saw the tip of his tongue touch his lips. He was interested, certainly. But was he interested enough?

"You are most eloquent, Colonel. There is still the matter of your traditional service with House Steiner."

"We were fired, remember? I'm sure Colonel Dillon, here, has filled you in on the board of inquiry."

"Mmm. Yes, he has. Tell me, Colonel, what about you?"

"What about me?"

"Where do your loyalties lie, if I might ask?"

"Not with House Steiner, that's for damned sure." Grayson sighed. "I don't really know, sir. I figured I'd stay with the Legion, maybe bossing one of the battalions, if that satisfies the adjudication board. There's not a lot else I *can* do."

"Would you consider working for me?"

Grayson's eyes widened. "You mean ... *not* with the Legion?"

"It occurs to me, Colonel, that we might indeed be able to work something out here. To tell you the truth, it would be most convenient if the Gray Death simply stayed where they were, but under *my* command instead of that of House Steiner. And you, well, sir, you have a certain reputation as a tactician and a strategist that may well surpass your Legion's reputation as a crack Battle-Mech regiment."

"You are ... too kind, sir."

"Not at all." Gareth waved a hand carelessly. "Not at all. I don't make idle flattery. Now, you do understand that I will have to take certain precautions?"

Grayson had been expecting something like this. "Of course. You think I might still be mad at you over your invasion of Glengarry."

He chuckled. "You don't seem to be the sort of man to carry a grudge, Carlyle. And you're too practical to be guided by something as cheap and as shallow as vengeance. No, Glengarry was, well, a part of doing business, and I think you are businessman enough to understand that. But we are on rather delicate ground here. This could be some sort of elaborate trap, you know, to get me to commit an act that Steiner could call treason. You're already under that cloud. I am not."

That was true enough. "So you want a guarantee that I

won't tell Katrina Steiner about what you're doing out here. That's fine. What did you have in mind, my family? Lori is running the Legion. In a sense, she's already hostage, since she would be working for you. My son, well . . ." He made a sour face.

"Alexander Carlyle resigned from the Legion at Tharkad, sir," Dillon put in. "He's been accepted in the First Royal Guard."

"So?" Gareth looked at Grayson with even more interest. "Interesting. Does this affect your feelings in the matter at all, Colonel?"

"You mean . . . the possibility that I might wind up fighting against my son?" Grayson shrugged again. "In the first place, it was his decision to leave the Legion because he thought he didn't have a future there. Maybe he was right. But, well, he'll have to accept the consequences of his decision, whatever they are. In the second place, the Royal Guard regiments generally stay on Tharkad. I can't see them being deployed clear out here for anything short of a complete breakdown of the border."

"I heard they were being held in reserve at Tharkad against a renewal of hostilities by the Clans," Dillon said.

"Whatever. In any case, I doubt we'll have to worry about shooting at one another."

"That's reasonable. Still, I didn't have hostages in mind. Do you think me a barbarian, Colonel?"

"Not at all. But you *are* practical."

"Thank you. No, I was thinking of something a little more . . . direct." Reaching out, Gareth touched a key on his desk console. "Lauren? Send him in, please."

A moment later, the door to Gareth's office slid aside and a major in a gaudily formal LAAF dress uniform entered. Grayson knew the man.

"Dupré!"

"Good morning, Colonel," the newcomer said. He was tall and capable-looking, with dark hair and a thin, aristocratic mustache. "I'm pleased you recognize me."

"Recognize you? Do you think I'd *forget*?" Until he'd recommended Dupré for promotion, Grayson had always considered himself a good judge of men.

Walter Dupré was the MechWarrior, newly signed on with the Legion, who'd won Grayson's confidence months before by seeming to foil an assassination plot, working his way into a position of trust. While piloting his *Zeus* at Falkirk, he'd slipped behind Grayson's *Victor* and opened fire. Grayson looked down at his left hand. *That*—and the fact that he would never again pilot a BattleMech—was Walter Dupré's doing. . . .

"Major Dupré has been a most valuable operative, Colonel," Gareth said. "And he is about to prove his worth once again."

"How? Your grace."

"By serving as your aide while you're working for me. And, of course, by reporting to me what you do, who you talk to, things of that nature."

Grayson eyed Dupré with distaste.

"Come, come, Colonel," Gareth chided. "I recognize that you may still harbor some ill will against the good major, but, as you say, I'm practical. And you are a good businessman. Major Dupré will be my insurance policy that this is not an elaborate hoax on your part. Do we have a deal?"

"A deal?" Grayson felt a fluttering of hope. "As in—"

Gareth nodded. "I will sign on the Gray Death Legion, a standard trial contract for . . . shall we say, one year? And I would like to sign a separate contract with you. I need a top strategist in my Operations Division. Are you interested?"

"*Am* I?" The relief Grayson felt surged like an incoming tide. The Legion would be *all right.* . . .

"As it happens," Gareth continued, "I *do* have need for a good mercenary BattleMech unit as well. I, ah, trust that when you tell me how attached your people are to Glengarry, you don't mean to say that they will refuse to serve elsewhere?"

"Of course not. They just need a place of their own to come home to."

"Understood." Gareth grinned. "Otherwise, they become rather hard to control, am I right?"

"Something like that. But if you sign their pay order, Field Marshal, they'll go anywhere you tell them to, in or out of the Inner Sphere!"

"I didn't have that extensive a voyage planned, actually. What I had in mind was . . . right here. On *this* world."

Grayson blinked. "Hesperus II?"

"That's it." Gareth nodded and touched a control on his desk. The viewscreen blanked, then showed a graphic—the organizational networks for three BattleMech units. Two were full regiments, Grayson saw. The third was an understrength local militia battalion, the Defiance Self-Protection Force, nicknamed the Catamounts.

Gareth indicated one of the regiments. "The Third Davion Guard," he said proudly, "is mine. *All* mine."

Grayson gave him a sidelong look. "And how did you manage *that,* your grace?"

He chuckled. "Wasn't hard. It might have been a Davion unit originally, but it's been here on Hesperus II for a long time. Those who didn't like living here rotated out long ago. Those that liked it, or who could tolerate it, at any rate, stayed. Like you said about your people, Carlyle. They put down roots. Married people living here in Maria's Elegy, or in the communities nearby. The place isn't much, but it's home to several million people."

"It didn't look that big from the air, your grace."

"Most of it's underground. With the factories. Who would want to live on the surface of this hell-rock? Anyway, I've been able to bring in a lot of my own people as well. The Third Davion is now at full strength, *despite* Caledonia and Glengarry, I might add. Marshal James Seymour in command, and he's part of . . . part of my organization.

"This other regiment is, well, let's say the Fifteenth Lyran Guard is *mostly* mine."

Grayson raised his eyebrows at that. "A Lyran Guard unit? They're usually pretty fanatical supporters of House Steiner."

Gareth smiled at the implied compliment. "Well, I've had a fair amount of say in having new MechWarriors and officers transferred into the unit in the past five years, and I've been able to nullify the, shall we say, *unreliable* companies by having them posted to several key defensive possessions scattered across different parts of Hesperus. The Melrose Valley. The shipyard facilities at the system's zenith point. Out-of-the-way spots like that. There's still a certain amount of devotion to the Steiners there, of course. It couldn't be otherwise. I remember, back during the Skye rebellion last year, some of them nearly mutinied against the Federated Commonwealth in favor of the separatist Steiner government. Well, you can imagine how wild they went when Katrina Steiner decided to secede from the Federated Commonwealth. The bars in Maria's Elegy are still trying to recover from their celebration. There have even been some incidents between members of the Third and the Fifteenth, including a couple of highly unauthorized duels.

"The real problem, though, is the Fifteenth's commander. Her name is Marshal Gina Ciampa, and I haven't been able to reach her. To make her see the common sense of our cause. Soon, the Third Davion Guard is going to deploy elsewhere. I will want your Legion, or a large part of it, at any rate, to redeploy temporarily to Hesperus II."

"To fight Ciampa?"

"Or block her. Whatever is necessary. Two of the Fifteenth Lyran's battalions are reliable and will do what I tell them to. Her First Battalion, though, is fanatically loyal to her. I'll want the Legion to block that battalion, as necessary, and to hold Hesperus II while my other forces execute the rest of the operation."

Grayson pointed at the DSPF militia's symbol on the screen. "And the Catamounts?"

"Pro-Lyran. Pro-Ciampa, I should say, since she's been working to upgrade their training, and a lot of their best people are former members of the Fifteenth. Definitely pro-Steiner. But they won't be a major factor. *Believe me.*"

"I do. I'm more concerned about Marshal Ciampa. If she's strongly pro-Steiner—" Grayson stopped and gave a wry grin. "Have you thought about assassination? You tried it on me a time or two." He glanced at Dupré. "Damn near carried it off, too."

"Hell, that wasn't *my* idea," Gareth said, looking surprised. "One of my subordinates, a marshal named Zellner, got a little, ah, *eager,* shall we say. He took things into his own hands, assuming that matters would go more smoothly if you were out of the way. But he died at Falkirk."

"I see."

"The problem with assassination as a tool of policy, Carlyle, is the fact that often the attempt fails. And that can end up being worse for your cause than the problem you were trying to correct. Even if you succeed, the victim can easily become a martyr to those most dedicated to him, or her, in this case. Ideally, I'd like to swing Miss Ciampa around to our cause. Failing that, your people will be more than sufficient to keep her from getting into any mischief."

"I see," Grayson said, thoughtful. "And just what *is* your cause, your grace?"

Gareth gave him a shuttered look. "In time, Colonel. All in good time. For now, all you need to know is that there is indeed such a cause, that it is called, as you somehow learned, Excalibur, and that it will change forever the shape of politics in this part of the Inner Sphere."

Grayson nodded slowly. "Your grace, I have no doubt about that whatsoever."

Isamu Yoshitomi looked up from his computer screen in Operations as the officers walked in. There were three of them—two, Dupré and Dillon, wore LAAF uniforms. The third, Yoshitomi would have recognized as a military officer despite the civilian clothing even if he hadn't known the man already. Grayson Carlyle's military bearing, that something about the way he carried himself and the look in his eyes, suggested a man used to giving commands and having them carried out.

He'd already seen Carlyle's name on the list of passengers aboard the incoming DropShip, so his presence was no surprise. His arrival here, however, suggested that he had indeed talked Gareth into hiring him and that Gareth was posting him here, in Ops.

Excellent. . . .

18

Castle Hill, Dunkeld
Glengarry, Virginia Shire
Lyran Alliance
1350 hours (standard), 17 November 3057

Major Davis McCall accepted the data storage cube from the comm tech. "Thanks, Maria."

"No problem, sir. I had it up on my screen as it came through. It looks like a lot of gibberish to me."

"Aye, lass. That's the whole point a' the thing, isn't it?"

"And you don't even trust *us*?" She grinned as she said the words, robbing them of any sting or accusation.

"Wi' this, lass, I would nae trust my ain poor auld maithair," Davis said with a twinkle, rolling his Rs and giving it his broadest Scot's burr. "But th' beauty of a cipher as opposed to a code is aye it's a hell of a lot harder for the opposition to break."

"No code or cipher is unbreakable, sir. Especially if you have a decent computer on your side."

"Perhaps." He tossed the small, plastic cube in the air, then caught it again. "Perhaps. But I'm willing to trust the Legion's future t' this one. The lad tha' worked it oot is a genius a' this sort of thing."

"Whatever you say, sir."

McCall walked back to his office, whistling tunelessly. The fact of the matter was, they *were* trusting the Legion's future to this cipher, and it made him more nervous than he cared to admit, even to himself.

In his office once more, he took the data cube and set it into the receiver on his computer. It was his own machine, one not hooked up to the Castle Hill network, an added piece of security that Isamu Yoshitomi had insisted on. He tapped out a coded entry, then waited as the computer processed the data.

In the murky world of cryptography, there was actually a fine and often blurred line between codes, which tended to retain a linguistic structure that could be analyzed, and ciphers, which did not. While no encryption could be one hundred percent secure, the best and most unbeatable ciphers were those that replied on a key unknown to any prospective enemy. This one used a computer encryption algorithm drawn from Glengarry's tide tables, an obscure source of constantly changing numbers guaranteed to keep any would-be eavesdroppers guessing for a long time. Yoshitomi had the same set of tables—disguised in his computer as part of a local time-conversion table— which allowed him to encode messages for HPG transmission with little chance of having them intercepted and read.

Of course, there was always the chance that Yoshitomi had been caught and the code tables drugged or tortured out of him, but even with that possibility, he'd left a safety hatch. Any message that did not include the name of a fruit at the end—and always a different one, to avoid giving Gareth's cryptoanalysts anything to work on— would tell McCall that his agent on Hesperus had been taken, and the coded messages were either being transmitted by Gareth's people, or by Yoshitomi himself under duress.

Yoshitomi, McCall reflected, had possessed a remarkably fatalistic demeanor about that, the knowledge that no one could hold out indefinitely against the mixture of drugs and physical persuasion common in the intelligence services of all of the Houses, and most independent military units as well. He thought again about the small, quiet Japanese mercenary; planting him in Gareth's organization six months earlier had been, McCall decided, one of the sharper moves of his career. The man had already been worth his weight in iridium in both the quality and the quantity of information he'd returned. He shook his head. No matter how you cut it, this whole op would have been impossible without decent intel.

His door chimed. "Aye?" he called "Who is it?"

"Lori."

He pressed a key at his desk console, unlocking the door. It slid aside and Lori came in. "They notified me in comm. You've got it?"

"Aye, lass, I do. It's runnin' through noo."

"This ought to be the one."

"Aye."

With a small beep and the spoken words "Task completed," the computer signaled its readiness. The coded message showed on the screen, a solid mass of letters, numerals, and characters with no hint of individual words, headers, or structure—as Maria had said, complete gibberish. Then the coded letter dissolved, replacing itself with a normal letter. There was no initial to, from, or date header; such would provide too many clues for a code-breaking computer program.

The message was curt and to the point.

CARLYLE REPORTS THAT GARETH IS AS EXPECTED PLANNING A MILITARY COUP. GARETH CLAIMS 3RD DAVION AND TWO BATTALIONS 15TH LYRAN UNDER HIS CONTROL. SUSPECT OTHER UNITS IN REGION AS WELL. NOTED NINE *EXCALIBUR* DROPSHIPS AT MORNINGSTAR. . . .

Side by side, McCall and Lori leaned close to the computer display, reading the words transmitted by Yoshitomi, but obviously coming from Grayson himself.

Evidence that he was still alive. . . .

Grayson, Davis knew now, was playing a role, an elaborate and dangerous role in a deadly game, with the survival of the new Lyran Alliance at stake. The court-martial on Tharkad, the loss of his title, the disgrace of the Legion in the wake of Falkirk, all had been planned in advance with Katrina Steiner in the hope of drawing Brandal Gareth out and learning just how deeply his cabal had penetrated the understructure of the Steiner government.

McCall had first discussed the possibility with Grayson only a few days after he was revived from the medical coma. It was clear then that Gareth—commander of the two regiments always stationed in defense of Hesperus II—was up to something. Wilmarth, that madman governor on Caledonia, had been getting too much help and encouragement in his campaign against the locals, and the response by the Third Davion Guards at Falkirk had been too swift and well-organized; McCall had been convinced from the beginning that the Third Guards' response had been choreographed in advance.

The real giveaway, though, had been the speed of the response by the Fifteenth Lyran Guard against Glengarry; they'd have had to have been on the way long before word of the Gray Death's "treason" could possibly have reached Hesperus II. In fact, the only way McCall could figure it was that they'd already made it as far as the Gladius jump point and had simply been waiting there until they were alerted by HPG transmission from either Caledonia or Hesperus II.

Grayson had thought then, and McCall had agreed with him, that Gareth had to be the one behind it all, if only because he was the one man in charge of both the Third and the Fifteenth. Obviously Gareth wanted Glengarry, though they couldn't come up with any decent reason why; the world was not a rich one. A secondary possibility was that the real target was the Gray Death Legion, though again, neither Grayson nor McCall could come up with a working theory as to why Gareth wanted the merc unit destroyed. One way or the other, though, it was clear that in Brandal Gareth the Legion had acquired an extraordinarily powerful and dangerous enemy.

The terrifying part of the whole situation, though, had been Grayson's depression as he grappled with the knowledge that he would never pilot a BattleMech again. More than once he'd told McCall it would be up to him and Lori to keep the Legion going, that he simply wasn't up to it. Thank God, McCall thought with a small grin, for Jonathan Frye. Sometimes, it took the viewpoint of someone who'd already walked that trail to put things in perspective for those who had to go the same way.

"Marshal Seymour's in it," Lori said, pointing to one of Yoshitomi's paragraphs.

"Aye, lass. But not the CO of the Fifteenth. We can use that."

They still didn't know exactly what Gareth intended to do, nor did they know the extent of his conspiracy. That was why Colonel Schubert had approached Grayson on Tharkad. *"Katrina Steiner doesn't know how far the rot has spread,"* he'd told them the night before the trial. *"That's why she doesn't want to use any of our regular troops. But she does believe that you, the Legion, can be trusted. . . ."*

When you don't know who to trust, call in the mercenaries. It was not a sentiment often heard anywhere within the Inner Sphere. But perhaps during the course of the past thirty-odd years, the Legion had earned that trust, after all.

McCall continued reading the missive from Yoshitomi. Not only was Marshal Seymour in on it, but obviously several key battalion and company commanders in the Fifteenth Lyran Guard. That Gareth was planning on taking over Hesperus II was clear enough. In fact, he'd already taken over that world in everything but name. All that remained was for him to make some sort of formal and final declaration of independence.

Anyone who could snatch Hesperus II and that world's Defiance Industries facilities away from Lyran control would, by God, have the whole Alliance by the short hairs. From the sound of Yoshitomi's report, Gareth was figuring on grabbing at least a dozen or so more systems, in an arc from Hesperus and Caledonia all the way to the Draconis Combine border, and possibly even including Skye itself. McCall wasn't sure the Lyran Alliance could survive such a loss. Losing Hesperus II would be bad enough; it would also plant an unfriendly force squarely across the Steiner LOC, their lines of communications, with the former Sarna March, that region beyond Terra that was now the scene of a bitterly fought war.

Added to this was the problem of the Lyon's thumb. Katrina Steiner's attempt to reinforce these worlds that poked into the Draconis Combine like an intrusive thumb had so perturbed Theodore Kurita that he'd persuaded ComStar to let him station forces on them as ComStar "peacekeepers."

Briefly, McCall wondered if Gareth was collaborating with Victor Steiner-Davion on this one, or with Marik and Liao. Unlikely bedmates, all of them, but blocking the Lyran LOCs between Tharkad and the old Sarna March that way would play directly into the hands of all three and could well be a long-term goal one or several of them had been covertly supporting for years.

Clearly, though, Gareth had been working at this for as much as ten years, bringing in troops loyal to him and placing them where they would do the most good. It was unthinkable that Victor Davion would be trying to sabotage his own Federated Commonwealth. Either Marik or Liao was a definite possibility, however, since either or both of them had a lot to gain from the FedCom losing a huge chunk of territory between Marik and Draconis space, not to mention the factories of Hesperus II. It was possible—said McCall's naturally suspicious mind—that some sort of deal had been worked out between Gareth and either Marik or Liao. BattleMechs from Defiance Industries in exchange for military or political help.

Whatever the truth there, however, they had enough information now to let them move against Gareth. He reached the end of the message.

CARLYLE SAYS NEW CONTRACT AND ORDERS DIRECTING AT LEAST TWO LEGION BATTALIONS TO HESPERUS II WILL BE TRANSMITTED WITHIN TWO DAYS. HE SUGGESTS 1ST AND 3RD BATTALIONS BUT LEAVES DECISION TO LEGION CO. HE SAYS, QUOTE, I'LL BE WAITING AT THE SPACEPORT. I'M LOOKING FORWARD TO SEEING ALL OF YOU AGAIN. UNQUOTE.

THARKAN BERRY APPLES. END MESSAGE.

McCall blanked the screen with the touch of a key, then leaned back in his seat. "It looks to me, lass, like it's aye aboot time t' get the show on the road."

"It does indeed," she said. She placed one slim hand on his shoulder patting lightly. "Well done, Davis."

"It was th' Colonel, Lori. The Colonel workin' so tight an' close he had us all thinkin' he was gone 'round the bend."

"Yes. I'm going to have words with him about that too, believe me. If he ever pulls this kind of stunt again—"

"I dinnae think he had much choice, lass."

"Possibly not. I'm still going to kill him, though."

That had, arguably, been the roughest part of this whole deception. Rough on Lori. Rough on Grayson. *"The hell of it is,"* Grayson had told McCall once, during one of their long, late walks with Schubert before the trial, *"that we can't bring Lori in on this. Not right away. Once I pass command of the Legion on to her, she becomes a target for any of Gareth's people here on Tharkad who might want to verify that I'm ready to give up on the Steiners."*

"Your wife is certainly under close observation," Schubert had replied. *"And your whole suite, as I've told you, is monitored for vid, sound, and truth assessment. If they even pick up her relief that this is all a sham—"*

"What about me?" Grayson had asked with a grin. *"They'll pick up on my relief too, won't they?"*

"Wi' all due respect, Colonel," McCall had told him, *"you've been actin' sae screwed up in th' head, I vurra much doubt they'll see anythin amiss at all."*

Grayson had laughed at that, the first genuine laughter McCall had heard out of him for a very long time. And afterward, he'd been ... *changed,* somehow. More alive. More interested in life, in himself, and in his beloved Legion.

At that point, neither Grayson nor McCall had known exactly what was going to be expected of them. Schubert had been able to tell them only that things would be arranged so that Grayson would lose his command and his barony, that no one could be trusted, and that Katrina Steiner herself had requested that Lori and other members of the Legion not be told. The reason for that gentle piece of deception was clear enough now. If Lori was in command of the Gray Death Legion and was seen to be *happy* about that, after her husband's disgrace ...

But McCall knew that it had been damned hard on the couple, who'd always shared *everything.*

"How soon can the lads an' lassies be ready for boost, d'y'ken?" he asked thoughtfully.

"The 'Mechs are loaded," Lori replied. "And we already have an agreement with a JumpShip at Glengarry zenith. The free trader *Durandel.*"

"Aye, we've used the *Durandel* before. A good ship an' a sharp captain. Perhaps, then, it's time we were thinking about wha' we're taking wi' us."

"I'm way ahead of you, Davis. I passed the word for First and Third Battalions to start boarding ship ten minutes ago, just as soon as I heard that Yoshitomi's next message had arrived. The DropShip skippers all report they'll be ready for boost inside of five hours. Major Frye says Third Batt's ready to move and I *know* First Batt's readiness. It's time we got ourselves to Hesperus and kicked Gareth's butt for him."

McCall grinned. They'd been expecting that this would be the message giving them the go-ahead to depart for Hesperus, a judgment based on the tenor of the last communiqués from the spy indicating that negotiations were going well. "You'll nae be wantin' to jump the gun too much, lass," he told her. "Remember tha' that's exactly what gave Gareth away in the first place, when he seemed t' make it to Glengarry from Hesperus before th' battle smoke a' Falkirk had had time t' clear away."

"Mechdrek," she replied, tossing her head. "It'll take almost a week just to reach the jump point. We'll have both contract and orders long before then, and I'm damned if I'm going to sit around here on my hands waiting for Gareth's bureaucracy to move the wheel another notch."

He nodded, face solemn again. "I know exactly what you mean, Colonel. Come on. Let's get our kits together. An' maybe a first wee stop at Operations, to coordinate things with the Ops staff."

"With you, Major. Locked, loaded, and weapons at the ready."

"One good thing," McCall added. "Yoshitomi says th' Colonel spotted nine *Excalibur* DropShips, and we can assume he has some smaller ones as well."

"He had plenty of *Union*s and a couple of *Overlord*s at Glengarry."

"Aye. We can be grateful he doesn't have the fleet of JumpShips he'd need to haul 'em all at once."

"He could contract with private traders. Hell, all he'd need would be one *Monolith*."

"Maybe. But *Monolith*s are God-awful rare, and when you don't have your own fleet, it's always a bear trying to get more than three or four JumpShips together when you need 'em. Gareth obviously has access to a couple of JumpShips, the ones he used at Caledonia and Glengarry. Signing long-term contracts wi' more than two or three others wold be hard to pull off. And hiring them jump by jump, even mission by mission, is going to play merry hell with his logistical planning."

It was nice to know there was at least one area where Gareth's superiority in numbers was going to slow him down. The Legion didn't have many other advantages in this confrontation.

Together, they headed for Ops, the bunker far below the fortress of Castle Hill.

"Captain to the bridge" blared from the *Caliban*'s loudspeaker system as Mindy Cain hand-over-handed herself down the long, curving passageway from the JumpShip's carousel toward the bridge. "Captain to the bridge, please."

"Always the worst possible time," she muttered to herself as she palmed open the bridge doors. She was clad in shorts and T-shirt, extremely *rank* shorts and T-shirt, since the emergency call had sounded while she was in the middle of her workout routine in the ship's gym. She arrived on the bridge still mopping glistening droplets of sweat from her face, trying to catch them all before a sudden movement sent them adrift, jittering through the air like tiny, silvery planetary systems.

George Petrucci, her exec, was floating next to the scanner suite, clinging to the back of the scanner chief's seat. "Sorry to roust you on your down time, Skipper," he told her. "But it looks like we're going to have company soon."

"What company?"

Petrucci nodded toward the main bridge data screen. A newly arrived *Invader* Class JumpShip was centered on the display, pinned in place by ranging and targeting brackets. Alphanumerics scrolling down the left side of the screen gave the ship's dimensions, mass, and other data; the range was registering as just over twenty-four hundred kilometers. Slightly closer to the Laiakan sun than the *Caliban,* it was sharply backlit, most of the near side of that half-kilometer-long hull lost in midnight shadow and only the edges showing brightly lit surfaces. Two smaller ships, sphere-shaped, showed as crescents drifting slowly in space between the *Caliban* and the newcomer here at the system's zenith point.

"He just jumped in?" Mindy asked. The *Invader*'s sail was still deploying, an immense doughnut of ink-black material slowly unfolding as it rotated astern of the ship. Petrucci's eyes shifted to a time readout on the bulkhead. "Fourteen minutes ago, Skipper. I decided to call you when he launched those DropShips."

"Look like *Union*s. How about it, Sandy?" she asked the scanner chief. "Headed our way?"

"Yup." Sanders Kruychuk adjusted the gain on the screen image, trying to get it crisper. "At one-point-five Gs, too. They're in a hurry, whoever they are."

She turned, holding onto the scanner chief's seat so she wouldn't drift away. "Mahmud!" she called. "Try hailing them!"

"I've been trying, Skipper. No response."

"Drek." This didn't look good. "Give me an enhancement on that image."

"Aye, Captain," the scanner chief said.

The JumpShip's image zoomed in closer, then sharpened, the shadowed portions becoming lighter and showing greater contrast.

"Is that an emblem?" Petrucci asked. "There, on the prow."

"Looks like it might be," Mindy replied. "And a name . . ."

"I'll give the enhancement another pass," Kruychuk said. "How's that?"

The image on the JumpShip's prow appeared to be a mailed hand gripping the hilt of a sword thrust into the sky. It was no design Mindy had ever seen before. After a quick check with the *Caliban*'s library computer, she was convinced that no one else had ever seen it before either.

"So, what do you think?" she asked her exec. "Pirates?"

"Possibly. If they've taken to raiding JumpShips, though, they're pretty damned desperate."

"I don't know about that. I can't imagine most bandits care for the niceties of civilization. The Ares Conventions wouldn't mean squat to 'em."

JumpShips were large, complex, and expensive, and the technology required for manufacturing their Kearny-Fuchida hyperdrives precarious indeed. They were also hard to build and hard to repair—increasingly so as the warring armies of the Inner Sphere had fought over the factories and high-tech production centers capable of handling JumpShip technologies and, as often as not, destroying them. Long ago, the various Houses had agreed among themselves that JumpShips were off-limits when it came to combat. As tempting as such large and vulnerable targets might be, for the most part JumpShips were inviolate. There were plenty of stories of House-owned JumpShips of opposing forces drifting peacefully within a few thousand kilometers of one another at a system's jump point, while the 'Mech forces they'd ferried in fought themselves into bloody wreckage on one of the system's planets.

Pirates and bandits—most often the starveling inhabitants of little-known and isolated worlds out in the Periphery beyond the borders of the great Houses, but sometimes rebels or lawless forces within the Inner Sphere as well—did not always play by the rules. Neither did the Clans. Still possessing genuine WarShips when the last Inner Sphere WarShip had been scrapped long ago, the invading Clans had been known to attack JumpShips, much to the horror and outrage of their more civilized opponents.

Mindy didn't like the way those DropShips were closing on the *Caliban*. JumpShips were never well-armed. *Caliban,* intended as a civilian merchantman, carried no weapons at all, not even as meteor defense, and even that big *Invader* Class out there only mounted a pair of PPCs. These *Union* Class Droppers, though, were bad news. Each mounted multiple batteries of LRMs, particle projection cannons, lasers, and autocannons, enough to shred the thin-skinned *Caliban* if that's what they wanted.

More likely, though, they wanted the *Caliban* as a prize.

"Captain?" Mahmud said. "We're getting an intercom message from *Miranda*. They've been watching what's going on out there, and they want to cast off."

"Um," Mindy said, unsurprised. "Thought they might. Permission granted." She'd been pretty sure that Joshua Ramier, skipper of the commercial *Mule* Class DropShip *Miranda,* hadn't been telling her everything about his cargo. His cargo manifests had been a bit too neat and too precise . . . and smuggling was common everywhere in human-traversed space.

There was a dull, distant thump as the *Miranda* cast off from *Caliban*'s drive spine. She watched its departure on a second, smaller monitor, watched its drive flare blue-white, watched it dwindle as it began accelerating at nearly two Gs, heading for Laiaka. *Miranda* had been *Caliban*'s only rider on this voyage, an easy plotter from Skye to Furillo that had dropped them into the Laiaka system four days ago for a routine charge.

So much for the routine. She wished Ramier and his crew well. There wasn't a lot in this system; Laiaka itself was mostly ocean, its population living in nomadic drift-cities, getting along by harvesting and exporting the vast, gene-tailored algae mats adrift in the upper reaches of its sunlit seas.

There weren't many places to hide, assuming Ramier even made it that far.

"Uh-oh," someone on the bridge said. "Our visitor's not having any of that."

"What are they?"

"*Corsairs.*" A dozen of the sleek aerospace craft had spilled from the *Invader* JumpShip or, possibly, from a DropShip still anchored to the starship's spine. Drives flaring, they were moving in pursuit of the fleeing *Mule.*

"Where the hell did a pirate get *Corsairs?*" Mahmud wanted to know.

"The same place they get DropShips or JumpShips," Mindy said. It was impossible to keep the bitter acid out of her voice. "They steal them."

The *Corsairs* didn't have the fuel or range of a *Mule* Class DropShip, but they had considerably greater acceleration. In moments, the *Corsairs* had overtaken the *Miranda.* The *Caliban*'s bridge crew waited breathlessly, wondering if there would be a battle.

There would not. The *Miranda*'s drives cut out, the big sphere rolled end-over-end, and the drives lit off again, killing the velocity toward Laiaka it had already generated, then beginning to move the vessel slowly toward the patiently waiting *Invader.*

The two DropShips, meanwhile, continued their approach, closing rapidly. "JumpShip *Caliban,*" a voice announced some minutes later. "This is the DropShip *Ravager.* Our weapons are trained on your command section. You will immediately signal your readiness to surrender."

"*Ravager,* this is the free trader *Caliban.* Who the hell do you think you are, anyway? You have no right—"

Laser light flared, a dazzling pinpoint winking from one of the DropShip's numerous turrets, instantly matched by an answering cascade of reflected light and vaporizing metal on *Caliban*'s hull. The hit was forward, well clear of the drive systems and fuel reserves, apparently targeted against one of the bow sections's hydroponics domes, though the hit had actually scored on the command module's lower deck. The beam, cut off after an instant at low power, did not, thank God, penetrate the hull.

Mindy found herself shaking. The sheer, unmitigated *arrogance* of these bastards!

She had to wait for a moment, swallowing hard, to make certain her voice would be under control. "Any damage?" she asked Petrucci.

He looked back at her, eyes very dark against skin gone pale. "No, ma'am. Nothing serious. But he . . . he . . ."

"He shot us. I know." She closed her eyes. As captain of the *Caliban,* she had more than just the ship to think about. The ship's crew consisted of twenty men and women, all of them friends, many of them people who'd served the Jumper when Mindy's father was captain. She couldn't let harm come to them, not when there wasn't a damn thing she could do to stop it, save one. . . .

"Okay, *Ravager.* You've made your point. What do you want from us?"

"The immediate and unconditional surrender of your vessel" was the reply. "Stand by to be boarded."

"We will offer no resistance," she said.

Twenty minutes later, the *Ravager* hung ominously off *Caliban*'s stern quarter, positioned equally well for a shot against the JumpShip herself or against the huge and delicately vulnerable expanse of her collection sail. The second Dropper, which identified herself as the *Lightning,* had locked down on one of *Caliban*'s two docking collars.

The door to the bridge sighed open. Men in dark, mottled-green combat armor crowded in from the passageway beyond, brandishing hand-laser weapons. She saw again the device they'd spotted on the JumpShip's prow, on shoulder and chest patches, a mailed fist—why was it rising out of what looked like the water of a lake?—holding a long, straight sword aloft.

"Captain Cain?" one of the armored men said, the voice distorted through his helmet speakers.

"I'm Cain," she said.

"And I am Group-Captain O'Leary of the Free Star Republic. I hereby requisition your JumpShip in the Republic's service."

Oh, God, no, Mindy thought. *Not again!*

19

Morningstar Spaceport, Maria's Elegy
Hesperus II, Rahneshire
Lyran Alliance
0910 hours (local), 13 December 3057

Grayson was waiting, Dupré a silent shadow, as the first of the Gray Death Legion DropShips began descending from the cloudy Hesperan sky. They waited inside the air-conditioning of the spaceport terminal, where the light from sky and shrunken, arc-brilliant sun was filtered to a softer glow. Even so, he wore goggles, which at the moment were hanging around his neck, and a light T-shirt and shorts against the sweltering heat outside.

As the DropShip thunder rolled overhead, Grayson happened to glance to his right. A large, bronze plaque was embedded in the terminal wall, together with a bas-relief profile of a Lyran marshal.

TO SAY THAT THE BATTLEMECH FACTORIES ON HESPERUS II ARE VITAL TO OUR CONTINUED EXISTENCE IS TO STATE THE OBVIOUS. DEFIANCE INDUSTRIES IS RESPONSIBLE FOR OVER THIRTY PERCENT OF OUR BATTLEMECH PRODUCTION. WITH THE LOSS OF OUR FACTORIES ON SUDETEN AND YED POSTERIOR, THAT PERCENTAGE CAN ONLY CLIMB HIGHER. HESPERUS ISN'T JUST VITAL; IT'S EVERYTHING.

— FROM STRATEGIC POINTS OF DEFENSE WITHIN THE COMMONWEALTH, BY GENERAL TAKASHI MYOO, 2789

Takashi Myoo—funny last name, Grayson thought; it didn't sound Japanese and so didn't seem to go together with the name Takashi; he wondered what its derivation was. Whatever his background, General Myoo had been one of the great strategists of the early days of the Lyran Commonwealth and was remembered, even revered, for his victory on Phecda at the Battle of the Chartrain Sea. His campaigns and his writings were studied at all of the Inner Sphere military academies.

Eventually, the mountain range within which most of the Defiance Industries complex lay buried had been re-named after Takashi Myoo. The original name had been much more bland, the South Whitland Highlands, or something of the sort. The name *Myoo Mountains,* Gray-son thought, had an interesting character to it.

Grayson had memorized most of the man's shorter essays and waded through all of the longer works. Battle-Mechs, by their nature, had changed little in six centuries or so, and that meant that tactics had changed little as well. In the case of Hesperus, the world today was, if anything, more vital now than Takashi Myoo could have dreamed.

Myoo's original assessment of the importance of Hes-perus II, however, hadn't required tactical or strategic brilliance for its genesis. His analysis was as demonstra-bly true today as it had been in the twenty-eighth century.

That, in fact, was why Grayson had decided to play this game with Gareth. If the new Lyran Alliance lost Hesperus II just now, it would be in very serious trouble indeed. The Alliance—like the Lyran Commonwealth of House Steiner from which it had originally sprung—was incomprehensibly vast, embracing some three hundred in-habited star systems, with hundreds, possibly thousands more occupied by nothing more than outposts and way stations. Yet despite the sheer scope of Steiner power, the state's very size made it vulnerable—to assault by House Marik from one side, to attack by her ancient enemy, the Draconis Combine, from another. And now, within the past seven years, to invasion by the warrior Clans from beyond the Periphery, with technologies far beyond any-thing seen in the Inner Sphere for well over two centu-ries. Without the high-tech supplied by Defiance Industries—and that went far beyond BattleMechs—the

Lyran Alliance would find itself subjected to constant, stinging attacks from three sides and to dissolution from within. The contract between any governing power and the people it governed was always a fragile thing, sensitive to any threat, actual or imagined. Once unable to defend itself, the Steiner government would swiftly fall as world after world aligned with some closer, more powerful warlord who could offer immediate protection from the attacks from without.

It hadn't been hard to figure out that Brandal Gareth was looking to create a little empire of his own in this part of Lyran space, and at the expense of the new Lyran Alliance. Others in the past had tried similar moves, political and military, to create smaller states like this new Free Star Republic.

Grayson cast a sidelong glance at Walter Dupré. He doubted that Dupré or Gareth or any of the other officers involved in this cabal thought of their activities as *destructive,* per se. It was Grayson's experience that the opposition in any military campaign—the "bad guys" in popular military slang—never thought of themselves as "bad guys." Certainly not! It was conceivable that Gareth saw himself as a kind of savior, bringing order to his small corner of the crumbing facade of Steiner power. At worst, he saw here a chance to grab power for himself, but he would never think of his actions as the first strike by the barbarians hammering at the gates of civilization.

Grayson, however, was a firm believer in the benefits of civilization, which made him all too aware of how fragile civilization really was. The Lyran state and the Steiner family were not perfect. Far from it. Ill-advised, venal, stupid, damnable, callous, and downright malicious acts had been perpetrated by both time and again throughout the past centuries, but the same could be said of any government that had ever existed in the long and bloody history of humankind.

Still, House Steiner had offered stability—which was necessary for education, a secure economy, and public security. By and large, Lyran citizens enjoyed as much individual and personal freedom as any people within the Inner Sphere, and that was the meterstick Grayson had always used to judge a government's stature, to determine whether or not that government was worth fighting for.

And if House Steiner fell, the alternative would be . . . what? Possibly assimilation by the Federated Commonwealth—not a completely unattractive prospect, perhaps, since the FedCom offered its citizens the same freedoms guaranteed those of the Lyran states. But Victor Davion had problems of his own, just now. Far more likely would be a succession of warlords and petty conquerors. Gareth would be but the first, and his Free Star Republic would likely fall to the squabbles of his generals once he died or was killed. Other "Free Star Republics" would rise, then fall, while external enemies like the Combine and the Clan struck deep into Lyran territory, dismembering the fast-rotting corpse.

There would be no hope at all for freedom in such anarchy, no education, no learning.

And no hope of anything better for centuries to come. . . .

Normally, something as monumental as the destruction of civilization was far beyond the efforts of any one man or even of any one small group. Ancient Rome had withstood two centuries of inept rule and wave after wave of barbarian invasion before the empty shell collapsed at last. House Steiner had withstood more serious assaults than this one, both from within and without, and this one small cabal of disaffected officers would normally have had little effect on a government spanning three hundred star systems.

The problem was that Gareth was a powerful man, with plenty of friends both on Tharkad and on Hesperus II. That, coupled with the timing of his coup, just when Katrina Steiner was trying to disentangle her realm from Victor's wars, meant Gareth had found himself with one of those rare opportunities that can mean the difference between obscurity and fame for any would-be conqueror. And his friends had given him a power base secure enough to make his ambitious dreams a reality.

The most dangerous of those friends, almost certainly, was Daniel Brewer. Though the young heir to the Brewer empire was rarely seen in public, his few personal appearances and all of his email and televid correspondence suggested both that he was still a free agent and that he thoroughly approved of Brandal Gareth and what he was doing. Hell, he'd insisted on naming Gareth as his personal advisor and rarely saw anyone else at all, not even those members of his own family who were running the various departments and holdings of Defiance Industries.

Grayson had tried to see the Duke of Hesperus II on the pretext of a social call but had been curtly rebuffed by Gareth. No one saw the duke, it seemed, unless Gareth himself authorized it. "His grace is really extremely busy these days" had been Gareth's explanation.

Amid billowing clouds of smoke, the first DropShip touched down on the spaceport tarmac, balancing in on a flaming pillar of white-hot plasma, its howling, deafening roar the thunder of an erupting volcano. Even from a kilometer away, Grayson could read the name on her prow, picked out in dark gray script above the white-on-black skull emblem of the Gray Death: *Phobos*. A *Union* Class DropShip, she carried one company of Battle-Mechs, plus ancillary techs, support personnel, and equipment.

The *Phobos* was generally the ship tagged to carry First Company, First Battalion, the First of the First, the Legion's headquarters company. The DropShip settled to the ground, its hydraulic landing jacks yielding somewhat beneath its 3,500-ton mass—almost 4,700 tons in this gravity, Grayson reminded himself. Steam vented in shrill-hissing clouds, outgassing valves popped and hissed, and even at this distance Grayson thought he could hear the sharp *ping* of rapidly cooling metal. A ramp lowered to the ground, and the first BattleMechs began striding down out into the dazzling light.

A *Zeus*. That was a new addition to the First of the First's line-up. That would be Lori's new 'Mech. A *Highlander*—Davis's 'Mech; Grayson could see the number three on its shoulder and pick out the painting of a set of bagpipes high on the torso. A *Centurion* . . . MechWarrior Caitlin DeVries. A *Vindicator*. That one, from the hull numerals and the camouflage scheme, looked like Veronica Tassone's machine, indicating a transfer for her from Third Company's combat lance up to First Company's command lance. There would have been a lot of reshuffling necessary in First Company since both Grayson and Alex had left the unit.

Other 'Mechs continued spilling from the ship. Lieutenant Denniken's *Cataphract*. Erica Carver's *Dervish*. The oddly shaped, menacing form of a PTR-4D *Penetrator,* a brand-new 75-ton 'Mech design only now beginning to appear on the battlefields of the Inner Sphere in the wake of the Clan invasion. Grayson wasn't sure who was piloting that one. There was Lieutenant Bergstrom's *Valkyrie* from First Company's recon lance.

Strange how comforting it was, he thought, to see his comrades again, arrayed in full panoply of war. He'd been alone, it seemed, for so very long. . . .

"Well, let's get out there and meet them," Grayson told Dupré. He grinned wickedly. "Unless you *want* to give me a chance to talk to them by myself."

"No way, Colonel," Dupré replied. "Gareth and his cronies, *they* may trust you, but they haven't worked with you before. I have, and I wouldn't trust you to wave at them without an escort."

"So nice to know that someone cares," Grayson said.

They boarded a wheeled transport outside the terminal, which took them swiftly across the tarmac to the grounded DropShip. Both the *Highlander* and the *Zeus* pivoted at the low-slung, streamlined vehicle's approach. Grayson stepped off the ground transport before it had rolled to a halt. "Davis!" he yelled, cupping his hands to make himself heard. "Lori!"

The *Zeus* slowly lowered its right-arm LRM battery swinging down to aim at Grayson's face. For a moment, he stared up into the multiple, flame-blackened openings of the weapon's muzzle. "You and I are going to have words," Lori's voice said, booming from the external speakers. "You ran off to find us work and didn't tell me word one!"

Grayson raised his hands. "I, ah, am glad you're the forgiving sort, Lori."

"I'm not sure we've established that," she shot back. The *Zeus* raised its LRM a few millimeters, gesturing, the servos giving a shrill whine as they moved. "And what about him?"

"He's part of the package, Lori. Gareth's insurance."

There was a pause, and then the *Zeus*'s greenhouse canopy head split apart, the upper half swinging up and back. Lori's head and shoulders appeared above the

'Mech's cockpit. She kept her neurohelmet on, using its visor as eye protection from the Hesperan sun.

"I'll fry him up for you right now," Lori called. "Poetic justice, right?" She patted her *Zeus*'s cockpit frame affectionately. Dupré had been piloting a *Zeus* when he'd wounded Grayson with his betrayal at Falkirk.

Grayson appeared to consider this. Dupré swallowed heavily, his face clouding with anger and possibly a touch of fear.

"Ah, I don't think this time, Lori," he called up to her. "We need him. For now."

"Go ahead and have your laugh, Colonel," Dupré said, glowering. "Remember, if Gareth gets the idea you're not useful to him anymore . . ." He made the age-old you're-dead sign, drawing his forefinger across his throat.

Swiftly, Lori swung her legs over the side of her 'Mech's head, descended the footholds leading down the flank and side, and lowered herself to the ground. Grayson found himself wanting to warn her about the higher gravity, but obviously she was as aware of that fact as he was, and was prepared for it.

He met her as she dropped the last meter to the ground, taking the impact on slightly bent knees. "Don't break anything," he told her.

"Just hearts," she replied. " 'Cause I'm already spoken for. . . ."

They embraced. He kissed her, savoring the taste of her mouth, the smell of her hair. "It's been too long," he whispered in her ear.

"I'll give you too long," she told him sweetly, "if you ever pull that kind of stunt again!"

He shrugged, pulling back. "I didn't have much choice." He shifted his eyes toward Dupré, warning her. *People are listening.*

She nodded. "Yeah, well. I guess I'll forgive you. *This* time."

A second DropShip was gentling itself to the tarmac a kilometer away. The *Endeavor,* one of Third Battalion's DropShips. "How many Droppers?" he asked her.

"Six *Union*s for the two battalions," she told him. "*Phobos, Deimos,* and *Utopia* for First Batt. *Endeavor, Valiant,* and *Defiant* for Third Batt. Plus *Io, Ganymede,* and *Europa* for infantry and support vehicles."

Grayson nodded. Those last three were *Leopard* Class DropShips, chunky, 1,720-ton aerodynes that could carry four 'Mechs and two aerospace fighters to be converted to haul a fair-sized complement of battle-armored infantry and heavy vehicles to and from a planet's surface.

"Unfortunately," Lori continued, "we've got a bit of trouble with one of the *Leopard*s."

"What trouble?"

She glanced at Dupré, a dark look passing across her features.

"It's all right, Lori," Grayson said. "This guy's going to be in our belt pouches for a while. What's the trouble?"

"Mutiny," Lori said.

"What?"

She shrugged. "Mutiny. The *Io* was carrying Second Platoon of the I/A support battalion. Lots of them are pro-Steiner." She cast another dark look at Dupré. "The word got around, somehow, that this op's aimed against the Lyran Alliance, and they don't want any part of it."

Dupré laughed.

"What's so funny?" Grayson asked him.

"Ha! It's just funny to hear that the great Grayson Carlyle has trouble with recalcitrant troops too, once in a while. Usually all anyone hears is how beloved you are by your people. Maybe ops like this one aren't always as smooth as they make out, even for heroes, huh?"

"They never are. So. What's it going to be, Dupré?"

"What do you mean?"

"I need that DropShip, and I need the armor on board. I have two choices." Grayson jerked his thumb toward the sky. "I can order one of my DropShips here back up to the jump point to slag the mutinous scum, or I can go back myself and straighten this thing out. I'd prefer the second, obviously. Like I say, I need that equipment. So that leaves you with a choice, doesn't it?"

"What choice?"

"You can stay here and watch Colonel Kalmar here deploy my 'Mechs, or you can come keep an eye on me. Your call."

"Oh, no. We've got people here to watch your 'Mechs. *My* orders are to stick with you, no matter what. You're not arranging for private access to an HPG transmitter, not while I'm on you."

Grayson shrugged. "Suit yourself. I hope you don't mind high-G, though."

"Why's that?"

This time Grayson laughed. "Because, Dupré, I'm going to burn back to the jump point at the highest G-factor one of my Droppers can manage, and it's *not* going to be a pleasant trip."

It had been two days since Grayson's abrupt departure for the Hesperan nadir jump point, and Lori missed him terribly. Somehow, it seemed like most of their life recently had been a series of near-misses and brief encounters, interspersed with long, long separations.

She was on a walking tour of Defiance Industries Plant 16 with a group of other newcomers to Hesperus II. Davis McCall and Jonathan Frye were the only other military personnel present. The rest were correspondents for various Inner Sphere news services, both planetary nets and HPG-transmission vids. Their guide on the tour was none other than Brandal Gareth himself, escorted by several smartly uniformed troopers. She was interested in the fact that the guards were wearing not traditional Lyran uniforms but black and gray livery somewhat similar to the Gray Death's own, right down to the black berets. Instead of the skull emblem of the Legion, however, these men wore what looked like the Steiner mailed fist, rising from a pool of water and clutching the hilt of an upthrust sword.

Lori had never seen the Defiance facilities before, not in person, anyway. She'd seen vids of parts of them a time or two. This floor, in Bay 70, was a lot like any BattleMech assembly area, a vast and echoingly cavernous steel chamber, with walls and ceiling all but lost in a complex maze of pipes, conduits, power cables, gantries, catwalks, mobile cranes, and supports. Gareth had summoned her and her two battalion commanders early that morning, saying that he was going to be delivering an important announcement later that day, and would she and her officers like to attend the press conference?

She'd accepted, of course. She and Davis both had already heard about it from Yoshitomi.

She glanced down at her wristcomp, a slim, black plastic ornament riding on her left wrist, its dark LED screen showing both standard and local time and the date. It was truly amazing how much microcircuitry could be packed into a single, tiny chip.

The devices had been introduced by Yoshitomi before he'd departed for Hesperus. Both the spy and Legion intelligence had been well aware that some form of secure communications would be necessary if Yoshitomi was to get any of the information he uncovered on Hesperus back to McCall where it would do some good. The cipher for the HPG transmissions had been his idea; so had the wristcomps.

A very great deal of information, it turned out, could be stored in a microcomputer chip that, when analyzed, seemed to do nothing more complicated than tell the time or handle four-function arithmetic. Yoshitomi had used the tiny, built-in keyboard to type out his observations, storing them as binary files that were automatically encoded in a cipher that could be broken only by adding the correct numbers taken from out-of-date Glengarry tide tables. A direct cable link could upload the coded message to an HPG transmission buffer; it could even be disguised as a part of a completely open and innocent message, just in case Yoshitomi was being closely monitored at the time.

The real problem, though, had been to find a way for Yoshitomi to communicate with Grayson, Lori, and Davis once they joined him on Hesperus II. Obviously, no overt meeting could be arranged; that would be as suspicious as hell.

But that morning, as Lori had entered the lobby of the Hotel Hesperanis, where she and the other Legion senior officers were staying until suitable quarters could be found for them, he'd made contact. She was on her way to breakfast when her wristcomp had chirped.

It was a tiny sound, the sort made by a simple alarm setting. When she'd looked up, she'd caught sight of Yoshitomi, standing on a balcony overlooking the main lobby from the second floor, just turning away.

As long as you could see the person you wanted to make contact with, a touch of a button could transmit a rapid-fire series of coded infrared pulses, the same sort of beam used to turn on remote-control vidscreens and the like. The entire message had been compressed into a tenth-second burst; a person could literally communicate with another simply by waving at him from across the room.

And that was how Grayson had been communicating with Yoshitomi, despite that bastard traitor Dupré's constant presence, literally by waving, since his microchip and the tiny IR transmitter-receiver unit were built into his artificial left hand. That was how Lori and Davis shared messages with each other and with Yoshitomi, even though they had to assume that microcameras and voice pickups were monitoring damn near everything they did and said. No unseen watcher would think twice about Lori programming her wristcomp alarm or checking the time; monitors would pick up unauthorized radio broadcasts easily, but IR pulses were all but masked by human body heat, and were in any case nearly invisible among all of the remote control pulses used in everyday life, for everything from programming vidplayers to opening automatic doors.

The message—she'd read it while walking down a passageway toward the dining room and breakfast—had been brief and to the point.

GARETH TO LAUNCH EXCALIBUR TODAY OR TOMORROW LATEST. PROBABLE ANNOUNCEMENT TO NEWS MEDIA.

SNOWCHERRY. Y.

Davis, it turned out, had gotten the same message. A news announcement would mean Gareth was ready to go *now*. They'd had to guess at the timing up until now; Grayson's flight out to the jump point had been arranged to make sure he was where he would be needed at the right time, but even then, not he, not McCall, not Yoshitomi had been able to say for sure exactly when Gareth was going to initiate the final phase of Excalibur.

She was damned glad they'd moved when they had. Everything depended now on timing, and if Grayson had been trapped on Hesperus . . .

The press group numbered about fifteen reporters, most equipped with either hand-held or wrist recorders or the more advanced data helmets that captured everything the wearer said and heard. They'd already been shown the usual sights in the big factory complex—the materials manufactory where ferrofiber weave was cooked up in its enormous, steaming vats; the circuit assembly plant with its ultrasterile clean rooms; the forging bay, a steel plant housing enormous crucibles of steaming, liquid metal; the main assembly line where 'Mechs slowly materialized under the constant ministrations of hundreds of workers and specialized assembler bots. Lori could sense, though, that their guide was building up to something big as he led them across the seemingly endless factory floor.

At the end of the factory bay, access gantries and support struts created a dense forest of interlacing steel beams and girders. Caught in that steel web were four tall and imposing machines, brand new BattleMechs awaiting their final trial. Lori recognized a *Hatchetman,* a *Nightsky,* and a towering, massive *Atlas* with its grinning, round skull of a head. The fourth, though, she didn't know . . . and she was in the habit of keeping close tabs on the latest 'Mech designs.

Lori was sure she'd never seen this one before, even as an engineering concept. It was somewhat reminiscent of the old *Warhammer* series, with the big PPCs mounted like arms, but the legs had a digitigrade suspension, like a *Marauder* or a *Stalker,* and the torso was lower-slung, less anthropoid, and somehow more menacing than any of the upright, humanoid 'Mechs. It hadn't been primed or painted yet, and its hull was still the shiny silver of a machine right off the assembly line.

"Okay, *Defiance* Zero-zero-one!" Gareth called, grinning. "Come out and take a bow!"

Gantry sections slid aside, exposing the huge machine's torso, arms, and legs. It took Lori a moment to spot the cockpit area, which was well shielded by heavy armor blocks. There was a buzzing whine of servomotors, and the machine bobbed slightly, then took a hesitant step forward. The sound of its armored sole coming down on the steel deck of the factory bay was loud enough to echo throughout that cavernous building. The 'Mech took a second step, dipping to its left, the hydraulics compensating for the changing balance. Steam chirped from a release valve, as sliding pistons hissed; a vacuum pump closed an interior valve with a dull *thup.* Then the huge machine took one more step, stopping immediately in front of the group of visitors.

"The designation is the DFN-3C," Gareth said with the air of the lecturer. "We've tentatively named it the *Defiance,* after the manufactory, of course. Its inspiration, you might say, was the old WHM-series *Warhammer,* though in terms of armament, it has more in common, I think, with KaliYama's HRC-LS *Hercules* series. Extended-range PPCs in arm mounts, left and right. An LB 10-X autocannon system built into the right-side torso. Two medium pulse lasers, a pair of SRM 6 pods, two small lasers, and a rotary chain gun for anti-infantry work. Plenty of armor. Weighing in at seventy-five tons, with a top speed of better than eighty-six kilometers per hour. This baby was already on the boards, of course, when the Clans attacked. Once we had samples of Clan tech to work from, though, we uprated everything we could. We're confident that the *Defiance* is going to be a powerful and valuable asset in any future conflicts we may have with the Clans, or any other potential opponent, for that matter."

"How soon will you be going into production?" a newswoman called out.

"We're already in production," Gareth replied. "We should be turning out four to five of these a month, starting this January."

Lori's eyebrows arched at that one. It was always possible that a new 'Mech design could be developed in secret by one of the other Houses—especially the secretive Draconis Combine or Sun-Tzu's Capellan Confederation—but she found it impossible to believe that House Steiner could have been developing a new heavy 'Mech design right here on Hesperus II without either her or Grayson ever hearing a single whisper about it. That suggested that Gareth had been doing a lot on Hesperus without Katrina Steiner's knowledge. It could well be that he didn't want her to know about the DFN-3C *Defiance,* for the simple reason that he didn't intend for her to take delivery on a single machine.

Which told Lori something more about Gareth's timetable, too. He wouldn't be announcing this development to the entire Inner Sphere if he wasn't already on the move.

"Tha' wee laddie's up t' somethin' noo," Davis said by her side. Gareth was continuing to talk about the *Defi-*

ance, having its pilot rotate and deploy the enormous PPCs, unfolding the small lasers tucked into the left torso, popping the chain gun out of its housing alongside the 'Mech's head.

"I'll go along with that. But what?"

"He's grandstanding," Frye said. "*Look* at him. He's on stage before a captive audience. Uh oh. Watch it. Here it comes. . . ."

"That's splendid!" Gareth said, loud enough for all to hear. "Why don't you give us a bow, Daniel, and then come out and introduce yourself!"

The huge 'Mech performed a stiff bow, dipping at the hip and knee suspensions in a maneuver that Lori thought was just a bit clumsy, as though the pilot weren't all that experienced. A moment later, the escape hatch popped open with the hiss of a breaking vacuum seal, and a young, black-skinned man in pigtails popped head and shoulders up through the opening.

"Ladies and gentlemen," Gareth said. "May I have the great privilege and honor of introducing his grace, the Duke of Hesperus II, Daniel Brewer. Today, his grace is formally taking command of a brand new BattleMech unit, the Ironhand Regiment."

Low murmured voices buzzed and chattered through the reporter group. Every scanner, every helmet pickup, was trained on Gareth now, despite his more well-known associate, still standing in the BattleMech cockpit ten meters above their heads.

"The Ironhand has been created out of the original Third Davion Guard, men and women who, for the most part, were stranded here by Katrina Steiner's summary announcement that she was dissolving her political alliance with Victor. We are augmenting that regiment, however, with a number of new 'Mechs from the Defiance factories, including"—he reached up and slapped the leg of the 'Mech behind him—"this baby right here."

A dozen voices gabbled out as one. "Field Marshal Gareth! Field Marshal!"

"Field Marshal!" One woman, wearing a data helmet, managed to outshout the rest. "This seems to be a rather . . . a rather unusual assumption of authority on your part. How do you think Katrina Steiner will react to this?"

Gareth's bland smile never wandered. "To hell with

Katrina Steiner. She has violated the trust of her subjects by summarily breaking with Victor, by destroying the great power forged here by Hanse Davion and her mother thirty years ago. When a firm hand was needed at the helm of government, she waffled . . . and failed to meet the challenge.

"I, therefore, am declaring a new government, the Free Star Republic. It will be a republic where the ideals of the Federated Commonwealth, indeed, the original ideals of the old Lyran Commonwealth, can be brought to full and abundant bloom." He raised his hand, gesturing toward young Brewer. "His grace, the Duke of Hesperus, is behind me on this. Obviously, because of his age and because of various political complications, he will have no part in the government of the republic, at least, not yet. But like a certain ancestor of his, he seems to have great talent as a 'Mech pilot, and he will command the republic's first BattleMech regiment, with help from myself and my colleagues, of course.

"I have called this press conference today to publicly announce the creation of the Free Star Republic and to issue an invitation to all MechWarriors, to all Davion military personnel still stranded in Steiner space, to all worlds and people who resent Katrina's iron-fisted rule . . . come! Join us! Join us in the triumph that will at last bring peace to this sector!"

"How big is this republic of yours?" someone called out. "Are you saying Hesperus II is part of it?"

"Hesperus II, yes. And Glengarry, which I already rule, as you well know. The Senate of Gladius and the High Council of Laiaka have both formally petitioned me for admittance to the Republic. There are . . . other world governments, let us say, interested in throwing off the Steiner yoke once and for all." Gareth flashed a dazzling smile at the vid pick-ups. "And this is your opportunity to rise, throw off the Steiner yoke, and enjoy the abundance and the prosperity of peace, security, and power!"

Lori glanced at Frye, then at McCall. Both men caught her look and nodded slightly in reply.

This was most definitely the proverbial *it.* . . .

20

Defiance Industries Complex, Maria's Elegy
Hesperus II, Rahneshire
Lyran Alliance
0312 hours (local), 18 December 3057

Davis McCall slowly pivoted his *Highlander*, scanning the complex of walls and battlements before him. It was dark, the pitch blackness of the Hesperan night relieved only slightly by the dim, cold glow of the world's auroras. Those slow-shifting curtains of red and green in the southern sky were not so bright or spectacular as the auroral effects on Tharkad—the planet's magnetic field was not so strong as that of the Lyran capital—but the Hesperan sun was powerful enough to bathe the world in charged particles even at this distance.

Too, the nearer and larger of the two Hesperan moons was aloft, its battered silver face half full and still subtending nearly five degrees of arc, ten times the apparent diameter of Terra's single satellite, its blue-tinted reflected light strong enough to cast sharp-edged shadows, strong enough to read by even, or to navigate a BattleMech without switching on light enhancement or infrared. Each detail of the stone work around McCall was sharply visible, picked out in pale light and deepest black.

A sign showed up ahead, block letters painted on board rather than projected holographically, identifying Gate 2. The gate itself was an enormous structure, eighteen me-

ters tall and six wide, easily large enough for the largest
BattleMech to walk through. At its base was a smaller
door, sized for mere humans.

There would be guards in there.

To his right, a dozen shadows separated from the
deeper shadows along the base of one of the walls, dashing forward like black wraiths. Ahead, a pair of Ironhand
troopers was just stepping out of a brightly lit guardhouse, staring at the 'Mech-shaped apparition looming
out of the night.

"Halt!" The guard's voice, picked up by McCall's external mikes, was sharp and a bit shrill. "Where the hell
do you think you're going, buddy? We don't have authorization for any—"

A shadow materialized behind each of the guards, arms
coming up around their throats from behind, knives—the
blades night-black and invisible at this range—slashing.
The two guards went down as one, slumping to the pavement. More shadows appeared, some dragging the bodies
aside, others taking up position on either side of the
guardhouse's open doorway, then rolling through, weapons at the ready. McCall tensed, waiting for the sound of
gunfire or a base alarm, but none came.

"We're in," a voice called in the headset, the first radio
transmission allowed since the beginning of the op.
"Opening up."

With a grumbling rumble, the massive, eighteen-meter
gate beyond the guardhouse split down the middle, then
slowly the two halves ground apart, spilling yellow light
into the outer courtyard. McCall braced himself; sometimes, a 'Mech would be stationed behind such entryways
to provide additional security, but this time, at least, the
defenders were relying on the usual contingent of sen-
tries, guardposts, alarms, and security cameras.

With Gate 2 open now, none of that really mattered.
McCall urged his *Highlander* forward toward the opening
wall.

To his left, Lori was advancing in her *Zeus*, her torso
rotated slightly away from him to cover the team's left-
forward firing arc. Behind her came the rest of First Battalion's First Company, spread out in open squad
formation. Every one of the Gray Death 'Mechs on Hesperus II had a specific task this night, with First Battalion

responsible for securing the three approaches to the main factory complex, and Third Battalion acting as mobile reserve and strike force outside the mountain. The Fourth Battalion's infantry/armor support group was serving in the infantry assault role, moving in ahead of the 'Mechs to clear out manned guardposts, bunker garrisons, and other non-'Mech units that might spread the alarm.

It was a complex op, and one requiring perfect timing. The roughest part of the whole operation was the fact that developing the plan had to wait until the Legion was actually on Hesperus II and the exact situation was known, plus the unpleasant fact that the Legion would be under close observation by their hosts. It would be hard enough for Legion team members to communicate with one another without raising the suspicions of Gareth's people; working out a detailed battle plan and rehearsing it would be impossible.

And so, as was so often the case in combat, the Legion was working with a compromise. Colonel Schubert had provided them with detailed three-D plans of the Defiance Industries underground complex, and these had been further updated and annotated by Yoshitomi over the past few months. Several different detailed operational plans had been worked out back on Glengarry, practiced in simulation, then further refined during the trip from Glengarry to Hesperus II. The trouble was, no amount of simulation or planning could prepare them for or even anticipate everything that could go wrong. Taking metal-plated, ten-meter, multi-ton monsters like BattleMechs and moving them around quietly ... *covertly* ... was always one of the worst problems 'Mech tacticians faced. Position and surprise were all-important when staging a battle with any element of preliminary control. It was tough enough out in the woods or in a rocky canyon; trying to sneak inside an enemy fortress unseen—McCall had the sudden mental image of a line of BattleMechs proceeding on tiptoe and stifled the urge to laugh—was next to impossible.

McCall corrected himself as he stepped through the open door. In fact it *was* impossible. Sooner or later they would trip someone's alarm or appear on a security monitor that was being watched, and the alert would be out. The only reason they'd gotten as far as they had at this point was the fact that the Legion was supposed to be part of Gareth's defensive force—the equivalent of a palace guard sneaking into the palace it was supposed to be guarding.

The alert hadn't been given yet, though, and the longer they could keep it that way . . .

The harsh bray of a perimeter alarm rasped through the tunnel opening behind the massive double doors, echoing down the long passageway as red lights mounted in the ceiling began strobing with urgent pulses of light. Behind McCall, the doors began sliding shut. Lori had already followed him through, with Caitlin DeVries's *Centurion* close behind, but the rest were about to be trapped outside, which would leave the three of them cut off and helpless inside.

McCall turned, looking for 'Mech-sized controls, then spotted one, a meter-wide pressure plate six meters off the tunnel floor, painted in diagonal strips of yellow alternating with black. He reached out and tapped the plate with his *Highlander*'s left hand. The doors rumbled to a halt, squeaked, then reversed themselves, sliding open once again. Another 'Mech, Bruce Sadler's *JagerMech,* pushed through, along with a scattering of infantry troops leapfrogging past the ponderous 'Mechs with lasers and flamers at the ready.

Gunfire snapped from down the tunnel—light stuff, probably small arms. McCall pivoted clear of the door controls, raising his left arm to point down the dark passageway. Targeting cross hairs appeared on his HUD, but there wasn't light enough for him to get a target lock or even tell what the target was. With a muttered *"Sassannach!"* he triggered one SRM, then another. The two missiles shrieked down the stone-walled tunnel, each riding its own tiny sun trailing flame. At the far end of the tunnel, they hit *something;* the twin explosions banished darkness in close-spaced pulses of light and raw noise. The shock wave, focused and amplified by the tunnel, rattled against McCall's *Highlander* like a strong wind. As the echo subsided, a clear, piercing shriek sounded from the regathered darkness.

"Okay, people!" Lori's voice called over the tactical net. "Check it out! Quicktime! Move!"

McCall swung into the lead. The tunnel was only about

ten meters wide, and would swiftly become blocked by a tangled and impassable traffic jam as more and more 'Mechs dashed through the open doors, unless those already inside dispersed. Thirty meters down the tunnel, he found the remnants of a checkpoint—a desk overturned and smashed, a trio of barely recognizable bodies on the floor.

Engagements between BattleMechs and unsupported infantry rarely ended satisfactorily from the infantry's point of view.

At least the screaming had stopped. Either the wounded man had died and was one of these three or he'd managed to get away. McCall switched to infrared long enough to scan the tunnel floor for the still-glowing traces of people who might have passed that way, footprints outlined in body heat or even droplets of fresh-fallen blood. Nothing but a muddle of recent tracks, to be expected in a public corridor like this one.

He had to assume that the warning was thoroughly given now and that reinforcements would be showing up at any moment.

Beyond the checkpoint, the corridor branched in three directions. McCall strode past, smashing the remnants of the desk underfoot as he did so, swinging left and heading for Bay 73. According to the intelligence they had on the facility's layout, 73 was a testing and maintenance facility for newly activated 'Mechs coming off the main assembly line. Another massive sliding door yielded at a touch from his 'Mech's hand, and he was greeted by a withering blast of gunfire and small, shoulder-launched rockets from the other side.

Crouching slightly, he rode out the initial attack, explosions gouging chunks of armor from his torso and right arm and cratering the wall beside him. He checked the readouts for the two lasers mounted in his right torso, then targeted them and returned fire, snapping off a quick-paced volley of coherent light bolts that splashed and flared in the dim lighting of the huge chamber beyond the doors.

Another rocket slammed against his torso, punching a crater into his breastplate armor. "Get the hell out of that doorway, Davis!" Lori yelled over the tactical frequency.

McCall had been about to do just that, lunging forward,

continuing to sweep the room with laser fire, moving fas to avoid making too perfect a target of himself. The as sembly room was huge, with a ceiling reaching far above the *Highlander*'s head, the walls cluttered by gantries cranes, and walkways, which cast confusing shadows ev erywhere. Thirty meters away, in the middle of the room something *big* moved in those shadows. . . .

It opened fire on Lori's *Zeus* as she burst into the room By the rippling flash of its lasers, McCall saw enough o head and torso outline to recognize it as a 50-ton TBT-5N *Trebuchet*, partly concealed behind the tangled struts and girders of a repair access gantry. McCall brought his righ arm up, taking aim with the powerful M-7 Gauss rifl mounted there. He squeezed the firing trigger as the tar geting cross hairs drifted up and across the *Treb*'s head magnetic fields pulsed, hurling a massive slug of deplete uranium encased in a ferrous durasteel jacket at hyper sonic velocities. The round sliced through a girder like vibroblade through plastic, then slammed into the *Trebu chet*'s right shoulder, just above the LRM battery mounted in its upper chest. The sonic crack of the projec tile, the shattering impact of the round converting kineti energy into white heat and molten ferrofibrous armor was staggering in that enclosed space.

The *Treb* flinched from the impact, staggering back step as part of the gantry collapsed. Pivoting its uppe torso, it fired on McCall's *Highlander* with the twin bar rels of the paired lasers in its right arm just as Lor opened up with the big Defiance autocannon in her *Zeus* left arm.

Cannon fire thundered, rounds cracking and explodin as spent casings spun through the air from the breech o Lori's weapon. McCall added to the thundering destruc tion with a second mag-driven Gauss round, then trig gered his torso lasers for follow-up.

The *Trebuchet* was badly outclassed in this firefight, 50-ton medium 'Mech facing McCall's 90-ton *High lander* and Lori's 80-ton *Zeus*. With a mass disadvantag of one to three point four, the *Treb* pilot simply couldn' maintain position for very long without having his 'Mec shredded around him. A trio of savage explosions rippe across his already damaged right shoulder, exposing th inner mechanism and a dancing cascade of white spark from severed power feeds and cables. Another of McCall's Gauss rounds ripped that arm out by its roots, sending the massive appendage spinning away to crash violently into the chamber's back wall. Sustained laser and projectile fire from both Legion 'Mechs flared and exploded around the unfortunate *Trebuchet* while misses and ricochets smashed into the gantry towers nearby.

More Legion 'Mechs were moving through the open door now, and the *Treb* didn't have a chance. Desperately, it tried to take cover behind the assembly line's main conveyer, an enormous belt constructed from plates of ferroweave that bore the prone and partially assembled torsos of two *Nightsky*s. McCall and Lori both kept firing, tracking the *Treb* as it moved. The room was completely black now, with every overhead spot and lighting panel blown out, but the flares and muzzle flashes of the firefight provided an unsteadily flickering light, its rapid strobing making the 'Mech movements appear jerky, almost comic, like the flicker of an ancient 2-D silent film.

BattleMech combat was a phenomenon of open spaces, of maneuver and cover, something never intended to be loosed inside a manmade structure. The sheer destructiveness of that brief exchange of volleys shattered the room's fixtures and access structures. Huge rectangles of insulation and soundproofing rained from the ceiling, occasionally bringing with them lighting fixtures, sections of power cable and conduits, and support struts and girders. A catwalk suspended across the middle of the assembly bay jumped and twisted under the shock wave of a Gauss round as it missed the *Treb* and slammed into a pillar. A dozen uniformed men clung desperately to the walk as it swayed; several lost their weapons and began scrambling for safety, trying to stay clear of several severed steam hoses that hissed and shrilled and danced meters above their heads.

Then a load of LRMs stored in the *Treb*'s left torso cooked off, the missiles banging and thumping wildly, some triggering accidentally and shrieking through that enclosed space and erupting noisily across gantry struts as the stricken *Trebuchet*'s hull disintegrated in a dozen places. The catwalk parted then, spilling its human cargo into empty air. The *Treb* exploded an instant later, the blast deafening inside the factory bay.

McCall stooped, lowering the *Highlander*'s head so that the protective armor plate shielding the cockpit like a visor took the brunt of that hailstorm of shrapnel. A gantry tower near where the *Treb* had been standing buckled, then collapsed with a roar; smoke boiled through the room, reducing visibility to a meter or two at best, save where the searing flame eating the stricken 'Mech's guts glowed like a sun in the heart of a nebula.

Infantry dashed through the wreckage cluttering the floor, flushing surviving defenders. A handful resisted to the death, blazing away with assault rifles and lasers until they were cut down by gunfire or flamers; most, stunned by having been close witnesses of the battle of the titans above them, surrendered, many with blood streaming from their ears and noses. The noise levels experienced by unprotected ears must have been horrible, even deadly. McCall had heard stories of people killed in church belfries by the pealing of big bells at close hand; this would have been far worse.

He switched on his *Highlander*'s chest lights, illuminating the fog of smoke wreathing the darkened assembly bay. Carefully, he picked his way through the tangle of fallen wreckage; all he needed now was to be trapped by a falling gantry tower, leaving him unscathed but trapped for the rest of the battle. Getting clear of the worst of the wreckage, he performed a sweep along the far side of the room. Several more Free Star troopers materialized out of the smoky gloom, hands raised. He herded them together in one spot with peremptory gestures of his *Highlander*'s arms, then held them there under his 'Mech's guns until Legion foot soldiers could come up and take them in hand.

"Everybody in?" Lori called over First Company's tactical frequency.

"That's affirmative, Colonel," Carlucci, with First Company's Recon Lance, reported. "Everybody's in and the door's slammed."

"How's the rest of the Batt doing?" Caitlin asked. Her voice sounded distant, and ragged with static. Her team had deployed right at the intersection in order to block the way up from the lower factory levels, and her signal was having to be passed along through small portable relay units strewn along the way.

"Feed's coming through now," Lori replied.

McCall glanced at his situation screen, which had been set to show the three-D graphic of the factory's approaches. First Company of First Battalion was inside now; it looked like Second Company was inside their gate as well, while Third Company still battled at the approaches.

"Something's holding up Third Company," he said. "I'd better get over there and see if I can help out." His computer showed the best route, a winding path marked in red, threading its way through the factory maze.

"Affirmative," Lori said. "DeVries. Carver. Jorgenson. Go with him."

The four 'Mechs, a *Centurion,* a *Dervish,* and a *JagerMech,* with McCall's *Highlander* in the lead, hurried back through the door and along the passageway they'd followed to get here.

They passed columns of Legion troops dispersing through the facility, as well as a couple of their own 'Mechs, standing guard at key intersections. McCall winced when he saw part of a wall collapsed in a tangle of twisted steel and a cascade of smashed-up rubble.

The point of this operation, of course, was to *protect* the factory, not shoot it to pieces. Forewarned, the Lyran Alliance military could have simply sent in a quick-response force to land on Hesperus II and retake the Defiance plant, but that would almost guarantee the factory's complete destruction. Recapturing the place would be worth nothing if the precious 'Mech facilities were reduced to smoking scrap and slag in the process.

The idea was elegant in its simplicity. First Battalion would force its way into the Defiance main plant through each of three main gates, one company to each gate. Third Battalion would act as strategic reserve and deploy to break up any determined effort by Gareth to breach First Battalion's perimeter defense.

Gareth would have to attack, or concede the factory—unthinkable since his entire strategic concept must depend on holding the complex. The Legion would hang on, fighting a purely defensive action, forcing Gareth to grind up his forces in frontal attacks against narrow target fronts.

Grayson, meanwhile, would be seeing about bringing

in some reinforcements. If the reinforcements—or at least the threat of reinforcements—arrived, Gareth would be forced to surrender, and the threat posed by the Free Star Republic would be ended.

But first they had to get all of First Battalion inside the damned factory, or it would be cut to bits outside. Fortunately, the Gareth forces—what was it they called themselves? Ironhands. The Ironhands wouldn't be expecting supporting attacks from *inside* the factory tunnels.

Defiance Industries was literally a maze, but the computer three-D diagram on McCall's secondary display guided him through each twist and turn. Twice, he scattered small groups of unarmed men—workers, probably—and once someone let fly at them with a shoulder-launched missile. This was going to be a particularly nasty fight; there were only the three gates large enough for BattleMechs, but there were any number of ways in for infantry, and Gareth would likely commit everything he had.

This was *not* going to be pleasant.

McCall burst around the final corner, to find less than twenty meters separating him from four 'Mechs, enemy 'Mechs, engaged in defending a tumble-down barricade against Legion forces still outside. The main door here had been breached by explosives—according to the plan devised if the defenders managed to get the doors sealed before any Legion 'Mechs got through. Possibly St. Dennis had been spotted during his approach. Possibly he'd had the bad luck to encounter 'Mechs coming out while he was trying to go in. Whatever the cause, the Legion 'Mechs had been locked out; infantry troops had blown the eighteen-meter doors part way out of their tracks, and now four of Gareth's 'Mechs were hunkered down behind them, ready to hold the Legion off all day if need be.

What they hadn't counted on was the possibility of attack from inside their own fortress. McCall opened fire with his Gauss rifle, slamming a round into the back of an enemy *Vindicator*. The machine turned, clumsily, and caught a hail of missile fire from Carver's *Dervish* just coming up beside McCall's *Highlander*.

A *Hatchetman* pushed past the stricken *Vindie*, charging McCall. It was, he saw, brand new, still wearing its silver-gray hull undercoating and otherwise unpainted. Its right hand, brandishing its massive, armor-cleaving hatchet, was coming up, and McCall realized it was going to try to attack him with that rather than with gunfire.

"Y' wee, bluidy idiot," McCall muttered under his breath, shifting his Gauss cannon to this new target and triggering a round, then another, then another. In rapid succession, the mag-hurled slugs ripped through the *Hatchetman*'s armor like bullets through tissue, gouging out chunks the size of a man's head. At nearly pointblank range then, he ripple-fired all of his available weapons, six SRMs, twenty LRMs, and one burst apiece from his paired torso lasers. The *Hatchetman* staggered in mid-step; the hatchet, swinging high, stuck the ferrocrete ceiling in a flashing cascade of dazzling sparks and the shriek of tortured metal. An explosion gutted the machine, blasting out the weakly armored back like an erupting volcano, and the charging 'Mech toppled over backward, trailing black smoke.

Carver's *Dervish,* meanwhile, had sprayed the *Vindie* and a short, stubby *UrbanMech* with missiles, and the flashing, thundering explosions had torn down a section of the tunnel wall, an avalanche that partly buried the struggling Gareth 'Mechs. The last defender was a CDA-2A *Cicada,* a 40-ton recon 'Mech whose greatest asset on the battlefield was its speed. Unfortunately, there was no way to use that speed in the tunnels, and the hail of rocket and laser fire from the advancing Legion 'Mechs knocked it over backward, legs still clawing uselessly at the air.

The *UrbanMech* and *Vindicator* were still very much alive, if a bit scraped up by the avalanche, and obviously ready and willing to prolong the fight as long as they could, but in the next moment, a violent explosion from the half-open, twisted gate doors knocked both defenders to the side. Smoke boiled through the opening, followed a moment later by Captain Turner St. Dennis in his brand new *JagerMech.* Those quad-mounted autocannon, two to each arm, thundered and bellowed inside the narrow passageway, chewing great chains of craters in the crumbling wall, smashing both Gareth 'Mechs down and hammering at them until the *UrbanMech* was ripped open and burning, and the *Vindicator* had raised its hands, signaling surrender.

"Welcome to Mount Defiance, Captain," McCall said as the *JagerMech* shoved its way through the partial opening, its feet crunching on the spilled gravel on the floor.

"Sorry we got held up, Major," Turner St. Dennis, Third Company's CO, replied. "Someone spotted us before we even made it to the courtyard."

"Well, come on in and sit by the fire."

St. Dennis chuckled as he moved to one side, clearing the way for the rest of First Battalion's Third Company to come through the breach. "I don't know, Major. Seems to me it's going to get plenty damned hot in here, and fast!"

"Aye, lad, you may have a point."

McCall peered past St. Dennis's *JagerMech* into the unfriendly night beyond.

From this point on, it all depended on how long the Legion could hold out against whatever Gareth was able to send against them.

The next few hours, especially, were going to be particularly interesting.

=== 21 ===

DropShip Europa *Approaching Nadir Jump Point*
Hesperus System, Rahneshire
Lyran Alliance
1245 hours (local), 21 December 3057

Acceleration ceased, at long, long last. Grayson, his head swimming in the sudden, blessed relief of zero-gravity, drew a deep breath, then blinked against the spots still drifting past his field of vision. Eight days of lying in that couch, feeling as though five men each his size or bigger were stacked up one on top of the other with him at the bottom of the pile, had been much more than enough.

There'd been occasional breaks in the routine, of course; eating and drinking at five gravities was doable, if dangerous, but walking was simply not possible. A young man, Grayson thought, might manage it, but if he fell he would almost certainly break a leg and his pelvis and, quite possibly, his spine. For a fifty-six-year-old man just recovered from massive burns, trauma, and amputation, even standing in the 1.34 Gs of Hesperus was unpleasantly difficult—while trying to go to the toilet or swallow paste food at the two Gs *Europa* pulled on its periods of reduced acceleration were almost more than he could manage.

Somehow he *had* managed, though, if for no better reason than that there were simply no alternatives. He scratched at the stubble of beard on his face, then winced at the tender patches around his eyes. His nose was plugged and congested, and he hurt all over.

Dupré, strapped into the acceleration couch next to Grayson's, fumbled unsuccessfully with his harness safeties. "I think . . ." he said, his voice weak. Suddenly, he turned his head away, retched once, and then was explosively sick. Grayson managed to conceal a smile. Dupré was at least twenty years his junior but hadn't handled the voyage nearly as well. There was a reason for that, of course. . . .

Deftly, Grayson unhooked his harness and floated free in the cabin.

"Need help in here, Colonel?" a sergeant said, using a handhold on one bulkhead to propel himself into the compartment. The man was as unshaven and bruised as Grayson felt, with a pair of black eyes and a swollen nose that made it look as though he'd been in a fist fight, and lost.

"I don't think so, Ray," he replied. "The major isn't feeling so well."

"I'll get someone in to clean it up," Sergeant Ray Coulter said, wrinkling his nose. "Malf! What a mess."

"After eight days of almost constant five Gs, I don't much blame him." The flight had been brutal. Grayson felt as though he'd been worked over head to toe with a blunt BattleMech—one with large, powered hands capable of kneading him up into a small ball and smearing him about under its thumb. He hadn't slept much during the past week, and he felt death-tired. Drugs had helped him grab sleep in small chunks when he could, but he'd never really rested. His ears were ringing and his pulse racing; everyone on board a transport accelerating at high Gs for any serious length of time was supposed to take a whole pharmacopoeia of drugs tailored to soften the effects of the body's system, reducing blood pressure, increasing heart efficiency, accelerating muscle tissue repair and replacement, but no drugs could completely prepare the body for that kind of abuse.

The only part of him that didn't hurt right now was his artificial left arm.

"I'm on my way to the main lounge, Major," he told Dupré. "Coming along?"

The man's eyes seemed to be trying to lock onto Grayson's face, but they didn't really connect. They stared like dull holes out of a paste-white face, uncomprehending, almost empty. Globules of vomit drifted about his head like moonlets orbiting a world; others clung to his face and the week's growth of beard that had invaded his face. He opened his mouth, but all that emerged was a weak, almost inaudible groan.

"No?" Grayson asked solicitously. "Well, that's all right. You won't miss anything. Sergeant? Take care of him, will you?"

"It'll be my pleasure, Colonel."

"How about his men?"

"All secure, sir. The medtechs have them in hand."

Grayson stretched, trying to work out the kinks in his back. "Judging from the way I feel right now, I hate to think what they feel like."

"That's a roger, Colonel. Right now I feel like I could hibernate for a month."

"Unfortunately, I'm afraid we just don't have the time."

That really had been a dirty trick he'd played on Dupré, Grayson thought, almost feeling sorry for the guy. The drugs *Europa*'s crew had been administering to Dupré and the fifteen troopers who'd come along with him as a security force had been the real thing the first couple of times, just in case they'd brought along pharmacological scanners to check the drugs given to them, but after that, after their minds were already numbed by the constant, hammering acceleration, each injection had been a placebo. For the past five days or so, they'd been enduring a minor hell of bruising, crushing acceleration, with no sleep and no pharmacological support for their body functions and comfort.

Hell, it was a wonder they were even still alive.

Using the bulkhead handholds, Grayson made his way forward to the DropShip's flight deck, where Lieutenant Charlene Henry was in the portside seat; copilot, flight engineer, commtech, and navigator occupied the other four seats in the surprisingly cramped enclosure of the bridge. "Permission to come on deck, Captain?" Grayson asked from the hatchway aft. Charlene might work for him and he might technically outrank her, but by very ancient and quite proper tradition, a ship's captain was God and had complete authority over who might enter the *sanctus sanctorum* of the ship's bridge during flight operations.

"Abso-damn-lutely," she said, turning in her seat. Her face was bruised too, from the passage, though she sounded chipper enough. Women tended to endure high accelerations for long periods better than did men. "Come on up, Colonel."

"What've we got?"

"Looks like a convention up there. You know, Colonel, I think the Star Republic's starting up a collection. I don't think I've ever seen that many JumpShips gathered in one spot, or herded so close together."

Three days earlier, they'd picked up the vid broadcast from Hesperus II announcing the official creation of the Free Star Republic. The *Europa* was at full thrust at the time, and Grayson wasn't in any shape to take more than a passing interest in the transmission, but during the next low-G break, he'd replayed the broadcast.

Actually, he'd replayed it several times, but for strictly nonprofessional reasons. Most of the time, the cameras in the group of reporters in the Defiance Industries's Bay 70 had been aimed at Gareth, at his new 'Mech, or at Daniel Brewer, but there'd been a handful of times when the transmitting camera panned across the media people and caught Lori, McCall, and Jon Frye standing together at the rear of the group, listening closely.

God, he missed her. . . .

Despite the distraction, the import of Gareth's announcement had not been lost on him. Gareth was obviously moving, and moving quickly. Grayson only hoped that he and the Legion could move more quickly still.

As he floated on the *Europa*'s flight deck between the pilot and copilot stations and looked out through the cockpit's forward windows, he realized he was seeing a confirmation both of Gareth's speed and of his determination. There were five JumpShips hanging in space at the Hesperus nadir jump point, three *Merchant*s and two *Invader*s. All had their collector sails fully deployed and aligned with the distant, fierce sun, which lay over six billion kilometers below the venturis of their station-keeping drives.

Solar collection sails were space-black, the obvious effect of a material designed to trap every photon of energy that struck it rather than lose anything to reflection. Long ago, however, the custom of placing corporate logos or national emblems on the insides of the sails, the side facing the ship and opposite the starward surface, had arisen—first among the Great Houses, then among the lesser states and organizations that also owned Jump-Ships. Since most collector sails were well over a kilometer in diameter, they made excellent displays of the vessel's registry and allegiance.

The livery displays on the JumpShip sails ahead indicated that two of the five were civilian vessels, owned and operated by civilian shipping or transport corporations. Two more were unmarked and were probably privately owned, free traders or independent transport contractors. The fifth JumpShip bore the fist-in-sun device of the Federated Commonwealth on the inside of its space-black sail. There was no way to tell whether that JumpShip was still in FedCom service, or if it now worked for the Lyran Alliance; energy collection sails were huge and delicate things, and removing the old livery and replacing it with the new was a tricky and time-consuming process, one best done in a well-equipped shipyard. It had been three months since Katrina Steiner's speech, but it was likely that at least half of the JumpShips now in her service still bore the old FedCom colors.

"Where are we in relation to the *Olympus*?" Grayson asked. That was the most important question right now. According to the data Yoshitomi had provided, Gareth's people were keeping the captured JumpShips under the recharge station's observation.

"Have a look," Charlene said. She touched a thruster control; Grayson felt the slight thump through the hull as a jet fired, followed by a brief, slight surge of acceleration. *Europa* yawed to starboard under the kick, and Grayson watched the gathered JumpShips and their vast, circular sails, all aligned the same way and bearing on the distant spark of the Hesperan sun, slide to the left. A second, opposing thump killed the yaw, and the stars and ships arrayed outside were motionless once more.

Centered in the view now, just beyond the gathering of JumpShips, was an *Olympus* Class recharge station.

It was a huge construction, easily three times the length

of even the *Overlord* Class JumpShips nearby, a ponderous, massive collection of parts and structures and fairings, a deep-space station fully a kilometer and a half from station-keeping thrusters to bluntly rounded prow. Like a JumpShip, it had an energy-collection sail deployed aft; like a JumpShip, the station was balanced on an invisible stream of charged particles providing thrust enough to keep it aloft at the star's jump point without actually having to be in orbit around the distant star. Over six billion kilometers from the south pole of the Hesperan sun, the station and the ships gathered at the jump point felt the star's gravitational field as a force of .000008 G, an acceleration of about eight-hundredths of one millimeter per second squared. For all practical purposes, that was zero-G. If you released something in midair in your cabin, you had to watch it a long time to realize that yes, it *was* falling, albeit very slowly. Still, even at that low acceleration, you could fall thirty thousand kilometers in a week, and a long, long way in a century or two. That was why all jump-point facilities—like the JumpShips that parked there for a week or more at a time and unlike conventional space stations that orbited a star or world— had to have station-keeping thrusters.

The idea behind recharge stations was simple. They hung in space at the jump points, continuously collecting energy from the local sun and storing it in array upon array of lithium-dithorium-iridium storage cells. JumpShips newly arrived in-system could be quick-charged directly from those cells, either by a power conduit physically connecting station and ship, or through less efficient beamed microwaves. The process allowed JumpShips to make the next leg of a multisystem jaunt after a delay of only hours instead of days.

Unfortunately, there weren't many *Olympus* stations left. Once, during the Star League era, there'd been hundreds of them, one apiece at least for the zenith and nadir jump points of every important system in the Inner Sphere, and the majority of the less important systems as well. Few had ever been directly attacked, since the stored energy reserves could be used by attackers as well as defenders, and, as technical abilities and training began to slip with year upon passing year of unrelenting war, everyone recognized the importance of these technological treasure-troves. Many, however, had been the targets of covert raids aimed at looting them of precious communications gear, computers, or electronic circuitry. The sensor suites and long-range scanners of a number of the big stations had been deliberately sabotaged or damaged in sneak raids, with the idea that blinded, the hovering behemoths could no longer serve their owners in a reconnaissance role.

Far more, though, had been lost through the years to mechanical failure or human error. None of the huge stations was less than two and a half centuries old, and equipment failure was inevitable. The trouble was that it had become harder and harder with the passing, war-torn centuries to repair or replace malfunctioning parts. When a plasma thruster failed on one of the *Olympus* stations, it was doomed unless the thruster could be brought back on line within a very few months. Hundreds of the massive *Olympus* recharge stations had perished through the years when their drives had failed and the local star's gravity, held for so long at bay, again took command.

Those that remained were showing their years.

Another vessel was visible now, adrift between the *Olympus* and the *Europa*. It was another *Leopard* Class DropShip, thick-bodied, boxy-looking, with stubby wings and a tiny bridge mounted high up on top of the blunt prow.

"We're in position to dock with the *Io*," Charlene said. "Shall we?"

"By all means," Grayson replied. "How about the station? Have they noticed us?"

"Ohhhhh, yes," Charlene said. "They've been calling every few hours for the past day or so, mostly by optical maser or high-gain maser. We've been maintaining radio silence, feigning LOS and no laser receptors."

Grayson nodded. The second half of the *Europa*'s six-billion-kilometer-plus odyssey had been made with the DropShip's main drives aimed almost directly at the station, its plasma thrusters going at full blast. Radio signals couldn't penetrate the cloud of charged particles, which created a loss-of-signal cone, or LOS region, astern of the ship. Laser comms and masers could usually punch through the cloud, but not all DropShips possessed communications gear that sophisticated and expensive.

"I imagine they're trying radio again now."

"As a matter of fact, Colonel," the bridge commtech said, "they're flagging us again. Want to hear?"

"Pipe it through. Let's hear what they have to say."

". . . class DropShip! You are ordered to communicate with this facility at once. If you approach to within one hundred kilometers without proper authorization, we shall fire on you. Do you copy? Over!"

Grayson accepted a hand mike from the comm tech and held it to his mouth. "*Olympus* Station, this is the DropShip *Europa*. We read you. Go ahead."

"DropShip *Europa*, this is *Olympus* Station. What are your intentions here? Over."

"*Olympus,* this is Major Walter Dupré, aboard the DropShip *Europa*. I am here as Field Marshal Gareth's personal representative, to assist in putting down a mutiny aboard the DropShip *Io*. We do not intend to approach your station at this time. Over."

There was a long hesitation. "*Europa* . . . does this have anything to do with the reports of fighting back on Hesperus II? Things sound pretty confused there, and they haven't told us a damned thing."

Grayson chuckled into the microphone. "It's always that way, isn't it? We left before the trouble started, but we heard about it, what, yesterday, I guess it was. We were going to ask *you* what was going on."

"Maybe someday somebody will tell us who won," the voice from *Olympus* Station said. He sounded a bit exasperated. "Listen, in view of the hostilities back on Hesperus II, we're going to have to check out your story. Or do you have an authentication code for us?"

"Negative on the authentication code, *Olympus*. Like I said, we left a week before any trouble broke out back there, and we didn't expect to need it. But you can check out the story with Field Marshal Gareth if you like. Give him my name . . . Walter Dupré. Or use my voice for authentication. They can compare it with my records back in Maria's Elegy and tell you it's a match."

"Roger, *Europa*. We'll do that. Meanwhile, we'll have to ask you to stay clear of this station."

"Roger that. We understand. While we're waiting, we're going to see what we can do with the *Io* over there. Call us when you hear from Gareth. Over."

"Roger that, *Europa*. And good luck. *Olympus* Station out."

The other five men and women on the tiny bridge watched Grayson intently as he handed the mike back to the comm tech. "Okay, people," he said brightly. "The clock is running. We have eleven hours, fifty-two minutes before they find out I'm *not* Walter Dupré."

"We're committed now," Charlene said.

The six billion-plus kilometers from Hesperus II to the jump point could also be measured by the time it took light to cross that gulf—356 minutes. It would take that long for the recharge station's query to make it all the way back to Hesperus, and that long again—assuming that the battle there didn't delay the response even more—before Gareth's reply could crawl back to the jump point. Almost twelve hours.

Grayson hoped it would be enough.

22

Autocannon fire thundered and spat, slamming rounds into the scoured-bare face of the cliff just above the partially opened doorway and sending a cascade of broken rock down across the opening. Lori crouched lower in her *Zeus,* making herself as small a target as possible behind the barricades as the cracking fire walked lower. Several rounds howled over her head, detonating inside the tunnel behind her.

Access to the Mount Defiance plant was sharply limited by terrain and by the high stone walls ringing the courtyard. That was deliberate, of course, a means of funneling would-be attackers into a narrow kill zone in front of the gate, enabling a handful of BattleMechs inside the tunnel mouth to hold off a much larger force outside. So far, the engineering behind the factory approaches had proven to be nothing less than brilliant. BattleMechs and 'Mech fragments littered the blasted and cratered stone court outside the gate, some still burning, others reduced to charred and twisted skeletons of endosteel and ferrofibrous armor.

They lay in cords where they'd fallen. A 20-ton *Wasp*

and two 40-ton *Cicada*s. They'd been part of a light 'Mech reconnaissance lance, sent up the hill to probe the gateway two days ago. A 30-ton *Valkyrie,* a 55-ton *Shadow Hawk,* two 55-ton *Wolverine*s, a 75-ton *Marauder.* The *Shadow Hawk* and one of the *Wolverine*s were still burning, part of a major 'Mech assault only a few hours earlier. Oily black smoke hung above the courtyard like a blanket. The *Hawk* lay sprawled on its back, one great, metal hand still clutching at the sky. Nothing was left of the *Marauder* but the digitigrade legs, still standing upright, and part of the torso chassis. Its power plant had blown while it was trying to rally the Ironhand 'Mechs for another all-out assault, and the fragments of its torso and arms were scattered all over the court.

And not only 'Mechs littered that courtyard of death. A company of hover armor had made an assault seven hours ago during the depths of the Hesperan night, howling up the sloping road that wound up the face of the mountain from the town below. That had been akin to target practice; the sturdy Pegasus and several Packrat scout cars had brewed up one after another as highly accurate blasts of laser or PPC fire and volleys of rockets had swept like a fiery hailstorm across the stone pavement. Several of those were still burning too.

And the courtyard itself had been all but completely razed. Walls had been smashed, towers and radar masts toppled, gun turrets exploded like overripe fruit. The guardhouse that had been the focus of the initial assault three days before was gone, with nothing but a scar on the ground to mark where it had been.

The Legion was holding, was *still* holding after three solid days of combat. Casualties, overall, had been light—five 'Mechs knocked out of action in the whole battalion, and twenty-seven men killed or wounded. Enemy losses included at least twenty 'Mechs destroyed so far, dozens of vehicles, and no one could guess at how many troops. Lori didn't expect their luck to hold; Major Frye, maneuvering his Third Battalion in and around the town of Maria's Elegy, had blocked two major thrusts toward Mount Defiance but had reported a buildup of Star Republic 'Mechs near Morningstar Spaceport.

Morningstar, unfortunately, had not fallen to Frye's attack three nights ago. That hadn't been his fault, or the fault of his people. An infantry patrol had simply been in the wrong place at the wrong time, and the warning had alerted an Ironhand BattleMech company that was likewise out of position. A lucky break for Gareth there, and a bad one for the Legion.

In combat, as Lori knew very well, even the best-laid and rehearsed and simulated plans *always* went wrong somewhere. Generally, the victor in a battle was the side that makes the fewest mistakes.

A flurry of rockets—small, shoulder-launched stuff— hissed through the air from the rubble a hundred meters off and banged noisily away at cliff and barricade. Several large boulders, weakened earlier in the fighting, were dislodged by the relatively small detonations and crashed down the cliff face to the right of the gate in a thundering avalanche of dirt and rock. Lori pulled back slightly, using the gate's archway for shelter in case the avalanche expanded, but the rockfall swiftly died away. *A few more like that,* she thought, *and we won't have to worry about keeping them out. We'll be sealed inside.*

The key to the Gray Death's battle plan was to keep Gareth's 'Mechs out of the main Defiance Industries complex, and they were managing that by barricading each of the three main gates capable of admitting BattleMechs to the primary facility.

In fact, the blockade had been a lot more difficult to master than that. The Defiance Industries facility—just this one plant in this one mountain—consisted of literally hundreds of kilometers of passageways in a three-dimensional maze that honeycombed much of the mountain, connecting no fewer than 150 major caverns and bays and countless smaller rooms, workers' barracks, storage areas, and workshops.

What the Legion's First Battalion had done was grab the central core of the plant, which was accessed by only the three outer gates. Interior passageways, however, would give access to the central core, both for troops and for BattleMechs. Lori had deployed the infantry—'Mech-hunter platoons and commando squads from her armor/ infantry support battalion—to several dozen specific points throughout the fortresslike interior of the factory complex, following a plan worked out on computer using the data transmitted by Yoshitomi. Road blocks had been set up at key intersections, designed to trap or at least slow 'Mechs trying to infiltrate the Legion perimeter. Roving patrols searched for infiltrating infantry and served as mobile reinforcements for roadblocks calling for help.

There'd been several pitched battles inside the factory complex already. Lori hated that—each battle caused more damage to the factory, and with enough damage the complex would become useless to both sides. Some clashes, however, were inevitable.

The trick was to try to keep the enemy 'Mechs outside. Once Gareth managed to slip even a few BattleMechs into the maze of tunnels and chambers within the heart of the mountain, sooner or later each roadblock, each Legion 'Mech fire team, would be isolated, pinned down, and crushed in turn.

At first, the Legion forces had relied on the huge double doors of the gates themselves, watching enemy movements outside both over the security cameras already in place and through microcameras positioned by Gray Death commandos during the first hour or two of the assault. Soon, though, Ironhand engineers had braved auto weapons fire from firing slits and bunkers, rushing forward to plant shaped charges against the outsides of all three gates. The explosions had sprung the gates, knocking them off their tracks and forcing openings big enough for one or two 'Mechs to pass through at a time. Ironhand 'Mechs had rushed the openings then, trying to shoulder their way inside.

They'd been stopped, barely. That first battle had lasted for over two hours, and at one point had been a hand-to-hand affair at the very thresholds of the gates, but the Legion positioning—and the fact that each 'Mech manning the barricade could rotate back in safety to rearm and cool off periodically—had given them a tremendous advantage. They'd used wreckage from the Gareth 'Mechs littering the three courtyards after the first attack to build barricades, five- to eight-meter-tall walls composed of BattleMech slab armor and body parts.

Lori had lost track of how many times they'd come since that first, wild rush. Some of the attacks had overlapped one another, as Gareth tried to carry at least one of the gates by wave assault.

That hadn't worked either, and by now, Gareth must be getting more than a little frantic. If he couldn't recapture the central portion of the factory complex soon, he could become vulnerable to counterattacks by LAAF reinforcements, which surely would be entering the Hesperan system just as soon as they got word of Gareth's insurrection. No doubt, his plan had called for *him* to be inside these tunnels if and when the Lyrans showed up.

"Colonel!" a voice snapped in her headset. It was Orloffski, in the 80-ton *Victor* holding the gate with her at the moment. "I've got movement! On the left, one hundred meters!"

Lori turned slightly, scanning the smoky ruin there. Yes, she saw them. 'Mechs were moving again beyond the spill of fire-blackened rubble that once had been the far wall of the courtyard. A *Trebuchet* hulked behind the tumble-down wall opposite. As it strode closer, it paused, left and right arms raised to volley-fire their three lasers in rippling spurts of brilliant white light. Other 'Mechs, shadowy figures in the clinging, opaque smoke, moved closer.

Gunfire spat from the shadows as infantry tried to rush the gate under cover of their larger and more deadly comrades. Lori loosed a flight of missiles, the explosions tearing through the tight-knit clots of running men and scattering them like torn, ragged cloth dolls.

Then the 'Mechs closed in, another rush. The *Trebuchet* came out of the battle fog in the lead, followed closely by an *UrbanMech* and a pair of 65-ton *Catapult*s. Lori raised her right arm, moving her HUD's targeting cross hairs onto the lead *Catapult,* tagging it as the most dangerous of the quartet. As autocannons roared and lasers hissed, she triggered a full volley from her LRM-15 pack. The warheads shrieked and whined across a range too short for decent accuracy in a long-ranged missile, but better than half of the volley caught the target in a thundering fusillade of explosions rippling across its legs and torso. Several of the LRMs that missed their intended target slashed into the second *Catapult* coming up behind the first. Lori had her left-hand Defiance autocannon in action now, the solid, rippling thunder of the heavy weapon hurling high-explosive charges into the oncoming 'Mechs with a booming, wild and terrifying randomness.

Orloffski had his *Victor* in action at the barricades to her left, sending a devasting avalanche of heavy autocannon fire into the attackers, concentrating on the two lighter 'Mechs Lori had ignored, the *Treb* and the *UrbanMech*.

Laser fire sparked and seared. Lori took a deep hit in her *Zeus*'s torso, the burn scoring across armor and gouging deep into steel and ferrofibrous plate. She pivoted, firing back, sending a quick volley of laser bolts back along the path the incoming lasers had followed. Her heat levels were starting to rise, but she ignored the gauge, concentrating on managing her fire in short but accurate bursts.

One of the *Catapult*s loosed both LRM-15 pods in a ripple-fire volley from a range of ninety meters, and suddenly the air was filled with writhing, lancing contrails and the crack and thump of detonating warheads. One explosion cracked sharply alongside her head; a second and a third rocket struck her right arm close to the muzzle of her missile launcher. Still another LRM flashed in through the smoke, striking the damaged spot on her armor with a sharp, ringing *bang* that staggered Lori, knocking her *Zeus* back a step. Four more missiles followed the first into the same general area, a savage, deadly clustering of explosions low in her side that peeled back a meter-wide section of plate armor and exposed a tangle of wiring and power conduits inside.

Sparks crackled and flashed from severed cables. Red warning lights flickered on her console. Power to the medium laser in the *Zeus*'s center torso mount had just been cut, the primary feed severed by the detonation of an LRM warhead inside the protective swaddling of her armor. She searched for a way to reroute the feed, but the damage in her midsection was bad, too bad for a programmed field repair, maybe even too bad for battlefield maintenance to handle. She decided to ignore the downgrudged laser; she still had the large laser in her left torso, her autocannon, and eight missiles remaining for her LRM launcher.

Scratch that . . . *damn*! One of those winking red lights

was a downgrudge warning on her right-arm LRM launch system.

Two of her weapons down now, leaving her with a single large laser mounted forward, plus the medium Martell in its rear mount—and her left-arm autocannon, of course, though she was down to just three cassettes of A/C ammo now. Three more five-round bursts, and the Defiance autocannon would be dry.

She had a more pressing problem than expendables, though. Since the onset of this latest attack, her heat levels had been building rapidly, climbing each time she triggered a weapon or took serious damage, and the multiple-warhead hit she'd just taken in her torso had smashed two more of her heat sinks, which would make heat management all the more difficult now. Still, she kept firing, triggering the large laser, then letting her heat gauge drop back a few points on the readout before she fired it again. She held the autocannon in reserve for a decent target.

At her side, Orloffski's *Victor* kept up its full, devastating broadside of fire, his armor marred and torn in places by the *Catapult*'s LRM volley but his weapons still fully functional and his rate of fire undiminished. The Gareth *UrbanMech*, a 30-tonner armed only with a small laser and an autocannon, thoroughly outclassed, outmatched, and outgunned, went down in a shrill clattering of parts, a severed leg, a fragmenting sheet of plate steel. An instant later, the *Trebuchet* lurched sideways, smashing into a wall, bouncing off, and collapsing, as an avalanche of stone and rock pelted it from the cliff face above.

Which left the *Catapult*s, steadily mincing across the fire-torn courtyard, slowing to pick their way past the steel carcasses of fallen comrades. They'd already taken their share of damage in the brief battle so far but they were continuing to press forward. Each was a heavy 'Mech, massing 65 tons and mounting no fewer than four Martell medium lasers and two LRM-15 racks in the place of arms.

"Colonel!" Orloffski called. "You all right?"

"I'm fine, but I'm down to only two weapons," she replied. "Davis! You read me?"

"I'm here, Colonel. How bad is it?"

"Bad enough. I'm going to need someone to replace me up here while I get patched up and reloaded."

"Aye. DeVries, are y' ready to move up?"

Another volley of LRMs thundered around Lori's machine, most of the warheads striking the ruin of the gate doors and the rock face above her, but some of the missiles smashing into her right arm and already damaged torso. "Negative, Davis!" she called. "We're facing two *Catapult*s up here. Caitlin's *Centurion* wouldn't last three minutes!"

"It sounds like you're in worse shape."

"Who do we have with a heavy? Denniken?"

"His *Cataphract*'s still down. Looks like it's time for me to take th' watch again. Hang on, lassie! I'm on m' way!"

Lori caught her lower lip between her teeth. If they hadn't yet suffered heavy casualties among their 'Mech force yet, they'd nonetheless taken a hell of a lot of damage. And most of that damage was cumulative, weapons smashed and armor torn that they wouldn't be able to replace or repair on the battlefield. Davis's *Highlander* had taken a beating already, and she'd hoped he'd be able to complete repairs to his leg and torso armor before bringing it to the front again.

But it looked like he wasn't going to get that chance. Any moment now, Legion 'Mechs were going to start dying as the relentless pounding they'd been taking for three days finally caught up with them.

Not good. Not good at *all*. . . .

Like dancers in a slow and exquisite ballet, the pair of *Leopard* DropShips closed with one another at the Hesperus nadir point, *Europa* rotating during her approach so that the two ships were aligned back to back. When they'd closed to within ten meters of one another, the *Europa* extruded a collapsible docking tunnel that locked home to the docking collar encircling the *Io*'s dorsal personnel transfer hatch. With a thump that echoed through both vessels, followed by the rapid-fire rattle of magnetic locks slamming home in sequence, the two *Leopard*s established a solid lock.

Minutes later, Grayson was gliding through the connecting tunnel, hauling himself hand-over-hand. The tunnel walls, in vacuum just moments before, were still frigid to the touch, and Grayson's breath came in small puffs of white vapor.

Lieutenant David Longo, the *Io*'s skipper, was waiting for him by the open hatch. "Welcome aboard, Colonel."

"Hey, Lieutenant. What's this I hear about a mutiny?"

Longo chuckled. "Ah. Is that the story you used?"

"It is. Haven't you been listening in on our chatter with the station?"

"Oh, certainly. But we know better than to believe everything we hear over the comm channels."

"Well, I'm here to personally put down this dreadful and unlawful insurrection against my legal authority."

The *Io*'s captain looked past Grayson into the tunnel. "Where's your shadow? Or do they trust you out on your own?"

"Oh, I've got one. But he's indisposed right now." Grayson stuck a forefinger into his open mouth, moving it quickly in and out several times.

"Gotcha. Well, come aboard and make yourself at home."

"You have my armor?"

"As specified. Colonel. And you'll be wanting to see the boys and girls."

Longo led the way into the *Io*'s main lounge, the only compartment aboard the cramped little *Leopard* large enough for everyone to assemble at once. It was considerably warmer inside. Fifty men and women were waiting there, showing a remarkable uniformity considering the fact that in microgravity the tendency was for people to orient themselves in any direction that felt convenient at the moment. These people, however, had aligned themselves in ranks, as though posing for a school photograph, though each looked more like a robotic machine than like a human being. They hadn't sealed their helmets yet, so the heads that turned to face Grayson as he floated into the compartment were human. Their bodies, however, were encased in bulky armor, layers of plastic-diacarb laminate as tough—if considerably thinner—as the armor plate on a BattleMech. All were painted in camouflage colors, a mottled gray and black that would break up the suit's outline both in the blackness of space and in the gray-painted sameness of a space station's interior passageways.

"Welcome, sir," Captain Matthew Gerard, the CO of the Legion's special infantry assault group, said. "It's good to see you again."

"It's good to be here." Grayson's eyes narrowed, reading the unit device on Gerard's chest.

It was a new unit logo, one he'd not seen before. On each shoulder and left breast was the Gray Death's white-on-gray skull; around it were the words "Carlyle's Commandos," in black-outlined red.

Grayson didn't trust himself to speak for a moment. He floated there, clinging to a bulkhead handhold, and wondered whether it would be too obvious if he tried reaching up and wiping his eyes. *Carlyle's Commandos.* That had been the name of his dad's mercenary BattleMech unit, a good many years ago now.

"Who thought up the name?" he asked, trying to steady his voice.

Lieutenant Chrissie MacGiver, her short blond hair seeming out of place framing her head against the gray and black menace of her armor, grinned at him. "That was Major McCall's idea, sir. He thought you'd approve."

"Well, I'll tell you," Grayson said slowly, "that particular name belonged to another unit, another mercenary unit, about forty years ago. Do you all know about that?"

Half of the men and women in the compartment were grinning, and Grayson saw several nodding their heads. Trust McCall to think about giving them a history lesson that went back to his dad's old regiment. Hell, most of these kids hadn't even been born back then.

"Well, then," he continued, "if you people are going to take that name, you're going to have to demonstrate to me, right now, that you've earned it. Will you do that for me?"

The cheer that answered him, ringing off deck and overhead and bulkheads, was deafening.

"Lieutenant?" he said. "Let's see a screen."

"Sure thing, Colonel."

A display screen on the bulkhead winked on, showing a computer-generated map that plotted, in three dimensions, the locations of each ship at the jump point in relation to the big *Olympus* Station. The five JumpShips

266 **William H. Keith, Jr.**

were crowded together—a cluster much tighter than their skippers must care for, with the constant danger of one ship entangling or tearing the running rigging or sail of another. Circling warily outside that group was a single Star Republic DropShip—a *Union* Class vessel named *Ravager* that appeared to be guarding the JumpShip cluster like a sheep dog watching over a flock of sheep. They'd already monitored several radioed warnings from the *Ravager* to one JumpShip that seemed to be having difficulty keeping station.

"Our ultimate goal, of course," he told them, "is the recharge station. But they're alert, thanks to the fighting back on Hesperus, and if we just go charging in there directly, we're going to take some heavy losses."

As he spoke, a 3-D diagram of the *Olympus* station appeared in one corner of the screen, a long-stemmed mushroom shape drawn in lines of green light, along with a column of text describing its systems, its defenses, and its dimensions. The list of weapons alone was a long one, scrolling off the screen, including dozens of lasers of all sizes, short- and long-range missiles, twelve particle projection cannons, and a number of autocannons, a bristling defensive array that would make the station a very tough nut to crack.

"We are, therefore," Grayson continued, "going to take the *indirect* route." He indicated one of the JumpShips, the vessel closest to the *Olympus* and farthest from the sheep-dog *Union* DropShip.

"This," he said, "is *Merchant* Class JumpShip *Caliban*, Mindy Cain, commanding.

"And we're going to pay her a little visit. . . ."

23

Defiance Industries Complex, Maria's Elegy
Hesperus II, Rahneshire
Lyran Alliance
1345 hours (local), 21 December 3057

"**A**ll right, Lori," Davis McCall's voice said in her headset phones. "On my mark, duck back and I'll step in, coming from your left."

"Rog!"

The two *Catapult*s had planted themselves fifty meters away from the mouth of the tunnel and were hammering away at the barricade now. Lori thought they were concentrating more on the barricade, in fact, than on the defenders, no doubt with the notion of smashing the pile of junk out of the way so that more 'Mechs could rush the place.

"And three!" McCall called.

Lori raised herself above the barricade, bringing her autocannon to bear on the more damaged of the two Ironhand BattleMechs. As her targeting cross hairs connected with the smoke-blurred image, she thumbed the autocannon trigger, cutting loose a banging fusillade of high-explosive shells. Her first burst of five rounds walked up the *Cat*'s right side and smashed into its right LRM pack, ripping the boxy structure open, then tearing it from the machine's shoulder in a spinning tangle of shredded wires and circuitry.

"And two!"

Unfortunately, the 'Mech's LRM supply had already been exhausted in the first few minutes of its attack. The *Catapult* rocked to the left, pivoting, and opened fire with all four lasers, with Lori's battered *Zeus* as its target. She kept holding down the trigger, ignoring the fast-climbing temperature indicator on her console. The empty autocannon cassette spun clear of its breech, and a fresh mag slammed home. Five more rounds rammed into the *Catapult,* hitting it high in its bullet-shaped fuselage, rocking it back on its hydraulics.

"And one!" McCall called, still counting down. "And . . . mark!"

Still she kept pressing the autocannon's trigger. The cassette clicked dry and was ejected; a fresh magazine—her last—snapped home and engaged. McCall was moving past her on her left. Lori took two steps backward as the right arm of his *Highlander* clashed noisily across the pauldron of her left arm. She kept her left arm raised and steady, however, still drawing a bead on the hapless *Catapult,* which was now backpedaling to move out of the field of her deadly, accurate fire.

Five more times in rapid succession her autocannon barked, smashing bits of armor off the *Cat*'s side and left leg in sprays of shrapnel. Her autocannon snapped empty, this time for good, the last of her ammo expended. She fired her remaining weapon, the left-torso laser, mangling an already cratered stretch of armor on the target just above and behind the cockpit, before turning and moving back into the cool, dark depths of the tunnel, letting McCall take her place.

"Take tha', y' bluidy damned heathen Sassannach!" she heard him yell over the tactical channel, a battle cry abruptly lost in a burst of static as his Gauss rifle's magnetics fired. Sassannach or not, she was damned glad to be off the firing line for the moment. Her heat indicator was showing well into the red and was coming down too damned slow. The mere act of *walking* down that tunnel drove her heat levels a point or two higher, eliciting a warning buzzer and the threat of immediate power-plant shut-down.

The heat wasn't critical yet, however; her *Zeus,* she'd learned, had a pretty generous safety margin in its heat envelope. She hit the shutdown override and kept walking, maneuvering her damaged 'Mech deeper into the mountain. Turning left at the intersection and moving past a roadblock of Legion troops, she reached the assembly bay, scene of the first 'Mech fighting three days ago.

"Hey, Colonel!" A man wearing the comm headset and green coveralls of a maintenance technician stepped into her path. "You're not looking so hot."

"A little too hot, actually, Paul. Heat's at one-four."

The tech signaled with his hands, waving her toward the right. "Head up that way. We've got a cold brew waiting for you."

"Sounds good to me."

The "cold brew" was fresh coolant, just chilled by an injection of liquid nitrogen into the tanks, ready to be piped through a 'Mech's cooling system to flush excess heat buildup. When the coolant personnel—identified by their purple jerseys—had completed hooking up the hoses to her *Zeus*'s system intakes and outlets and begun flushing out her coolant system, she locked the machine down, popped her canopy, and clambered out. Her senior tech, Sergeant Johnny Wallhauser, met her when she dropped down to the floor.

"Good God, Colonel, what'd you do to my *baby*?"

She glanced up the towering height of the 80-ton *Zeus* and felt a small shock. The damage looked a lot worse out here. The 'Mech's legs, protected behind the barricade, were largely untouched, but from the hips up, nearly all the paint had been scoured away, the skin was peppered with fist-sized craters and holes, and the area from her left-side taces plating at the hip to her left breastplate was completely open, the armor and support structure stripped away, exposing the black tangle of wiring, conduits, and tubing within. Silicarb lubricant was dripping from ruptured circulator pipes, and steam was spilling from a cracked injector valve. The rounded end of her right-arm missile launcher looked as though it had been savagely dented by an enormous club.

"I guess I scratched the paint up a bit, huh, Sarge?"

"I guess you did." He considered the wreckage a moment, wiping carbon-blacked hands on a towel already just as black. "We might have some spares, though, stuff to patch you up with," he said. Then he cracked a grin.

"This is a scrounger's paradise, I tell you! Especially for Defiance-built 'Mechs!"

She nodded. They'd taken that into account during the ops planning, but she'd not expected such a dramatic demonstration of the idea. The *Zeus* was one of the BattleMech models manufactured by Defiance Industries. It stood to reason that there would be plenty of spares of whatever she might need.

Still, there wouldn't be time for anything fancy. "Just get her up and running again, Sarge," she told Wallhauser. "I don't have the time for you to burnish all of the bolt heads."

Normally, he would have made some sort of a joke about what she could do with her bolt heads, but this time he merely shook his head. "We'll do what we can, Colonel. No promises."

"I don't want promises, Johnny," she replied, grinning. "All I want from you is the impossible."

"You got it."

The bay was quiet, empty of all activity. Good.

Daniel Brewer, in a MechWarrior's uniform of shorts and sneakers, T-shirt and cooling vest, stepped out of the elevator, looked around the darkened chamber, then hurried ahead, slipping silently through the shadows of Bay 70. He'd reached the bay through the secret passageway that Field Marshal Gareth had shown him the other day, during the press conference in this same room. It had been an exciting journey; once he'd had to lie in the dusty darkness of the narrow passageway for fifteen minutes as a Gray Death Legion infantry patrol moved through, checking all of the dark corners for just such intruders as himself.

Intruders? His mouth tightened. This was *his* factory, damn it, and he was about to show the Legion intruders just what a Brewer could do behind the controls of a BattleMech.

Years ago, Gareth had, at Daniel's request, had a BattleMech simulator installed in his apartment. That piece of hardware was going to pay off now, by Blake. He could handle a simulated 'Mech like an extension of his own body and had practiced close-'Mech combat for hour upon hour. He was *ready*. . . .

He would have to work fast, though. There was no way of predicting when another Legion patrol would pass through this area. His advantage lay in the fact that there couldn't be that many enemy troops inside the factory complex, and it was a very *large* factory, too large for them to guard everything at once.

Daniel paused, listening carefully. The chamber was not totally quiet after all; in the distance, he could hear the dull, muffled booming of gunfire, like the thunder of a far-off summer's storm. But there were no guards, no soldiers present to see as he darted out of the surrounding gloom. His 'Mech rested in the dark gathering of shadows at the north end of the room.

His 'Mech, the towering silver-gray form of a *Defiance*, still stood where he'd left it, enfolded in the cold grip of its access gantry. Taking a quick look around, confirming once more that the room wasn't guarded, he started up the gantry ladder alongside the 'Mech, wincing as each step caused the structure to clatter and squeak. At the top, a touch swung the cockpit hatch up and back with a sigh, and Daniel stepped down into the close-fitting embrace of the cockpit. Swiftly, he pulled his neurohelmet off its rack, checked the fittings and feed cable, then lowered it down over his head until the carved and thick-padded saddle rode comfortably on his shoulders, just as the field marshal had taught him.

He'd done this in simulation more times than he could remember . . . and for real once. He knew the checklist by heart . . .

Power plant . . . switch on. Power to operational parameters. Go.

Gyros . . . running . . . up to speed.

Engine . . . ready to engage.

Targeting system and HUD. Go.

Comm system. Go.

Tactical. On.

Weapons systems . . .

PPCs. Weapons on safe, power nominal, green light.

SRM. Unloaded and off-line.

Lasers, power connect green. Core temperature green. Safeties set . . .

Neurohelmet feedback . . . nominal.

He was just reaching for the switch that would open

the gantry restraints and permit him to walk out, when a sound, caught by his external mikes, froze him in mid-motion. A half dozen soldiers were entering the far door. He couldn't see their faces behind their helmet visors, but their hunched attitudes, the way they gripped their weapons, told them that they were on the alert, ready for anything.

Soldiers he could handle. One burst from his PPC would sweep them away like dust before a broom, but that would alert the invaders too early. He waited, scarcely breathing, as the squad moved through Bay 70, poking into corners, checking behind gantries and structural supports.

"What the hell are we lookin' for, Sergeant?" one soldier called out.

"Something making noise" was the reply. "Security picked up some rattling, or something. Now shut your trap and look!"

The search continued for several minutes. Twice, Gray Death soldiers passed close enough to his position that they could have reached out and touched his *Defiance*'s leg, but none gave his machine more than a passing glance. They'd not thought, apparently, of the possibility that someone was actually inside one of the huge, lifeless 'Mechs caged in their gantry towers.

Daniel tried to decide what to do. Brandal was going to be furious with him if he found out he'd come down here on his own. Right now, the field marshal was organizing an assault team of 'Mechs to hit the plant through Gate One, up by the main surface factory facility, and he hadn't been willing to listen when Daniel tried to call him from the apartment with his idea.

Fine. He would surprise the field marshal. It was painfully obvious by now that the invaders, by holding the three key BattleMech gates, could hold onto the most important part of the Defiance complex until doomsday if they wanted to—or, at best, could be broken only by taking extremely high casualties in the assault. However, if the Gray Death Legion 'Mechs defending Gate One were suddenly and unexpectedly attacked from the rear by a BattleMech already inside the complex, the entire picture would change.

And Brandal only needed to push through one of the

defended gates to have full access to the entire factory. . . .

"Hold it, guys!" the noncom in command of the search team shouted. He paused, one hand to the side of his helmet, listening. "Oh, drek! Out! Everybody out! Quick time!"

"Hey, Sarge!" someone replied as the troops began trotting toward the distant doorway. "What's up?"

"Security just called! Seems like they picked up some other noises in here and just analyzed 'em."

"Like what?"

"Like a 'Mech powering up! Now quit yapping and *move* it!"

They knew he was in here. Daniel felt a cold stab of fear. BattleMechs must already have been alerted, must already be on the way to hunt him down and trap him.

Well, he wasn't going to *let* himself be trapped.

He hit the switch, and the gantry opened up like a garment being unzipped. He leaned forward, and the *Defiance* took a ponderous first step onto the Bay 70 floor, the footfall ringing and echoing through the cavern.

"Watch out!" someone yelled. "It's activated! It's *moving*!"

One of the soldiers turned, raised his weapon, and opened fire, a chattering, yammering full-auto burst from a T&K assault rifle. Daniel was momentarily entranced by the sudden, sequential appearance of a half-dozen gray smears on his canopy—bullets bouncing off the tough transplas window. He increased speed, striding rapidly across the bay. Legion soldiers scattered before him; one dashed toward him—whether with some plan in mind or out of blind panic, he couldn't tell—and Brewer dropped his right-arm PPC, swinging the heavy, long-barreled weapon through a whistling arc that connected with the man's helmeted head and kept going with the follow-through. The helmet and what was left of the head inside clattered off the far wall; the body took another step, then sagged and collapsed, as a crimson spray of blood fountained up from the stump of the neck.

More gunshots shrieked and whined as they ricocheted from his armor. Daniel, suddenly, felt a surge of confidence, of sheer, raw power. He was a titan, a colossus astride the bloody field of battle. Three of the puny enemy troops had stopped at the doorway, one fumbling with a man-portable rocket launcher. Raising his right PPC, he activated the weapon's targeting cross hairs on his HUD, letting it drift across the doorway, then squeezed the trigger.

A blue-white bolt of living fire leapt from the PPC's muzzle to the doorway, passing above the huddle of soldiers and impacting with a wall just beyond. For one searing, blinding instant, the Legion soldiers were outlined by that light as skeletal shapes in rapidly dissolving body armor, their flesh vaporized by the artificial lightning passing so close overhead. Then the blast from the wall caught them, and their bones and equipment were scattered like dried leaves in a whirlwind.

Daniel advanced toward the open door with three-meter strides. According to his console map, the pathway to Gate One lay *that* way. . . .

"Colonel!" Captain Boychenko, Lori's tactical aide, shouted over her headset on the private channel. "We got trouble!"

"What is it, Boy?"

"Just had a report from Infantry Team Seven. There's a 'Mech loose in Bay 70! It just chewed through the squad, and now it's headed for Gate One!"

"Wait one," she snapped. "Paul! Get me a tacpad!"

Lori was down in Bay 73, the testing and maintenance area, drinking a cup of caff and gnawing on some rations while Wallhauser and his tech gang refurbished her *Zeus*. She chugged the last of the caff, then tossed the cup aside as one of the techs handed her a small, portable noteputer, already linked to the Legion's tactical network and showing a scaled-down version of the tactical display in her cockpit. She used the page key to work up through several levels of the image, until she found the one she wanted, a schematic of the levels showing Bay 70 and the factory complex's main entrance. It was two levels above the Bay 73 level, and perhaps a kilometer to the north.

She listed her available assets . . . and there were none.

Well, not quite correct. A full company of Battle-Mechs, the 'Mechs in Henri Villiers's Second Company, was assigned to Gate One; unfortunately, those twelve 'Mechs were widely scattered. The physical layout, different from that of the courtyard fronting Gate Two, re-

quired more 'Mechs to cover all possible approaches, and
several of Second Company's machines had been detailed
to cover a number of minor entrances to the east and
west. There were four 'Mechs in a forging bay behind the
entrance, being rearmed and armored; they might be able
to stop the sneak attack from their rear.

"Sarge!" she bellowed, handing the tacpad back.
"Sarge!"

"What is it, Colonel?"

"I'm going. Pull the plug and tack down anything
loose."

"Scag it, Colonel! We don't have it in place yet!" He
gestured, and she looked up. Her *Zeus*'s side was still
gaping open; a shaped mass of ferrofibrous armor taken
from another *Zeus* found in the complex hung suspended
from an overhead gantry crane on a series of chains and
pulleys as techs tried to guide it into place.

"No time," she told him. "Am I loaded up?"

He checked his own tacpad, scrolling through several
screens' worth of data. "No missiles yet. That's okay,
though, 'cause we haven't swapped out your right-arm
launcher yet. But your autocannon reloads are in and
ready to go."

"That'll do," she told him, pushing past, grabbing onto
a foothold and starting up the side of her machine.

It would *have* to.

"Io!" The radio voice of the communications officer
aboard the *Olympus* station was sharp—and worried. *"Io!*
This is *Olympus*. What the hell are you doing?"

Grayson was ready, microphone in hand. *"Olympus* recharge station, this is Major Walter Dupré, aboard the
DropShip *Io*. Do you read? Over."

"Major Dupré! *Olympus*. We saw your DropShip dock
with the *Io* twenty minutes ago, and now you've separated again. *Io* appears to be accelerating toward this station. What's going on over there?"

"Sharp eyes, *Olympus*. Don't worry. Everything's
under control."

"Yes," the voice shot back. "It is. Both DropShips are
now locked into the targeting cross hairs of this station's
primary weaponry. You will both maneuver to cancel all

velocity relative to this station and wait while a ship comes over to check things out."

As he spoke, a *Union* Class DropShip separated from a docking bay beneath the *Olympus* station's huge, mushroom-shaped head. Drives flared briefly, and it began drifting toward the two smaller *Leopards*.

"Roger that, *Olympus*. We copy. We request permission, however, to dock immediately with the JumpShip *Caliban*."

There was a long hesitation. "Ah, repeat that, please, *Io*."

"We request permission to dock with *Caliban*, immediately. We have an emergency here."

"Ah, what is the nature of your emergency, *Io*?"

"*Olympus* station, there was a bit of a firefight here. *Io* gave us permission to come aboard, but several of the mutineers ambushed my troops as they came through the docking tunnel. The troops returned fire and stormed the DropShip's engineering and bridge sections. The mutineers are dead now, and the *Io* has been secured, but it looks like a wild laser bolt down in engineering took out our only QVW-280."

There was a longer hesitation this time. "Ah, we copy, *Io*. What is a QBW-280? Over."

"*Olympus*, damn it, I don't have time to discuss emergency fusion-plant repair with you. If you don't know, I suggest you find someone in your maintenance and repair department who knows what the hell they're about and—"

"Okay, *Io*. I've got it on my screen here." There was a pause. Then, "Holy Mother of God. . . ."

"The QVW-280 is a timing regulator circuit on the fusor coil's magnetic field focus array," Grayson told him, stressing the V in the designation. "Without it, the magnetic bottle containing the ship's fusion core reaction is going to start to degrade. Now unless you would like another small star in your immediate vicinity, we need to replace that part."

"But why the *Caliban*?"

"Because *Merchant* Class JumpShips also use two-eighties on their fusor plants, and they always carry plenty of spares!" They *had* to, since they never touched a planet's surface, and it might be years between visits to one of the handful of deep-space or jump-point ship repair facilities left in the Inner Sphere.

"What about that other *Leopard* out there?"

"Already checked. *Europa* doesn't have a spare. Believe me, Field Marshal Gareth is going to crucify her exec and her engineering officer because of it. Besides, we need to dock with a ship or a facility with a bigger power plant than we have, because we're going to have to rig a parasite power feed to keep our mag bottle up and healthy while the engineers swap out the part. That's why I didn't just ask you guys to run the part out in one of your work boats. Right?"

"Ah, affirmative, *Io*." Grayson could hear the wheels turning in the officer's head. The recharge station's commander wouldn't be thrilled about allowing a damaged, potentially deadly fusion reaction anywhere near his facility. And coming up with volunteers to work on the *Io* would be a problem too.

"Now, the way I figure it," Grayson said, "you can let us dock with *Caliban* and repair the problem from their stock of spares, or you can let us dock with the *Olympus* station, and your techs can patch me up with *your* spares. Which'll it be?"

"*Io,* this is Admiral Barnes," a new voice said over the channel. "I am the commanding officer of this facility. You have permission to dock with the *Caliban,* and I will issue orders to the troops on board her that her captain is to cooperate fully with you and provide everything you need. Under no circumstances, I repeat, under no circumstances, will you bring your damaged craft closer than within fifteen kilometers of this station." The way he said it, Grayson had the idea that the man would have preferred maintaining a distance of fifteen hundred kilometers, but the figure named was the current separation between the station and the *Caliban*.

"The DropShip *Lightning* will escort you in," Barnes continued. "We will not have final authentication on your voiceprints for another ten hours, or so. I trust, Major, that you understand the necessity for security out here."

"Of course, Admiral. And, if I may say so, I believe Field Marshal Gareth would approve of your measures in full, and I will report your cooperation and vigilance to him when I see him again."

"Thank you, Major." He still sounded more worried than appreciative. Having a potential fusion explosion in your backyard, even a small one, was guaranteed to ruin any ship or station CO's day. "*Io,* you may proceed. *Olympus* Station out."

Grayson glanced across at the *Caliban,* now hanging in space just to the left of the more distant *Olympus.* Her skipper wasn't going to be happy about this at *all*. . . .

Lori strode rapidly through the corridors of the Defiance factory, following the glowing green line of light zigzagging across the map on her center console screen. She doubted that she could reach Gate One before the newly activated BattleMech from Bay 70 did, but she would be close on its heels. She'd already flashed word ahead to the defenders at the gate, but the 'Mech—tentatively identified by the surviving infantryman as the prototype *Defiance*—was big enough and mean enough to cause real problems.

She wondered if there were other enemy MechWarriors infiltrating the Legion's perimeter inside the factory, moving to power up deactivated 'Mechs. It was a clever ploy with only one real disadvantage that she could see: it would be impossible for the infiltrators to coordinate attacks between different 'Mechs in widely separated parts of the complex, and that would mean high casualties for the attacker.

But if they could disrupt the Legion's defense at the gates for even a few critical moments, that might be all Gareth's forces would need, causing sufficient confusion to allow them to barge through and gain a solid beachhead inside the mountain. Just the lone *Defiance* itself might be enough to do the trick.

She'd grasped the tactics of the situation at once, as soon as she'd seen the layout on the tacpad. The *Defiance* would first be entering the bay where Second Company's 'Mechs were re-arming and receiving maintenance; if it could blast its way through at that point relatively undamaged, it would emerge moments later from a short tunnel squarely behind the main gate . . . and in an ideal position to disrupt the Legion perimeter.

But if she could get her *Zeus* to the forging bay, even

damaged as it was, then possibly they could trap the infiltrator and bring him down there.

There was only a little farther to go now. . . .

Daniel Brewer emerged in Forging Bay 1, a broad, high-ceilinged room housing blast furnaces and the enormous buckets that poured molten titanium-steel alloy into armor casts. The factory had been working at full capacity when the Legion had struck, so the buckets, though unmoving now, each still contained thousands of liters of molten metal, ready for casting. Three days was not enough by far for the liquid to cool. The room was darkened, but the light from the white-hot metal in the casting vats set a wavering, eerie glow across the walls, lighting the crisscrossing traceries of gantries and crane struts that seemed to float beneath the ceiling high overhead.

It was hot; his temperature gauge began rising even as he stepped into the room. He could see a large, mobile cooling tank off to the left, where 'Mechs coming down from the firing line could have their systems flushed.

Men in colored jerseys were dashing back and forth, and several soldiers were running toward him, missile launchers in hand. The area had been alerted to his approach, but he'd expected that. A *JagerMech,* an *Enforcer,* and a *Centurion* were present, already facing in his direction, weapons ready and armed.

The hail of autocannon fire that met him as he burst into the room was devastating . . . and stunning in both its suddenness and ferocity. Daniel had thought he'd known what to expect from his hours in simulator runs, but *this*! The noise was unbearable, a slamming, crashing thunder; the impact was savage, a steady pounding against his torso that forced him back a step . . . and then another. Ground troops with shoulder-fired missile launchers ran in close, loosing rockets that arrowed up at him on twisted white contrails of smoke.

But he leaned into that hail of fire and raised both left and right arms. His 'Mech's twin PPCs were fully charged, and in this close space and at a range of only ninety meters there was scarcely even any need to take aim. He triggered first his left arm, then the right; the bolts seared the eye even with HUD safety cutouts, and the sheer kinetic energy of those particle clouds generated a recoil that rocked him back on his feet.

Lightning spat and arced, coiling around the *Enforcer*'s torso, then venting itself against the metal gantries and cooling pipes to either side. Smoke spilled from a crater in the *Enforcer*'s chest and shoulder, and the machine seemed to be having trouble moving its right arm. Infantrymen—those who'd not been electrocuted by the grounding arcs that had filled that part of the room—scattered wildly, many dropping their weapons to run faster.

Daniel fired at the *Enforcer* once more, then shifted aim to the *JagerMech*—by far the most deadly of his opponents. He cursed himself for not targeting it first; that brief lapse of judgment might well cost him in the next few moments.

But as he strode forward again, shrugging off the hail of autocannon fire sleeting across the factory floor, he noted that all three Legion 'Mechs were heavily damaged—the *JagerMech* missing its right arm, the *Enforcer* showing a blackened, burnt-through patch on its right shoulder and side, the *Centurion* missing its left hand. They must have been using this bay, he realized with a flash of insight, to re-arm and repair 'Mechs emptied or damaged on the firing line up by the main gate. He might be up against twice his own 'Mech's mass, but he still had the advantage both in firepower and in untouched armor.

For a moment, the battle raged inside the foundry, stray rounds flashing as they struck steel struts or the rust-darkened walls. Daniel took cover behind a gantry that absorbed some of the fire, hesitated, then lunged around the other side and charged.

He triggered his PPCs left . . . right . . . then when the recharge cycled through, left again, then right again, each bolt searing into the *JagerMech* with devastating effect. The 'Mech twisted to the left, stumbling, and Daniel saw yellow flame spurting from a burn-through high on its torso. He triggered a laser burst . . . missed, but then connected with the second try. The *JagerMech* fell, the crash as 65 tons of Kalon Royalstar armor smashed into the steel floor a deafening, shrieking cacophony.

His confidence surged once more, a heady, delirious

feeling of joy mingled with terror and a pulsing eagerness that was almost sexual in its intensity. This was easier than he'd thought, and infinitely more exciting! The other two 'Mechs continued firing as he strode past, but fitfully, the shots scattered and poorly aimed. He chose to ignore them, focusing his attention on the 'Mechs that would be facing Brandal at the gate. The *Centurion* tried to step into his path, but he bashed it aside with one sweep of his left arm, the barrel of the PPC smashing the lighter 'Mech's shoulder bearing and knocking it aside with clattering ease.

The open door leading to Gate One was just ahead. . . .

24

Forging Bay 1, Defiance Factory Complex
Maria's Elegy, Hesperus II
Rahneshire, Lyran Alliance
1402 hours (local), 21 December 3057

Lori entered the forging bay from the south just as the *Defiance* was leaving to the north. She could see the big 'Mech almost a hundred meters away, partly blocked by a forest of gantries, towers, cranes, and spillways. The facility had been savagely wrecked; one gantry was canted far over to the side and looked like it was in danger of crashing to the floor. One of the huge foundry buckets had been hit, the joint on its massive hinges smashed, the bucket tilted at a precarious angle. Smoke filled the room, so thick it was hard to see, and the air was so hot that infrared imaging was useless.

The *Defiance* was getting away.

Lori raised her right hand, intending to fire her missiles, then countermanded the move, aware that she no longer had a launcher there. Smoothly, she shifted to her left-hand autocannon. Cannon shells splashed across the *Defiance*'s low-slung torso, the explosions dazzling and unsatisfyingly superficial. That monster's armor had scarcely been touched. She turned slightly, lining up her large laser, and triggered a burst, then another, targeting the other 'Mech's back, while continuing to clamp down on the autocannon trigger. Five autocannon rounds burned off in quick succession, the empty cassette popped clear, and then five more rounds chased one another across the foundry floor. Missed shots slammed into the wall with searing, crater-punching explosions; others smashed the *Defiance* in the rear of its low-slung torso and scissoring legs. The 'Mech paused, bobbing as it absorbed the impact, then turned in place, looking for all the world like a very large, very angry flightless bird. Lori kept firing, slamming autocannon rounds into the enemy machine, but its armor was thick and mostly intact, and she was doing little but scratching at the surface.

The *Defiance* fired, a single bolt of man-made lightning that slashed across the foundry floor and struck Lori's right arm, sending a shower of sparks dancing across her cockpit and smaller lightnings cascading to the ground as the excess charge bled off. She emptied another five-round autocannon cassette at the intruder, scoring some minor hits, then dodged to the left, putting the drunkenly lopsided gantry between her and her foe. The *Defiance* fired its laser, the beam slicing through some catwalks and support struts, bringing them down with a crash. She waited as her autocannon reloaded, then opened fire again. She knew she was hitting the damned thing, the rounds detonating across legs and torso, but that scagging monster was just shrugging them off.

Combat one-on-one between heavy 'Mechs was, more often than not, a drawn-out match of brawn against brawn, of armor against armor, with victory going to the machine that could stand up the longest under the steady, armor-blasting attrition of its opponent's assault. The trouble with this situation, as Lori quickly realized, was that her *Zeus,* though bearing a five-ton advantage over the infiltrator's 'Mech, was so badly torn up that a very few shots—just *one* shot if it was a lucky one—would be enough to kill her, while it would take many, many solid hits from her one working laser and her autocannon to knock out a 'Mech as well-armored as the *Defiance.* With many 'Mechs, there were weaknesses experienced MechWarriors could exploit—the *Hatchetman*'s weak rear armor, for instance, or the weak rear-flank armor on the *JagerMech*—but the *Defiance* was completely unknown to her. Beyond its mass of seventy-five tons, and the weapons she'd seen on the machine during the press conference a few days before, she knew nothing about the beast, nothing about where concentrated fire might be the most effective.

It would be a battle of attrition, a war of the numbers, and the numbers didn't lie. She'd never be able to survive more than a mere few seconds in a standup fight against the *Defiance*.

Not unless she could find a way to inflict a hell of a lot of damage on that machine in very short order. . . .

Daniel Brewer pushed forward, smashing into chest-high catwalks and railings suspended across the huge chamber of Forging Bay 1, brushing them aside like spiders' webs, edging to his left, trying to get a clear line of sight on the battered *Zeus* that had attacked him from behind. The *Centurion*, standing to his right and at half the range, opened fire again with its autocannon, jolting the *Defiance* savagely.

He spun right, raising both arms and triggering a double PPC bast. The charges caught the *Centurion* high in its chest, sending the smaller 'Mech sprawling backward.

A warning buzzer sounded, a repeating, pulsing rasp, startling him. His eyes shifted back and forth on the console. Now what?

Temperature, that was it. His heat gauge had been climbing with each discharge of his PPCs, with each laser shot, even with each step he took, and the temperature of the air in this room was so high that his heat sinks were having some difficulty dealing with it.

The enemy *Zeus* reappeared, its autocannon blazing. Shells detonated against his torso, and he chanced another PPC bolt in reply.

His heat indicator jumped up another ten points, well into the red. Alphanumerics scrolled across his HUD, warning of immediate power shutdown, an enforced cooling-off period that would leave him helpless and immobile.

He certainly couldn't stand still for that, not with enemy 'Mechs closing on him, guns blazing. He hit the auto shutdown override, gambling that the heat buildup in the *Defiance* wasn't going to overload his systems. He wasn't carrying missiles for his launcher, so there should be no risk of fire or ammo explosion.

His best move, he decided, would be to avoid further combat with these 'Mechs and go hit the defenders at Gate One while he still could. Otherwise, he risked being trapped here, a bear worried by a pack of slavering dogs. As autocannon fire roared and boomed, he turned toward the door to the foundry bay.

The *Defiance* was turning away again, lumbering toward the door. Lori kept firing, then abruptly raised her autocannon. She wouldn't be able to stop him before he got away. Damn, this was *not* going to work. . . .

She glanced to the right, and up. The titanic shape of a suspended bucket of molten metal hung from the complex tangle of overhead cranes and struts, just above a set of rails designed to slide molds into position. It gave her an idea, something faster than trying to wear that bastard's armor down centimeter by stubborn centimeter.

Lori brought her autocannon up to high point, centering the targeting cross hairs on the joint connecting the bucket with the supporting chains and beams overhead, then cutting loose with a long, rolling volley of high-explosive mayhem. Shells detonated against the bucket's massive, titanium-steel-encrusted sides. The bucket's contents sloshed with the repeated, hammering impact, sending splashes of dazzlingly bright orange liquid arcing through the air; where they hit steel, they splattered again in showers of sparks, sending up acrid clouds of gray smoke.

Lori kept firing, praying that all the techs on the floor had fled at the first appearance of the *Defiance*. Another cassette ran empty and popped clear of the autocannon's breech; a fresh magazine slammed home and she kept firing, watching as more and more fiery streamers of liquid metal splashed over the bucket's jarring, trembling rim. Craters punched through the encrusted metal, and bright, yellow-white-orange metal cascaded toward the floor. In almost the same instant, the chains holding the bucket suspended gave way on one side, and the bucket canted sharply to the side, spilling its contents in a volcanic waterfall of liquid fire.

The bucket was no closer than fifty meters from the *Defiance*'s position, and if any of the preliminary splashes had touched it, there was no sign. But when half the bucketload of liquid titanium-steel alloy hit the conveyer tracks and the floor, a wall of molten metal splashed out across the room, accompanied by a wave of heat that was literally palpable, driving a hot wind before it that jarred Lori's *Zeus* back a step as it struck.

Only a part of the splash caught the *Defiance*, a few droplets and splatters that clung to its hull, sizzling and smoking, but Lori guessed that the other MechWarrior must be having trouble with heat; he couldn't keep triggering double and triple and even quadruple bursts from those huge, twin PPCs of his without sending his 'Mech's heat levels straight out the top of the 'Mech's canopy. Then the hot liquid flowing along the floor hit the *Defiance*'s feet.

Smoke arose in a searing cloud, obscuring the other 'Mech while a waterfall of noise assaulted her ears. Lori moved forward, probing ahead cautiously, autocannon leveled, but she could no longer see her opponent, could hardly see anything at all through the thick, orange-illuminated smoke. Steel was burning in there; even steel burns when subjected to high enough temperatures and plenty of oxygen. She could see the flames roaring inside the roiling smoke and decided she'd better step back before she started overheating her own circuits. Her 'Mech's heat sinks were strained to the limit already. Much more and her systems would shut themselves down.

The *Defiance* stumbled forward, moving out of the smoke, smashing into a catwalk and bursting through in a spray of metal and parting cables. Its right arm was burning, and smoke was curling off its steel-gray hide. Lori took another step back, bringing her autocannon to bear, but before she could open fire, the top of the *Defiance*'s canopy exploded up and back, and an instant later the pilot rocketed into the air, flame stabbing from the base of his ejection seat.

"You idiot!" she yelled, though of course he couldn't hear her. She'd never, ever heard of anyone ejecting *inside* a building before. . . .

The closer the *Io* drew to the JumpShip *Caliban*, the closer, too, she drew to the Hesperan nadir recharge facility, and the older and more corroded—*rusty* was the word that came to Grayson's mind—the *Olympus* station looked. Like a JumpShip, it was long and slender, with an array of rigging spars extended at the stern around the plasma drive venturi, and a bulbous nose, roughly mushroom-shaped. As the *Io* drew closer still, Grayson could see the station's carousel rotating slowly within the nose, a slender band moving against stationary gray metal. *Olympus* stations possessed the largest of all known grav carousels, wheels measuring a good twelve hundred meters across and rotating several times a minute to provide a constant out-is-down artificial gravity—a necessity for crews who might live aboard the station for a year at a time, or longer.

"How many people you figure Gareth has aboard, Colonel?" Captain Gerard asked. They were again in the *Io*'s lounge with the other armored troopers, watching the scene revealed by the DropShip's nose camera as they drifted toward the *Caliban*.

"*Olympus* stations are rated at a crew of one hundred fifty, Matt," Grayson said, "and about a hundred, a hundred twenty-five passengers."

"Huh." Gerard eyed the monster station dubiously. "You'd think something that big could pack a good many more people on board, wouldn't you?"

"Oh, there's plenty of room on the thing," Grayson told him.

"You've been on one?"

"Couple of times. That's one reason I volunteered myself for this mission. Large space structures like the *Olympus* generally have room to spare. Of course, a lot of the space in the habitat module forward is taken up by repair bays and such. It's got twelve holds, and room for, oh, something like a hundred sixty thousand tons of cargo. That's why they're often used as transshipment points. The whole station masses about a million tons."

"So why so few people on board? That thing's big enough for a small city."

"A small city's population eats a hell of a lot, Matt," Grayson said. "Not to mention water, which is usually the reaction mass they burn in their plasma drives too. And life support—atmosphere-generation, humidity and temperature control, all of that—becomes more difficult with every warm body you add to the place. Of course, Gareth's not likely to be that worried about long-term life support. If he's worried at all about someone trying to pull what we're about to pull, he could have packed a small army onto that thing, and we'd never know until we kicked in the door."

"How do we know he didn't?"

"We don't. Still, it's not likely he'd risk putting a major strain on the station's life support and expendables for an indefinite but long period of time, just on the chance of a raid like this one. I don't think we have much to worry about."

"Hope you know what the hell you're talking about, Colonel."

Grayson paused for dramatic effect, then nodded sagely. "So do I."

Gerard laughed, and Grayson and some of the other commandos near enough to overhear joined in. They were good people, Grayson thought. High morale. Well trained. Eager. Confident.

He tried not to think about the fact that some of them were about to die, or the even more disturbing idea that he might have misjudged the situation completely and be about to lead them all into a bloody slaughter.

"Five minutes, Colonel," Longo called over the intercom from the bridge. "Better start getting ready."

Grayson exchanged glances, grins, and winks with Gerard and with Lieutenant MacGiver. "We're all set down here, Captain," he replied. "Just make it look like you're a crip."

"You got it, Colonel. Just call me ol' gimpy. . . ."

Grayson looked down at his chest, checking the readouts on the small display implanted inside the ring connector for his helmet. He was at full power, and ready to boost, jets on safe, environment settings go.

A few years before, the Gray Death Legion had become the very first Inner Sphere mercenary unit to be equipped with the new power armor suits, blatant copies, in most respects, of the battle armor worn by Clan elementals. The Legion used two different types—an infantry suit that bore weapon hardpoints and thick armor, and a reconnaissance suit that carried less armor and had no built-in weapons but was lighter and easier to use, less like riding a small BattleMech, more like wearing a space suit.

It was the second type of suit that Grayson had ordered prepared for this operation, Mark I reconnaissance suits, equipped with jump packs that would serve as propulsion units in microgravity. He'd had seventy of them broken out and prepped for this operation, each one tuned and balanced to serve both as combat armor and as spacesuits. They were finely tooled, intricate, and very expensive mechanisms—Davis McCall referred to them as his "wee bairns"—purchased from the FedCom NAIS in New Avalon.

Grayson wondered how much longer the Legion would be able to get parts for the things, now that the Lyrans had split off from the FedCom once more.

But this wasn't the moment to worry about that. He disconnected his helmet from the tether he'd used to tie it to his equipment harness, settled the thick metal bowl over his head, and clicked it into place with a half turn. All around him, the rest of Carlyle's Commandos were doing the same.

"This is it, people!" Grayson called to the waiting cadre of armored men and women. "Everybody check yourself and then check your neighbor. Weapons. Connectors. Valve settings. Then turn around and check the guy behind you." For the next few moments, the team busied itself with its precombat checks. The idea was to stay too busy to think much about what was coming up.

Grayson was carrying a gyrojet carbine. About half of the commandos were packing either gyrojet carbines or the larger g-jet rifles, while the rest were packing lasers. The gyrojet was an ancient design, first experimented with over a thousand years before, back in the mid-twentieth century, but abandoned because the rocket-powered rounds simply couldn't build up thrust enough to carry much stopping power at short ranges. Modern gyrojets had more efficient rockets coupled with explosive warheads; the design was ideal, in fact, for combat in microgravity. The recoil from a conventional rifle or pistol would kick the firer backward in a vivid demonstration of Newton's third law, and likely impart a vicious spin as well. A gyrojet kicked the rocket round clear of the firing chamber with almost no recoil; by the time the round was a meter or two clear of the muzzle, however, it had already accelerated to about one hundred meters per second, fast enough to do some serious damage to whatever it hit, even without the warhead's explosive charge. Grayson's Star King carbine packed twenty rockets into a banana clip magazine in a bullpup receiver; he had three more loaded mags packed into various pockets in his suit's combat harness. He also carried a bangbomb, a small grenade designed to explode with a series of deafening reports and eye-dazzling flashes. That weapon, too, was a very old one.

"Okay, Colonel," Longo's voice said in his helmet's earphones. "We're coming up on the *Caliban,* forward docking ring. We've received permission to dock, but I get the feeling that this lady doesn't like us."

"Can't really blame her," Grayson replied. "Give me a count-off on the distance, will you?"

"Affirmative. We're at fifty meters now. Thirty. Twenty. Ten meters." There was a thump and a nudge of acceleration as Longo cut the *Io*'s speed by another fraction. "Five meters. Three . . . two . . . one . . ."

A loud clang sounded through the DropShip, accompanied by a gentle surge of deceleration that sent the entire group of armored men and women drifting toward the hatch. "Contact!" Longo cried over the tacnet, needlessly.

"Everybody set?" Gerard asked them. He was answered by a chorus of shouts and calls. "Good. Let's just have Squad One up here. Line up by the numbers, right here in front of the hatch."

The *Io* was now docked with the *Caliban.* DropShip passengers normally remained in the rider vessel rather than venturing aboard the JumpShip. However, docking tunnels could be rigged to permit passenger transfer; since this rendezvous was being set up specifically to allow technicians to come aboard from the *Caliban,* the tunnel was being extruded now from the *Caliban*'s spine to the DropShip's aft dorsal hatch.

"Tunnel is secure," Longo announced. "Pressurizing . . . Tunnel pressure matched and equalized. You are free to crack the hatch."

Captain Gerard slapped a control on the bulkhead beside him, and the hatch door cycled open. He motioned to the waiting boarders. "Squad One only! Let's go!"

"Follow me!" Grayson cried, launching himself headfirst into the opening. He sailed through and down the short tunnel beyond, just as the hatchway on the Jump-Ship *Caliban* began cycling open. As he sailed along the tunnel, he armed the bangbomb by pressing a trigger plate with his thumb, then launched it forward toward the yawning hatch. It sailed through; seconds later, the circle of darkness beyond the hatch lit up in a dazzling, blue-white strobe effect, accompanied by a rippling pattern of blasts that would have been ear-splitting if the attackers hadn't been wearing helmets with noise-suppression circuits in their external mike electronics.

His trajectory was off a hair, and he slammed into the ring of metal encircling the *Caliban*'s hatch. He was able to push free and crowd his way inside, however, before the next Legion trooper in line collided with him. Inside, a dozen men and women were adrift in a large passageway. Grayson tucked and rolled, bringing his feet up against the bulkhead opposite the hatch and absorbing the impact on flexing knees. Most of the people gathered there, he saw, were civilians in shipboard jumpsuits and coveralls; floating alongside one was a brand new QVW-280, still in its clear plastic factory wrappings.

Two of the people, though, were in armor—lighter weight than Grayson's and painted jet black. They were helmeted and they were armed, and their helmets had protected them from the bangbomb's effects.

Still, the suddenness of the attack had taken them by surprise. They were only now beginning to react to Grayson's precipitous arrival, bringing their laser rifles to bear. Grayson triggered his gyrojet carbine from the hip. There was a shrill hiss and a slight kick to his weapon, followed an instant later by the ragged sound of tearing cloth. His target was floating in mid-air only about four meters away. The round was approaching the sound barrier by the time it reached the man, striking him high in the chest and exploding with a sharp crack of the projectile's detonation.

The second man fired his laser from a range of three meters. The beam struck Grayson in the side of his helmet, but the suit's optics cut out the sudden, blinding glare and the armor ablated most of the heat. Grayson felt his head growing suddenly quite warm, but the armor held. He had his weapon ready when his visor cleared, but by the time he had a target again, the man was dead, cut down by the next couple of Legion troopers in line who'd just sailed through the hatch.

It wasn't until that moment that Grayson realized that he'd been the first one through that hatch, that he'd deliberately taken the number one slot with an arrogant assumption of prerogative. Damn, colonels weren't supposed to lead crazy-assed frontal charges!

No time to think of that now. They had no idea how many of Gareth's troops might be aboard the JumpShip, and they needed to find and take them all down before they could communicate with the *Olympus*.

After taking a moment to orient themselves, the assault squad turned and headed up the main corridor toward the bridge. Along the way, they encountered two more black-armored soldiers wearing the sword-in-hand device of the new Free Star Republic, both of whom surrendered immediately rather than trying to put up a fight. One Legionnaire stayed behind to watch them while the rest kept moving. Ahead, the main bridge hatch waited. If the enemy had managed to barricade himself in there, it was already too late.

The hatch slid open and Grayson pulled himself through. A tall, slender woman with short-cut blond hair floated just inside the entrance, watching him narrowly.

"Captain Cain?" he said, reading the merchant rank badge on her collar. "How many more of Gareth's people are on board? We've accounted for four."

"Then you got 'em all, fella."

He felt an inward sag of relief. "Good." He nodded. "I'm Grayson Carlyle."

"Well, *the* Carlyle in person," the woman replied, eyes widening. "I suppose I should thank you for rescuing my ship."

"No thanks necessary."

"Wasn't planning on giving you any. Damn it, you people could have breached my hull! What kind of a hare-brained rescue was this, anyway?"

"Well, to tell you the truth, ma'am," he told her with a wry smile, "it wasn't a rescue."

"Oh? What do you call it, then?"

"How about impressment? We need to borrow your ship for a few moments."

The woman closed her eyes. "Oh, *no*! Not again!"

* * *

"Go, men! Go now!"

Captain Michael Kaminski turned the upper torso of his 95-ton *Banshee* to the left, waving his 'Mechs forward. Behind him, partially hidden among the war-shattered ruin of the factory, a dozen more heavy and assault 'Mechs began lumbering forward, breaking cover for a last, desperate attempt to force their way into the bloody mountain.

Their surroundings were a tumble-down shambles of twisted steel and burned-out buildings. The main structure was little more than a shell now, parts of it collapsed and still smoking, other parts standing, a forest of steel beams and sheet metal, of gantries, traveling cranes, and towers. This part of the Defiance factory complex was in the open air, outside the mountain, with a broad ramp leading up to Gate One. That ramp, some fifty meters long and thirty broad, had been a killing field for the hidden Legion 'Mechs inside the mountain for the past three days, and now it was going to be a killing field again. Frontal charges were rarely worth the cost, no matter how vital the prize at the end.

Still, Field Marshal Gareth seemed to have hit on a good idea here, one that had a fair chance of carrying the day. He'd rounded up the heaviest 'Mechs available in the Ironhands, most from the old Third Davion Guards, but a few too from the Fifteenth Lyran Guards and even the Catamounts, whose MechWarriors had thrown in with Gareth because he'd told them only that Hesperus II was in danger, and that no matter whether they loved the Lyran Alliance or the Federated Commonwealth, they would fight the invaders to save their world.

And, amazingly, there'd been no shortage of volunteers. The men loved Gareth, Kaminski knew, and would follow him into hell itself if he gave them the word. The idea was appallingly simple. Six heavy BattleMechs—Kaminski's *Banshee,* an ungainly 90-ton *Cyclops,* two 80-ton *Victor*s, a 75-ton *Orion,* and a *Catapult*—would line up side by side and advance up that ramp. There was no way the enemy could miss, but those six 'Mechs possessed one hell of a lot of armor and would take some killing. Sometimes, Kaminski thought, modern Battle-Mech warfare seemed to be a throwback to the eighteenth

century, when troops lined up facing one another in par-
allel rows and just blazed away until something broke.
The assault line would close with the Legion barricades,
firing constantly, trading damage for damage, forcing the
defenders back from the gate by sheer mass and firepower.

It ought to work. The Legion was keeping two and
sometimes three 'Mechs behind the crude barricade at the
top of the ramp, and other Legion 'Mechs had made occasional forays into the near portions of the factory, ha-
rassing and raiding. They'd been taking a lot of damage
over the past three days, however, and must be getting
pretty ragged by this time. One good, last push, and the
heavies would have the way open. More 'Mechs were
waiting, then, to rush the gate as soon as the heavies had
seized it, pushing past and into the depths of Mount Defiance.

And that would be the end of the Legion forces holding
the factory complex.

Cannon fire cracked; lasers sizzled among the ruins.
Kaminski's *Banshee* took a laser hit in the arm, but he
shrugged it off and kept moving. He reached the foot of
the ramp, pausing a moment as the others joined him. The
fire from above redoubled, sweeping down the ramp,
striking the assault 'Mechs, gouging pieces from their armor but doing no serious damage. "All right, men!"
Kaminski called. "Quicktime . . . march!"

With a clanking as loud as the trumpet announcing the
Final Judgment, the six 'Mechs broke into a lumbering
trot, charging up that fire-swept ramp toward the factory
gate.

25

**Defiance Industries Complex, Maria's Elegy
Hesperus II, Rahneshire,
Lyran Alliance
1415 hours (local), 21 December 3057**

Lori had been forced back by the fierce heat of the fire in
the forging bay, but after several minutes, the blaze had
dwindled, too hot, too intense to support itself for long
with no fuel better than steel and the carcass of a wrecked
BattleMech. As the heat died away in wavering curtains
of air turned translucent and shimmery, she was able to
edge past the spill, where the liquid metal, puddled on the
floor now with a much larger surface area than it had had
in the bucket, was already cooling enough to form a
glowing, orange-brown crust. Once she was into the passageway beyond, the air temperature had fallen swiftly,
and with it her 'Mech's heat indicator had begun falling
as well. It had been a literal furnace in there, with an air
temperature reaching hundreds of degrees near the fire,
and her *Zeus* could not have survived much more expo-
sure to that kind of heat.

Thirty meters from that flame-seared doorway, the corridor opened into a broad anteroom just behind what had
been a massive set of eighteen-meter gates, identical to
those across the facility at Gate Two. Second Company,
under the able and experienced command of Captain
Guillaume Henri Villiers, had set up their command post

there, scant meters behind the barricades at the blast-shattered gate. His 75-ton *Marauder,* missing its left arm, was standing by a stairway leading to the factory's upper levels, shouting commands over the company's tac frequency to his troops. The scene was one of organized chaos, with dozens of foot infantry, several badly damaged 'Mechs undergoing emergency repairs, and a J27 transport offloading missiles for Legion 'Mechs in need of a reload. If that *Defiance* had managed to smash its way through and open fire in this crowded area ...

"Colonel Kalmar!" Villiers called, recognizing the markings on her *Zeus.* He spoke with a rich, Gallic accent. "What in the hell happened to you?"

"A run-in with an angry creditor, Henri. What's the sit?"

"They are coming, *mon cher colonel.* They are coming and they are coming in hot!"

Lori moved toward the barricade, where an *Apollo,* a *JagerMech,* and an *Enforcer* were standing practically shoulder to shoulder behind a pile of wrecked 'Mechs and vehicles five meters tall—waist high for a BattleMech—firing all of their weapons as rapidly as they could. The *Apollo* was firing flights of missiles, providing long-range fire support, while the other two rattled away with their autocannons, laying down a savage curtain of fire.

When she peered past the defenders' shoulders, she was greeted by an awesome sight—two heavy and four assault BattleMechs, lined up as though on parade, advancing side by side up the broad ramp leading to Gate One. As the ramp narrowed, the line of six was squeezed down to a line of four followed by a line of two, the *Orion* and the *Catapult*—the heavies—following the *Cyclops,* the two *Victor*s, and the savage-looking *Banshee.*

That *Banshee* was the leader's 'Mech, the body paint and decoration giving it away. While 'Mech pilots tended to be an individualistic bunch who often decorated their machines with unauthorized nose art, paint designs, and war trophies, it was usually the company commanders who took particular pains to dress up their 'Mechs for full psychological effect.

The *Banshee* was already an anthropoid design, and this one's head had been crafted to look like an angular, sharp-cornered skull. The pilot had enhanced that image by applying paint and tack-on plate armor; the head was painted bone white in the image of a screaming skull, while the rest of the machine was painted death-black in startling contrast.

As a professional, though, Lori was more concerned by the clues in design and weapons mounts that indicated this *Banshee* was a BNC-S, a House Steiner variant of a machine that originally had been ludicrously over-armored and under-gunned. One of the oldest of all BattleMech designs, the original *Banshee* had carried only one PPC, an autocannon, and a Magna Mark I light laser. The Steiner variant, however, had swapped out the original heavy GM 380 fusion power plant and replaced it with the smaller Pitban 285, freeing up space and mass enough to add a second PPC and a second small laser, four medium lasers, and a short-range missile launcher. The new version was slow and it tended to overheat rapidly in combat, especially if its pilot got too free with those twin Magna Hellstar PPCs.

Lori dwelt on none of this; she recognized the model and knew that with that kind of firepower in a 95-ton BattleMech, the defensive perimeter at Gate One was in serious danger.

"Davis!" she called over her private comm channel. "Davis, we've got trouble up here at One."

"Whatcha got, lass? Tha' wee infiltrator?"

"He's down. No problem. But there's a major assault forming up here, and I don't think we can hold them. What's the sit at Gates Two and Three?"

"Three is in a firefight noo, but holding. It's quiet for the moment at Two."

"Then round up anybody you can spare and send them over to Gate One. We're going to need to fall back here when the assault carries the barricades."

"Aye, lass. We're on it. We're on our way."

She hoped they would be in time.

Mindy Cain had been, if anything, less enthusiastic about Grayson's plan than she'd been about a DropShip with a damaged fusion reactor docking with her ship. Still, the tall, grave man in the gray combat armor had given her no choice. "You can do it, ma'am, or I have people with me who can. I assume, though, that you'd rather not be relieved of your command."

The guy certainly knew how ship captains thought ... and how they felt about their vessels.

He'd moved himself and several of his people onto *Caliban*'s bridge, still wearing gray combat armor as they took up positions at several of the work stations, not interfering with her crew but keeping a close watch on them. Then he'd given her very specific and precise instructions as to how to move her ship.

Not a jump, no. Nothing so *simple*. What Carlyle wanted her to do was yaw the big starship to starboard, swinging tail and collector sail together to port, toward the *Olympus* station, a tricky enough maneuver in the best of circumstances. The *Caliban* was now swinging about slightly, shifting its orientation with respect both to the distant Hesperan sun and to the small fleet of vessels gathered in its shadow.

Moving a JumpShip with its sail unfurled was always a difficult, and sometimes a dangerous, maneuver. The sail's tension was maintained both by the JumpShip's low-G thrust and by rotation, which created the centrifugal force that held the sail stretched taut when maneuvers were necessary. This far from the local sun, though, very little thrust was required to keep the ship on station—just eight-hundredths of a millimeter per second. Mindy was relying on the sail's rotation to keep it furled, while swinging it with the ship, all the while having to watch that the running rigging and powerfeed cables weren't fouled.

"*Caliban,* this is *Ravager,*" came a radio call seconds after the JumpShip began its maneuver. "Cease acceleration at once!"

"Ah, *Ravager,* we've got a problem over here," Mindy shot back. "Give us a second. . . ." She switched off. "That'll keep 'em guessing for a moment or two, anyway."

"Good," Carlyle said. The mercenary colonel sounded distracted. He was studying the navigational repeater screen with an almost ferocious intensity, watching the alignment of the blips displayed there in three dimensions. Once, he adjusted the controls to rotate the image on one axis, until he could look along *Caliban*'s length from prow to stern, and toward her sail. Mindy's eyes widened. Until that moment, she'd not been sure what the merc was trying to do, but she saw now that he was turning her ship so that *Caliban*'s broad, circular, jet-black sail would block the *Olympus* station's view of what was going on near the JumpShip's hull. That sail now completely blocked the line of sight between itself and the recharge station.

"Okay, Matt," Carlyle said, holding his headset's needle mike to his lips. "You're masked, both from the station and from the Droppers. You've got three minutes. Launch!"

"Roger that," a voice came back over the console speakers. "Here goes."

Mindy saw the launch unfold on one of the console monitors. Ports in the *Leopard* DropShip's sides slid open, and with a thump that echoed through the JumpShip's hull, a quartet of jet-black spheres spilled from the smaller vessel's aerospace fighter tubes.

She recognized the small craft, even though they were devilishly hard to see against the black of space. They were NL-42 troop transports, "battle taxis" in popular parlance. She noted that not only was their launch hidden from the *Olympus* station by the sail, but the *Leopard* DropShip's hull and part of the *Caliban*'s spine structure blocked the launch from the perspective of both the *Ravager* and the *Lightning*. Sneaking up on a JumpShip or a large space station was virtually impossible, thanks to radar and high-tech sensor suites that would render even those black-on-black battle spheroids visible.

But this guy was contriving to do just that.

"How many people do you have on those things?" she asked Carlyle.

He gave her an appraising look, as though trying to decide whether or not to answer. Then he shrugged. "There's room aboard each for ten men in full battle armor," he said.

The four NL-42s sped silently past the *Caliban*'s stern, neatly clearing the rigging spars and the rigging itself, their approach now completely masked by the sail. For a moment, Mindy wondered if the bastards had miscalculated. It looked to her as though those accelerating projectiles were going to punch four neat, round holes right through the third quadrant of her sail, out near the rim, but then, as *Caliban* kept turning, the edge of the sail drifted out of their path in a closely choreographed display of precision flying and calculation. The transports skimmed past the edge of the sail, their course aligned perfectly with the mushroom-prow of the *Olympus* station, their plasma drives setting the thin material of the sail to fluttering violently as if in a sudden, hard wind.

"If you people tear my sail," she said in a low voice, "you're going to pay for a new one."

"Of course," Carlyle said. "Actually, I was originally considering having the taxis punch right *through* the sail. It would be harder to see them coming that way, and that approach would be completely unexpected."

"Why didn't you?"

The mercenary colonel made a face before answering. "Mostly I don't like the destruction of high-tech assets," he said. "We don't have enough of them as it is, and every time we lose one, it takes us another notch or two on the downward road toward barbarism."

She wasn't sure what he was talking about, and shook her head. "What?"

"Put it this way," he said, turning those hard, gray eyes on her. "If this stunt goes down, I'm going to have a job for you. One involving a jump to another system. Interested?"

"Are you coming along?"

He blinked. "No. My place is here."

"Good. The farther away I can get from you, the better I like it! Sure, if the price is right, I'll do it."

"Fine. We'll talk about it after the battle." He looked at the tactical display again. "Okay, Captain. Cease rotation."

Mindy gave the necessary orders, and the JumpShip slowed, then stopped. When she looked at the display, she saw that the *Caliban*'s primary drives were now aimed directly at the *Olympus* station, some fifteen kilometers distant.

"Caliban!" Admiral Barnes called over the radio. "What the bloody hell are you—"

"Admiral Barnes, this is Colonel Grayson Death Carlyle, commander of the Gray Death Legion. We are here in support of the military and political interests of House Steiner and the Lyran Alliance."

There was a pause. "Carlyle! But you . . . you were disgraced . . . not with the Legion anymore . . ."

"I regret the deception, Admiral, but it was necessary. I assure you that I have the full support and complete authority of Archon Katrina Steiner."

The two DropShips were moving now, closing on *Caliban*. Mindy was beginning to sweat, the atmosphere on the bridge now close and uncomfortably warm.

"That JumpShip is no match for two *Union* Class DropShips!" Barnes said, a blustering verbal advance. "Surrender!"

"Admiral," Carlyle said quietly, "I suggest you take a look at the way we've aligned this JumpShip. The *Caliban* can manage two tenths' of a G acceleration for short periods. I suggest you think about what a tightly focused beam of high-velocity hydrogen ions would do to your command if I engaged this vessel's primary drive."

Mindy blinked in the long silence that followed. She'd not seen that possibility herself, though she'd wondered about Carlyle's maneuver. The drive exhaust on a JumpShip's station-keeping drives was deadly to any vessel downstream, and spacecraft piloting conventions always kept the vessel's drive venturis well clear of any other ship or facility.

Grayson Carlyle had just turned her *Caliban* into a half-kilometer-long particle projection cannon, the biggest damned PPC in the Inner Sphere. "You're crazy, you know," she told him.

"It's one of my more endearing traits," he replied, killing his lip mike.

"Have they spotted the taxis yet?"

"I don't know. They're damned near invisible optically, but they'd show on radar. I'm hoping our friends over there are more worried just now about *Caliban*. We need time to let our people get over there."

"*Caliban*," Barnes said. "You're bluffing! You wouldn't fry a recharge station. You'd be branded as a heretic and an outlaw on every civilized planet. I have your bio up on the screen in front of me, and it says you have a thing for lostech and preserving technology.

"Now if you want to preserve the technology of that

damned JumpShip, you will maneuver it around to aim your drive somewhere else, well clear of this station. Next, you will surrender to my DropShips, or they will open fire at my command and cut your vessel to scrap."

Mindy shivered a bit at that. JumpShips were supposed to be inviolate, though she'd heard stories of the Clans defying the bans and destroying Jumpers. But then, large-scale facilities like recharge stations were supposed to be inviolate too.

What was happening to the universe?

"*Caliban!* This is *Olympus* station! Do you copy? Surrender or—"

The voice was cut off abruptly, almost in mid-word. Mindy heard some indistinct sounds from the speaker, and something that might have been Barnes's muffled voice in the background, saying "*What?*"

"I think," Grayson said slowly, grinning, "that they just spotted the taxis." He checked a time readout on the console. "They should be decelerating now, and the station will be looking right up their drive flares."

"What, you're using them as PPCs too?"

"Not powerful enough to be worth the effort, though at full thrust they'd definitely do some damage. No, I don't want to fry that facility. And we won't have to." He shifted channels on his mike. "*Io!* You're clear to launch. Execute defensive pattern Bravo-sierra."

"Ah, roger, *Caliban!* Bravo-sierra. Watch my jets!"

On one of the monitor screens, the *Leopard* Class DropShip broke free from the *Caliban*'s magnetic grasp, an emergency jettison that sent the docking tunnel spinning slowly off into space in a sparkling cloud of frozen vapor and left several fuel and power leads writhing in space like slender black serpents. Elsewhere, farther out in space, the DropShip *Europa,* hanging unnoticed ever since Carlyle had boarded the *Io,* suddenly engaged its primary drives, accelerating at four Gs toward the developing space battle.

The *Ravager* fired first with one of its PPCs—the beam invisible in the vacuum of space, but detectable aboard the *Caliban* by the surge of its magnetic field. The target, however, was not the JumpShip as Mindy had feared, but the *Io,* now maneuvering half a kilometer away. A spot on the *Leopard*'s dorsal armor grew white hot, spraying a fine mist of glowing particles into space; an instant later, the *Io* replied, firing her two bow-mounted PPCs and following those invisible bolts of lightning with a volley of long-range missiles.

"*Io*," Grayson said into his mike. "Work well clear of the *Caliban*. I don't want civilians catching the ones that miss you."

"Affirmative, *Caliban*." The *Leopard*'s stern thrusters lit up with white plasma fire; the *Caliban*'s sail fluttered in that charged particle wind, and Mindy saw the energy flow readout surge upward, as the collector sail snagged a percentage of the energy spilling from the *Io*'s main drive.

A gift from the battle raging in the vacuum outside.

Carlyle's concern for her command and her people surprised her. She'd not thought of mercs as being particularly interested in whether civilians lived or died, especially in a case like this, where his actions had already placed her command in danger. It gave her a new and slightly unsettling perspective of the man, with the idea that he was doing what he had to do to win his fight but not particularly enjoying what he did, and all the while taking precautions to reduce . . . what was that delightfully understated militarism? *Collateral damage.* That was it.

It wasn't enough to make her change her mind about him, but damn if it wasn't making her think.

26

Gate One, Defiance Industries Complex
Maria's Elegy, Hesperus II
Rahneshire, Lyran Alliance
1421 hours (local), 21 December 3057

The three Legion 'Mechs on the barricade were firing, *had* been firing for long minutes now, as temperature gauges rose, the spent brass from their autocannons piling up around their feet like a glittering carpet of golden snow. For a time, their concentrated fire had stopped the enemy advance, but now the assault 'Mechs were grinding forward once more, slowly, step by step carrying the ramp.

The defenders were concentrating on the *Banshee,* recognizing that the 95-ton monster was going to be their most serious problem, but sparing plenty of firepower for the others as well. One of the *Victors* had taken a bad hit in the left arm already, rendering the twin Sorenstein V medium lasers there useless.

The *Cyclops* was taking plenty of hits too. The CP 10-Z *Cyclops* had originally been designed as a commander's 'Mech, with a lot of space devoted to its sophisticated communications and sensor suites. This particular machine was old and war-battered, with corrosion showing on exposed armor and the paint streaked and scratched—more likely the BattleMech of a down-on-his-luck mercenary who'd signed on recently with the Ironhands than of an Ironhand senior officer. Still, the *Cyclops* was a decent 'Mech with heavy armor and adequate weaponry, and a serious danger in that four-abreast charge lumbering up the ramp. It also had a weakness exploited by every experienced 'Mech pilot who faced it. That odd, even funny-looking head with its staring Tacticon scanner disk that gave it the appearance of a one-eyed giant was vulnerable, and knocking it out could cripple the entire fire-control system.

The *Apollo,* the *Enforcer,* and the *JagerMech* kept up a constant, savage fire, laser bursts and autocannon rounds smashing and cracking among the advancing assault 'Mechs. The *Cyclops* staggered once as a barrage of missiles from the *Apollo* washed across its legs and torso, raising a dense cloud of smoke and flying gravel and making the big 'Mech stumble. Return fire blasted into the barricade, hurling fragments of white-hot metal into the air and across the crouching Legion 'Mechs. The *Enforcer* staggered back, smoke spilling from a deep, flame-scorched wound in its left shoulder. It righted itself, raised its autocannon again, and kept firing.

"Pull out of there, Dimitri," Lori called. "Let me in and have a crack at them!"

MechWarrior Dimitri Oretsov emptied the last of a cassette at the advancing 'Mechs, then stepped back out of the way. "Give 'em hell, Colonel!" he called.

She moved past him, taking her place alongside Sergeant Martha O'Dell's *JagerMech,* taking aim with her autocannon, and opening fire with scarcely a missed beat. She concentrated on the *Banshee* and then, as the enemy 'Mechs moved still closer, ponderously advancing into that hail of fire, she shifted to the *Cyclops,* which was almost directly opposite her position.

Cannon fire sparked and sang and chattered, the thunder of the battle now so deafening that nothing at all existed save raw, Voice-of-God noise and the enemy himself, a wall of steel-alloy and blazing weapons a scant forty meters away.

"Henri!" Lori yelled, still firing. "Start organizing every 'Mech back there! Line them up, three abreast. We'll take it as a shooting withdrawal, by the numbers!"

"Roger that, my Colonel!" He pronounced "Roger" like "row-share."

Lori held her place in the line, as laser fire clipped past her head or buried itself in puffs of expanding vapor erupting from her armor. She was slamming round after round into the *Cyclops,* which was on the extreme right of the enemy's line—to her left as Lori looked at him. The assault 'Mechs were now well up the ramp leading to Gate One and the ramp was narrowing. Under that incessant, devastating fire, the *Cyclops* missed its next step, its foot grating down the side of the ramp, causing the big machine to lurch suddenly forward.

Lori rode the target down with her targeting cross hairs, hurling high explosives into the now fully exposed top of the enemy 'Mech's head. Smoke swirled past, momentarily blocking her view though she continued firing nonetheless. As the smoke cleared, she saw the *Cyclops* on the ground next to the ramp, struggling to rise; its head had been blown clean away, leaving nothing on its shoulders but a sparking stump of wires and cables.

It seemed odd for the 'Mech to be still moving after complete decapitation, but the *Cyclops* had been designed with its cockpit sheltered inside its upper torso, and nothing but sensors and electronics packed into the diminutive, one-eyed head. The pilot was still alive, but with the tracking and scanning gear gone, the *Cyclops* was as helplessly blind as its mythological predecessor Polyphemus, the original Cyclops who'd encountered the Greek hero Odysseus in Homer's epic. She immediately shifted to her right, targeting the *Banshee.*

Her ammo was down to three cassettes, and her heat was building again. She wouldn't be able to stay up here much longer.

She opened a new channel. "Jonathan!" she called. "What's your position now?"

"On our way to help you, Colonel" was Major Frye's reply. "Major McCall said to come in from the west and try to help you out. We're about two kilometers from Gate One, but we're hitting damned tough resistance."

"Roger that. Break through if you can. I think they're about to force the barricade."

"We'll do our best. Hold on, Colonel!"

The *Banshee* was now less than thirty meters away, leaning forward as if braced against a high wind from its front. Its head had taken a number of hits, and the skull-paint and tack-welded armor had been stripped away. What was left was, if anything, uglier than any artist could have possibly portrayed it, a dark gray, angular skull with bright splashes of lead mingled with streaks of paint, and a smear of green coolant leaking from a ruptured pipe like BattleMech's blood. She aimed her autocannon directly into that face at near pointblank range and emptied one cassette, then another, then a third, the rounds sparking and flashing as they struck head and shoulders and upper torso, a firestorm of high explosives washing across the machine's upper works. It fired both PPCs in reply, the bolts striking Lori's *Zeus* hard, one high, one low, sending blue lightning arcing across her legs and into the cordwood stack of dead 'Mechs and wreckage in front of her.

"Front rank!" Villiers yelled suddenly. "Fall back!"

Lori tried to take a step back, then felt cold horror when she realized she couldn't; the right thigh of her *Zeus,* the part of her armor called the cuisse, had become arc-welded to the barricade itself by the jolt of grounding electricity.

She was trapped, about to become the sole standing 'Mech remaining directly in the middle of two opposing fields of fire.

The *Banshee* seemed to be grinning at her as it took another step, then fired a deadly, savage, rippling barrage of PPC and laser fire into Lori's *Zeus*. The blast staggered her, ripping armor from her hull, carrying away her already shattered right arm, mauling her right leg, then smashing her free of the spotweld with an explosion so powerful she felt as though she'd just been given a hard kick in the tail.

"Punch out, Colonel!" someone was yelling over the taccom. "Punch out!"

Her *Zeus* wasn't dead yet, but damned near. Systems were failing, the heat at critical levels. She tried to fire the autocannon, but yet another red warning discrete lit up, announcing a feed jam, probably caused when half the breech had been blown away or the barrel twisted in the fusillade of fire. All Lori had now was her laser; she fired it directly into that grinning face.

Useless. The monster kept coming . . . coming for *her,* its arms reaching out as though its pilot intended to smash her 'Mech to scrap, with her still trapped inside. The thing suddenly vented a shrill, piercing ululation, an eerie, hackles-raising screech of rage and battle lust, a scream played from an onboard recorder, the sound amplified and projected as a kind of psychological terror weapon.

She took a step back, and her right leg started to give way, refusing to support her any longer.

Lori knew better than to press her luck any further. "Davis!" she yelled. "You've got command!" Then she slammed her fist down on the eject sequence key.

Her *Zeus*'s canopy flipped up, back, and away, suddenly exposing her to the brilliant light and roaring thunder of battle outside. The *Banshee*'s great, steel hand was reaching for her, as though intending to pluck her from the cockpit when her ejection seat's rockets fired, carrying her into the sky. If she thought she'd been kicked in the tail before, this was a thousand times worse, the acceleration hammering at her, the wind tearing at her bare legs and cooling vest and the heavy neurohelmet still resting on her shoulders.

Then her chute deployed, and she had a dizzying, swirling view of the battle from above.

Villiers's line of 'Mechs waited as the *JagerMech* and *Enforcer* slipped through their line, then fired a single, devastating volley at the enemy assault 'Mechs just as they reached the barricade. Lori's *Zeus*, still standing at an odd, listing angle, was picked up and carried along in that blast, smashing into the *Banshee*. One of the *Victors* went down; the other stopped, pivoting to deliver a missile barrage, and then the front rank of Legion 'Mechs broke and moved to the rear, taking up position behind still another rank of waiting, fully armed BattleMechs.

The *Banshee* collapsed as the next rank fired, its right arm blasted away, its head a mass of puckered craters and shredded armor. The remaining, damaged *Victor* withstood the fire for only a moment, then began backing away from the barricade, nearly colliding with the *Catapult* and the *Orion* to its rear. In another moment, the three survivors of that charge up the long ramp were moving way, in full retreat.

Seconds later, Lori saw other 'Mechs emerging from the shadows of the gateway's mouth, Davis McCall's

Highlander in the lead. Retreat became a rout, the surviving Star Republic 'Mechs scattering wildly back through the outside factory complex, their panic infecting those 'Mechs still waiting there for their turn to attack.

It looked to her as though the heart simply went out of the Gareth forces in that moment, when their assault line broke at the barricade.

Lori drifted to the ground a hundred meters from the gate, hitting hard and rolling, then working swiftly to unhook her harness and draw her holdout pistol, checking to see it was charged. She was down in enemy territory, but she wasn't going to make her capture easy.

She heard a whine from the left and turned to face the source, dropping to one knee. A Pegasus hovertank approached, its ducted fans shrieking as they spat gravel and dust. The vehicle drew closer, angling to meet her; she held the pistol on target—a pathetic gesture and no more against that armor, then suddenly raised the weapon and stood up.

"Jonathan!" she cried, pulling off her helmet so he would recognize her.

The Pegasus settled to the ground ten meters away, the whine of its fans dwindling to silence. A hatch popped open on the vehicle, which was close enough now that she could see the gray skull emblem of the Legion and the unit markings for Third Battalion. Major Jonathan Frye stood up in the hatch, grinning and waving.

"Lori! Are you all right?"

"Fine. What the hell are you doing out here?"

What she meant by that, of course, was what Frye was doing in his light scout hovertank so far in advance of the rest of Third Battalion's 'Mechs. He was dangerously exposed, an easy target for any heavy weapon that challenged his right of way.

He shrugged, the movement shifting his heavy black combat vest on his shoulders. "It was the fastest way to get somebody in here," he told her. Leaning forward, he extended a hand and helped her mount the tank, then ducked down to clear the way for her to wiggle into the hatch. Inside, the cabin was cramped, but there was space enough for her to squeeze in next to Frye's commander's seat. The fans shrilled to life again, the vehicle lurched heavily, and then the hovertank was flying, supported on its own cushion of air, howling through the wreckage of the factory.

The devastation was pretty bad, though it appeared to have been limited to a few tightly bounded areas. But if the fighting continued much longer ...

"In any case," Frye said, shouting to make himself heard above the racket, "I think we've beat them." He pointed, indicating a display screen on the bulkhead above the main console. Though the image danced and jittered with the tank's movement, she could make out a shadowy line of BattleMechs advancing through more or less intact cooling towers and factory stacks. A little closer, and she could see unit markings. It was the Third Battalion, entering the factory complex from the west.

"The bad guys have been pulling back ever since we began moving into the complex," Frye explained. "I think you had them so worn down already, they decided to pack up and leave rather than hang around and face us."

"Makes sense," she said. "You ... you made it just in time."

He shook his head. "Wasn't me, Colonel. *You* did it, by holding the perimeter. If it was up to me, I'd have to say you just won the battle."

Lori turned, looking at a rear display monitor that showed part of the factory devastated by the battle, storage tanks burned out, gantry towers toppled, whole mountains of twisted, burning wreckage.

"It sure doesn't feel like a victory," she said. "And if Grayson doesn't pull off his part, out at the jump point, it won't be."

"Which is something we can't do a damned thing about," Frye said. "Don't worry, Lori. He'll pull it off if anybody can do it."

She smiled. "I know."

Minutes had passed, for Grayson an agony of waiting and wondering. If this didn't work ...

Though smaller and considerably less well-armed than the *Union* DropShips, the two *Leopards* were more maneuverable, and the *Europa* had had the advantage of being able to pick her initial position as the battle began. The *Ravager* was under heavy fire from both the *Europa* and the *Io*, while the *Lightning*, blocked from the fight by the JumpShip's hull, tried to work her way in closer. A hole had been opened in the *Ravager*'s side, a gaping crater from which atmosphere and water were spilling in a vast, expanding cloud of cascading flecks of ice. Several of the weapons mounts on that flank of the vessel had been knocked out, and both Legion DropShips were maintaining position on that side, a cheap way of keeping enemy return fire to a minimum.

The end, when it came, was so sudden that it caught everyone on the *Caliban*'s bridge by surprise. *"Caliban!"* a voice announced. "This is Gerard."

"Go ahead, Matt," Grayson said.

"The station is secured."

The Legion people floating on *Caliban*'s bridge erupted in a volley of cheers—all save Grayson, who merely smiled. The relief he felt, however, was overwhelming. The gamble had paid off. He had to work to keep his voice from shaking. "Good work, people. *Damned* good work."

"Thanks, Colonel. Admiral Barnes surrendered to me personally just a few moments ago, when we broke into the operations center. There may be some holdouts in the lower levels and cargo bays, but we've got the bridge, Ops, Engineering, and the command staff."

Seconds later, both *Union* DropShips aligned their prows with distant Hesperus and lit their main drives, accelerating at maximum gravs.

"Should we go after 'em?" David Longo wanted to know.

"That's negative, Captain," Grayson replied. "They'll be a week or ten days getting back to Hesperus II, and by then it'll be all over. *Io,* return to *Caliban* to pick me up. *Europa,* you go rendezvous with the station. Put more troops aboard, and watch out for lurkers." He turned to face *Caliban*'s captain, who was looking at him with a thoughtful expression. "Captain? I'll be leaving your ship soon. Again, I apologize for the danger, but if it's any consolation, your ship helped me save the lives of a fair number of my people."

"That's important to you, isn't it, Colonel? Saving lives, I mean."

"Yes, it is. Does that surprise you?"

"I guess it does. You know what they say about soldiers. They're trained to kill people and break things."

"Generally speaking, that's true. But a wise tactician once pointed out that the *real* victory came in winning a battle without killing anybody, yours or theirs."

"Who said that?"

"Sun-Tzu. Early fourth century B.C., about thirty-three hundred years ago. Some things just can't be improved on."

"War without killing? That doesn't make much sense."

"I think he meant that it was better to win your victories without leaving them to chance on the battlefield. Battles," he said, rubbing his eyes, "are messy. So much can go wrong, so much that you can't possibly foresee."

She nodded, but her expression suggested that she didn't really understand. "You wanted me to do something for you?"

Grayson nodded. "That's right." He fumbled with the belt harness on his armor, extracting a small computer memory block. "I want you to jump for Furillo, as fast as you can. Zenith jump point. And when you get there, here's what I want you to do...."

As he spoke, though, his mind was on Hesperus II, wondering how Lori was doing, wondering if she had even survived.

It was strange, he thought. He'd been so depressed at losing the ability to pilot BattleMechs, as though that particular talent was all that was needed to be a successful warrior. He knew differently now; the tactics he'd applied here, in space, had been similar in spirit if not in execution to tactics he'd employed dozens of times as a MechWarrior.

Grayson Carlyle was a warrior; he could not escape that.

And yet, for all of that, he was realizing afresh how very much he hated war, its destructiveness, its tragedy, its capacity for ultimately devouring the entire human species, with all its accomplishments, arts, and science.

There must be, he thought, a better way.

He just couldn't imagine what that way might be.

Epilogue

Royal Palace, Tharkad City
Tharkad, District of Donegal
Lyran Alliance
1015 hours (local), 3 January 3058

"**C**olonel Grayson Death Carlyle, Baron Glengarry and commander of the Gray Death Legion!"

The fanfare was majestic, a soul-stirring martial air rich with the voices of two hundred brass pieces. Grayson stood, resplendent in his full-dress uniform, then strode up the steps toward the waiting Katrina Steiner. Behind him, the crowd erupted into applause, a growing, throbbing torrent of noise that nearly drowned out the brass fanfare. He'd already been through one ceremony today, the formal re-investiture of his full rights and privileges as Baron of Glengarry. This, however, was something more.

He stood at attention before the Archon, delivering a crisp salute. Katrina acknowledged with a slight, cool bow.

"Colonel Lori Kalmar-Carlyle," Katrina said, her amplified voice booming across the vast and colorful mob of people—civilian nobles, military officers of all ranks, government officials, even ordinary Tharkans, most wearing furs and heavy cloaks, all gathered this morning in the Grand Hall of the Palace to witness this presentation. In the front ranks, Lori stepped forward and hurried up the steps. She took her place at Grayson's left side, facing the Archon with him. Her warm breath puffed like smoke in the chilly air.

For some reason, it reminded Grayson of a wedding ceremony; his marriage to Lori had been a small and informal affair. This, however, was very much larger. The two *Griffins* that guarded the Archon's throne stood impassively, towering overhead, symbols of military power and the stability of long tradition.

"Colonel Carlyle . . . and Colonel Kalmar," Katrina said, nodding to each in turn. "It is my very great pleasure to make this presentation today, an honor that is rarely extended even to my officers within the Lyran military, much less to mercenaries. You, however, Baron Glengarry, and you, Colonel Kalmar, have both more than amply demonstrated your loyalty to me, to the Lyran Alliance, and more, to the civilization we hope to maintain here, despite the savage desecration of war.

"Therefore, for actions above and beyond the call of duty, for particular brilliance in both strategy and tactics in the service of the Lyran Alliance, for the tactical expertise and effectiveness shown on and before 21 December 3057 in the defense of Alliance interests on the world of Hesperus II, it is my very great privilege and pleasure to present you *both* with the McKennsy Hammer."

The Archon gestured, and two aides stepped forward from the wings, each carrying a green velvet pillow with a heavy, square-headed silver hammer resting on it. Katrina turned, took the first hammer, and passed it to Grayson. He hefted it, feeling its nine-kilo mass, as Katrina handed the second hammer to Lori. It was hard to believe how much had happened in the past few months, concluding with Katrina putting a command circuit of JumpShips at their disposal so that this ceremony could take place at the soonest possible moment.

"I should point out," Katrina was saying, "that this is the first time in history this award has been handed out in a double ceremony. Perhaps the most impressive aspect of the Battle of Hesperus, however, was the way the two of you worked together, Grayson in space, Lori on the ground.

"Grayson Carlyle, Lori Carlyle . . . the Lyran Alliance

is grateful." Katrina Steiner rendered a perfect, militarily precise salute. "We salute you!"

On cue, then, they turned to face the multitude, holding the heavy hammers aloft. The crowd went wild. . . .

The award should have gone to the entire Legion, Grayson thought, to the men and women who'd really pulled this difficult action off and made it work, even when he'd been forced to plan almost all of it in the dark, with frighteningly little intelligence. They'd pulled together when they'd had to; they'd made the difference. Gareth's cabal was broken.

Of Gareth himself, there'd been no sign, though a number of *Excalibur* DropShips had fled from Morningstar Spaceport after the battle. Lori had simply not had the available ships and men to stop them. No doubt Brandal Gareth and his senior officers had jumped out aboard one of the waiting JumpShips at the Hesperan zenith point. Grayson regretted his escape, but there'd been no way to stop it; Gareth had no more authority now within the Alliance, though, and would either be forced to flee to the service of another House, or turn pirate. Sooner or later he would show his face again, and then he'd be cut down.

More important than Gareth, though, was the security of Hesperus II. The Defiance industrial complex was back on-line at seventy percent capacity, despite the damage suffered. The new acting manager at the plant promised to have production up to one hundred percent within another month.

That brought to mind a strange twist to events. Daniel Brewer, the young CEO of Defiance Industries and the would-be 'Mech pilot who had nearly breached the Legion's defenses single-handedly, had been found after the battle, alive. His chute had deployed as he'd ejected, then become tangled in the crisscrossing maze of struts and spars high up in the foundry bay. He'd hung there for hours until someone spotted him and brought him down.

He should be in the crowd here today . . . yes, there he was. Standing in the front row, next to a grinning Davis McCall. Katrina had recognized that he'd been deceived by Gareth and decided not to punish him; it was equally clear that he couldn't go back to running Defiance Industries. Lori had suggested an alternative.

Daniel Brewer, hereditary head of Defiance Industries, had at Archon Katrina's order been enlisted in the Gray Death as a cadet MechWarrior. During his tour with the Legion, the next-in-line-of-succession would run Defiance Industries and the planet; Daniel, however, would retain the title of Duke of Hesperus II. Someday, when he was a bit more mature, a bit wiser, perhaps, he would return and take up the reins of his family's business once again. In the meantime, he had his fondest wish . . . to be a MechWarrior.

Grayson hoped he didn't regret it. It was certainly an advantageous alliance for the Legion, since it virtually guaranteed the unit an unlimited supply of parts, ammo, and new 'Mechs.

Grayson spotted Alex in the crowd, standing next to Caitlin. He looked quite handsome in his new green and blue dress uniform of the Royal Guard. There was another one who would benefit from some seasoning, who might return to the Legion someday as a senior officer, with new skills and experience to strengthen the unit. When *Caliban* had jumped to Furillo, she'd emerged almost in the middle of the Lyran fleet that Katrina had been assembling there, awaiting only the word from Grayson to make the final jump into Hesperan space. The arrival of the First Royal Guard—including Alexander Carlyle—had been the final blow to Gareth's rebellion.

Mindy Cain had asked to sign on with the Legion, bringing her ship and crew with her. Grayson couldn't refuse that offer; there were several JumpShips that the Legion worked with on a fairly regular basis, but since the departure of the *Invidious* a year or two ago, they'd had to rely entirely on commercial lines.

It would be good to add *Caliban* to the Legion's TO&E. Grayson wished, though, that he knew what had changed Mindy's mind about the military.

Maybe she figured that she'd be less likely to be impressed into service again if she actually joined up.

Or maybe she just liked what she'd seen of the Gray Death Legion.

As for Grayson, his own doubts were dispelled. If he couldn't pilot a BattleMech any longer, there were other ways to extend his talent for tactics into the arena of war. He'd demonstrated that at the Hesperan jump point.

Slowly, he lowered the hammer as the cheering subsided. The band could be heard again, playing the Lyran anthem, and he and Lori stood to attention, facing the Lyran Alliance banner hanging to the side of the stage. It was a thrilling, a *glorious* moment. . . .

Why, he wondered, did humanity, after all these millennia of bloody-handed savagery, still associate glory with the barbarism of war?

Someday, he thought, his grip squeezing tighter on the shaft of the heavy silver hammer, *we'll find a way to stop this madness.*

But when that would be, or how it would come about, Grayson still had no idea.

In the meantime, he was content to remain what he'd always been . . .

. . . a *MechWarrior.*

About the Author

William H. Keith, Jr. under his own name and several pseudonyms, has written, at this point in the space-time continuum at least, forty-some novels ranging from science fiction to action-adventure to fast paced military technothrillers. He is a popular BattleTech author who has been writing in the BattleTech universe from the very beginning. His trilogy of novels—*Decision at Thunder Rift, Mercenary's Star, The Price of Glory*—introduced the now infamous Gray Death Legion and kicked off FASA's line of BattleTech novels. *Operation Excalibur* continues the story begun in Keith's *Tactics of Duty*, which was published in August of 1995. More adventures of the Gray Death will be published in 1997.

His expertise in military tactics, technology, and the epic theme of men at war have been showcased in several long-running series following modern aircraft carrier combat and the exploits of the U.S. Navy SEALs. *Warstrider*, a military-SF book series, explores the ultimate interface of man, machine, and alien. Keith's first love, however, is hard SF in the tradition of Arthur C. Clarke and Robert Heinlein.

Keith lives in the mountains of western Pennsylvania with his tactical coordinator wife, his combat-ready daughter, and four ninja-assassin cats.

Salamander

Apollo

Nightsky

Enforcer

Zeus

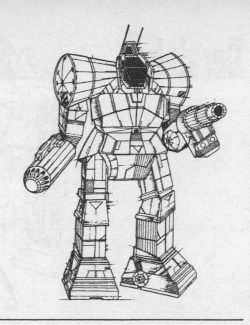

Cataphract

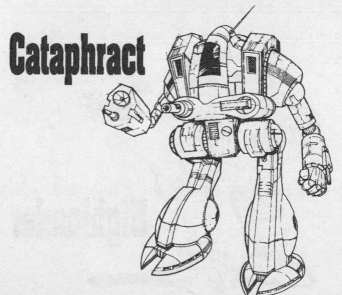

Dervish

Highlander

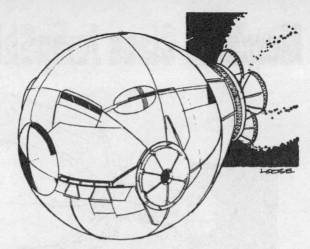

NL-42 Battle Taxi

Olympus Class
Recharge Station

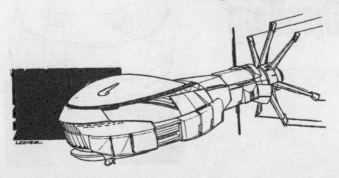

Merchant Class JumpShip

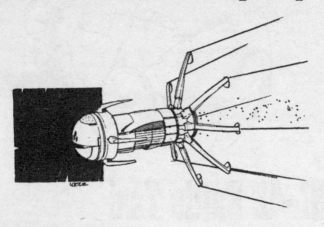

Excalibur Class DropShip

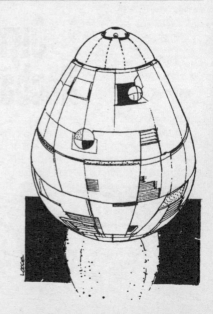

Moons Viewing Pavilion, outside Deber City
Benjamin
Benjamin Military District, Draconis Combine
20 December 3058

"We must have revenge!"

The speaker whose fervently hissed words chased one another like rats up the square-sectioned wooden uprights and on among the exposed rafters of the great pavilion, was no young man. But a greater weight than years alone stooped his thin shoulders and bent his back.

His tall spare frame was draped in a heavy robe like an acolyte of the Order of the Five Pillars. His cowl was thrown defiantly back, revealing a long haggard face with graying hair drawn into a topknot.

With burning eyes he glared about at the score of men kneeling about the long, low table. Like him they were robed, but their hoods were in place and so hid their faces.

The cowls were pure formality. These men controlled substantial resources, not least in the gathering of intelligence. Each knew who the others were. They were leaders of the Draconis Combine's still tightly regulated business community, of the Draconis Combine Mustered Soldiery, and of the yakuza crime organizations which constituted—in the yakuzas' minds at least—the Combine's shadow government. Together they formed the ruling council of Kokuryu-*kai,* the ancient Black Dragon Society. The current regime proscribed the Society, and the black-clad hounds of the Internal Security Force were ruthless in sniffing out and extirpating its members. Hence the masks, to serve as constant reminder that discovery was death.

Behind each man, still and silent as statues by the shadowed walls, stood a single bodyguard. By ancient usage firearms were prohibited within the precincts of the Pavilion. Each guard was an adept at both the armed or unarmed variety of hand-fighting: karate, jujutsu, taekwon-do, ryukyu kobujutsu, savate, shorinji kempo, escrima, and Ryu-bujutsu, the Dragon's Warrior-Techniques and official hand-to-hand combat form of the DCMS. Each had taken at least one life in face-to-face combat, and each was implicitly trusted to be ready at an instant's notice to lay down his own life for his lord.

Outside the stressed-cement walls, the Moons marched across the sky, huge and red as bloodshot eyes. The moons were vast reflectors, like JumpShip collecting sails, placed in orbit to augment the feeble shine of Benjamin's type-M sun. They strewed multiple oblongs of light like fanned cards across the floor and the occupants of the cathedral space, and the shadows they cast were tinted green.

Hiraoke Toyama stared at each of his compatriots in turn, as if to see through their cowls to the depths of their souls. Then he turned to face the head of the chamber, gestured with a small black controller in his hand.

In a large holotank filled with color and movement, a magnificently muscled man with blond hair hanging unbound around great shoulders, clad only in the cooling trunks of a Kurita MechWarrior, knelt before the bulk of a fallen BattleMech. He stared contemplatively down at the naked *wakizashi* in his hand. Behind him stood a slender young woman holding a drawn *katana,* her hair seared short and smoking like the black garments she wore, and her face burned red by intolerable heat.

The watchers gasped in sympathetic reaction as the kneeling man plunged the steel into his washboard belly.

"The full three cuts," murmured a man the others affected not to know was a ranking officer within the DCMS. Despite the popularity among the Combine's soldiers of Coordinator Theodore Kurita, who had been a distinguished MechWarrior and Gunji no Kanrei before ascending to the Dragon Throne, not all of its military leadership approved of his liberalization of Draconian society. "*Bishonen* Kusunoki knew how to die like a man."

The young woman struck. The blond man's head sprang from its shoulders as blood spouted from the stump of his neck. Toyama froze the holovid display.

"As a result of our attempts to seize Towne for the Dragon, and our so-called leaders' dilatoriness in taking advantage of the confusion which reigns among our age-old enemies, untold lives were lost, including that of *Taisho* Jeffrey Kusunoki, whose death we have just witnessed as it was broadcast to the planet. Four regiments of DCMS regulars were disarmed and returned to the Combine in disgrace; two regiments of our own Black Dragon *kobun* were virtually wiped out. I myself lost my son, Taisuke, and my most trusted advisor, Edwin Kimura, who committed honorable *seppuku* after transmitting a hyperpulse message describing the catastropic end to our heroic undertaking."

He held up his left hand. The little finger was absent. "I myself have performed *yubitsume,* offering my finger to this Council to atone for my own role in this shameful failure, and if the Black Dragon so demands, I shall give over my life as well. But blood cries out for blood. I beseech you, my brothers, permit me to live long enough to see the shedding of so many Dragon's Tears avenged!"

"Your, ah, your fervor is noted, Brother," said a figure, turning his cowl nervously this way and that as if to try to gauge his comrades' reactions from their postures, "but avenged against *whom,* precisely?"

He was an important industrialist, whose company was involved in the manufacture of vital BattleMech components. Like many Draconian corporate magnates, he felt Theodore's reforms were sapping the morale and productivity of Combine workers—not to mention the near feudal prerogatives of Combine CEOs.

"Against the traitor Chandrasekhar, who dishonors his noble surname, which I will not speak in the same breath as his given name," rasped a man who like Toyama was a noted oyabun. "Not to mention his *gaijin* hirelings—like this one whose filthy claws besmirch the *Tai-sho*'s sword."

"Besmirch may be too strong," the DCMS officer said. "She wields a blade like a warrior. She severed the neck at a stroke, which not many can do, even with a blade as fine as poor Jeffrey's. Her style's not much too speak of, but her *makoto* is impeccable." *Makoto* meant, roughly, *sincerity,* and was the artistic attribute prized above all. It signified a work, such as a painting or a bit of calligraphy, which was executed directly from the heart, without self or thought interfering.

"Still, she must pay—she and her money-grubbing comrades, and their fat paymaster!" Toyama cried, his voice ringing like a temple gong.

"And why," a voice asked from the entryway, "do you not name the party ultimately responsible?"

Hooded heads snapped around. A figure stood in the open doorway, a shadow edged green in the light of false red moons. It wore a floor-length black *hakama* and a padded gray jacket with great flared shoulders, making its exact height and build impossible to distinguish. Its head and face were concealed in a black cloth mask such as those associated in the popular consciousness with the ancient ninja. Its voice was a highly sexless baritone, obviously run through some sort of speech synthesizer.

"Who are you?" demanded the seated oyabun. "How dare you interrupt Kokuryu-*kai*?"

"As to who I am," the figure said, "you may think of me as *Kaga,* the Shadow. As to how I dare—"

It gestured with black-gloved hands. Two figures slipped inside to stand flanking the Shadowed One. They were clothed in form-fitting black, and from behind the left shoulder of each protruded the hilt of a *ninjato,* the straight-bladed ninja sword with the square *tsuba* or hand-guard. Each wore a helmet of some black synthetic, and their faces were obscured by red visors.

"ISF!" somebody shouted. "We're betrayed!"

Laughing, the Shadow held up its hand. "Do not be disturbed. Had I wished you dead, none of you would still be breathing. Not all within Internal Security are under the sway of the archtraitor Subhash Indrahar."

The council members settled back to the floor, exchanging hooded looks. The intruder had just given definite corroboration to his—or her—sincerity. For an internal security agent to refer to the Smiling One, the ISF chief, in such a way would mean death if Indrahar ever learned about it.

"What do you want?" Toyama asked.

"The same thing you want. To return the steel to the Combine's spine and to expunge the traitors who weaken the Dragon: the Smiling One, his red-headed whelp Ninyu Kerai, and the real author of your miseries, Theodore Kurita."

The men gathered around the table gasped, and not just the council members. The businessman who had spoken earlier shot to his feet.

"I won't hear such treason!" he shouted.

The Shadowed One turned its hidden face to him and nodded. "*So ka*, Duirkovich-*san*?"

The hooded Black Dragon sagged at use of his real name. "Yes, I know you," the Shadowed One said. "I know much about you. Perhaps more than you know yourself. For example, Park, your bodyguard there."

The intruder nodded again at the square-bodied and square-jawed man who stood behind Durkovich. "He is a member of *Tosei-kai*, the Voice of the East Syndicate."

Durkovich's hooded head turned briefly back towards his guard, then toward the Shadowed One. "What of it? Lots of oyabun use them for security. They're known for loyalty and impartiality."

"Impartiality in the petty struggles among gang leaders, yes," the Shadowed One said. "But the Korean dogs feel they owe their greatest loyalty to the First Lord, who has given them much of what he stripped away from the Dragon's true servants. Your man, there, is a pipeline to ISF; you are lucky indeed to have a friend in position to divert the flow from the eyes of Indrahar and Ninyu Kerai."

Park glared, dropped into fighting stance, blocky fists raised. Kaga laughed again, whipped out his right hand. A seven-pointed *shuriken* leapt from his fingers and spun toward the bodyguard. The Korean leapt back with a litheness belying his bulk, so that the throwing-star rebounded from the wall with a musical clang.

The bodyguard's leap took him in front of a window. At once his chest exploded in a geyser of blood, rich wine-dark in the Moons' light.

"I have honored the prohibition against bringing weapons into the Pavilion," the Shadowed One said as Park collapsed to the concrete floor. The delayed report of a Zeus Long Rifle shot rolled like thunder through the window. "But my sniper, located a kilometer from the grounds, is under no such judicature."

Durkovich jumped away from the sprawled corpse of his guard. His hood fell away, revealing a jowly, panic-stricken face.

Once again the figure looked toward the arms manufacturing executive. "You are careless, Durkovich-*san*," it said in its neutered voice. "That makes you an unacceptable liability."

A black-clothed figure dropped to the floor behind Durkovich. Before the magnate could move, it had encircled his throat with the curved blade of a *kyotetsu-shogi*, a traditional ninja weapon resembling a knife crossed with a sickle and attached to a rope.

The ninja stepped back. Two more descended from above, holding the ring on the end of the rope attached to the *kyotetsu-shogi*, which had been looped over a rafter. Their combined body weights jerked Durkovich's body into the air. His blood showered his comrades as the blade bit into this thick throat.

The Shadowed One gazed up until the blood-spray and kicking had subsided. It nodded to the operators, who released the rope. The corpse fell across the table with a sodden thump. The operators retrieved the weapon and stepped back against the wall.

"Now that we have winnowed weakness from our midst," the Shadowed One said, "permit me to tell you a tale—rather, a truth. The story was put about that the old Coordinator, Takashi, Theodore's father, died in his sleep of heart failure. This was a lie.

"There is a conspiracy, coiled like a serpent around the Dragon's heart. Its members presume to call themselves the Sons of the Dragon. In truth, they are no more than servants to the will of the demonic spy-master Subhash Indrahar.

"Among their sworn number is Theodore Kurita, Coordinator of the Draconis Combine."

The Black Dragons stirred uneasily, their cloaks rustling like autumn leaves. "I have heard rumors to this effect," the DCMS officer said in half-grudging tones.

"Those rumors are true. Look at what has befallen the Combine during the rise of Theodore Kurita, and you will see the hand of the conspirator on every side. A conspiracy to gnaw the Dragon's heart out from within!

"Takashi Kurita was a *bushi*. More than a mere warrior, he was also a samurai, who devoted his whole being to selfless service of the Dragon, who is greater than any individual—greater, indeed, than the First Lord, Takashi-*sama* stood for the traditional virtues of the Dragon. He grew sickened by the way his son was drawing the spine out of the Draconis Combine with his so-called reforms. He intended to put a stop to them once and for all. Before he could act, the Smiling One, Subhash Indrahar, and his devil-pup Ninyu murdered him—with the connivance of Theodore Kurita."

Deadly silence filled the Moons Viewing Pavilion. "How can we know you're telling the truth?" the hooded DCMS officer asked in a subdued voice.

"Your tone answers your question," the Shadowed One said. "Your very passivity answers the question. If you doubted my words, you would leap to slay me, despite knowing my operators wait all around, and in the rafters above your heads. For you are true sons of the Dragon, who would not hesitate to sacrifice your lives to bring down one who dared falsely accuse the First Lord.

"But you do nothing. Because in your *hara,* in the center of you, you know the truth of what I say. You've known it for a long time, though you would not face it."

Hiraoke Toyama dropped to his knees. "He's right," the oyabun said. "For too long we've hidden behind the myth that Th—that the Coordinator was being misled by evil advisors. We can hide no longer. The evil lies at the very core."

He looked at the Shadowed One, and there were tear tracks gleaming down his grief-ravaged cheeks. "What can we *do*?"

"Theodore and his reforms are a cancer, eating away at the Combine from within," the figure said. "You must act quickly and decisively to expunge that cancer before it is too late.

"And I will help."

MORE HARD-HITTING ACTION
FROM BATTLETECH®

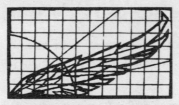

YOUR OPINION CAN MAKE A DIFFERENCE!
LET US KNOW WHAT *YOU* THINK.

Send this completed survey to us and enter a weekly drawing to win a special prize!

1.) Do you play any of the following role-playing games?
   Shadowrun _____ Earthdawn _____ BattleTech _____

2.) Did you play any of the games before you read the novels?
   Yes _____ No _____

3.) How many novels have you read in each of the following series?
   Shadowrun _____ Earthdawn _____ BattleTech _____

4.) What other game novel lines do you read?
   TSR _____ White Wolf _____ Other (Specify) _____

5.) Who is your favorite FASA author?
_____

6.) Which book did you take this survey from?
_____

7.) Where did you buy this book?
   Bookstore _____ Game Store _____ Comic Store _____
   FASA Mail Order _____ Other (Specify) _____

8.) Your opinion of the book (please print)
_____
_____
_____

Name _____ Age _____ Gender _____
Address _____
City _____ State _____ Country _____ Zip _____

Send this page or a photocopy of it to:
FASA Corporation
Editorial/Novels
1100 W. Cermak Suite B-305
Chicago, IL 60608